SPUTNIK SUMMER

SPUTNIK SUMMER

by Paul Castellani

Pyramid Publishing, Inc.
Utica, New York

Printed in the United States of America

ISBN 978-1-886166-39-4

Pyramid Publishing Inc.
PO Box 8339
Utica, New York 13505

www.pyramidpublishingservices.com

For Donna

ACKNOWLEDGEMENTS

SEVERAL PEOPLE CONTRIBUTED to the completion of this novel. Wayne Lindeman and Tina Lincer read many drafts and provided sound advice and generous support. Gay Malin read late drafts and made many valuable suggestions. As always, Donna Castellani provided encouragement and fierce editing.

Wednesday June 25, 1958

VANGUARD FAILS TO PUT SATELLITE INTO ORBIT

'52 DeSoto. $75. Needs Work. Will Dicker.

ONE THOUSAND, TWO HUNDRED AND TWENTY MILES under the orbit of Sputnik, Kevin Boyle tracked the route of a fisherman trolling for trout on Uncas Lake. At Byrd's Seaplane Rides and Marina, a half-filled windsock drooped. It was dead quiet. But hidden by a thick cover of hemlock the residents of Hawk Cove hurried to complete their final preparations in the countdown to Saturday when carloads of tourists would fill freshly-scrubbed cottages and take their first splash in the lake before fanning out to the gift shops to buy balsam-stuffed pillows and rubber-tipped tomahawks. The beach at Iroquois Lodge would ring with shouts of brothers cannon-balling off the dock at shrieking sisters, mothers calling to toddlers to be careful, and the slap of water skis jumping the wake.

From the first day of the season until Labor Day, Kevin would have to act as though every guest staying at the Lodge was his best friend or favorite aunt and uncle. And every night after supper, he would have to pull his cart behind their cottages and collect the trash barrels that stank of rotting corncobs, coffee grounds, and watermelon rinds. They were on vacation, he was the help.

He'd help his parents prep the Lodge next June then leave town as soon as possible for his freshman year at college. But this summer he had to do something besides watching traffic from the steps of the Red &

White. It was either a re-run of last year with his old friends – or the Rock.

At the Rock, guys parked their cars and drank beer around beach fires with girls whose parents didn't know or didn't care. At the Rock, guys took dares to dive far enough off the top to miss the outcropping of boulders at the base and knife into the black water. At the end of every June, kids hoping to join that crowd lurked at the edge of the clearing until the guys in charge either told them to beat it or let them in to serve their probation, keeping their mouths shut, not laughing too loudly at the dirty jokes, and being in the right spot when one of the girls needed a light or a guy wanted another beer.

He'd been wondering how he was going to pull it off when yesterday in the town hall parking lot Buck Duncan appeared like a lucky charm. Kevin had joined the pack leaning under the hood of Jimmie Nelson's '52 Mercury when Buck slid in next to him. Buck's older brother was a regular at the Rock before taking off for Star Lake, and Kevin was sure Buck was going to try to get into the Rock.

Jimmie pulled the throttle arm under the four-barrel and slammed down the hood muttering, "Thanks," when Kevin said, "Smokin' wheels, Jimmie."

As they watched the Merc lay a strip of rubber out the entrance, Kevin said, "Jimmie's our ticket into the Rock."

Buck stepped back to look Kevin over. "I didn't figure you for the Rock."

Kevin was sick of being easily figured out. "Tomorrow night. Seven. Wait at the end of my driveway," he'd told Buck.

"LET'S BREAK FOR LUNCH," Kevin's father called from the front steps of Cayuga.

Kevin grabbed the broom he'd been using to sweep the screened porch of Oneida. The six cottages at Iroquois Lodge were almost ready for the families from Utica, Syracuse, and Rochester who would rent them for one or two weeks. Twenty-two mattresses laid on dusted springs; eighty-seven windows washed; six toilet bowls scoured; dozens of screens brushed; hundreds of dishes, glasses, cups, knives, forks, and spoons washed. Could his father think of anything else that had to be done before Saturday? Bet on it, he thought as his father headed toward the Longhouse at the top of the triangle of the cottages.

Everything was going to be double time for the next two days. Falling in behind his father, Kevin watched his head swivel as he went through an inspection of the grounds. Badminton net inspected for rips? Check. Rackets and shuttlecocks in their racks? Check. Horseshoes cleaned? Check. Firewood stacked under the tarp next to the fire pit? Kevin had made absolutely sure nothing was going to keep him from slipping out the door after supper.

Kevin turned from making sure the picnic tables he'd wiped down that morning would pass muster and almost ran up the back of his father's legs. He'd come to a dead stop and was staring at his mother standing on the steps of the Longhouse waving a letter.

His father dropped the bottle of window cleaner in a bucket and snatched it from her hand. "How can the Barkers cancel? They're supposed to be here next Saturday." He turned the letter over as though there might be some explanation on the back. "They've been renting Seneca since fifty-one."

"That's what it says." She cocked her head toward the door. "Lunch is on the table."

"How can I eat?" He grabbed the bucket and stomped off to the workshop.

Kevin was sure his father was already cooking up one of his projects magically guaranteed to solve any predicament. "Want me to help?"

"Go have lunch."

AFTER HASTILY EATING, Kevin figured he'd better help his father with whatever scheme he was concocting to make up for the Barkers' stab in the back.

The second Kevin stepped into the workshop, his father said, "We've got to get this diving board back on the dock. Steady the end while I see if I can drill out these stripped screws."

Seeing the old diving board that had been leaning against the back wall of the storeroom for two years now on the workbench surprised Kevin. His father kept the bench as clean as an operating table, and the moldy diving board was shedding burlap dust all over the place.

"You said we weren't going to put this back on the dock," Kevin said. "Remember, right after that Anderson kid broke his wrist?"

"Horsing around. Lucky we didn't get sued. And I hear Indian Point Cottages put in *two* new boards."

Kevin's father took a drill from the peg board. Each drawer of the racks next to its ghost outline was labeled with punch tape: blue for every type of screw; red for the nails. Green labels read: Drill bits - up to ½; Yellow for Drill bits - less than ½. The whole workshop was one of his father's life lessons: *A place for everything, and everything in its place.*

As his father inspected a bit before slipping it into the drill, Kevin switched on the portable radio perched on the windowsill. Fiddling with the dial, he finally picked up the top 40s on WSYR. The kids from Syracuse who stayed at the Lodge said he was the luckiest guy in the world to live in the middle of the Adirondacks. But how would they like to be stuck in a town where everybody knew if you blew a fart and every song came in with static?

"I can't think with that rock and roll blaring," his father said.

Kevin poked at the tattered burlap. "Probably a million dried cooties in there. Just add water, and it'll be like the movie with the fire ants that ate those guys in the jungle."

"Our people catch wind of the new high-dive board at the Point, and we'll have more cancellations. *Damn it!* I told you to hold the end. Now

I've snapped off the bit, and I don't know if I've got another three-eighths."

The news came on. Kevin's father shook his head. "The Ruskies launch a satellite bigger than a Lincoln Continental, and we can't get a grapefruit off Cape Canaveral."

"That wasn't my fault either."

"Why do you think our rockets go up fifty feet and topple over like a drunk falling off a barstool? Somebody left a broken-off drill bit in a vital part. A too-smart Clarkson engineer forgot to turn off a valve. Everything counts, Kevin. Little things add up."

"Cripes, Dad, I'm going to get a brain tumor worrying about somebody falling off our diving board and suing us."

"You're right about the burlap. I want you to strip it off and sand the board. You get to it after supper, and you can shellac it tomorrow afternoon. That way we can get new burlap on before Saturday. No matter how many times I tell people that check-in is at two, somebody always comes early."

"Don't I get a night off?"

"Help me flip this over."

"Dad, I'll get up early and start sanding. This will be the best diving board in the entire Adirondacks. But tonight, I've got to get out."

―――――

AFTER SUPPER, Kevin finished putting away the dishes and read the newspaper at the kitchen table as he waited for his parents to settle down. At ten minutes to seven, he quietly stood against the frame of the door between the kitchen and the living room. Beyond the Franklin stove on his right, his father sat at a roll-top desk pulling out drawers, aligning papers into neat piles, and checking the sharpness of the dozen number two pencils sticking out of a jar. His mother was opening a jig-saw puzzle at the card table under the hanging lamp. "I'm going to lay out what I need to refinish the diving board early tomorrow morning and then head up to town for a few minutes," he said in an after-thought tone he hoped wouldn't set off his father's *where to?* and *who with?* alarm. He was definitely going to the Rock, but he didn't want to have an argument about it. He grabbed his jacket off the peg next to the door to the porch.

Kevin's father looked up. "Where are you going?"

"Out." Kevin waved to a blank space between his mother and father. "You said it was okay."

What about the….?"

"Good night, Dad, Mom," Kevin said as he headed out the door. "I know, Behave *yourself*," he and his father said at the same time.

FIFTEEN MINUTES LATER, walking backwards along Spruce Road and waving his arms, Buck continued his story. "And then he says, 'You think your shit don't stink.' And you know, Kev, I had one of those moments when the bulb goes off. Does everybody's shit stink? Or does it stink different – like over there in China, where all they eat is rice or a hunk of dog? And how come it stinks anyway? You eat a nice juicy steak, a baked potato. What do you get? Stinky shit. That's a question they'd never ask Mr. Wizard. But I figured since you always get a hundred in science, I'd ask you. So what..."

"For chrissakes, Buck, you ever hear someone say, 'Eat shit and die?'"

Maybe this wasn't such a good idea, Kevin thought. Buck's a good guy. But every time one of his other friends caught him talking to Buck, they gave him a funny look. Buck's sideburns were already below the school's mid-ear limit. Why did he have to choose sides? It's summer. The rules changed.

"Yeah, I heard that."

"Okay. Shit's poison. If it tasted good, people might eat it – and die. So God made it stink so they wouldn't."

"I'm lucky to be friends with you, Kev."

Checking out the Rock with Buck didn't mean he joined the after-school-detention crowd. He caught a whiff of horse manure drifting in from the Hemlock Island Boys Camp stable, one of a string of rich-kid summer camps in the area. He'd seen the trailers delivering the horses to the fenced-off stables last week. A lingering smell of black fly spray laid down by the town fogger still hung in the air.

At the end of the rutted tracks in the scruffy pines, Jimmie's Merc and Chink Perrotti's Hornet were pulled in front of a rough lean-to. As they reached the edge of the clearing, Buck said, "I hope they don't pull a weird imitation rite on us. My brother told me they made one guy stay all night in the lean-to – naked, with honey rubbed all over him."

Kevin had been thinking more about getting into the Rock, not what he'd do there. He imagined letting his other buddies at the town beach know that he was copasetic with the guys at the Rock. And maybe girls might find him more exciting than a guy they could count on to behave himself. "He was yanking your chain."

"Could be, but I'd stay naked all night in the lean-to if they threw in one of the girls for company." Buck swung his arm around Kevin's shoulders. "We'd have to get real close to stay warm."

Kevin pushed Buck's arm away. "You'd be too busy slapping mosquitoes."

Through the low-hanging branches, Kevin could make out a pit fire backlighting a clump of figures on the beach. From a portable radio, Chuck Berry cranked out, 'Go, Johnny Go. Go, *Go Johnny B. Goode.*' One of the guys yelled, "Who's that?"

"It's us – Buck Duncan and Kevin Boyle," Buck shouted.

"Duncan and Boyle?" Jimmie called out to a chorus of snickers. "You get lost on your way home from the playground?"

He called us by name, Kevin thought. He listened: murmurs, a laugh, a beer bottle being chucked into the weeds.

Kevin nudged Buck, and they slowly treaded out of the bushes. They neared the fire, and he could feel the stares. But Kevin sauntered to the water's edge like he did this every night.

In the flickering light, Kevin could make out Jimmie, Chink and three girls in battered lawn chairs clustered around the smoky fire. Twenty feet beyond, four guys he couldn't identify were sitting on a log facing the lake.

Buck nodded in their direction. "I'm going to see if I know somebody over there and get some beer."

The girl sitting across from Jimmie stood up and stretched. She strolled over to where Kevin was trying to act like he belonged there. "Hi, I'm Maxine."

Maxine twirled a long-necked beer bottle in one hand. With the other she pushed back the blonde hair that slid over her face. Her nipples stood out like small corks under her tee-shirt. He could tell she was older than him, eighteen or even nineteen.

"Kevin," he said with a hitch in his voice.

"Don't give yourself a headache trying to guess who I am. I just got into town. Jimmie's cousin. His old man and mine are brothers." Nodding in Jimmie's direction, she said, "Mr. Manners ain't going out of his way to make introductions, so I figured I'd better do it myself." She stepped so close to Kevin that he stumbled back.

Coughing and waving away smoke from the fire, Kevin said, "How long are you visiting the Nelsons?"

Maxine looked as though she was sizing him up. "The season. On Saturday, I start at the Acropolis in Inlet."

Kevin straightened; tried to look taller. "Where from?" He glanced toward the cluster around the fire, feeling her eyes still on him.

"Outer space," she laughed. "Minerva. Same thing."

"It's not like Hawk Cove is a real resort like Lake Placid."

"Whether they were going to waitress in Placid or Lake George after

8

senior year was like the most important decision my friends had to make."

"Why didn't you go?"

Maxine shrugged. "Mom thought I'd be better off here with Jimmie's family."

"Why's that?"

"Long story," Maxine said. "Anyway, here I am. Jimmie's fifth wheel."

One of the guys huddled around the fire let out a long belch. "At least, Jimmie took you to Hawk Cove's swanky spot." Kevin stared at the front of Maxine's tee-shirt as she tucked the beer bottle under her arm and fished around in the pocket of her Bermuda shorts.

"You ever see tits before?" Maxine said as she dug first in one then the other pocket.

"I, ah...." Kevin stuttered, feeling a burn on the back of his neck.

"Forget it. Got a cigarette? Mine must have fallen out someplace."

Kevin pointed to the dark shapes at the far end of the clearing. "My friend Buck's got mine."

"Sorry I ragged on you about checking out my you-know-whats."

"It's okay, I..."

"Don't sweat it. I got to learn to act nicer. You Hawk Cove guys probably got more couth than the Minerva jerks."

"It's the water."

Maxine gave Kevin a punch on the arm. "I like you. Want a swig?" She held out the bottle.

"Sure." Kevin took a sip.

"I need a smoke. I'm going to bum a cigarette from Jimmie. Don't run away on me."

Kevin watched Maxine walk back to the fire. She told him not to run away, so maybe he didn't sound like a total dork. What would he say when she came back? Jimmie and the others stood, and Maxine returned. "Jimmie's hot to bug out. You want me to ask him if you can come?"

"Me? Ah... Jeez. Where? I mean..."

Maxine eyed Kevin. "Your choice."

"That'd be great, but I promised some guys I'd meet them later. Next time. Here. The Acropolis. Around."

"Sure thing, Ken. I'll look up, and there'll you be – scoping out my ba-zoom."

"You never know," Kevin said as coolly as he could manage. Could he be a guy who could get in a car and just go someplace with a girl who talked like that?

Maxine put her hand on Kevin's shoulder. Leaning close to him, she said, "I don't usually ask twice, so we'll see what happens next time." She squeezed his shoulder and let her hand drop. "Later, alligator."

Maxine joined Chink and Jimmie's girlfriend, Noel, on their way to the cars. Hearing a snort, Kevin turned and flinched. Jimmie was staring up at him with a murderous glare on his face. Jimmie scared Kevin. He scared everybody. It was as though Jimmie had started out at six-three and was mad as hell for being hammered into a five-seven bull-dog. With biceps like hams and a permanent I-dare-you-to-call-me-short sneer on his flat face, Jimmie looked as though he was about to pound him. "What's with you and my cousin?"

"Jeez, Jimmie. I just said hello."

"Just cause I didn't kick your ass out of here tonight, don't mean you're top stud."

"I didn't think that, Jimmie. I was trying to be nice."

Jimmie gave Kevin a head-to-toe sneering look. "If I was you, Boyle, I'd be careful who I was nice to." He let out a barking laugh. "I don't know whether to warn you off or watch you get your sorry ass in a sling. See you around – Kennie."

Buck came up next to Kevin. "Who was the girl you were talking to?"

"Jimmie's cousin."

"What'd Jimmie say?"

"I'm not sure."

Thursday June 26

RUSSIANS PULL OUT OF GENEVA A-TALKS

Acquire Law Degrees at Home.

BOUNDING INTO THE KITCHEN, Kevin leaned over his mother standing at the sink and kissed her on the cheek. "Morning, Mom."

Joyce wiped her hands on the front of a blue paisley apron. "You're the chipper one this morning. I was wondering where you were." She sniffed the air. "You smell like paint."

"Shellac. I put the first coat on Dad's new plan to put Indian Point out of business." Kevin pulled a bottle of milk from the refrigerator and slid into a chair across from his father at the kitchen table in the long end of the L-shaped room. He poured milk into a bowl of Cheerios. "Our boards will be so unreal; we'll host the 1960 Olympic diving championships. Right, Dad?"

"A smart mouth is going to get you into trouble one of these days. And if you weren't out gallivanting, you could have put the first coat on last night and you'd be finished by now."

Kevin was pleased his father was stewing about the diving board instead of giving him the third degree about where he was last night, even though he had a couple of pretty good alibis tucked in his back pocket. He looked over his father's shoulder through the windows facing the beach. With the curtains pulled back, sunlight poured in, warming the room. But on Saturday, the curtains would be pulled, shielding the family from the view of the passing guests. "Mom, didn't people

11

stop gallivanting around 1938?"

"Your father's right, young man."

Thomas rattled the newspaper and turned it so Kevin could see it. "Khrushchev's riding high because of the huge rocket that launched his new satellite. If we don't start graduating more engineers and scientists, there won't be a 1960 anything. With your math and science grades, you could go into either one."

Lately, it seemed to Kevin his father found an important career lesson in every headline. The old Philco at the end of the table was on. "Mom, you tune in SYR and get those stupid chipmunk songs or Perry Como and don't listen." He turned up the volume and twisted the dial until he got Elvis' *Wear Your Ring Around My Neck*. "That's music."

"You'll end up a disk jockey if you don't start working on your college applications," Thomas said.

Kevin imagined Maxine hanging on his arm at the dance as he spun the records. "Dad, it's only June."

"You have to think ahead, Kevin. The Pattersons arrive next Saturday, and Marty went to Clarkson. I want you to ask him to write a recommendation. It's not what you know, but who you know."

"Dad, I do not want to be an engineer."

"What about a doctor or maybe a dentist? People are always getting cavities."

"What's so important about a profession?"

"You become a professional, and people need you. With the Barkers cancelling, we've got a hole in the schedule we might not fill. The *Farmers' Almanac* says it's going to be a rainy August, and we get more vacancies. Carrier goes on strike, and everybody from Syracuse stays home." Thomas pushed back his chair and stood, grimacing as his knees, hips and back aligned into place as though each needed oiling. "You don't understand what it's like to always depend on somebody else for your living. Things drop out of nowhere to mess you up." He pushed in the tail of his plaid shirt. "Early bird, Kevin. Early bird."

"It's the early worm that gets eaten, Dad."

"This is not funny, son. You've barely got enough saved for one of the state schools, and we can't afford the private colleges without a scholarship. We need to use whatever pull we've got. You with me on this?"

"Yeah, I'm with you," Kevin muttered.

Friday June 27

BIG JET TANKER CRASHES ON TEST: 15 Dead

Opportunities Await You In Scientific Crime Detection Work.

SITTING BACKWARD ON A PICNIC TABLE tucked in a grassy patch between Mohawk and Oneida, Kevin put *The Scapegoat* on the table top and took a bite of his sandwich. I wouldn't mind switching places with a French nobleman, he thought: *Chateaubriand*, the *Moulin Rouge*, Brigitte Bardot. He leaned back on his elbows and looked up. A blue jay perched on a branch of a pine, then flew down to the grass fifteen feet in front of him. He slowly picked a shard of crust from his sandwich and tossed it toward the bird. Eyeing him suspiciously, the bird hopped toward the crust and pecked at it. If I stay here very quietly, maybe Dad won't find me right away. He picked another piece of bread from his sandwich and tossed it toward the bird.

Kevin let out a small sigh. It would be great to have a real vacation. Not at a place like Iroquois Lodge with scads of kids running around, moms and dads yelling at them to stop throwing sand, but someplace quiet. Two weeks, even one, all to himself. Maybe the ocean, on a beach where he could sit back in a chair with a stack of books, read for a couple of hours, splash in the waves, read some more, find a funky clam shack for supper, meet some girls, go to…

"Kevin, where are you?" Thomas called.

Kevin glanced at his watch. *Exactly* thirty minutes since they took their lunch break. His father ought to put in one of those time-clocks.

"*Kevin?*"

"I'm *coming*." He tore off another piece of crust, but the bird had taken off. He finished the chocolate milk in his thermos, tucked the book under his arm, and headed in the direction of his father's voice.

Nodding toward the book, Thomas said, "You'd rather read than eat, but we've got a load of things left to do. Twenty-four hours until the first guests arrive."

Kevin stuffed the last of the sandwich in his mouth and set the thermos and book next to a tree.

"We need to push that double bed against the wall in Oneida and make sure the paint's dry on the window sill in Mohawk," Thomas said. "But first, we'll get a crescent wrench and some washers out of the workshop. You can take them over to the bathroom in Seneca while I see if the shut-off on new pump's working."

Heading to the workshop, Kevin and Thomas passed in front of Onondaga where Joyce was on the front steps shaking a dust mop. Without looking at her, Thomas said, "Are all the propone tanks turned on?"

A sharp crack of the handle of the dust mop hitting the top step made the two wheel around. Joyce pointed the mop toward Thomas. Slowly enunciating each word, she said, "As you requested, I checked them yesterday afternoon. I checked them this morning – as you asked once more. I am *not* going to check them yet again. In fact, I am going to take a nap. I suggest you cool your jets – even if that means jumping in the lake."

"Sorry, I…" Thomas said to Joyce's back as she stalked into Onondaga.

"Dad, why don't I run up to town and pick up the mail? And I've got a couple of books due at the library. Be back in an hour."

"What about….? Maybe that's a good idea."

IN THE POST OFFICE in the south end of the Red & White, Kevin pulled a stack of envelopes rubber-banded in a Sears catalog supplement from the Iroquois Lodge box. As he was about to close the brass door, he heard "Is that a Boyle?"

Realizing the voice came from the post box, Kevin peered in. Framed eight inches at the other end were the beady eyes and pointy nose of Postmistress Ethel Ricketts.

"Hold your horses," she said.

Through the narrow slot, Kevin watched her shuffle through piles of mail on a long table. Knocking a cup set on the end, coffee sloshed over a stack of letters. She picked up a postcard, read it and tossed it back on the table. She grabbed a handful of letters, flipped through them, and turned to where Kevin was waiting. "Here," she said, thrusting her hand through the box. "Return address says Penfield. Isn't that near Rochester?"

"I think so," Kevin said, as he peeled the brown-stained, damp letter from the one underneath.

"I expect it's one of those new suburbs full of tract houses. But you can't blame folks for wanting to get out of the city."

"Thank you, Mrs. Ricketts." Kevin looked at the return address: Michael Byron, 57 Baird Road. He hoped it was a request for one of the vacant cottages.

WAITING ON THE SHOULDER OF ROUTE 28 for a black Ford to pass, Kevin jumped back, startled, as Slim's dog darted out from behind the steps of the post office and chased the car to the driveway of the Knotty Pine, barking and snarling at the right back wheel as though he wanted to tear it off. The dirty brown mutt kept his eyes on the Ford until it disappeared around the bend before trotting back to its hide-out to rest for another ambush.

I hope that dog doesn't die of a heart attack like Slim, or after tomorrow, get mashed by a station wagon full of tourists, he thought. He heard folks in town chewing over whose cars got chased most or not at all;

needling the ones that did about Slim's ghost in the trunk.

Kevin cut through the parking lot behind the high school to the town library. He pushed through the doors, waved to Warren Marsh, the librarian, standing behind the circulation desk, and headed into the non-fiction room. He picked up a biography of Adenauer from the new books display. His father insisted the lives of great men had lessons for success. More important, Kevin knew having his face in a book, especially non-fiction, was a free pass from one of the chores his father invented to fill idle time.

Back in the periodical section, Kevin pulled a three-day-old copy of the *New York Times* from a stack of newspapers and sat at a round table. Hawk Cove might be a tiny dot on the map, but it had a great library – and a mail subscription to the *Times*. He loved reading about what was going on in the world; fascinated by the stories about places, and people and events he'd never thought about, even knew existed. He would miss the library, but he was sure the college he'd be going to would have one larger than this. He also hoped it would be a place where he could get away; be by himself to imagine traveling to countries he'd read about.

Beaming a wide smile, Warren Marsh stacked an armful of books on the shelving cart and, finishing the last notes of a tune, joined Kevin at the table. "Scouting out one of Hawk Cove's top tourist attractions for your guests?"

Mr. Marsh was always smiling and humming, Kevin thought. It was like he had his own radio station playing in his head. "I'm taking a break before everything gets wild tomorrow."

"And I'll be playing the slow song on the flip side until Labor Day," Mr. Marsh said. "I came over to remind you our group will meet a half hour earlier on the seventh. Okay?"

"I'll be there." When Kevin hinted he might quit the book club before summer, Mr. Marsh talked him into staying, telling him they needed a young person's view. And now they might meet on a night he could be at the Rock with Maxine. Lying wide awake in bed last night and sanding the diving board earlier, he'd rehearsed a dozen better answers to Maxine's dig about seeing tits before. He couldn't make a casual, "You kidding?" sound believable. He tried "Sure thing," and "Get out of here," with different pauses and gestures. He'd even practiced a laugh and, "Not as nice as those," but didn't see pulling that off in a million years. Still, she'd asked him if he wanted to go along with her and Jimmie and Noel. But she also said she didn't ask twice, so he'd better be ready next time.

Pointing at the newspaper in front of Kevin, Mr. Marsh said, "Keeping up on current affairs?"

Kevin had been imagining Maxine's face on the model wearing the *Escapade* bra in the Macy's lingerie ad. "Cuban rebels, Russian rockets, riots in France: a new crisis every day."

"You ought to consider joining the Foreign Service after college."

"I'll add it to the long list my dad carries around: lawyer, doctor, engineer, *dentist*. I'm not ready to make all these choices."

"Don't knock it. Not everyone has your potential, and the people that care for you want you to have a shot at whatever you want to do."

"It sounds so simple, like picking up a menu and deciding whether you want a cheeseburger or a hot dog. Mr. Carlson in the guidance office pulls out these tests I took a hundred years ago, studies the pin-holes for about ten seconds, and says I have an aptitude for being a scientist. Did you have an aptitude for being a librarian?"

Removing his wire-rimmed glasses, Mr. Marsh huffed a film of breath on them and polished the lenses with a red polka-dot handkerchief he'd pulled from the breast pocket of his sports jacket. "I don't know about that," Mr. Marsh smiled. "But, I fell in love with books. "And," he said with a sweep of his arm, "this is where the books are."

"You're not from Hawk Cove, but you decided to come here and be the librarian. You're different from most people. You decided – didn't you?"

Mr. Marsh stacked the magazines left on the table into a neat pile. "I suppose, but who you are is more than a job."

Folding the *Times*, Kevin said, "I'd be a janitor if I could live in New York."

"I have friends in the city. One is an actor; another is a literary agent. They all don't have exciting occupations, even though they'd kill themselves if they didn't get to the latest play or opera at the Met. They kid me about my quiet life as a librarian, my mineral collection. Oh, I forgot to show you my latest discovery."

Mr. Marsh strode to the bookcase along the wall where his displays of minerals were lined across the top, each in its own glass-topped box: garnet crystals from Gore Mountain; quartz from Indian Lake; tourmaline from Cranberry. Kevin had seen Mr. Marsh coming and going from his excursions wearing sturdy hiking boots, a heavy canvass bag hanging from his shoulder, and a leather holster for his short-handled pickax. Returning to the table with a new box, he said, "Look at this beauty: labadorite: a trove not far off the trail from Tahawus to Newcomb Lake. Rare this far south."

"Neat," Kevin said. He never imagined that there were such beautiful things under the gray rocks of the mountains until Mr. Marsh started his collection.

"I estimate that I can collect the best specimen of every mineral in the *Adirondack Rockhound Guide* by – say, 1995," Mr. Marsh said. "I tell my friends that everyone else in the world isn't miserable because they don't live in New York City." He placed the box on the table. "I'm happy here."

"I hope I can figure out what I would like to do for the rest of my life. You're lucky. You love being a librarian, and you've got a hobby that will last a life-time."

Smiling, Mr. Marsh said, "I'm not *that* old. I always take two specimens. One for the display," he said gesturing toward the bookcases.

"And the other, I keep at home. I'll pick one and just hold it in my hand while I'm reading. Sometimes I think I'm absorbing energy stored for thousands of years in those crystals."

"Geologist," Kevin said. "Another one for my dad's list."

Looking toward the circulation desk, where Ida Rayburn fidgeted, Mr. Marsh said, "Back to work. I have to show Mrs. Rayburn my aptitude for stamping the due dates neatly within each box. See you on the seventh at seven."

Mr. Marsh stood, grasped the lapels of his jacket and shook it until it sat neatly on his shoulders, then straightened his tie. Humming the theme from *The Long Hot Summer*, he walked toward Mrs. Rayburn as though he'd been waiting all day for her to arrive.

Sunday June 29

"AND HOW DOES GODLESS COMMUNISM gain a foothold in America?" Father Francis Xavier Donovan asked from the pulpit of St Mary of the Woods. Seconds ticked as Father Donovan swept his eyes over the faces of the squirming tourists and year-round parishioners filling the church at ten o'clock Mass on this first Sunday of the season. A baby squawked. Feet shuffled under the kneelers.

In their usual spot five rows from the front, Kevin and his mother were squeezed in a pew with a man and woman he didn't recognize and Mr. and Mrs. Matthews who'd pushed in grumbling about a family of tourists who had poached their regular pew. As the priest continued his sermon, Kevin supposed the returning tourists were surprised by Father Donovan. He wasn't at all like the priests usually sent up from the retirement home in Utica to help Father Petroska with the summer spike. Compared to those old men, Father Donovan was a movie star.

Kevin slunk down behind Mrs. Tomlinson, seated in front of him, hoping that he was camouflaged in the silver vines and leaves on her dress. He didn't want to be noticed by Father Donovan who seemed to be scanning the congregation for the answer to his question.

"*Moral rot*," Father Donovan shouted as he pointed at Floyd and Edna Tucker. As the congregation's eyes followed the accusing finger, Kevin wondered what sins the red-faced, middle-aged owners of

Adirondack Gifts and Crafts had committed and whether they too had gone to Father Donovan for Confession. After his Confession, two weeks ago, Kevin hoped he could lay low for the next ten weeks until Donovan left and make sure it was Father Petroska, *not* Father Donovan in the confessional.

Waving his arm toward the clot of whispering men at the back of the church waiting to duck out early, Father Donovan said, "Rot *underneath* what we see, like cancer eating the core of sick trees in our beautiful forests."

Hunching down further, Kevin feared that Father Donovan was going to point at him and announce that he'd been thinking about what was underneath Maxine's tee-shirt.

When he'd knelt in the confessional two weeks ago, Kevin was expecting Father Petroska in the booth. But when the grill slid open, and he heard 'Yes, my son?' as though the priest was really going to listen, he'd felt uneasy. He wanted his routine Confession with Father Petroska, not a conversation about his sins.

He'd tried to get a muttered 'impure thoughts and deeds, about seven times, Father,' buried between 'missing my evening prayers, about six times,' when the voice cut him off and asked, "Are you masturbating my son?"

"Yes," he'd finally conceded, cringing at the word Father Petroska never used.

Then Father Donovan asked him *when* he masturbated. After quickly trying to estimate the number of times he done it in the morning and afternoon, he'd finally settled on 'mostly at night," hoping this would satisfy this priest. But then the priest asked him *where* he masturbated. He remembered thinking that this was some new kind of Confession the church invented that hadn't yet reached Hawk Cove. Images of himself in dozens of places with his thing in his right hand had flashed through his mind before he whispered, "In the bathroom."

And when this priest asked him what were his impure thoughts when he masturbated, he'd considered backing out of the booth. As it was, his mother and the others waiting in line were probably thinking he was confessing to a murder or robbery for being in the booth so long. He recalled how the flowery smell of aftershave seeping through the grill had made him gag. How was he supposed to tell this priest about picturing Linda pulling her slip over her head, taking off her bra and panties; them doing stuff with their clothes off? He'd decided on, "Mostly naked girls."

Finally, after the priest warned him that he was violating the sanctity of his body *and* the sanctity of those whom his lust defiled and he'd packed as much contrition as he could into "I'm very sorry and will try harder to be good," the priest gave him absolution and his penance – the rosary instead of the ten Hail Marys and ten Our Fathers he always got from Father Petroska. If his mother or father saw him saying the rosary, they'd know he'd done something really terrible. He'd have to find that rosary and say it at night.

Orin Matthews snorted, and Kevin shook away the recollection of that Confession. He hoped he wouldn't be singled out for not paying attention as Father Donovan continued his sermon. Next to Mr. Matthews, his wife Eunice was staring up at the pulpit as though she wanted to capture every one of Father Donovan's words in her open mouth.

"The *masters of deceit* will steal into the core of America concealed in magazines and movies that subvert our morals, books that promote so-called *progressive* ideas that cleverly try to undermine our way of life."

Fingering her rosary beads, Mrs. Matthews nodded.

"They employ quiet, almost invisible, gatherings where they hatch plans to infiltrate our schools, the organs of government, and even our churches. Oh Father, that's in New York City, Washington, and Hollywood," Father Donovan said with an exaggerated shake of his head. He brushed back a lock of his thick wavy white hair, and his eyes crinkled under lush eyebrows that curled up at their ends as he beamed a broad grin around the church.

Kevin joined the rest of the congregation in a chuckle. He had to admit that Father Donovan was funny. He told jokes. Not joke, jokes, but stuff that made people smile. And he'd stand outside after Mass shaking hands with the men, talking to the ladies, remembering their names even though he'd been around only for a month.

"Sadly, that's true, my friends. But, Communists know that subverting the moral fiber and steadfast patriotism of good people in small towns will be their most difficult challenge, and that is why they send their most clever and patient agents, plant their deepest cells, and use their *best* plans in these seemingly innocent places."

Father Donovan gazed around the congregation, seeming to scrutinize each pew for a spy. "My dear friends, if the tide of Godless Communism is to be turned back, it will be in Old Forge, Long Lake and Hawk Cove. It will be the patriots in small towns who will show America how to fight Communism." Lifting his arms, he said, "Let us pray to our Lord and Savior Jesus Christ and the Blessed Virgin Mary to give us the strength for this battle," and then he wheeled around and descended the pulpit.

The congregation released a collective sigh. Eunice Matthew's palms stopped an inch before coming together in applause. 'Our own Bishop Sheen,' she'd told his mother.

Kevin followed his mother to the Communion railing. He'd tried to be better – for the first week after that Confession, but being a sex maniac made it hard. "Corpus Christi," Father Donovan said as he held the host a moment before Kevin's face. Kevin closed his eyes, stuck out his tongue, and said, "Amen."

After Father Donovan gave the congregation the final blessing and his mother chatted with folks she didn't see except at Sunday Mass, Kevin stopped to read the Legion of Decency flier tacked up on the bulletin board in the vestibule. He zeroed in on the group at the bottom, "C – Condemned" and scanned the titles for new additions: *And God Created Woman, Artists and Models, Chicago Confidential.* Would he ever live someplace where he could see a Condemned movie?

Kevin slipped around the clot standing in front of Father Donovan and out onto the front lawn. He was staying as far away from Donovan as he could. But then he spied Father Donovan talking to his mother. Not just a 'Nice to see you' but *talking*. He hid behind a group of people until his mother found him.

"Kevin. There you are," his mother said. "I was beginning to think you'd headed home without me. I had a nice chat with Father Donovan, and there's something he'd like you to do."

"Me? How does he know me?"

"I don't know, but that's not important. He has a project and needs assistance. He asked if you would help."

"What project? What would I do? I'm really busy."

"Now, Kevin, don't get ahead of yourself. Besides, he offered to pay you *three* dollars an hour."

"Three bucks an hour to do what?"

"Folding brochures, stuffing envelopes, setting up a mailing list."

"I don't know anything about setting up mailing lists. Besides, I've got my chores around the Lodge."

"Your father isn't going to mind you spending a couple of hours on Tuesday afternoons earning three dollars an hour for stuffing envelopes. Your college fund could use the extra money."

"Jeez, I don't know."

"Kevin, we aren't fifty feet from the house of our Lord. I wish you wouldn't use that language."

"It's not swearing."

"I don't know whether a mangling of the name of our Lord is technically swearing, but at a minimum, it's crude. Let's go."

"Did you tell Donovan I'd do it?"

"*Father* Donovan. And yes I did."

"Don't I get a say in this?"

Pointing at the white-haired priest who was handing a baby back to its mother, Joyce said, "You can go up there and tell him you're not going to do it. Or go to the rectory Tuesday at two o'clock. If it turns out to be such a huge burden, you can quit after that. But I don't see how doing a good deed and getting a very good pay for it ought to be a problem for you."

Monday June 30

HOFFA WINS ACQUITTAL ON WIRETAP CHARGE.

Meat Cutting Offers You Success and Security. People Must Eat.

"Hey, Kev! Over here!" From the alley between Tallon's Propane and Adirondack Gifts and Crafts, Buck waved at Kevin. "Come on over."

Kevin waited for several cars to go by before dashing across the road. "Cripes, we go from being able to sit on the white line for an hour to this," he said, gesturing to the line of cars snaking through town.

"Where the hell you been hiding?" Buck said. "I haven't seen you since last week. We got to get back to the Rock before Jimmie and the guys forget they let us in."

"It's been raining almost every night, and my dad's driving me nuts with chores. I hate the start of the season."

Buck twirled his head around and rubbed his shoulder. "I swear those propane tanks got heavier this year. I'm going to be sore for the next two months." He pointed to a car full of tourists pulling into the gift shop. "Busting our asses for them – for peanuts. Mom's already pooped, doing double shifts at the Knotty Pine. They ought to give her the twenty weeks in ten."

"Yeah," Kevin said. Buck's mom scrabbled like many Hawk Covers for twenty weeks on the books to qualify for the unemployment checks that would barely carry them through the winter. Kevin's dad went back to teaching after the season – even if he complained about the low pay.

"I hope I won't be doing this next year," Buck said. "What Creepy

27

Carlson called my aptitude for the manual arts."

"You going to be the only person who ever went to Hamilton High who listened to him?"

"You don't have to worry. You're tail lights next year," Buck said. "Off to college."

"What are you going to do?"

"Join the Navy."

"You never said anything about the Navy. Everybody else around here joins the Air Force."

"I never said it before. I just read it: an ad in *Outdoor Life*. 'Join the Navy and see the world.' I thought, hey, that's not a bad idea. I've never been farther away from Hawk Cove than when I went to my grandmother's funeral out near Buffalo. Cheektowaga." Buck laughed. "Where you from? *Cheek taa whag a.* That'd be hard to get over."

"Never farther than Buffalo?"

"Nope. Anyway, they won't let me join. I've never even seen the ocean, just the rusty lake near my grandmother's house," Buck said. "I'll probably end up in Star Lake with my old man. He says they're hiring again at the mine."

"Star Lake's smaller than Hawk Cove."

"I might like being a mechanic," Buck said. "Harry Simpson would give me a job pumping gas; change tires; even replace a set of plugs. But he'd lay me off come October. No way I'd get my twenty weeks."

"You could get into mechanics at Canton, or something at Paul Smith's, work part-time."

"What about you?" Buck said. "Remember when Rat-faced Riley yelled at you when you didn't have that assignment done? '*Young man*,' he said in a falsetto, 'someone with your possibilities should not let them slip away.' I can't believe Riley belongs to the same half of the human race as Kim Novak. And speaking of babes, what about Jimmie's cousin? She's hot for you."

"Is sex all you think about?"

"Yeah," Buck said. "What do you think about?"

"I don't have to *think* about it."

"Hey, I get off at four tomorrow. You want to take a boat out, buzz by the new batch of rich kids on Hemlock Island?" Buck said.

"I can't. I got to help the new priest. My mom set up this job with him. Never asked me."

"That's better than loading propane. Maybe I'll be a priest. Better than the manual arts," Buck said as he pumped his fist at his crotch.

"You aren't even Catholic."

"You can commute, right?" Buck said. "You told me your mother's a commuter."

"Convert."

"So I'll be a convertible. Yeah, priest would be the life for me. Put in a couple of hours on Sunday, rake in the loot from the collection basket, then take a nap while old lady Pulaski makes me supper." Buck pulled a pack of cigarettes out of his breast pocket, tapped one out and held the pack toward Kevin.

Kevin shook his head. "You still have to go to the seminary. It's like college."

"I'll study for a change." Buck lit the cigarette, snapped the lid of the lighter closed and blew a smoke ring.

"Celibacy," Kevin said. "Ever heard of it? Priests are celibate."

"I'll get all my screwing in before I join you mackerel smackers."

"Yeah, Buck, the women of Hawk Cove will be begging for mercy by Thanksgiving."

Kevin and Buck watched traffic, then began a contest of pitching small stones at a coffee can across the alley.

Buck said, "The three kings brought gold, frankenstein, and myrtle to Baby Jesus, right?"

"What?"

29

"I was thinking about this priest business, and I remembered the front lawn of your church every Christmas. You know, Baby Jesus freezing his ass off laying in a tub with nothing on but a diaper and everybody else standing around staring at him. The three kings holding pots of gold. You know."

"It's called a manger." Kevin held out his hand. "Give me a drag."

"You want one?"

"Just a drag." Kevin took a short pull on the cigarette and blew the smoke out his nose. "And it's not frankenstein. It's frankincense."

"But gold's gold, right?"

"What's the question?"

"What did Joseph and Mary do with the loot?"

"Probably gave it to poor people. How should I know?"

"Why don't you ask this priest you're working for," Buck said. He glanced down the alley, where Jim Tallon had poked out his head out the side door. "I got to go." Buck levered himself up and flicked his cigarette into the dirt. Since school ended, he'd also let his black hair grow out into a DA. "We got to get back to the Rock real soon, Kev. Your new girlfriend's going to find someone else."

As Buck walked along the side of the building with that rocking saunter, Kevin remembered Mrs. Riley's scold. 'Don't you dare sashay in after the bell again, Mister Duncan.' Buck, like his older brother, Duke, had a way of pissing people off just by the way he walked.

Kevin dashed back across the road. Slim's dog stood on the shoulder. "Figured you'd be road kill by now." He started walking toward Tamarack Road. Hearing a low growl, he turned to see the dog behind him. "Beat it," he shouted, but the dog stood, staring at him.

"I'm not feeding you," Kevin said as he continued toward the intersection of Tamarack and Route 28, where he'd turn and head for the Lodge. He'd heard Slim's neighbors had started feeding the dog; others had argued that the old dog ought to be put down. It had been the dog's wailing and baying all day and into the night that had brought the clos-est neighbors to discover Slim's body in his workshop behind the Polka Dot Cottage. No one could remember when the flat boards of Slim's extended shack hadn't been covered with large red, yellow, and blue cir-cles painted on the dull gray background. At the end of a long sandy path lined with dozens of Slim's whirligigs perched on posts, nailed to trees, and sitting on stumps, the Polka Dot Cottage was one of the few things Hawk Covers kept mostly to themselves. Around the age of six, every kid in Hawk Cove had been led up the path by a parent to marvel at the shack that seemed to have jumped off the page of a nursery rhyme, be introduced to the tall, stooped and bearded "Mr. Carrington," and shown around the workshop by the taciturn man who seemed to be torn between a need to be left alone and the momentary pleasure he showed when watching the child choose one of his whirligigs from the tantaliz-ing array on his workbench. Kevin's cardinal had twirled on its post next to the Longhouse with wings that wind-milled in the slightest breeze until a falling limb in a thunderstorm crushed it. Now, the one-winged bird lay buried in the cardboard box in the back of his closet. No replacements for lost or broken whirligigs seemed to be the unspoken rule; no whirligigs for tourists who'd heard about the Polka Dot Cottage off Eagle Pond Road and parked at the end of the path for a glimpse; held at bay by Slim's growling dog.

Kevin wondered what would become of the Polka Dot Cottage. Old-timers said there was a cousin out in Ohio, and someone was trying to locate him. In the meantime, he hoped no one trashed the place or stole the whirligigs.

At the corner, Kevin heard the dog following him. He picked up a stone and cocked his arm. The dog dropped back a few feet. "I'm telling you; I'm not feeding you." Kevin pointed at a passing station wagon. "Go chase that car."

Tuesday July 1

TURKS INVADE GREEK QUARTERS ON CYPRUS
Private Elvis Presley on Furlough

ON THE SIDEWALK IN FRONT ST MARY'S, Kevin automatically bowed his head at the point he figured was in front of the tabernacle and continued on to the rectory. His first day, and already this job his mother set up had become a pain. She made him scrub down after lunch and put on chinos and a good shirt, checking him over as though he was a kid who couldn't be trusted to wash behind his ears. And when his father grumbled about not having Kevin's help cleaning the storeroom, she reminded him of the boost the job would be to Kevin's college fund. He could get hepped-up if the money was going towards buying a car, but his college fund was this space alien growing in the vault at Thendara Savings and Loan. Even if he got a scholarship his father figured was in the back pocket of one of the guests, his parents still weren't going to let him spend it on a car.

He mounted the three stairs, stepped through the wide screened porch with its wicker chairs and swing and reached out to grasp the lion-faced knocker on the door. The door jerked open to yank him into the rectory where he almost stumbled into Mrs. Pulaski.

"Mighty Dinah! You'll send me to an early grave, young man."

"Sorry. I'm here to help. My mother. Mrs. Boyle. Father Donovan. Sorry."

"I *know* who your mother is. And as far as helping, the Father has

32

completely taken over the dining room," Mrs. Pulaski said, waving a large floppy straw bag. "Cleared everything off the table for his project." Filling the doorway, she straightened the scarf tied under her chin and pulled her faded blue cardigan sweater tighter across her enormous bust. "Now if you will kindly let go of the door, I have to be in Old Forge in a half of an hour, and the roads are jammed with tourists."

Squeezing against the door frame, Kevin managed to avoid rubbing against Mrs. Pulaski as she bustled out. Inside the rectory, he heard someone singing. He walked down the carpeted hallway and peered into the formal dining room. At the far end of an eight-foot mahogany table, Father Donovan, dressed in a short-sleeved pleated front dickey and Roman collar, bent over a stack of papers. A waxy aroma of furniture polish hung in the air.

"*When Irish eyes are smiling,*" Father Donovan crooned in a rich baritone. He glanced up and greeted Kevin with a 500-watt smile.

"Well, well. You must be Master Kevin Boyle or someone doing a marvelous impersonation of him."

"Yes, Father."

"Kevin Boyle – or an impersonator?"

"Ah, it's me. I'm the real Kevin Boyle."

Father Donovan's eyes settled on Kevin. "I'll accept that for the moment. But now, the real or presumptive Kevin Boyle, I have to ask you one of the most important questions you will ever have to answer."

Oh, no, Kevin thought. He knows I lied in Confession; that I didn't try harder to not do it.

"Yankees or Red Sox?

Kevin's mouth opened and closed as he tried to make sense of what Father Donovan had said.

"Take your time. Your life may depend on your answer."

The New York Yankees or the Boston Red Sox? His life? Should he tell the priest he liked the Dodgers? But that wasn't one of the choices.

He guessed that if it was just the American League, he'd better pick one. He hated that stuck-up Mantle, so he finally said, "Red Sox."

"The *Boston* Red Sox? You are *absolutely* sure?"

It's a trick, Kevin thought. Father Donovan was trying to trap him into confessing he hadn't stopped masturbating. He should have known. Finally, he weakly uttered, "I'm sure."

With two great strides, Father Donovan bore down on Kevin. His right hand rose from his side, and Kevin flinched, expecting a blow on the head.

When no blow came, Kevin was surprised to see Father Donovan grinning as he held out his hand for Kevin to shake.

"Put'er there, my boy!"

Kevin let Father Donovan take his hand and give it three grand shakes.

"My prayers have been answered," Father Donovan said. "A true fan amid these heathen hordes of Yankee fans."

Rooted to the carpet, Kevin felt relieved at not being exposed as a serial masturbator.

"But, you can't have everything, can you my son?" Father Donovan said, clapping Kevin on the back and guiding him to the dining room table. "But while we could spend the afternoon discussing why Ted Williams is the greatest player of our era, there's work to do."

Father Donovan explained that the sheets of paper stacked at one end of the dining room table needed to be neatly folded in thirds and slid into the envelopes he addressed. Kevin should then carefully seal the envelope with a swipe across the wet sponge sitting in one of the china luncheon plates. Finally, the stamps were to licked and affixed in exact alignment in the upper right hand corner of each envelope.

Under intense scrutiny that made his hands shake, Kevin began folding the papers and slipping them in the envelopes as though he were packing his own parachute.

"I greatly appreciate the care you're taking young man," Father Donovan said. "But I'm afraid you'll never turn the double play at that speed. Here," he said as he leaned over Kevin to demonstrate how to set an empty envelope in front of the paper as a guide, "See if this helps."

Kevin crouched closer to the table as Father Donovan's arms draped over his shoulders. The flowery aroma of aftershave reminded Kevin of that terrible Confession as he tried to concentrate on Father Donovan's instructions. After several run-throughs, the priest allowed Kevin to continue on his own.

Getting the hang of it, Kevin folded and slid the sheets into the envelopes with enough routine dexterity to allow him to read what was printed on them. 'Impeach Earl Warren,' proclaimed the headline of the column on the left of the sheet. 'Communism – 90 Miles Away,' read the headline over the story on the right. 'State Department Rife with Reds' cried the heading of the story below the fold.

Father Donovan sat at the end of the table humming as he checked a long list of names before writing out the addresses with a black fountain pen. "We're doing the Lord's work, my son." After a few moments, he asked, "I don't suppose you have heard of John Birch from your history teachers?"

"No, Father."

"I can't say I'm surprised. But if we persevere, more true Americans will learn about the first victim of World War III – murdered by the Chinese Communists put into power by our State Department."

Kevin had been standing for almost an hour and needed to pee. He shuffled his feet and fumbled a fold. He squirmed from leg to leg, "Ah, excuse me Father, but I need to use the bathroom."

"Of course, of course. I'm not running a slave labor camp. Right around the corner and on the left before you get to the kitchen."

Slipping out of the dining room, Kevin found the bathroom with its toilet and small sink behind the heavy oak door. He sighed as he let go a long stream of pee. What's with this commie stuff? he wondered. He finished, washed his hands, and zipped up. He opened the door to find Father Donovan standing in front of him. "Excuse me," Kevin stammered.

"Taking Holy Orders does not mean one is released from the natural order of things."

Kevin ducked around him and hurried to the dining room and continued stuffing envelopes. After a few minutes Father Donovan returned.

"You've done a fine job, young man," he said. "But I don't suppose someone as bright as you yearns for a job in the post office?"

"No, Father."

"Have you given any thought to the priesthood?"

"No, Father."

"I don't want to seem too forward, seeing as how we've just met. But you will be entering your senior year in September, and I understand you're at the top of your class."

"Yes, Father." Kevin wondered how this priest who'd only been in town a month knew that.

"I'm sure you've been getting a lot of advice about careers and thinking about what you'd like to do."

"Yes, Father."

"Well, I want to get an oar in here. The priesthood is a wonderful life, even with its challenges. There may be a vocation out there with your name on it." Father Donovan paused. "You will listen for it, my son? Ask God in your prayers if He is calling you?"

"Yes, Father." Was lying to a priest a mortal sin, he wondered?

Father Donovan stared at Kevin for several seconds, as Kevin tried not to look away. The priest seemed satisfied and returned to addressing the envelopes. After a half hour of stuffing, addressing, and stamping, Father Donovan called a halt to their work. "Would you join me on the porch for a glass of lemonade and some of Mrs. Pulaski's wonderful molasses cookies?"

Kevin wanted to tell him he needed to get back to the Lodge, that he had chores to do, but he nodded and went out to the porch and sat in a wicker chair. When Father Donovan came out the rectory door with two tall glasses of lemonade and a plate of cookies on a tray, Kevin jumped up.

"Thank you for the courtesy, young man," Father Donovan said, pointing to Kevin's chair. "I'm afraid that's one of the few drawbacks of the priesthood. 'Yes, Father,' 'No, Father,' and folks standing around as though they're expecting you're going to spring a High Mass on them any second."

Kevin perched on the edge of the chair as Father Donovan took a seat in the rocker across from him, handed Kevin one of the glasses of lemonade, and pointed to the cookies. Kevin took one and wondered how long he was expected to stay.

Father Donovan took a bite of his cookie. "Wonderful cook, Mrs. Pulaski." He patted his stomach and sighed. "Now if I can only convince her we don't have to have breakfasts every morning as though we're cutting timber or dine every evening as though Cardinal Spellman might pay a surprise visit."

Kevin drained his glass of lemonade.

"Engage the world! That's what the modern priest must do." Father Donovan slid forward and put his hand on Kevin's knee. "I tell you, young man – Kevin – the world is in turmoil; adrift without a moral anchor. We have to give people a strong hand on the tiller, guide them around the shoals. We need to be *in* the world, not in an isolated monastery: not that our saintly brothers do not have an important role in our salvation. But it's a messy world out there, isn't it?"

Father Donovan's hand slowly slid off Kevin's knee. Kevin said, "I guess."

"I think I'll start having breakfast at the Sunnyside Up." Father Donovan said. "Or perhaps I'll stroll into the Trading Post one night and have a Utica Club with a few of our parishioners – meet them in their real lives."

Kevin stifled a grin as he imagined Orin Matthews toppling off his bar stool if Father Donovan did that.

"Just joking, my son." He paused. "But the world isn't two hundred miles away. It's right out there on Route 28: the Red & White, Simpson's Garage, and the library. So, don't be too surprised if you see me at the Trading Post."

"I won't," Kevin murmured.

"Won't be surprised?"

"Ah, I won't be at the bar, Father. I'm seventeen."

"So, you'll just have to make do with the six packs your friends can get at Pauquette's," Father Donovan laughed. "Don't worry, my son. This is not the confessional, and I won't let tell-tale blushes go beyond the confines of this porch."

"Thank you, Father. I'd better be going. I've got chores to do before supper."

Father Donovan stood quickly. "Of course. But first, a workman's due his wages." He pulled a wallet from his back pocket. "Now, that's two hours at three dollars an hour." He handed Kevin a five and two ones.

"That's too much, Father. It's only six, and that's a lot more than minimum."

"Let's just say, it's a bonus from our benefactor. And if you want to do him a favor, have a Mars instead of a Snickers next time you're in the mood for a candy bar."

"Thank you, Father."

"And one more thing," Father Donovan said. "Wait here a moment." He went into the rectory and returned with a Polaroid camera. "I'm a sucker for gadgets." He pointed the camera at Kevin. "Smile."

Kevin blinked as the camera flashed, then stared at the shiny paper Father Donovan pulled from the back of the camera. Slowly, an image of a startled Kevin Boyle formed.

"I like to keep a record of partners in crime," Father Boyle chuckled. "See you next week, Master Boyle. And curse them *Damn Yankees*."

WALKING BACK TO THE LODGE, Kevin wondered what he'd gotten himself into. Yankees or Red Sox? Couldn't he do the job and go home instead of choosing a favorite team as though his life depended on it? Sure he was happy when Hawk Cove beat Blue Mountain or the other teams in the league. But it wasn't like he couldn't eat for a week when we lost. If he lived in New York or Boston or another real city, he could see rooting for the home team. Otherwise, what made it so important?

The only kid he knew who got juiced up about the Red Sox was Billy Fletcher. And that's because his father took him to a game at Fenway Park a couple of years ago and got an autograph from that weirdo Jimmy Piersall. Now he's a Red Sox fan forever. Billy and Father Donovan can sit on the rectory porch sipping lemonade telling each other how much they hate the *damn* Yankees. And you can't just be for your team; you got to hate the other guy's.

Kevin scooped up a stone and pitched it at the pine slab nailed to a tree at the end of a driveway – The Carpenters. Fairport, New York. It's not so awful to be proud of where you live, as long as you don't go around making sure everybody else ought to be pissing their pants because they don't live there, too. Still, if you lived in Hawk Cove, what were you besides screwed? Was he going to take the gas pipe if he ended up in St. Louis or Cincinnati or Denver? First, he had to get out of Hawk Cove. Then he'd worry about where next.

Kevin turned onto Cedar Road, and Slim's dog trotted out of the bushes and stood fifteen feet behind him. "What are you doing here?" He'd never seen Slim's dog in this part of town.

The dog snarled, and Kevin took a quick menacing step towards the dog. The dog didn't move. Kevin shook his head and continued walking toward the Lodge. "I'm not feeding you, so don't follow me expecting something to eat." When he reached the driveway to the Lodge, he glanced back. The dog was still fifteen feet behind him. "No food! Go!" Kevin pointed toward the direction they'd come. The dog continued staring at him, but stayed on the road as he walked down the driveway to the Lodge.

Friday July 4

SOVIETS REQUEST TALKS ON BARRING SURPRISE ATTACKS
Can Parents Prevent Teen-Age Petting?

AFTER SUPPER, KEVIN PRETENDED TO READ A BOOK as he waited for the right moment. He'd been dying to get back to the Rock, but a solid week of rain every night washed that out. Would Jimmie remember that he and Buck were cool? Would Maxine remember him? "I think I'll go out."

His father ignored him and waved the manila folder he used as a schedule at his mother, who was sitting at a card table across the room next to a matching green plaid, maple-armed sofa and chair. On the floor, an oval braid rug covered most of the gray-flecked linoleum. A pulley lamp cast a circle of light inside the square of the card table.

"Not only do the Barkers cancel at the last minute, but look at these other vacancies. Seneca is open the last week of July, and Mohawk and Cayuga are vacant both the second and third weeks of August. At this rate, I don't see how we're going to make the loan payment."

Joyce gazed at the almost-completed jigsaw puzzle of Monet's Rouen Cathedral as though it was the cover of a travel brochure. "*Qué será sera.*"

"I'll be back early," Kevin said.

"It's not just the Barkers," Thomas said. "We can't count on the same people coming back year after year. We need new blood."

Fitting one of the handful of sandstone-colored pieces left, Joyce said, "What about those people from Utica who stopped in last week? Didn't they want a cottage for the second week of August?"

"Fruit and vegetable hucksters. The missus looked like a gypsy princess with that mop of black curls and those dangly earrings and gold bracelets clanging every time she moved. They won't fit in."

"Up to the Red & White," Kevin said.

With a piece held in her fingers, Joyce peered at the puzzle. "We are not running a country club, Thomas."

Thomas stared at the schedule as if the empty squares would magically fill with the names of families eager to spend a week or two at Iroquois Lodge. He picked up the business card Salvatore Magretti had left. "Spaghetti," he muttered. "I'm calling them collect."

"April's *Ladies Home Journal* had a feature on pasta. It's very healthy and becoming fashionable."

"I'm talking about that Magretti who wanted a cottage."

"Just a couple of the guys," Kevin said.

"We should put colanders in the cottages," Joyce said. "If you want new blood, we have to keep up."

"For crying out loud, Joyce, as it is, I don't know where half the pots and pans in those cottages get to. I'm not going to add colanders to the kitchen supply warehouse we're running."

I'll leave, and they won't know I'm gone until next week. Kevin thought.

Joyce fitted a piece of the puzzle and stood. "I think I'll have a small cordial. Would you care for one? It might calm your nerves."

"My nerves are fine," Thomas said.

Joyce crossed the room, opened the sideboard, and stared at the rainbow of bottles. She removed a small stemmed glass and filled it with *Crème d' Menthe*. Taking a sip of the syrupy green liquid, she returned to her chair and looked at the thousand piece puzzle on the table under the hanging lamp, the first of the ten puzzles she would do before Labor Day. Later this evening, she would gaze at the blurry outlines of Rouen Cathedral for as long as it took to smoke a cigarette. Then the puzzle would be swept into its box and shelved in the store room next to the dozens of others.

Thomas pulled a bill from the stack and ripped a check from the book.

"See you later," Kevin said as he headed for the screen door.

"Be back by eleven," Thomas said.

"I'm too old for a curfew."

"What does that mean?"

"You said you wanted me to take more responsibility around the Lodge this year."

Thomas swiveled around in his chair and ran his hand through the few strands of hair left on top of his head. "I don't see what that has to do with coming in at a reasonable hour."

Kevin wondered if his father's shiny scalp warned of what he would look like before forty. He's looking at me, but he turned slowly, not with an angry jerk. "The other day you said I'm supposed to think for myself and do things without having to be asked. Okay, then I ought to decide what's a reasonable hour to come home."

"Thinking for yourself and staying out until all hours are not the same thing."

Opening his arms wide, Kevin said, "Where could I stay out until all hours in Hawk Cove?"

"That is not the point."

"Don't you want to see the fireworks?" Joyce said.

"I should have known better than say 'yes' to that Shannon guy when he asked if I minded if he brought in a few fireworks. Now he's set up some sort of frame on the dock, and there's a stack of boxes full of Roman candles and bottle rockets, and goodness knows what else on their porch. I hope we don't run into trouble."

"Thomas, you're such a worry-wort. It will be fun."

"We'll see who's laughing when a kid gets a finger blown off."

Kevin grabbed his jacket from the hook. "See you later."

"And where are you going?"

"Around."

"Tomorrow's turn-over day," Thomas said.

"And don't forget Confession tomorrow afternoon," Joyce added.

"I'm not planning on staying out all night."

"Kevin..."

WALKING UP LAKE ROAD five minutes later, Kevin couldn't shake his mother's reminder. She'd probably tell him that going to the Rock was an occasion of sin. Confession. Mass. Holy Days of Obligation. Easter Duty. Sometimes it seemed as though her reminders were meant to ricochet off him and hit his father: the Catholic – on an extended sabbatical, he said. Was anything going to happen tonight he'd have to confess?

He hoped Buck had taken care of business.

KEVIN HESITATED A MOMENT at the end of the track before he and Buck stepped into the clearing. They'd been given the okay – hadn't they? But even in the dim light he could make out Jimmie Nelson charging at them. Kevin and Buck cautiously held out the six-packs they'd brought.

"It's you two pussies," Jimmie snarled.

Kevin dangled the beer a little higher.

"Steal these from your old man?" Jimmie snatched the six-pack and looked Kevin up and down like he was thinking of bench-pressing him into the bushes for kicks. "Don't be a fuck-up, Boyle." He grabbed the carton Buck held. "That goes for you too, Bucky Beaver. You go puking your guts up in town and the fuzz comes around, you two are going to wish you stayed at the town beach with the other fairies." He pulled out two bottles, flipped off the caps with the edge of his belt buckle, and handed them to Kevin and Buck. "You better be cool," Jimmie said before stomping back to the fire.

44

"Whew," Buck said. "Popeye's going to let us stay."

"You let him hear you call him that, and you're mincemeat."

"Hey, there's Chink Perrotti," Buck said. "He owes me fifty cents. I got to get it off him. My half of the beer cleaned me out." Buck edged around the fire and headed for the guys standing near the base of the Rock.

Puffy Russell goosed Buck. Then Chink grabbed him in a hammer lock. Buck laughed as he wrestled his way out of Chink's grasp. The slant eyes Chink inherited from his Indian mother got him the handle in first grade. But along with his pointy nose set in his pinched chin-less face, Kevin thought he looked more like a mole than a chink.

When Puffy slapped Buck on the back, Kevin wondered if Puffy and Chink had already squared-off. Puffy had an empty head bigger than a watermelon and claimed his ability to fart *shave-and-a-hair-cut-two-bits* showed way more talent than Chink's *Up-yours-asshole* burp. Chink looked like he was working on adding another line when Hack Leroux handed Chink a beer. Probably full of rat poison, Kevin thought. Hack *looked* normal, but Hack was the only kid in school who got a visit from a psychologist sent all the way from Marcy. Because it was only Hack's sisters and younger girl cousins who he'd tie up naked and toss lit matches at kept Hack out of reform school. And that wasn't too strange in that clan of nutcases. Everybody steered wide of Hack who'd figured out how to get his way by putting on a far-away stare while making grunting and squealing noises in the back of his throat.

What was he doing hanging around with this crew? His father would have a bird. Would he start acting like these guys; looking like them, too? He hated the way his ears stuck out. After a summer at the Rock, they'd be calling him "Dumbo." Maybe getting into the Rock wasn't such a good idea.

But as Kevin turned over the idea of quietly slipping away, he spotted Maxine, wearing a pair of red Bermuda shorts, a white short-sleeved blouse and red tennis sneakers, walking toward him. It looked as though she was going to walk right into him, but she stopped inches from where he stood. She pressed one of the bottles of Carling's he'd brought against her cheek. "I was hot, and like John Wayne you rode in to save the day."

"I'm glad. It just…" Kevin glanced down at the gap in her blouse.

"Like I said, I'll look up, and there'll you be scoping out by ta-tas."

"I ah,…" He was about to apologize – again. But something about the way she stood with one hand on her hip, the sly smile on her lips, stopped him. "Well, there they are, so I thought I should introduce myself."

Maxine grabbed Kevin's arm and pulled him toward her. "You're a goof."

Jeez, he never thought he'd pull off something like that – and she liked it. "I guess."

Maxine picked up a stick, knelt and drew circles in the sand. "So, this is your regular hangout?"

"One of them."

Maxine ran the stick over the design she'd scratched in the sand. "I asked Jimmie about you – after we met last week."

"What did he say?"

"He was surprised you were here, your dad being a teacher. Said you owned a big-time resort."

"Just some cottages. Over around the point. So, you don't think Jimmie likes me?"

"He didn't say that. He said he knows your friend's brother."

"It's a small town."

"So's Minerva. Peyton Place."

"That's what everybody says about where they live. Did you like the book?"

"I saw the movie. I was thinking about reading the book, but I got sick of hearing every girl I knew practicing the line about sticking it in Allison."

A wind shift blew smoke at them. As Maxine turned away and flipped her hair, Kevin noticed a white line from the back of her left ear to the neckline of her blouse.

"What are you staring at?"

"Nothing. Well, I noticed the line on your neck."

"A scar is supposed to make a person mysterious."

"That's what I hear."

"Don't you want to know what's the mystery?"

"Okay."

"I'm not telling." Maxine poked he stick into Kevin's belly. "Or maybe I will – if…"

"If what?"

"If I want to." Maxine took another swig of beer. A bottle rocket whistled out from the beach and hissed into the lake.

Everybody Kevin could see in the dim light had a beer in their hand, holding it like it was what they did. He knew that right now, kids his age would be huddled at the far end of the town beach, away from the younger kids dangling off the jungle gym and the adults taking an evening stroll. Somebody might have a quart of beer tucked under their jacket, and they'd pass it around, like it was a big deal. Another bottle rocket whistled out over the water. Roman candles were shooting from somewhere beyond Injun Swamp, and the snap of firecrackers began to drift in. Yeah, this was okay. It wasn't like he planned on spending the rest of his life at the Trading Post bar with Jimmie, Chink and Puffy. It was time he decided things for himself, see what else was going on.

Bam. A firecracker went off at Maxine's feet. "*Jesus Christ!*" She jumped back, almost falling.

Chink and Jimmie were pointing at them. "Wet your pants, Boyle?" Chink shouted.

"That's not funny," Maxine shouted back.

"You two looked so lovey-dovey, we couldn't resist," Jimmie said.

Maxine grabbed Kevin's arm. "That is really, really not funny." She pulled him farther from the fire.

To Kevin she seemed more afraid than you would think from a fire-cracker going off. Chink tossed another fire-cracker at the group standing near the path to the lean-to. "Are you okay?"

They sat on a log at the far edge of the clearing and watched the guys toss firecrackers at each other.

"Bunch of jerks," Maxine said. "I told Jimmie before we came over. Yeah. Yeah. He thinks it's funny."

"You got a thing about firecrackers?" Kevin said.

"No. Guns."

"Guns?"

"Forget it."

A green starburst opened just above the tree line. Must be Mr. Shannon's fireworks. A double red and yellow starburst followed. "That's our place," Kevin said as he pointed toward the trees.

"What do you mean?"

"Those fireworks. A guy staying at our place brought them. They don't bother you, do they?"

"No, they're okay." Maxine picked up a handful of sand then let the grains slide through her fingers.

Kevin picked up some sand and tossed it on the grass. "So, how are things at the Acropolis?"

"You go from one thing to another, dontcha?"

"I just wondered how the job is working out for you."

"Sorry I snapped your head off," Maxine said. "I should have known when the Greek handed me a uniform that wouldn't cover my ass in a stiff breeze."

An image of Theo Dorakadis hip-bumping and shoulder-squeezing the waitresses jumped into Kevin's head. Maybe it was a Greek thing – or maybe it was because Theo's wife was the ugliest woman in the

Adirondacks.

"Has Theo done anything?"

"The first week I got what the other girls said was the usual: a *friend-ly* pat on the ass, a couple of cracks about banana splits and hot fudge." Maxine ran her fingers through her hair and looked off. "I'm like, you know, fly-paper to creeps."

"Did he do something else?"

"Wednesday, Theo corners me in the storeroom, pins me to the wall, and tells me a girl like me shouldn't act so high and mighty."

"*Jeez.*"

Maxine shrugged. "What's he got, radar for what he figures is an easy mark?"

"What do you mean?"

"Nothing. Forget it. And, hey, I didn't mean you when I said that about fly paper."

"That's all right," Kevin said, then took another swallow of beer. "So, are you going to get another job?"

"I need the money, and the best jobs are sewed up already." Maxine looked toward the lake. "Besides, it's always the same thing. And I've learned a couple of tricks. The Greek thinks all my brains are in my tits, so I took his slimy paws off them and said it was going to cost him." Maxine laughed. "I undid two more buttons on my uniform and told him I was going to scream and go running out front like that – unless I got a raise and better hours. You should of seen the look on his face. He said Athena did the payroll, so I had to settle for better hours."

"That's it?"

"For now. At first, he probably figured he'd made the deal of the cen-tury. But I think he's worried. The other girls are pissed I'm off week-end nights, but, hey, they can make their own deals. A girl's got to take care of herself, right?"

A couple of guys had climbed to the top of the Rock and were tossing firecrackers out over the water. Through the smoke blowing from the pit fire, Kevin could make out Jimmie with his arm draped over Noel Dupleiss's shoulder. A closing-time brawl at whatever bar would still let them in was the guys in the Dupleiss clan idea of a good way to end a day of logging. Noel had barely graduated in June, and from what he heard, Jimmie and Noel's dates were mostly parking somewhere.

Jimmie took his arm off of Noel and looked at Maxine and Kevin. Kevin tensed as Jimmie whispered something to Noel and pointed at Kevin and Maxine.

"Hey, want to be my date?" Maxine said.

"When?"

"Tonight. Double date."

"With Jimmie and Noel?"

"I either get a date, or Jimmie's going to drop me back at the house."

"You sure it's okay with Jimmie?"

"Come on. It'll be okay," Maxine said. "Jimmie's supposed to be nice to me, and if he's not, I'll tell his old man." She grabbed Kevin's arm and tugged him toward the fire. "Kevin's my date."

Jimmie scowled at Kevin. "Your mommy let you stay out past ten o'clock?"

How long *were* they planning on being out? Where were they going?

"Robbing the cradle?" Jimmie said to Maxine.

"Kevin is a very sweet guy,' Maxine said as she pulled Kevin closer. "Besides, you don't want to go all the way home to drop me off."

Buck came up next to Kevin.

"What do you want?" Jimmie said.

"Where are you going?" Buck said to Kevin.

"I'm, ah, going with Maxine."

"I thought we were going to do fireworks and stuff." Buck said.

Jimmie said to Kevin. "This ain't no kiddie parade. You going with Maxine here, or what?"

"Yeah, sure," Kevin said. "I'll catch you later. Tomorrow, Buck. Okay?"
Buck shuffled off.

"Christ," Jimmie said to Maxine and Kevin. "We got this sorted out,
or what?"

"For crying out loud, Jimmie. Don't make a federal case out of it,"
Maxine said.

"You girls get in the car," Jimmie said. "I got to have a word with
Boyle." Jimmie grabbed Kevin by the shoulder and held him back. "You
damn well better be cool with this. I don't need somebody shooting their
mouth off about my business: what I do, where I go."

"Sure, Jimmie." Kevin paused. "Where are we going?"

"I got to check on some property I'm taking care of. But I don't want
nobody knowing my business."

"Ah, Jimmie. I got to get up really early tomorrow. Need to fix the
dock. One of the damn drums is leaking. Hell of a lousy job with the
lake full."

Jimmie squeezed Kevin's shoulder until it hurt. "I'll get you back
before you turn into a pumpkin. Besides, I got to take care of Maxine.
She's got enough trouble." He pushed Kevin toward the cars.

Kevin glanced back to see Buck raise his hand, then let it drop as
Kevin ducked low to climb into the back seat of Jimmie's Merc. As soon
as Kevin got in, Maxine sidled next to him and took his hand. "This will
be fun."

In the front seat, Noel huddled next to Jimmie. Jimmie backed slowly out onto Cedar Road, then laid a strip of rubber up Lake Street as he
floored the souped-up V-8. With dual exhausts roaring, Jimmie careened
around corners in town until he shot across Route 28 onto Beaver Pond
Road. When he hit the straight-away a mile out of town, the trees were
a blur. After the road curved around Moss Lake, Jimmie took a hard right
into a dirt road and slammed on the brakes. "Time to earn your keep,
Boyle." The headlights lit a loggers' gate: two metal posts supporting a

long hollow metal bar with padlocks on the outside of each end.

As Noel pulled the seat forward, Jimmie handed Kevin a ring of keys.

"The one on the right," Jimmie said as Kevin clambered out of the car.

Kevin unlocked the padlock, pulled it out of the slot, and pushed the long hollow bar toward the other post. As the bar slid through the hole, it gained momentum and pulled Kevin along with it until it jammed his right hand against the post hole. "*Goddamnit!*" Kevin jumped back and tears welled as he unclasped his fingers to see blood smearing his ripped knuckles.

"For crissakes. Ain't you ever worked one of these before?" Jimmie shouted as he leaned out the window.

"I couldn't see. I'm okay."

"I should of known." Jimmie shook his head and drove five yards beyond the gate. Kevin clanged the rod off the post before he managed to get the prong through the slot. He snapped the padlock shut, pulled his handkerchief out of his back pocket, and wrapped his right hand in it. He climbed back into the back seat.

"Poor baby," Maxine cooed. "Let me see."

"Don't get no blood on the seat, asshole," Jimmie said.

"Just go, Jimmie. For crissakes." Maxine daubed at Kevin's torn knuckles as they drove along the dirt road. After about a mile, they pulled into a clearing. The headlights picked out a large house set back on a sloping lawn from a lake.

"The Pearson place," Jimmie said. He reached under the front seat and pulled out a flashlight, then grabbed a ring of keys from the glove compartment.

Kevin and Maxine followed Jimmie and Noel to the back door of the building. Jimmie unlocked the door, pulled the master arm next to the fuse box and flipped two switches. Bulbs along the rim of a large wooden circular chandelier lit the varnished stripped timbers that formed cross beams in the high open room. A stone fire place filled one wall.

Through a picture window, a strip of moonlight framed black silhouettes of pines lying across the lake.

"Holy smokes," Maxine said as she twirled around. "A mansion."

"There's a lot of these places," Jimmie said. "You got to know where they are."

"How come we're here?" Maxine said.

"My old man's looking after the place. He did work for the Pearsons last fall, and they asked him to keep an eye on the place this summer while they're in Paris, France."

"Wow," Maxine said. "They must be millionaires."

"I never heard of the Pearsons," Kevin said.

"They keep to themselves. There's places up on Raquette and Blue Mountain even got full-time managers and cooks. The less you know, the happier it makes them."

"And they just leave this place empty?" Maxine said. She stepped into the great room and gazed around. "Don't rent it out or nothing?"

"Like you said, dummy. These are rich people. They don't need the dough and don't want folks like them that rent from Boyle's old man leaving wet bathing suits on the couch. Some only come up for a few weeks. Other times they go to France or Europe and don't come at all."

"So what are you supposed to do?" Maxine said.

"See if any limbs fell on the roof, or windows got broke," Jimmie said as he smirked at Noel. "Make sure nobody's messing around." He glanced at his watch. "I don't want the lights on here too long. There's one other place across the lake, and I don't want them calling the cops if they think somebody is staying the night." He made a face at Kevin. "And Boyle here has got to be home for his beauty sleep."

Maxine gaped around the room. "This place is like a hotel."

"Yeah. And me and Noel are going to check out the honeymoon suite," Jimmie said nodding in the direction of a door to the right of the fireplace. "You guys can make sure everything's all right upstairs."

Jimmie handed Kevin the flashlight. "I'll let you know when we're done checking." He leaned close to Kevin and whispered, "The place has got to look *exactly* like it did when we got here. If you use the bed, remake it like you was in the Marines."

Kevin gawped at Jimmie, then shot a quick glance at Maxine bent over the fireplace.

"You could roast an ox in this," Maxine said.

"*Exactly*," Jimmie said to Kevin. "My old man finds out we've been messing around here, and I will personally drop you off the Rock with a hundred pound anchor around your neck. Got it?"

Jimmie and Noel disappeared through the door next to the fireplace.

Maxine walked over to Kevin and took his hand. She unwrapped the blood-stained handkerchief. "You did a nasty job on your knuckles." She kissed the knuckles. "Come on. Let's check out this place."

They poked in and out of two bedrooms off the landing that circled the living room. Maxine shone the flashlight on a door at the end of the landing. "I'll bet that's Pappa Bear's room."

Remake the bed? Kevin thought as he followed Maxine. He figured they we were going parking. Half-baked images of kissing Maxine – maybe his hands on her breasts – swirled in his head.

Maxine opened the door, shined the flashlight around the empty room. "It *is* Poppa Bear's room."

A large bed filled the left side of the room. On the right a small sofa, two chairs, side tables and a coffee table faced a picture window with a wide view of the lake. There was a bathroom behind the open door to the right. "And our own potty," Maxine said. "To hell with whoever's across the lake. I'm getting sick of this flashlight. Hit the lights."

As Kevin flipped the lights on, Maxine stretched out on the sofa. "I could get used to this. And it sure beats the back seat of Jimmie's hot rod."

The bed seemed to grow larger in Kevin's view.

"If you're worried Jimmie's going to bust in on us, you can lock the door."

"I don't think he will. Will he?"

"Who knows what Jimmie'll do? Sometimes I think he's got a screw loose."

"What do you mean?"

"Hey, you gonna stand over there all night? I won't bite, you know."

As he walked toward her, Kevin tried to ignore the bed, bigger than a double, with a white birch-branch headboard. The room's musty odor reminded Kevin of the cottages when they started cleaning them in the spring. And the room was nicer than the bedrooms in the cottages at Iroquois Lodge: wood paneling halfway up the walls, and real walls too instead of beaverboard.

"Wouldn't it be nice to have a place like this? Even a room like this?"

Kevin sat on the end of the sofa. It the first time he got a good look at Maxine away from the dim, smoky light at the Rock. She was thinner than he thought, and her skin lighter too. "So, what do you want to do?"

Maxine drew her legs up under her. "I don't do it on the first date."

"Me neither," he said after a second.

"That's what a lot of guys say." She swiveled around to face him. "Then they do what they want anyway."

"I won't." He met her eyes, then looked out the window. A breeze had come up, and the tops of the pines were swaying. When he turned back, she was staring at him.

"You ever been alone with a girl in a bedroom before?"

"What do you think I am, a kid?"

"Hey, I like that about you."

"That I'm a kid?"

"No, that you're not all over me like some creeps I know."

"Fly paper."

She made a face.

"I'm sorry. I didn't mean that you – well, I'm sorry."

"Just because I've had some problems, doesn't mean I'm like a pushover. You'd be in a nice room like this, sofa, lamps, moonlight through a big picture window, and a lot of guys they'd say, 'Yeah, sure,' and start pulling off your clothes." She gave him a sly smile. "But you wouldn't want to do that, would you? You're a gentleman."

"Yeah, sure."

"I think it would be nice to talk for a while. You know."

"So what do you want to talk about?"

"I don't know. Stuff."

"Okay. Tell me how you got the scar."

Her hand went to her left ear. "You don't want to know."

He slid along the sofa, put his hand behind Maxine's ear and traced the white line down as far as he dared. As her blouse parted, he caught a glimpse of the edge of her bra. "Yes, I do."

"You might not like it."

"Try me." His fingers rested on the nape of her neck, then inched forward along the neckline of her blouse.

"Okay. My boyfriend – *ex*-boyfriend tried to kill me."

His hand came off her neck as he bolted upright. "With a *knife*?"

"Yeah, one of those big Bowie knives. The one the son-of-a-bitch used to gut deer."

"Holy mackerel! Why would he want to do that?"

"You only get one mystery at a time. If I tell you all my secrets, then you won't want to be my date anymore."

He let out a nervous laugh. "I'm sorry. It's just that you want to have a nice talk, and you tell me your ex-boyfriend tried to kill you with a hunting knife. It's kind of funny. I mean weird."

"I suppose it isn't very romantic."

"And you won't tell me why?" A picture of Noel's older brother Frank, a three-fingered maniac, holding a knife tumbled through his brain. He almost pulled his hand away when Maxine reached out to take it in hers.

"If I told you, you might not want to – you know – be nice to me." She squeezed his hand. "So, maybe we shouldn't talk." She put her arms on his shoulders.

Kevin leaned in to kiss her. They both tilted in the same direction, giggled, then kissed, lips pressing, then pulling away, then again harder. He felt her tongue snaking between his lips, and when he opened his mouth, it darted in, first flicking around his tongue, then probing deeper. At first surprised, he struggled to keep up, pushing his tongue in, tasting beer, tobacco and Juicy Fruit gum. He felt her palms pushing him away. What had he done?

"Whew. I needed to come up for air."

The jam of his thing in his jeans forced him to sidle around. He shifted his legs trying to give it room, then moved in closer. They laughed again as they fumbled with where to put their arms.

"I don't think this is a love seat," she said as she pulled him off the sofa and onto the braid rug.

They lay alongside each other, kissing, then Kevin slid his hand from her shoulders to the edge of her breasts. He opened his eyes to see whether she was giving him a sign and saw her smile. She's going to let me, he realized. At first, his fingers skipped over her breasts, then began gently kneading them through her blouse as he tried to burn in the feel of them, arching his head to keep kissing her. He pressed them harder, then felt her push him away again. "I'm sorry."

Her smile told him he shouldn't be, and her hands nudged him to kneel beside her as she sat up. Then his eyes followed her fingers as she slowly unfastened one, then another, then another until her blouse slid open and she sat back on the palms of her hands.

He started to put his hands on her breasts, but she pushed them away. Before he could say he was sorry, again, she shrugged the blouse off her shoulders, reached behind her back to unclasp her bra, and let it slowly slide down her arms.

He took in her sly smile then feasted on her breasts, real tits on a real girl sitting two feet in front of him. Could he, his eyes asked?

Sure, why not? hers answered.

Kevin grinned and ran his fingers over her breasts, first letting them confirm he was really, really doing this. Next, he flicked his fingers across her nipples, holding them gently, relishing the feeling of them between his fingers. He was surprised by how the look on her face excited him as much as the feel of her breasts. Then he held them in the palms of his hands, lifting them, weighing them, squeezing them, stroking her nipples with his thumbs.

And when she leaned into him, grasped his tee-shirt in both hands, and pulled it over his head, he had to force himself to breathe. "Fair is fair," she murmured.

She lay back on the rug. Her breast slipped gently to her side. "You can take off my shorts if you'd like."

A whoosh of air came out of his mouth. He wondered if it hung open as he tried to hear those words again and again in his head. He didn't care. His eyes left hers and slowly tracked with his fingers down her body to the brass button on her red shorts. He felt her lift slightly as the button unfastened, and the tab of the zipper pulled down, peeling her shorts away from the white panties underneath. Somehow they were pushed down her legs and kicked off. "Leave my panties on."

His hyper-sensitive fingers ran across the front of her panties. His zoomed in on the tiny scalloped ridges along her waist, the dark tuft under the thin nylon; then pulling back to gaze at this girl lying in front of him wearing nothing but a pair of white panties and red tennis sneakers.

Maxine pulled herself up to rest on her forearms. "My turn." He kissed her. Her hand was on his cheek, then his neck, then walking down his chest. Then he let himself be pushed back onto the rug. He picked out a water stain on the white ceiling, like a small box turtle, focusing on it to let him concentrate on the feeling of her fingers fumbling with the button on his jeans. As she pulled the zipper down, he felt his hard thing un-spring. It hurt. He had hardly felt it before. Now, it was..... Oh, Jesus! *Oh, Jesus Christ!* A rushing, pulsing sensation sped through him as he struggled to get up.

"Oh, my," she said.

He covered her hands with his as his thing erupted into a spurting convulsion between his legs. "Oh, no." He pushed away and gaped at his thing shuddering under his shorts, feeling the sticky ooze spread through his hair.

She put her hands over his shorts and gently massaged his erection until it softened. "You've got a hair trigger."

"Oh, *Jeez*." He flopped back and stared at the ceiling as the sticky mess congealed.

"Poor baby got too excited."

His brain felt like the wet, sticky thing shriveling in his shorts as he sat up and rubbed his hands over his face. "I'm sorry." The excitement he'd felt moments ago drained away by a wide-open spigot; leaving nothing but dregs of shame and remorse. "I'm sorry."

"It happens to a lot of guys."

"I feel like a complete jerk." He closed his eyes: too embarrassed to look at her, still confused by what had happened, ashamed of what he'd done.

After what seemed like minutes to Kevin, Maxine leaned forward and kissed him on the forehead. "Are you, ah? You ever do this before?"

"Lose it like that?"

"No, silly. Be with a girl like this?"

"Oh sure, lots of times." He finally met her eyes. "No."

"That's sweet. I don't know many – really not any guys like you."

"What's that, a stupid jerk?"

"Hey, don't be hard on yourself. Next time, we'll go slow."

Next time? He didn't want to think about this time. "I've got to get cleaned up. I look stupid."

"It's okay. We both look kind of silly." She kissed him on the cheek as they both got to their feet. "You go first, but hurry up. I need to go to the potty."

In the bathroom, he avoided the mirror as tried to sop up the congealing mess in his pants. He stuffed a wad of toilet paper into his crotch, zipped himself and walked out into the room where Maxine had gotten her bra back on, blouse tucked in and shorts pulled up.

"I'll be out in a minute," she said, giving him a peck on the cheek as she headed to the bathroom.

Kevin slumped on the sofa. *Oh, Jeez.* He glanced around the room expecting to see Rod Serling standing in the corner explaining that just a few minutes ago one Kevin Boyle had been rocketed into the twilight zone of real sex – almost real sex. Had she kissed him first? He'd unbuttoned her blouse? He couldn't even remember what it had felt like; just the pulsing, then the cold, wet shame. Through the window, a light went on across the lake. Now someone will call the cops.

"Whatcha thinking?"

He started at the sound of her voice, then sat forward and let out a long sigh. "You must think I'm a moron."

"No I don't. At least you're a gentleman." She sat next to him on the sofa. "So, like you're whatever guys are that are virgins?"

Kevin shrugged. "I guess."

"Really? I don't think I know any guys that are."

"You, ah, know a lot of guys?"

"Hey, I'm no slut," She pulled her legs up, wrapped her arms around them. "I used to be, but I'm not anymore." She buried her chin between her knees. "We can start a new leaf. Like you're a virgin, and I'm going to only go out with nice guys like you. Maybe we'll be steadies."

Nice guys who don't try to slit your throat with a hunting knife. He wondered whether he should ask her why her ex-boyfriend tried to kill her, but then he wasn't' sure he wanted to know. He glanced at his watch: ten-fifteen. "I suppose we've got to wait until Jimmie and Noel are done?"

"Hey, you're not sorry are you?"

"No. It was nice, for as long as it lasted."

"Hey! You guys! Come on down," Jimmie shouted.

"You're not going to say anything to Jimmie about what happened?"

"Nope. I can keep a secret."

They joined Jimmie and Noel in the main room.

"Everything just the way you found it?" Jimmie said.

"We had to pee," Maxine said. "What's your old man going to do, feel if the toilet seats are warm?"

"You're sure?"

"For crissakes, we dusted the furniture and mopped the floors."

"Come on, Jimmie," Noel said. "Dad will kill me if I'm late."

Oh, shit, Kevin thought as an image of Noel's father swinging a tire iron, flashed through his head.

Jimmie grabbed Kevin's shoulder and held him back. "What did you do with the rubber?"

"Huh?"

"You dumb shit. You used a rubber didn't you? Maxine don't need no more trouble."

"Yeah, sure. What do you think?"

"So, it ain't laying on the floor?"

"No, I flushed it down the toilet."

"Asshole. My old man has to get Hansen over here to pump out the septic cause you clogged it up with a used rubber, and I'm going to personally murdalate you."

"No. It went down easy."

On the silent ride back to Hawk Cove, a thousand thoughts jangled through Kevin's head, but one kept repeating. Next time?

Saturday July 5

EVERY TIME KEVIN FELL INTO EXHAUSTED SLEEP, strange dreams startled him awake: naked Maxine kneeling in the confessional, whispering, 'I dreamed I jerked off Kevin Boyle in my Maidenform bra,' into Father Donovan's ear; Fred Hansen's honey wagon parked in front of the Longhouse with its "We haul milk on weekends" slogan in neon as thousands of gallons of used rubbers pumped out at his parents feet. Sweating, he lay holding his fingers close to his eyes trying to resurrect the feeling of them sliding over Maxine's nipples. Twisting in the damp sheets, re-runs of his thing spurting in his pants played on the dim bedroom wall. When the alarm jangled at seven, he felt like he'd been running up and back Beaver Pond road all night.

Sitting at the breakfast table, Kevin was barely able to keep his head erect. The cereal in his bowl had lost its snap and crackle. His father paced between the sink and the table noisily clearing dishes.

"How long does it take to eat a bowl of cereal?" his father muttered at the refrigerator.

Kevin's mother put her hand on Kevin's shoulder. "Thomas, let the boy finish his breakfast."

"Making his own decisions when to come home is a bunch of baloney if he can't pull his weight on change-over Saturday. If Mister *taking responsibility* would get a move on, we could get to the chores that need doing before the next guests arrive."

"Kevin and I are going to Confession this afternoon."

"We've got the broken porch swing in Seneca, and there's a rip in the back screen door in Cayuga."

"The Maddens and the Woodmans are both coming from Rochester, and they never arrive until late afternoon. There will be plenty of time for chores before and after Confession."

Kevin hunched forward and studied the side of the cereal box. Rice, modified corn starch, impure thoughts and deeds, sugar, salt, taking the Lord's name in vain, calcium carbonate.

————

AT FOUR THAT AFTERNOON, Kevin stood in the line outside the confessionals at the back of St. Mary's – after he'd made sure it was Father Petroska in the booth. He stepped into the narrow stall with its lingering aroma of perfume and sweat, squeezed his eyes shut and tried to concentrate as he heard the muffled mutterings from the other side.

When the grill slid open, Kevin recited his venial sins before slipping in "committing impure thoughts and actions eight times." As he waited for Father Petroska to speak, Kevin heard 'Next time, we'll go slow,' playing so loudly in his head, it seemed Maxine's words were echoing around the booth.

"Is that all, my son?" Father Petroska said.

What happened last night was just another kind of impure thought and action, Kevin thought. It's not like they did it. He was covered. "Yes, Father."

"I want you to try harder to remain pure."

"I will, Father."

"Good. For your penance, I want you to say ten Hail Marys and ten Our Fathers. Now make your Act of Contrition."

Kevin raced through his Act of Contrition and shot out of the booth.

"ARE YOU ALRIGHT?" his mother asked Kevin as they were walking from the church to the parking lot.

"Yeah, sure." She'd asked him that five times already.

"You seem distracted. I would have thought going to Confession would clear your mind."

His lies must be painted across his forehead, Kevin thought. "It's this college thing. I can't turn around without Dad getting on me about my applications. It's only July."

"Your father has your best interests at heart."

"He goes on about which guests went to what college and whether they'll write me a letter of recommendation. I'm afraid he's going to ask one them to adopt me if they'll get me into their alma mater."

"Don't you think you're exaggerating?"

"I'm caught in the middle, Mom. If I don't get a big scholarship, I won't have enough saved for the colleges Dad's talking about. And if I go to one of the state colleges, I won't need all I've got saved right away. So, why not use the money to pay Cousin Bob?"

"Kevin, your father and I appreciate your offer, but it's settled."

"You treat me like a kid. I'm supposed to take responsibility except when it's something important." For crying out loud, he hadn't known his mother's Cousin Bob owned Iroquois Lodge before his parents bought it from him.

"What will be, will be with Cousin Bob."

"You make it sound like we don't have anything to say about what happens. It's like in our blood or something."

"We Catholics don't believe in predestination, but you can't ignore your heritage."

Cripes, Kevin thought, she knows more about religion than the Pope, a heck of a lot more than Dad, the born Catholic. He guessed the church came out ahead: his mother converting and raising him Catholic, then his father sort of quitting. Two for one. He glanced back at the church: Baptism, First Communion, Confirmation. If you quit, really quit, did you have to write a letter or something? He'd seen those certificates with the gold seals, the Confirmation one with the bishop's signature, in the drawer where his mother kept important papers. He'd bet there were copies in a filing cabinet somewhere inside St. Mary's. It probably wasn't easy to officially quit. He imagined Father Petroska reading out his name from the pulpit; tacking it on the bulletin board next to the Legion of Decency list. And how could you quit your family?

He hardly remembered Grandpa Ward, and he only met cousin Bob once a long time ago. And most of Dad's family was dead, and the ones left lived near Chicago. Were they perverts, liars? From biology class, he remembered it was your mother's family that made you go bald, so maybe he would have a lot of hair – but inherit the Boyle gene for stealing or heart attacks.

Kevin picked up a rock and tossed it at a chipmunk. "So I'll just have to wait to see whether I'm a Boyle or a Ward?"

"Time will tell."

Sunday July 6

DULLES REJECTS DEGAULLE PLEA FOR A-BOMB DATA

Every Guy in Town Knew the Dame in *The Tattered Dress.*

"WELLS," Father Donovan said.

Kevin and the other parishioners at ten-o'clock Mass waited for him to continue.

Thirty seconds passed before Father Donovan leaned over the pulpit railing and said, "*Fluoride.*" He gazed around the church again. "What's the connection, you're wondering?"

Two hundred heads nodded.

"Under the guise of preventing tooth decay in our children, agents of international Communism – and their well-meaning dupes – are carrying out one of Communism's most insidious plots."

Should he go to Communion? He didn't exactly lie. And lying was only a venial sin. But was lying in Confession a mortal sin or one of those sacrileges? Kevin wished Father Donovan would give one of those seven-minute sermons like Father Petroska. He could remember when he didn't totally mind going to Mass; looked forward to the quiet that let him slip into daydreams. Now he was supposed to watch out for commies under the bed, and just seeing Father Donovan had him worrying about what kind of sins he'd committed.

"Towns like ours that get their drinking water from *wells* are safe from that tentacle of the Communist octopus," Father Donovan thundered.

His thing started spurting *before* she grabbed it, Kevin thought. So maybe he didn't actually *lie* in the confessional.

"Can we relax?" Father Donovan said as he shot his finger at the first row. Verna Nichols jumped as though she'd been goosed. She shook her head then beamed when the priest shouted, "Absolutely correct."

Father Donovan turned to the rest of the congregation. "No, my friends, we cannot relax. Our town may not be under assault from fluoride, but there are many other ways Communists are plotting to undermine our way of life."

Kevin was already sick of Father Donovan and his commie-crusade. He put on his pretend-to-be-listening face, and imagined being in the upstairs room at the Pearson Place. Maxine lounged on the love seat; her head tilted back as she blew a thin stream of smoke toward the ceiling. Red toenails peeked through the front of the backless high heel shoe dangling from her foot. Her draping arm pulled back the satin edge of her *peignoir*, exposing the curve of her neck. And then what? Were they really going to do *it* next time?

At first he didn't believe Donnie Fletcher's explanation of *it* that day, walking home from school when they were ten. And Donnie, with two sisters and a brother also claimed his parents had done it four times to Kevin's parents' once. Overhearing snatches from the older guys about 'banging' and 'fucking' really didn't help, and the comic book with cartoon characters doing *it*, and another magazine, he'd had a quick look at, with a picture of the guy's hairy butt between the legs of the women almost put him off the idea.

A couple of times doing it to himself, he tried jumping ahead, quickly stripping the clothes from Linda or Sue, and sticking his thing in there – trying to imagine how it would feel different from his hand, what Linda or Sue would look like while they did it. It never seemed right. He never seemed to understand what it would really be like.

And when he'd found *Ideal Marriage: Its Physiology and Technique* tucked behind the stack of old receipts and tax returns in the store room last March, he'd thought he'd lucked into something terrific. He remembered how excited he was when he leafed through it and realized this was going to really describe *it*. But it was like studying for a geometry exam. He should have known with an author named Th. H. Van de Velde, M.D. And there weren't any pictures of *it*. He'd gotten "First position: converse, face to face" quickly, but by the time he'd figured out "Second extension attitude, Suspensory (Variation B)," the whole idea soured. He'd made a couple of other trips to the back of the storeroom since then, but for every snippet that gave him the faintest buzz, tons of other stuff made the whole thing sound like an appendectomy. Besides, it was his father's book, and the idea of him and... And the book was so dusty, he was sure it hadn't been taken out in a while.

"People like you, and you, and you, and you are under attack," Father Donovan shouted said as he pointed at startled parishioners around the church. He stopped with his finger squarely aimed at the middle of Kevin's chest.

Kevin shook himself back to attention.

"If you believe Hawk Cove has been declared off-limits to Communism then you are sadly, sadly mistaken," Father Donovan said. "Sitting in church listening to my warnings – or indulging in the daydream that these problems will solve themselves is not enough. It is a time for *action*." Letting that last word hang for several seconds, he leaned over the edge of the pulpit and slowly swept his eyes over the congregation as though daring anyone to contradict him. Finally with a faint nod of his head, he said, "Let us pray to our Lord for the strength to defend America. Let us give thanks to Our Lady for Her Blessed Son."

Ten minutes later, when opening his mouth to take the Host on his tongue, Kevin felt Father Donovan staring right into his brain at his mortal sins, his lies – at the sacrilege he was committing, his plans for really doing it.

Monday Morning July 7

FINNISH REDS SCORE SURPRISING ADVANCE

Which twin has the Tony?

AFTER SETTING OUT THE LAWN CHAIRS ON THE BEACH, Kevin rounded the back corner of Oneida and caught the aroma of cinnamon toast wafting from an open kitchen window. Joseph Stalin is dead. Damn, he thought. There it is again. He ought to see a shrink. His brain is wired AC instead of DC or the other way around. Probably accounts for his over-active sex drive.

March 5, 1953. There wasn't anything else unusual about that morning except his mother sprinkling cinnamon on warm buttered toast as he walked into the kitchen. She rarely made cinnamon toast. But at the moment he smelled the spicy aroma, the announcer on WSYR said, "And to repeat today's top story. This morning, the Kremlin announced that Joseph Stalin, supreme ruler of the Soviet Union, has died." It was a big deal. He remembered the Korean War; how he and the guys traded accounts of MIGs shot down by Sabre Jets; the air raid drills; scanning the skies for Russian Bear and Bison Bombers on their way to drop A-Bombs on Syracuse.

His mom said she just felt like cinnamon toast. No special reason. Cinnamon buns didn't do it; or cinnamon anything else. But months would go by, and he'd be at Buck's house or sitting at a booth in the Sunnyside Up and *wham* – he'd smell cinnamon toast and he'd have to stop himself from saying out loud, "Joseph Stalin is dead." That would get him nominated for the funny farm. Yeah, and so is Abe Lincoln and FDR and Attila the Hun.

LATER THAT MORNING, Kevin nervously stood in Perkin's Pharmacy holding a bottle of aftershave lotion in each hand. Jimmie's question replayed in his mind for the hundredth time: *You used a rubber didn't you?* What had he gotten himself into? The only rubbers he'd ever seen were the dirty, deflated slugs thrown behind the lean-to at the Rock. Did they come singly or by the dozen? Were there instructions? His careful inspection of the aisles confirmed that if Perkins did sell them, they were behind the counter. What was he going to do, walk up to Mr. Perkins and ask for a package of *prophylactics?* 'Sure, Kevin. Will that be cash, or shall I put it on your family's charge?' He probably would-n't need one anyway. Not likely to be a next time, he thought, as he pictured Maxine yucking it up with Noel and Jimmie: the three of them slapping their knees as she told them about him coming in his pants.

Oh, no. Kevin spotted a head of thick red hair peeping over the top of the next aisle. Nobody but Linda Standish has hair like that. '*Auburn*' she insisted when anyone called her a red-head. Probably here for a gross of *Breck*. He shoved the bottles back on the shelf, knocking over one then the other, as he tried to align them. Linda wheeled around the end of the aisle and made a bee-line for Kevin. Any other time, he'd be glad to see Linda. They were sort of a couple toward the end of the school year and his date for the Junior Prom. It wasn't like there were that many guys at Hamilton High she'd go out with, so he wasn't sure she really liked him or figured she ought to date someone with good grades and no recent arrests.

"Careful, or you'll take out the whole shelf," Linda said.

Kevin blushed and righted the bottles. "Aftershave."

"I can see that."

"I ran out."

"I thought it might be disappearing lotion," Linda said, tossing her hair. "I haven't seen you since the last day of school."

"You're always hanging around with the summer people, Linda. You're a ghost to us poor Hawk Covers until Labor Day." Linda was a snob, Kevin thought. Still, he remembered the feel of her as they danced at the prom: the crinkle of the stiff green net sash over her bare shoulders, the tiny straps holding up the dress that billowed from the petticoats underneath. He also remembered her arm pinning his hand to her side as it crept around from her back.

Linda twirled a finger in her hair. "I was at the town beach on the Fourth. And I was there the week before. You're the one who's become a mystery man."

"I've been around."

"I heard you're swimming in another school."

Was she flirting, Kevin wondered? After the prom, he'd given up trying to be her boyfriend: too many, *I have to wash my hair tonight*. Kevin said, "I got tired of hanging out at the town beach."

"So, instead you're hanging around at the Rock?"

"I like to get to different places; meet different people."

"Chink Perrotti? Jimmie Nelson and that complete dimwit girlfriend of his. I heard her real name is Noelle, with an ell - ee, but she uses N - O -E- L because it's easier to spell."

"Lay off, Linda, she's nice. It's like we live in such a big town, we can only hang out with the seven kids who are going to college."

"I'm sure your new friends are a stimulating group."

"Let's not argue, Linda. Maybe we can see each other a little this summer. You know, without tying each other down."

Linda glanced at her watch. "I've got to run. I came over to tell you that Todd Wentworth's having a party on Saturday night. He asked if I wanted to bring along some friends."

"At the Wentworth *compound*?"

"Listen to who's being a snob."

"Am I your date?"

"It's not like that. If you want to come, come." Linda paused. "If you want to hang out with Jimmie and N-O-E-L and *Chink* – well, that's your decision."

"They're not invited?"

Linda poked a finger into Kevin's chest. "I don't know what game you're playing this summer. I've passed along the invitation. You decide." Linda started toward the door, turned and said, "Old Spice."

Monday Evening July 7

CUBA REBELS FREE 3 MORE AMERICANS

All Sorts of Sports Cavort in Cuba – Fly Cubana Airlines.

"Does anyone have anything else to add?" Warren Marsh asked.

Kevin surveyed the six other members of the bi-weekly book discussion group seated in a circle in the non-fiction room. Mr. Smithers' mouth started to open, but a scowl from his sister Winifred seemed to squelch whatever he wanted to say. Kevin wondered whether poor Mr. Smithers ever said anything without getting the go-ahead from his older sister. Everybody in town called the owners of Smithers Real Estate and Insurance Winnie and Ninnie behind their backs. Frank Smithers had been following his sister around town like the back end of a two-man bobsled team since they inherited the business from their widowed father in 1947.

"Did you want to say something, Frank?" Mr. Marsh asked.

"No, I think Doris said it best," Frank said after casting a cautious glance at his sister.

"I thought you said *I* had summed it up best," Steven Naylor said to Warren.

"I think everyone had excellent observations," Mr. Marsh said.

What am I doing here? Kevin thought. When Mr. Marsh and Miss Weaver asked him to join the book discussion group last winter, Kevin had been flattered, and his father said it would be an extracurricular activity other kids his age wouldn't have on their college applications.

He didn't need an excuse to read, but it got him out of the house another night. Now it was summer, and he was stuck with Warren Marsh, Winnie and Ninnie, Mr. Naylor, who must have been living in Hawk Cove when the Mohawks traded beaver skins, along with Gladys Perkins, and Doris Weaver.

Kevin liked Miss Weaver. This evening she wore an embroidered white cotton peasant blouse, billowing flowered skirt, and sandals with socks. Her gray hair was pulled back into a bun fastened by a leather thong. The responses to her letters to the *Central Adirondack Times* calling for banning the bomb, equal rights for Negroes, and population control were the liveliest reading in a newspaper that claimed 'All the news that fits, we print.' Kevin was a reluctant recruit in her latest campaign: promoting Esperanto as a key to world peace.

"I propose we read *Masters of Deceit* next time," Mrs. Perkins said.

Miss Weaver said, "Aren't we getting ahead of ourselves?"

"Well, that's next on the agenda," Mrs. Perkins said jutting her jaw at the others in the circle.

Gladys Perkins looks like J. Edgar Hoover in a dress, Kevin thought as he glanced at his watch. This excuse to get out of the house was worse than cleaning the workshop. Lately, they had been spending more time arguing about what book to read for the next session than discussing the book they'd read. Mrs. Four-by-Four was getting her marker down first.

Kevin stared over Mr. Marsh's head and tried to tune out the argument as the others waded in. Frank Smithers wanted *Please Don't Eat the Daises*, and Kevin was sure he saw '*Ninnie*' form soundlessly on Mr. Marsh's lips. He liked Mr. Naylor's suggestion of *Anatomy of a Murder*, but a scolding from both Gladys Perkins and Winifred Smithers about whether a novel about rape and murder would be appropriate in a public library discussion group squelched that idea. Kevin usually went along with whatever Miss Weaver promoted, but Vance Packer's *The Hidden Persuaders* was running into heavy resistance. What did he care, anyway? There was no way they'd pick *The Ginger Man*, even if there was a copy within a hundred miles of Hawk Cove. Besides Ninnie, Gladys Perkins, and Old Man Naylor would ruin what the *Times* called, 'The comic, amorous adventures of a red-bearded rogue.'

Around and around they went for another twenty minutes. A summit meeting with Khrushchev might be easier than this, Kevin thought. Finally, they agreed to Doris Weaver's compromise of *The Affluent Society* by John Kenneth Galbraith next time and *By Love Possessed* after that.

"*Gi kunveni estas multa laboro*," Miss Weaver said.

"Oh, Doris," Mr. Naylor said shaking his head.

"I simply said that meetings take a lot of work."

"Well, I sometimes get the feeling the joke's on us," Frank Smithers grumbled.

"Now, how could that be?" Doris said.

TEN MINUTES AFTER THE DISCUSSION GROUP BROKE UP, Kevin finished putting the chairs in order. Warren and Doris came out of the bathroom holding washed coffee cups.

"I think it's part of the stupid crusade that blow-hard priest is trying to start, and..." Doris said. She glanced at Kevin and closed her mouth.

He'd overheard Miss Weaver and Mr. Marsh talking about the other members of the group before. Sometimes they'd let him in on it – if it wasn't too malicious: a joke about something really, really stupid Mr. Naylor had said. And other times, there might be some tight-jawed comments if the discussion had been rancorous. Still a kid, he'd thought when that happened: Miss Weaver and Mr. Marsh telling him he was a full-fledged member of the group but not letting him in on the adult conversation when it got interesting.

"Sorry," Miss Weaver said to Kevin. "I didn't mean to. Well, actually I did. I get more than typically on my high horse when it comes to books. I don't want it to sound like I'm against your church." She smiled. "More than any other church." She glanced at Mr. Marsh. "Well, I didn't want to drag you into this."

"It's okay," Kevin said. "I guess Father Donovan's on a high horse too."

Miss Weaver glanced at Mr. Marsh before saying to Kevin, "It's just that you're a Catholic, and we're not, and we've been getting reports of this book thing second-hand. And we were wondering if Gladys Perkins pushing for the J. Edgar Hoover book had something to do with that priest."

"I don't know," Kevin said. He'd never thought of Gladys Perkins as a likely recruit in a crusade. Crazy images of Mrs. Four-by-Four wearing chain mail armor and a pointy-headed helmet with a nose protector flip-flopped with J. Edgar Hoover in a dress. Doris and Warren exchanged wary looks

Mr. Marsh leaned back against the table and folded his arms. "Kevin, I think I can be frank with you."

Kevin nodded uncertainly.

"We didn't want to drag you into something that I'm – well – we're, unclear about," Mr. Marsh said, then looked at Miss Weaver as though he was unsure about continuing. "But Gladys Perkins has been going through the card catalog, checking off items on a list she's carrying. I asked her if I could help her, and it was obvious she didn't want me to see what she was doing. But, I saw enough to realize she had a list of books, and I saw one or two titles. Nothing exotic, but what you – somebody – might label as books with a *liberal* bent."

Miss Weaver said, "Have you heard anything about a list of books coming from St. Mary's?"

Kevin shook his head. "Donovan. Father Donovan said something about subversive books in a sermon last week, but I didn't hear anything about a list."

"I'm sorry to put you in the middle like this," Mr. Marsh said. "You said something about having a part-time job at the rectory, so we, I, thought you might be able to shed some light on what Mrs. Perkins was up to."

"I didn't see any list."

"Well, let's not borrow trouble," Miss Weaver said. "I'll see you next time, if I don't run into you around town. *Havu bonan notkan.*"

"*Dankon. Bonon nokton a vin.*"

Kevin walked out of the library and jogged to the center of Route 28. Through the front window of the Trading Post he could barely make out figures sitting at the bar: locals complaining about the tourists. The rest of Hawk Cove was closed for the night. How could he be a rogue in this two-bit town?

Tuesday July 8

KEVIN STOOD ON THE FRONT STEPS OF THE RECTORY. He didn't care the job paid three dollars an hour. He didn't want to be here. He was sure Father Donovan knew he was a sacrilege-committing liar; that he'd been prowling around town wondering where he could get a rubber, and that he had been masturbating even though this was supposed to be the week he didn't do it.

His mother had insisted he come today, and if, foolishly, he didn't want this job, he would have to tell Father Donovan himself. He'd fold the brochures, eat his cookies, and tell him on the way out the door.

Mrs. Pulaski led Kevin into the dining room. It was the same set-up as the last time: Father Donovan standing at the end of the table next to a stack of newsletters waiting for Kevin to fold and insert into envelopes. Father Donovan looked up, scowling, as Kevin stopped in the doorway. *Oh, Jeez*, Kevin thought.

Father Donovan shook his head gravely. "It's a sad, sad day, isn't it my friend?"

What can he do – excommunicate me, he thought, as Father Donovan continued to stare at him? He was *not* telling him what happened with Maxine.

"Can it get any worse?" Father Donovan said.

"I suppose not," Kevin offered weakly.

Father Donovan let out a long sigh. "Well, we can stand here all after-noon trying to understand why these terrible things happen, but that won't make it better will it?"

"I guess not, Father."

"Even though we've known each other a short time, I hope you won't reveal what I'm going to tell you."

"No, Father."

"Kevin. My faith is tested. You're a mature young man. You are beginning to understand your parents, your teachers, and even your priests have flaws."

Kevin nodded awkwardly.

"Kevin, I have sinned. In a world awash in sin; in a great country being led astray by pinkos; and in a town that needs moral guidance, I have prayed for timely hits and inning-ending double plays." Father Donovan shook his head. "And God has punished me for these foolish ways. A six-game losing streak." Father Donovan looked at Kevin beseechingly.

Kevin wracked his brain. Oh, that, he thought as he remembered the story in this morning's *Observer-Dispatch*: 'Boston Drops Another: Errors Sink Sox.' Kevin said, "The Red Sox?"

"Of course!" Father Donovan gave a puzzled look at Kevin. "I hope I don't have reason to doubt your veracity: you were telling me the truth, weren't you?"

"Oh yes, Father. I *am* a fan of the Red Sox. I, uh, guess I might not be as big a fan as you, but I do like them better than the Yankees."

Father Donovan looked at Kevin for a few seconds. "Well then. Let's get to work. I trust you remember the drill?"

Kevin began folding the newsletters stacked at the end of the dining room table and inserting them into the envelopes. "New York City School Board Bans Suspected Reds," read the headline on one side of the newsletter. "Recognizing Fronts: Undermining Good Intentions," was the lead story on the other side.

"I see you've got faster hands this week," Father Donovan said. "You must have been practicing."

"No, Father." He felt a flush rising from his chest up to his neck as Father Donovan stared at him.

"Why don't you set those aside for a moment, Kevin. I'd like to talk to you." Father Donovan gestured at two dining room chairs pulled away from the table.

Kevin followed the arc of Father Donovan's arm toward the chairs. He can't make me confess, he thought. I never should have come here. I should have quit. He perched on the edge of the chair as Father Donovan pulled the other around and peered at Kevin over the steeple of fingers he'd formed in front of this face.

"I'm afraid I have a bad habit of catching people off-base," Father Donovan said. "My poor excuse for a joke about the Red Sox's losing streak," he said gesturing toward the doorway at the end of the dining room.

"That's alright, Father."

"Well, thank you for your understanding, Kevin. The reason I apologize is that I was teasing you, as though you were a child."

"It's okay."

"It's not okay if I need you to behave like the young adult you are."

He chanced a glance at Father Donovan and let himself relax.

Father Donovan pointed at the table. "Those newsletters. You're bright enough to fold, stuff, *and* read."

"I mostly look at the headlines."

"I understand you are a talented young man: straight A's, top of your class."

Kevin nodded.

Father Donovan smiled. "A *vociferous* reader: *catholic* tastes; biographies, world affairs, novels, perhaps one of the handful of regular readers of the *New York Times* in the entire Adirondacks."

Kevin blushed, wondering if the priest also knew how much time he spent scanning the lingerie ads.

"There I go again, teasing. Can you forgive me, Kevin?"

"Ah, yes, Father."

"Kevin, I'd like to take you into my confidence. I feel I can trust you to deal with adult matters. May I?"

"Yes, Father."

"Good." Father Donovan leaned forward in his chair. "You are what is known as an opinion-leader. Do you know that means?"

"Not really, Father."

"You're someone people look to; someone whose thoughts are taken seriously, a leader."

Kevin shrugged. He'd never thought of himself like that.

"Oh, I don't mean captain of the football team. I'm talking about someone who has a quiet, but powerful impact on the way people think and act."

"I don't know about that, Father."

"Don't underestimate your importance, Kevin. Weren't you invited to be a member of the book discussion group at the library?"

"Yes, Father."

"That's what I'm talking about. You may not think it's important, but it may have more significance than you imagine." Father Donovan nodded. "I do enjoy having an intelligent conversation with someone with your vocabulary." He looked toward the door to the kitchen. "Not that I'm denigrating the good folks of Hawk Cove. Solid, salt-of-the-earth. Perhaps not many as sophisticated as you. Take Mrs. Perkins." Father Donovan leaned forward, put his hand on Kevin's shoulder, and said, "I can trust your discretion in these matters?"

"Yes, Father." What matters, Kevin wondered? He didn't suppose Gladys Perkins told Father Donovan Kevin had been lurking in her husband's drugstore, obviously looking for prophylactics. Still. Kevin tensed, and Father Donovan took his hand away.

"I assure you this is not a breach of the seal of the confessional, but Mrs. Perkins brings me some disturbing news. It seems to Gladys – you don't mind if I refer to Mrs. Perkins by her Christian name do you?"

Kevin shook his head.

"It seems to Gladys the book discussion group has shifted – to the left. Do you get my drift?"

Kevin shook his head. "Ah, no, Father."

A disappointed look crept over Father Donovan's face. "Gladys tells me some members of the group seem to have an agenda – a pattern of promoting books that, shall we say, tend to undermine the moral fiber of the community." Father Donovan sat up and pointed his finger towards the ceiling. "Now, I'm not suggesting that everyone in your book group wants to read subversive literature. But, a sophisticated individual like you might understand how innocent people can be duped – beginning a slide down a slippery slope. Can't you?"

"I'm not sure what you mean, Father."

A deep sigh wheezed through Father Donovan's lips. "Kevin," he said in a firmer tone, don't expect our enemies to begin with *Das Kapital*. "No, first, it's a book with a few crude words; then a book that deals with a sensitive subject. Do we need a book that revolves around rape and murder and contains salacious material in the guise of a court-room drama? People become accustomed to reading these kinds of books, and before you know it, books that contain filth, books that tear down our great country are everywhere eating away at America's moral fiber." Father Donovan sat back. "I understand *The Affluent Society* has been selected as the next book for the group."

"Yes, Father."

"Did you know *Professor* Galbraith is a Canadian?"

"No, Father."

"Didn't it set off the tiniest warning in someone as sophisticated as you that this attack on American values might be written by a foreigner?"

"I didn't know that, Father."

"Well. There you have it," Father Donovan said as he clapped his hands. "I didn't know," he repeated in a mocking sing-song. "When we wake up some day to find our freedoms gone; our country under the heel of agents of International Communism, it won't be because we fought a great battle, Kevin. No, we'll wake up as puppets of the Kremlin and all shake our heads and moan, 'I didn't know.'"

Kevin stared at the fringe of the carpet. This was getting worse than Confession, he thought. What was he supposed to do? He didn't have anything really important to say about what books were read. "Sorry, Father."

Father Donovan reached forward and put his hand on Kevin's knee. "I hope I haven't been too harsh."

"It's alright," Kevin said as he looked at the red knuckles resting on his leg.

Father Donovan gave Kevin's knee a squeeze before lifting his hand and settling back in his chair. "Well, let's not go on and on. Here's what I'd like you to consider. Give Gladys some support. She means well, but, frankly Kevin, she doesn't have what you've got. She needs you. I need you. Kevin, America needs you."

Kevin gazed at the floor.

"No, don't be bashful. I'm not joking. It's young men like you that will be our bulwarks." He paused. "Can I count on you, Kevin?"

"Yes, Father."

"Good. Good. Enough of this palaver. You play ball?"

"I was on the basketball and baseball teams last year, Father."

"That's great."

"Just about anybody who tries out makes the team, Father. There aren't many of us in Hawk Cove. I was a sub, mostly."

"I'll bet you'll make first string. What's your position?"

"Mostly guard. Sometimes forward. I didn't usually get in until late in the game, so I sort of subbed for whoever needed a rest."

"You need to build your strength. Do you exercise, work out? Dumbbells, jumping jacks, throw the medicine ball around?"

"Coach has us do wind sprints."

Father Donovan shook his head. "Intellectual strength and physical strength go hand-in-hand, Kevin."

Kevin nodded and glanced at the stack of newsletters.

Father Donovan caught Kevin's glance, and made a dismissive wave.

"They'll wait. If you're going to be a consummate bulwark of freedom – and a starting guard on the varsity – you've got to begin now. Stand up, young man. Let's see what needs work." Father Donovan jumped to his feet.

Kevin slowly rose from his chair. Father Donovan loomed over him, barely two feet away.

"Make a muscle," Father Donovan said as he flexed his right arm.

Kevin did, then flinched as Father Donovan reached out and grasped his bicep.

"I'm afraid you're a bit flabby there, my friend. Definitely a need for upper body work. Come over here." Father Donovan walked to the corner of the dining room table. He pulled two chairs around and sat in one, rolled up his sleeve and planted his elbow on the table. He nodded toward the other chair. "Come on, Don't be afraid to hurt an old man."

Kevin cautiously slid into the chair and put his elbow on the table. Father Donovan grasped Kevin's hand.

"Go ahead. Let's see if you can pin me."

Kevin started to push against Father Donovan's arm, but it didn't move. He pushed harder and stared at the priest's fingers wrapped in his.

Slowly, but inexorably, Father Donovan pushed Kevin's arm down until it lay across the table. "You weren't giving me a free pass simply because I'm a priest were you?"

"No, Father."

"I didn't think so. Biceps. Forearms." Father Donovan's left hand came under the table and grasped Kevin's thigh. "Tighten that thigh muscle."

Kevin tried to tighten it, but Father Donovan's firm grasp made it hurt. He looked up to see Father Donovan shake his head. After several seconds, he removed his hand, and sat back. "You need work, young man. Have you ever heard of the Canadian Air Force Exercise Program?"

"I remember our junior high gym teacher saying something about them. Maybe we did some. I don't remember."

"A shame. We forget one good thing the Canadians gave us and read *tracts* by Haa-vaard Professor John Kenneth Galbraith. Well, that can be remedied. See the briefcase over there?" Father Donovan pointed to a large black briefcase next to the sideboard.

Kevin nodded.

"In the inside, on the right, I think, there's a side pocket. There's a copy of the exercises in there."

Kevin got out of his chair and stepped over to the briefcase. It was open. What looked like a missal and another black leather bound book were on the bottom. There were three or four file folders stuffed with papers. On the right side was a long zippered compartment. Kevin unzipped it and saw two mimeographed sheets among other papers. One had four or five rows of drawn figures: a man, rows of the same man, with black briefs, in various positions: hands over his head, hands extended out, bending. Kevin guessed this was what Father Donovan wanted. "The papers with the drawings of the man doing the exercises?" he said.

"That's it. There should be two sheets," Father Donovan said and turned back to the envelopes.

Kevin pulled the sheets out of the flap. Underneath was a glossy magazine. *Physical Culture*. The cover had a picture of two Charles Atlas-type guys in a tiny briefs standing in strongman poses: arm muscles flexed like they had thick ropes under their skin. Kevin quickly pulled his hand away and, without thinking shot a look at Father Donovan. He had his back to him, humming as his finger ran down a mailing list. The first magazine flopped forward, revealing a second. *Adon* were the only letters of the title Kevin could see, along with part of the flexed forearm of the man on the cover.

"Have you got them?"

"Yes, Father," Kevin said and quickly zipped the flap shut. He stepped toward the table, and Father Donovan swiveled around and pointed to the chair.

As Kevin sat, he tried to edge the chair back.

Father Donovan laid the two sheets out in front of Kevin. "This is what I mean," he said, pointing to the various figures. "Push ups. Squat thrusts. Chin-ups. Jumping Jacks. A systematic program. That's what this is, Kevin."

Kevin nodded.

"I can't force you – but it would make me very happy to know you were following this program." He stared into Kevin's eyes. "Will you give it a try?"

"Yes, Father." Kevin flushed as he felt Father Donovan's eyes on him.

"There is something else to consider." Father Donovan paused for several seconds. "If it were someone else, I might think it was too much. But you're special, Kevin. I've asked you to take on important responsibilities in your book group, and I've laid out an exercise program that will build your strength and agility for sports. That might be enough."

Kevin nodded.

"But there is one other thing. If Our Lord does have a vocation waiting for you, it is a joy – and an enormous challenge. You understand don't you?"

"I think so, Father."

"Holy Orders mean celibacy. You can't simply enter the seminary and expect a switch will be thrown. You need to become strong to resist the temptations of the fair sex. You have to prepare. I believe vigorous exercise is an excellent tonic." Father Donovan reached out and put his hands on Kevin's shoulders. "I'm putting a lot on these young shoulders, but I think I see someone who is ready to take on the challenge."

"I don't know if I want to be a priest, Father. I mean, it's not that I think it's a bad idea, I just don't know if I have a vocation."

Father Donovan laughed. "I resisted, but that's me. No, young man, I'm not Shanghai-ing you off to St. Bernard's. Let's just say, I'm preparing you for a number of contingencies. Goodness, how nice it is to converse with someone who doesn't blanch at a word like contingencies. I might like you for that alone – but I digress. No, I'm not in the business of selling vocations. Our Lord will do that. I'm in the business of preparing you, and I've put an awful lot on your plate, haven't I?"

"I guess."

"And speaking of plates, I'll tiptoe into the kitchen so I don't wake Mrs. Pulaski from the afternoon nap she takes in her rocking chair by the stove, and steal a few of her cookies."

"I didn't stuff many envelopes, Father."

Father Donovan waved toward the table. "Oh, don't worry about that, my friend. What we've done is much more important. Wait for me on the porch, and I'll bring you the pleasures of Mrs. Pulaski' baking."

TWENTY MINUTES LATER, Kevin plunked down on the bottom step of the stairs leading to the parking lot and put his head in his hands. His mind swirled. What had he said to Father Donovan? He didn't say he was thinking about being a priest, did he? He didn't understand what he was supposed to do with Mrs. Perkins at the book discussion group.

He put his hand under his T-shirt, feeling the place where Father Donovan touched him as he was leaving. 'Do those sit-ups, and you'll have a stomach that will bounce back bullets,' he'd said. Kevin thought he was going to quit. Now he's a bulwark. Varsity. Starting guard. Could he be? An image formed of Linda in her cheerleader outfit shouting through a megaphone, 'Kevin. Kevin. He's our man.' to a crowd cheering the two-handed set shot he'd made to put Hawk Cove into the lead.

Wednesday July 9

GOMULKA ABSENT AS REDS CONVENE
Stengel Baffles Senate Hearing

A BELL ECHOED from inside Harry Simpson's Garage as a green Plymouth pulled away from the pumps and rolled over the thin hose stretched across the two lanes. Kevin stepped into the narrow cluttered office on the left side of the long building. Harry slammed the register shut and retook his stand behind the counter. With a head that looked as though it had been squeezed between two flat boards and a tuft of red hair shooting from the top of his widow's peak, Harry looked like an angry woodpecker.

"A dollar of regular," Harry snarled. He twitched to un-kink his neck, then flicked a sideways glance at Kevin. "Come to town with a ten dollar bill and one shirt and don't change neither."

One good thing about stopping at Simpson's garage was that Harry gave Kevin the same unasked-for advice he gave adults: 'Never change your oil on a rainy day,' or 'Buy Fords in even years; Chevies in odd.' And Harry's advice wasn't limited to cars. Two weeks ago, he'd fixed Kevin with a serious look and said, 'Nobody but a frog ought ever use a double-bladed axe.'

Kevin pushed a dime into the battered red Coke machine, opened the long, narrow glass door and pulled an Orange Crush from its round slot. He slid the bottle into the opener, levered off the cap and took a swig. Letting out a long "Ahhh" he took another swig and stood in the doorway between the office and the three-bay garage before setting out for the only other good thing about Simpson's Garage.

Breathing in the aroma of grease, new rubber, burnt coffee, and exhaust fumes, Kevin watched Len Hastings wrestle a truck tire onto the changer in the first bay. In the second bay beyond the stack of tires, Danny Henderson pushed a bowl on a drum under the oil pan of a Plymouth. He knew Harry didn't like customers in the garage where they'd overhear Len's swearing or get dinged by the tire iron he'd toss behind his back, but he hadn't had a chance to check out July's calendar.

Kevin glanced over his shoulder to make sure Harry was still scowling at the cars that dared drive by without filling up and took one long step into the first bay. Len put a black-veined thumb against the side of his nose and hawked a gob of snot onto the cement floor. Kevin choked down the suddenly thick-feeling mouthful of soda and turned to look up over the workbench at the pinup on this month's Whitesboro Auto Supply calendar. "Going Up" read the caption under the long-legged blonde in high heels and stockings who had turned with a surprised 'Oh' to see her dress caught in an elevator door, leaving her pink panties with a dainty blue flowered embroidery along the leg on display for the lucky fellows who'd come upon her mishap. June's calendar had featured a tall brunette in wide-eyed astonishment that a revolving door had pulled off her skirt.

Elevators, revolving doors, movies, bookstores, cities where everybody didn't know you and your business. The clang of a tire iron hitting the cement floor warned Kevin to jump as it clattered toward him.

"Watch it," Len yelled.

Taking one last glance at "Going Up," Kevin shuffled back into the office, finished his soda, and dropped the empty into the wooden crate next to the machine. "See you, Mr. Simpson."

Kevin walked along the shoulder of 28 before hopping up on the front porch of Thibedeau's Hardware, where Claude Thibedeau was loading a hot water tank onto the back of his truck.

"Is Larry around, Mr. Thibedeau?" Kevin said.

"He's working."

"I know, but my mother asked me to give him a message. It won't take a second."

Claude Thibedeau nodded toward the door to the basement. "Tell your dad, the stove fittings he ordered are in."

Slipping around Mr. Thibedeau, Kevin went down the stairs, and took a few steps in the dim, airless cellar before spotting Larry Needham in the far corner stacking cardboard boxes. He was wearing a tattered tee-shirt more gray than white, and the stifling heat had pasted his lank blonde hair to his head. Kevin could hear Larry saying something, talking to himself. "Hey, Lar," Kevin shouted.

Larry looked up and peered toward Kevin through the bent frames of his thick glasses. "What?"

"It's me, Kevin. My mom wanted me to remind you that you and your mom are coming to dinner tonight."

After staring at Kevin for a few seconds, Larry asked, "Tonight?"

"Yeah. Mom says around five would be good." Kevin paused as Larry seemed to thinking about it. "You want my dad to pick you and your mom up at your place?"

"No," Larry said quickly. "I'll – we'll be there at five." He bent down and continued stacking the boxes.

TWENTY MINUTES LATER, as Kevin turned onto Cedar Road; Slim's dog slunk out of the woods and fell in behind Kevin.

"I can't believe you're still around." Kevin continued toward the Lodge. Reaching the end of the Lodge driveway, Kevin picked up a stone and feinted throwing it at the dog. The dog scampered for the bushes. When Kevin reached the back door of The Longhouse, his father was pointing over Kevin's shoulder.

"Why do you have Slim's dog with you?"

Kevin turned and shook his head. "I can't help it. He keeps following me."

"I can't tell you how many times I've had to enforce our no-pets policy. But poopsie is a member of the family," Thomas said in a sing-song. "I can't tell the guests they have to leave poopsie home when they see you with a dog."

"I didn't ask him to follow me. He just does."

Joyce stepped out of the kitchen door. "Isn't that Slim Carrington's dog?"

"Kevin's going to get rid of him."

"He's adorable. And I feel so awful about the poor man. I wonder what will happen to the Polka Dot Cottage."

Thomas said, "He had relatives out of state. They'll sell it. But I don't want Kevin adopting his dog."

"I'm not...."

Joyce ducked back into the house.

"You let him follow you, and you'll never get rid of him."

"*Dad*....

"Here," Joyce said, popping back out the door. She held out a paper plate with meat scraps.

"*Ohfogoodnesssakes*, Joyce."

"I'll feed him over by the trash barrels," Kevin said as he grabbed the dog by the collar and pulled him out the driveway.

"You are one lucky dog," Kevin said as the dog wolfed down the scraps.

———————

"KEVIN," Joyce called up the stairs, "would you please set the table. Mrs. Needham and Larry are coming to dinner at five."

"I'll be right down." Kevin couldn't remember when his parents had joined the families in Hawk Cove who invited Bunny and Larry

92

Needham to dinner. Twice a week, during the summer months and once a week during the school year when Larry got his free hot lunch at the cafeteria, several mothers in town took turns slipping a note under the door of the dilapidated trailer at the edge of town on Beaver Pond Road or sending their children to invite Bunny and Larry to dinner, knowing Larry would arrive with apologies for his mother who'd suffered a migraine attack, eat dinner next to the always empty place set for her, and take home a huge plate for his mother to heat up when she was feeling better.

Dinner was going to be ham, oven-baked chicken breasts, or something else portable and likely to last a few days in the Needhams' fridge. At dinner Kevin's mother would ask after Bunny as though they spent every Saturday morning together with the Altar and Rosary Society arranging flowers and dusting pews. And Kevin would have to act as though Larry was his friend. Larry wasn't anyone's friend. He was one of those free lunch kids who smelled like kerosene heaters. With his scraped and patchy home haircut, shirts and jackets with too-short or too-long sleeves, everything about Larry had come from somewhere else. No one made fun of him. Larry was just there.

After dinner, Larry would reluctantly take Thomas' offer to drive him home to drop off his mother's plate, and then Larry would head to the IGA to close up. From September to June, Larry pieced together odd jobs sweeping floors and hauling out trash in the shops that stayed open. During the summer, he worked a forty-hour, eight-to-four shift at Thibedeau's Hardware. On Saturdays Larry cleaned Rayburn's Cabins, and on Sundays he washed dishes at the Knotty Pine.

As far as Kevin knew, Bunny Needham sat in the trailer all day listening to the radio. 'Nervous breakdown' was what his father had called it, but he'd just shrugged when Kevin asked when and why it happened, and whether Mrs. Needham was ever going to get better. And Kevin wondered what would happen to Larry if she didn't.

Thursday July 10

U. S. FIRES ROCKET CARRYING MOUSE
Don't touch that dial.

"I CAN'T STAND READING THE NEWSPAPER," Thomas said. "Nothing but crises."

It's been building all day, Kevin thought, as he heard the jagged undertone in his father's complaint. It had to be *somebody's* fault. Whose? Just before dinner, it had been Kevin's when his father had waved a broken badminton racket in his face. "*They* don't take a shred of responsibility for other people's property." Kevin hadn't bothered to try to remember what he'd done recently to deserve having one of the guest's screw ups land on his head. Anyway, from the way his father frowned at his mother, Kevin could see it was going to be hers. He watched her slowly look up from her puzzle and, with the tiniest shake of her head, blow a puff of smoke in Thomas' direction before picking up a piece for careful inspection.

"Khrushchev is rattling sabers, Little Rock's about to explode: the world is awash in one crisis after another."

"Don't forget poor Princess Margaret," Joyce said without looking up. "Being forced to give up Captain Townsend simply because she's third or fifth in line for the throne is so unfair."

Sometimes she ignores him, and sometimes she'll do this, Kevin thought. Maybe he'd walk down to the beach. Damn. It had started to rain. Was it too early to go upstairs?

Joyce snapped the puzzle piece into place. "What's the use of being a princess, if you don't get to choose?"

"You take Princess Margaret," Thomas said. "I'll take Mr. Anthony knocking on our door to tell us we've been chosen to be millionaires."

A short intake of breath. An almost whistling sigh through clenched teeth. "Is this the long way back to *my* Cousin Bob – again?"

"Would you like me to tell you what I think about your cousin Bob?"

We're not two weeks into the season, and his father has brought up the loan payment a dozen times. Well, maybe not that many, but if he doesn't actually say it, he goes around like the guy in Lil' Abner with the black cloud over his head, Kevin thought. "Can we watch "*Have Gun Will Travel?*"

"I thought we agreed to watch *Father Knows Best*," Joyce said. "It's so instructive."

Thomas levered himself off the couch to turn on the television. Waiting for the tube to warm up, he said, "We'll watch whatever comes in best," as he twisted the dial between the snowy and slightly-less-snowy images on the screen. "I need to get on the roof and adjust the aerial again."

Joyce stabbed the ashtray with her cigarette. "If we can't get *Father Knows Best*, I'm going to work on my puzzle."

What was it like living where you get all three stations – without snow and constant adjustment of the horizontal hold, Kevin wondered? He watched his father fiddle with the knobs while his mother sighed. It was going to go on all night.

———

LYING BACK ON HIS BED, Kevin slipped his hand between his legs. He didn't care that Father Donovan said this would happen because he wasn't ever going to Confession to him again. He squinted at the gray beaver board ceiling as though it was the screen at the Gaiety and remembered the ad for Z-Ray glasses on the back page of Zap Comix: a guy's eyes popping out of his head as he stared at the curvy babe whose dress had been dissolved by the power of atomic research. He pictured himself slipping on the Z-Ray glasses as Maxine stood across the bedroom at the Pearsons' place. As he activated the super-spy lenses, Maxine's dress vanished. Then her slip and bra. Pressing the ultra-vision button, he zoomed on the lime-green embroidered "Thursday" over the frill of white lace along the leg of Maxine's yellow panties. He pressed the button again, and her panties dissolved. "*Go slow. Slow, Slow,* he muttered as his thing began to spasm. *Damn*, it's been faster, not slower. There probably won't be a next time, anyway, he thought as he wiped his deflating penis with the toilet paper stashed under the pillow.

Can your thing do it only so many times? Like you get ten thousand before it doesn't work anymore? He remembered his shock the first time it spurted as he lay in bed rubbing it as he thought about when Uncle Art and Aunt Lorraine were visiting and he walked into his parents' bedroom where his cousin Rosemary stood naked with her bathing suit in her hand. He must have been ten, and she was probably seventeen. "Get out of here, you brat!" she yelled as his eyes yo-yoed between her breasts and the black nest between her legs.

If he got only, say, ten thousand, and he'd been doing it for at least six years, and in the weeks like this one between communion and Confession he'd do it ....*jeez* he could run dry before he was twenty-five. Does it just stop shooting, or does it stop working altogether? Does anybody do it as much as me? Maybe Buck. He talks about it all the time, but you can't just ask even your best friend like how many times do you do it in a week. That would be pretty queer. Father Petroska never sounds shocked when I say 'about seven times,' but Father Petroska would never sound shocked about anything, and besides 'about seven times' might underestimate it a bit.

Kevin heard his father and mother rustling around in the bedroom below him. He put on his pajamas and pulled the covers over his head. Even though he wasn't at the listening end of the bed, he didn't want to hear the muffled voices of another argument. Shortly after he moved to this upstairs bedroom in the Longhouse, he discovered the spot between the head of his bed and the corner near the window that channeled the words and sounds from his parents' bedroom to his as though they were three feet away. He would lie there listening to his father talk about other teachers or what his mother said about what people in town did that were not for young ears. He would lie awake worrying after hearing them argue about having enough money to pay the bills. And now that he was older, he understood that other argument; those same words flying back and forth like shuttlecocks.

"Me, I'm just the son of a Mick carpenter,' his father would say. 'First in my family to go to college – not that a state teachers college counted much with your family.'

And his mother would cry, "If it wasn't for my family letting us buy the Lodge, where would we be?"

"Dumped it on us when the bottom started to drop out of the resort business."

"They got you your job at the school."

"The lowest salaries in the state."

And then, "My professors said I had promise."

"Takes two to tango."

Sometimes it stopped there. But they might get to Winter Carnival Weekend 1941. Could he ever ask? Did he need to?

From his parents' bedroom, Kevin heard his father's voice. A door slammed. Kevin pushed his head further into the pillow. He imagined himself on assignment as special correspondent for the *Times*, sipping an *espresso* in a café in Venice, Gina Lollobrigida chuckling at the wry comment he'd made.

Friday July 11

ROCKETED MOUSE IS HUNTED AT SEA

Pall Mall. So Friendly to Your Taste. No flat filtered-out flavor. You can light either end.

KEVIN PULLED ANOTHER SCREEN from the stack leaning against the side of the workshop. He poked at the blister the wire brush had raised on the inside of his thumb. After wiping the sweat on his forehead with the back of his hand, he took another long swig from the jug of Kool-Aid. Eight more screens, he thought. Even in the shade of the overhang, it was ninety. He knelt on one knee and began scraping the flaking paint.

Now, where was he? He'd stolen Blue Mountain's in-bound pass and was dribbling toward their basket. Ten seconds. One point behind. Blue Mountain's center and forward had dropped back down the court. A head fake sent the center sprawling. Linda and the other cheerleaders were bouncing on the balls of their feet, screaming his name. The forward raised his arms. Kevin pulled up. Cradling the ball in his left hand, he flexed his knees and launched his jump shot. The ball arced over the forward's outstretched arms. Linda's hands covered her mouth. The shot was....

"You've got visitors."

Kevin looked up to see four bare legs behind his father's.

Thomas cocked his head over his shoulder. "Noel *Dupleiss* – and her friend."

Noel and Maxine were stifling giggles. What are they doing here? If his father's introduction wasn't enough of a declaration that absolutely no Dupleiss – not Noel's crazy brothers, not her drunk of a father, not her mother – was welcome anywhere near Iroquois Lodge, the nasty look on his face hammered the point home.

"Hi." Kevin wiped his hands on his jeans and smiled weakly.

"Me and Noel was taking a ride, and she said your place was near, so we decided to stop and say hi."

Thomas' face screwed into a scowl.

Pulling a pack of cigarettes from the pocket of her shorts, Maxine held it out to Thomas. He sneered at the pack as though she'd offered him a dog turd. Maxine offered it to Kevin, who shook his head. Maxine shrugged, lit a cigarette, then dropped the match.

Thomas snatched the match out of the dirt. "You think it's out, but you never know," he scolded. He held the match out for their inspection as if he was the DA in front of a jury in an arson case. He pointed at Maxine's cigarette. "And make sure that's dunked in water. Insurance never covers your losses."

Maxine started to say something, then closed her mouth.

Chin raised, Thomas seemed to measure her face for enough sass to send her packing. After a few more seconds of stare-down, he wheeled on Kevin. "You need to get going on those screens so we can paint them. It might rain. And I need your help with the pump."

"We won't be long," Kevin said.

Thomas turned his glare on Noel as though he was recalling every misdemeanor committed by one of her brothers. He shook his head and stomped off.

Maxine said, "How come I get the feeling your old man don't like us?"

"What are you two doing here?"

"You said you'd stop in at the Acropolis. You haven't been there – unless you was in disguise."

"Chores."

Maxine nudged Noel. "Why don't you check out the lake." As Noel headed to the beach, Maxine said, "Am I going to see you again?"

"Do you want to?"

Maxine laid her hand on Kevin's forearm and stroked it. "You're hot." Her hand felt like a popsicle. "Ahh."

She ran her fingers up his arm, then spread her fingers across Kevin's forehead. "How does that feel?"

As Kevin glanced in the direction his father had left, she said, "You ashamed to be seen with me?"

"No." Breathing in the aroma of cigarette smoke and coconut suntan lotion, Kevin said, "I like the way *you* smell." He laughed. "I mean, you ..."

Maxine stepped closer. "I like the way you smell."

"I smell like sweat."

"I like that."

A flutter went through Kevin's chest. "I'm glad you want to see me again."

"That's why we came here." Lowering her voice, Maxine said, "There's going to be a little party tomorrow night. I want you to be my date."

"Where?"

"At Jimmie's – our place."

"What about his parents?"

Maxine put her finger to her lips. "They're going to Utica for a wedding – and staying over. *And* Donna-the-brat is going with them."

"Who's coming?"

"It's going to be a *very* intimate party." Maxine put her hand on Kevin's waist. "We can pick up where we left off."

A picture of Maxine lying almost naked on the rug at the Pearsons' place shot into Kevin's head. Does she mean? Could he? "Gee. That sounds great, Maxine," he said. "But Jimmie lives way on the other side of Inlet. I don't know how I can get there and back."

"You want to come don't you?"

"Sure."

"I'll get Jimmie to pick you up."

"No. I mean that might not be the best way to do it. My dad. You know. He…"

"He don't want you hanging around with the wrong crowd."

"He's had run-ins with them – Noel's brothers."

"How about I get Jimmie to swing by Ricketts around nine?"

"Make it the post office side."

Maxine kissed Kevin. "I'm glad you want to come. We'll have fun."

Kevin flushed. "Yeah."

"I better go get Noel before your old man puts her in detention."

"Want me to come with you?"

"You afraid I might scare the rich people you got staying at this high class place you own?"

"According to my father, we owe so much to my mom's cousin, we barely own it." Pointing at the stack of screens, he said, "Besides, I'm the help."

"You better finish scraping." Maxine looked up at the cloudless sky and laughed. "It might rain." She dropped her cigarette and ground it into the sand. "I better fetch Noel before she starts lifting wallets or stealing diamond rings."

Kevin picked up Maxine's cigarette butt and put it in his pocket as Maxine sauntered toward the beach.

A few minutes later, Maxine and Noel strolled by with Thomas trailing them as though he was escorting trespassers off the property. They waved at Kevin, and Maxine wordlessly mimed, *'Nine'* then puckered a kiss at him.

Thomas stopped next to Kevin as the girls got into the car parked next to the 'No Parking' sign.

"What was *that* all about?" Thomas demanded.

"Nothing. Just a girl I met. Jimmie Nelson's cousin." Kevin knelt and started scraping old paint from the screen.

"I don't want you seeing her – them: a Dupleiss or anybody with them."

"Noel's not her brothers – or her father. And the Nelsons are nice people."

"Don't start telling me what's what. Nothing good is come from hanging around with that crowd: smoking, drinking, and you know what."

Kevin flipped the screen over and muttered, "You know what."

"Watch your mouth."

"You're the one who's always said stuff like 'Don't judge a book by its cover' and 'Think for yourself,' and..."

Thomas grabbed Kevin's shoulder and pulled him around. "You listen to me. You think I've got my head in the sand; don't know what goes on with that Noel and her boyfriends. Jimmie Nelson'd better watch himself. *I* know what...." He stopped and stared at Kevin, eyes clouding. His hand fell away from Kevin's shoulder. "Get those screens done pronto. This place starts looking like a dump, and we'll never fill those vacancies." He took a few steps, then stopped and turned back to Kevin. "You remember what I said."

AFTER DINNER, Kevin pulled the wagon with the large trash cans he'd picked up from the back of the cottages to far end of the parking lot where the burn barrel and fifty-gallon drums were located. As he held his breath while tipping them over the drums and snagging tissues, paper towels, and anything that would burn, he thought he ought to join the Navy Frogmen since he'd managed to hold his breath until each trash can was empty. Even wearing the thickest work gloves Thibedeau sold, he hated pawing through maggoty steak fat, slimy pork chop bones, putrid lettuce, and the rest of other people's garbage that sometimes had him bent over gagging. But his father would yell at him if he saw stuff like tissue-wrapped Kotex that could have been burned when they were dumping the large drums at the dump. Every other night after supper, three, sometimes four trips around the back of the cottages; the stench of rotting garbage, stinging smoke in his eyes from the burn barrel; and chaining down the lids so the raccoons didn't strew the mess all over; before he could dash into the lake with a bar of soap to try to scrub off the stink.

His father was so damn worried the Lodge would look like a dump. So Kevin had to bust his ass and smell like a dump. Fifty-one days to Labor Day. Less than one year, and he was out of here.

As he came over the small rise, Kevin spotted Slim's dog sniffing around the barrels. "You knock them over, and I'll stick you in the burn barrel," he shouted. Damn dog. He'd figured someone else had taken up feeding him since he hadn't been around since his mother gave him those scraps. Looks scrawny. Kevin tipped the first can over the lip of the drum, and slid the garbage in more slowly than usual. He grabbed a half-eaten hot-dog and tossed it behind him. "I must be nuts to do this." The dog lunged at the hot dog, gulped it down and looked up at Kevin. "For chrissakes," he muttered. "Dad will shit a brick." Tough titties. Seventeen and his father figures he's got the right to veto who he can see. Get anywhere near Noel, and you'll end up stealing hub caps.

Kevin tilted another can over the drum and snatched at some soggy French fries. I'll hang around with who I want. "You want this crap?" The dog wolfed down the fries Kevin had tossed on the dirt. More slowly than usual, he tipped the cans and found more scraps he figured were edible. "You get sick and die, it's not my fault." I've got to haul garbage, pick up badminton rackets, and not be seen hanging around with the wrong crowd or I'll fall off the end of the earth. "Here." Kevin spilled a paper plate of potato chips in front of the dog. "Live it up."

———

AFTER COMING UP FROM THE LAKE and getting dressed, Kevin dashed out the door before his father could quiz him on where he was going. From barbecues in the back of the cottages, Kevin smelled hamburgers grilling. He wished he'd had a hot dog instead of the macaroni and cheese they'd had for dinner. Along Spruce Lane, laughter from the screened porches of the lakeside cottages drifted toward him. A little girl's shout of, 'Daddy's here!' greeted a car pulling into 'Hyde-a-Way' – the name burned into a slab of pine nailed to a birch tree arching over the driveway.

As Kevin neared Route 28, "Summer Fun," "Hawk Heaven" and the other cottages with names gave way to the gap-toothed row of the year-round houses of Hawk Covers. Next door to the Matthews' neat bungalow, piles of logs waiting to be split were heaped in Len Hopkins' front yard. Geraniums grew in white-painted truck tires on either side of the cement blocks that formed the steps to the porch. Floyd and Edna Tucker's green-shuttered house with its patch of sandy lawn faced Stew Rapp's double lot in which every car Stew owned since 1936 had been driven or pushed into a neat rank along the cedar hedge. A '39 Chevy sat on its rims. Next to it was the final resting place of the '46 Desoto in which Stew's wife, Blanche, had been killed: its concave grill matching the bridge abutment on the Uncas Road Blanche hit after another long evening at the Trading Post bar. Blanche's death car seemed to enjoy no special place between the Chevy and the '51 Ford wagon slumped on four flat tires.

At the side of Becker's, Kevin turned into the long dirt driveway leading to the cabin where Buck and his mother lived. Behind its sloping porch, the cabin at the back of the property was an exhausted shade of the red of Becker's newly painted two-story chalet. Buck and Thelma had moved in three years ago when the Beckers stopped renting to the couple who ran the Halfway House in the summer.

Becker's German Sheppard, Sammy, raced to the end of his lead and lunged at Kevin. Startled by the barking dog, Kevin side-stepped into a squishy patch of grass with a pong of septic.

Buck got off the old sofa on the porch, yelled at Sammy, and stepped into the yard. "How come you wanted to meet here?" Buck said. "Aren't we going to the Rock?"

"Later." Kevin looked around. "Your mom's working?"

"It's Friday night. She went in around four and won't be home until ten, ten-thirty."

"I need to talk." Kevin climbed up on the porch and flopped at the end of the sofa.

Propping his leg on a Coleman cooler next to the door, Buck said, "About what?"

Kevin drew a deep breath. "I need a rubber."

After staring at Kevin as though he hadn't heard his friend correctly, Buck slapped his knee. "Wow, Kev!" A rubber. Way to go!"

"Jeez, Buck. Keep it down will you."

"Who for? Not Linda. Oh yeah. Jimmie's cousin. Marlene."

"Maxine. I don't know exactly if I'll need one, but I was thinking I ought to have one. In case. You know."

"You do it with her yet?"

"I kind of got to third base."

"But you didn't get it in?"

"Almost. I mean she was going to let me, but..." Kevin paused. "But I decided I'd better not without a rubber."

"Wooo – eee! You had her clothes off? And yours too?"

"Yeah."

"I was wondering all week what happened when you left the Rock." Buck sat on the other end of the sofa. "So, what was it like? Come on. You can tell me."

"It was .. Look. You got to swear you won't say a word."

Buck crossed his heart. "You can trust me, Kev. Wow. Stark naked. Where did you go? The dirt road out near Limekiln?"

"Another place. I swore I wouldn't say."

"Okay. So you're parking, and making out, and – you tell me."

"We went to a house. No place you'd know. I took off her clothes. We were going to do it, but I forgot to take along a rubber."

"Holy Smokes. And, now you've got a date for the real thing?"

"It looks like it." Kevin picked up a twig, snapped it in two and tossed it into the yard. "I was thinking about the time. You know when we saw those used ones at the lean-to and you said something about..." He paused. "About the time your father came back from Star Lake and found..."

Buck stepped off the porch and threw at rock at the barking dog. *"Shut up!"* he yelled at Sammy, then remounting the steps of the porch, he said, "You want one of my mother's rubbers."

"Jeez, Buck. It's not like that. I was thinking maybe you knew some-place I could buy one."

"Like where? Perkins?"

"Not likely," Kevin said. "Maybe the drug store in Old Forge."

"What are you going to do, hitch to Old Forge and back? You think they sell rubbers to kids in the big town of Old Forge?" Buck picked at a loose thread on the sofa. "You want me to look?"

Kevin shrugged. "It's not like..."

"I don't know if she even has any," Buck said. "She ain't seeing any-body right now. At least not here."

"I'm sorry. This was a stupid idea." Kevin stood. "Want to go to the Rock?"

"I'll look."

"You don't have to if you don't want to."

"Come on," Buck said as he opened the screen door. "If we find one – even if we don't, I want a blow-by-blow description of *everything*: bra size, what her pussy looks like, what it feels like, *everything*."

Kevin thought looking for a rubber in Buck's mother's bedroom was kind of weird. While Buck shuffled through her underwear drawer,

Kevin looked through the night stand next to her bed.

"Bingo!" Buck said.

In the back corner of the drawer, under some bras, there were two foil packets of *Sheiks*. They stared at them. Finally, Buck said, "You better only take one. I don't know if she knows there's two here or what."

"I don't want you to get into trouble, Buck."

"What's she going to say? 'Buckey-boy, did you take one of the rubbers I was keeping for when Jim Haywood stops by.'

"What?" An image of Mr. Haywood, the tenth grade chemistry teacher at Hamilton, shot into Kevin's head; quickly followed by a second one of Mr. and Mrs. Haywood and their three children sitting at Sunday mass. "Come on. You're joking."

"Yeah. I'm joking," Buck said. He picked up one of the packets and tossed it to Kevin, patted down the underwear and slammed the drawer closed.

They walked back out to the porch and slumped onto the sofa.

Holding the silver packet up to the dim porch light, Kevin tried to make out the tiny print: 'Before using, read directions and warning on carton.' Damn. What carton?

Buck rapped a stick against the porch post.

"I'm sorry. This was a dumb idea," Kevin said.

"Hey. I'm just mad, because I'm the only one around here not getting any."

"Mr. Haywood, the chem teacher?"

"I shouldn't have said anything. I don't think they're seeing each other anymore – at least not here."

"Your dad been around lately?"

Buck laughed. "He only shows up when one of his girlfriends kicks him out, his unemployment's done, or he just misses kicking mom and me around. Manages to arrive about when mom's had it with him for good and might be seeing somebody. But Duke's around. He came by yesterday to *borrow* fifty bucks from mom."

"Is he staying here?"

"No. He made a show of hanging around long enough so Mom would think he might, but as soon as he got the money, he took off."

"Is he going to be at the game tomorrow? We could use Duke."

"Who knows," Buck said. "Besides, I'm getting sick of being a punching bag for the summer people. Most of the guys in town who play varsity are working tomorrow."

"I wish they'd all stay home," Kevin said. "Who needs them?"

"Me, you, my mom, your parents – about everybody in Hawk Cove. The other day, Ed Downey drove the ambulance to Utica with some jerk water skier who tried to jump a dock. Ed says the guy's yelling at him because Ed won't wait at Utica General while they put his leg in a cast."

"Some of these people forget to pack their brains when they go on vacation."

"Remember last August, the guy who set his garage on fire barbecuing inside in the rain? Fifteen volunteers trying to save the garage, and this guy's shouting he's going to sue the department if they don't hose down his cottage so the paint don't blister. So Stewie Rapp swings a five-incher around and blows out every window on the side of the place."

Buck and Kevin laughed and sat back on the sofa. After a few moments, Buck said, "I think I will play tomorrow." He paused. "And remember, I want to hear everything."

"Sure thing."

"Hey," Buck said. "I haven't had anything to eat since lunch. Let's go up to town and get a burger and fries."

"I'll have fries. Friday. No meat."

Saturday Afternoon July 12

SWISS WILL SEEK ATOMIC WEAPONS

Dodgers Lose Argument and Game to Braves

AT TEN MINUTES TO ONE, Kevin ducked under a branch at the end of the shortcut through the woods and stepped onto the edge of the ball field. It was fifteen minutes before the start of the big game. In front of him, the crowd on the visitors' side looked like a family reunion: women waving and hugging, men slapping each other on the back, and bunches of laughing kids running around.

Why shouldn't they be happy? They're here for the annual rout, Kevin thought. If he hadn't told Buck he'd come, he would have skipped it. No one he'd asked could remember when a pickup baseball game between the locals and summer visitors became *us versus them*. Except *us* was a bunch of kids, old fogies, and, he hated to admit, second-stringers like him. And *them* always included enough good ball-players on vacation to thoroughly trounce us. Around town in the week after every game, he would overhear 'our best players had to work' or 'picking little Georgie Fredericks off second base wasn't fair' or another excuse for why Hawk Cove always came up short – way short – year after year after year.

Hawk Cove would come up short against anyplace, Kevin thought. Did anyone live in Hawk Cove because they wanted to? If they didn't have a job like his father's or own a business that depended on tourists, why would they stay?

Besides, Maxine's invitation to tonight's "intimate" party was all he could think about. All morning flashbacks of what they did at the Pearsons' place and fantasies of what "We'll go slow" would be like flooded his mind and stiffened his thing. All this dumb baseball game might do is keep him from coming in his pants.

Kevin pushed through the crowd. Side-stepping a girl gyrating her bright green Hula Hoop, he imagined Maxine doing that with all her clothes off. As he started across the ball field, he heard someone calling and turned to see Linda Standish waving at him from the visitor's side.

"Are you coming tonight?

"Huh?"

"To Todd Wentworth's party."

"I don't know."

"It'll be fun," Linda said, nodding at the clots of people gathering on the home side. You might meet more sophisticated people."

"I guess."

"Well, Mister Hard-to-Get, when you've sorted through all your other invitations, see if you can fit us in."

What a snob. She's on the *sophisticated* side of the field. If he heard that word one more time from her, he was going to push her off the town dock. Would her family get invited to cocktail parties at the Wentworths' if her dad wasn't the town supervisor who might put in a good word when assessments came up in January? He watched Linda join the growing number of families on the visitors' side. Mothers were opening canvass chairs and handing kids sodas; men were hoisting red and green plastic tumblers with celery sticks. On the home side were a handful of Hawk Covers with nothing better to do. His head swiveled from visitors to home. Technicolor versus black and white.

Kevin saw his parents get out of their car. His father headed to the visitors' side where he shook hands with Mr. Slade, who was staying at Iroquois Lodge. His mother walked to the home side and opened her lawn chair next to Mrs. Talmadge. Kevin sighed. He knew it wasn't that simple. He used to complain his father wasn't being loyal to Hawk Cove when he spent most of the game on the visitors' side. But he supposed his dad had to be nice to the guests. As he scanned the visitors, he saw other Hawk Covers like his dad and Linda: folks who wanted to, had to, or maybe just pretended to be their friends. Were they stuck in the middle like him, stuck in this rinky-dink town?

But it wasn't just that Hawk Cove was a small town. It was two towns. From Labor Day to the first of July, it might be like any other small town in the middle of nowhere. Hawk Cove was so small, he was stuck with the same friends, the same teachers, and the same handful of people scurrying from their cars to their houses in dark sub-zero winter days, or ducking in and out of their houses in black fly season. But then there was Hawk Cove in *the season* – from the first of July to Labor Day when everything was turned upside down.

Was it upside down? No, as he watched his father shaking hands with one of the visitors, Kevin thought it was more of a muddle. With his father being a teacher, his family was better off than most. Now, he was over there sucking up. There were few Hawk Covers who didn't spend the season renting to, working for, or waiting on the visitors. "The natives," they call us, like we were a tribe gathering roots and berries until they discovered us. It's our town, and every July they show up and act like they own it.

"Hey, Kevin. You coming or are you going to stand in the middle of the field all day?" Buck called.

Kevin joined Buck in the group around Ade Harmon, custodian of the town dump and self-appointed coach.

Ade squinted at Kevin through the smoke rising from the Chesterfield permanently attached to his lip. He dug around in the duffel bag where he kept the "valuable stuff" he salvaged from the dump and pulled out a couple of taped bats and a ratty glove.

"Anybody need any equipment let me know," Ade said. His yellow tobacco-stained fingers tugged at his greasy cap. "Let's get lined up."

Buck said, "It's our year, Kev. You'll see. Duke's going to pitch a no-hitter. Probably hit a couple of homers too."

"Where is he?" Kevin looked around for Buck's older brother.

"He'll be here. Don't worry."

Kevin was worried. Being Hamilton High's best pitcher in anyone's memory was all that kept Duke from being flunked or thrown out of school. Duke might be trouble, but as Kevin sized up the rag-tag group surrounding Ade, he figured at least Duke might give them half a chance to win. A loud belch erupted from the one of the spectators on the home side, and a can of UC was tossed on the grass. What difference would it make, Kevin thought, if Duke showed up and we won?

Ade called out the line-up. Kevin was assigned to center field; Buck was in left. Gerry Prindle was the starting pitcher. "Where's Duke?" he asked Buck.

"He said he'd be here," Buck said, scanning the highway.

Why was he so anxious for his jerk of a brother to show up? He used to feel sorry for Buck whenever Duke got into trouble. He didn't think anybody in town, including Buck, was sorry when Duke took off for Star Lake. Now Buck acted like they were waiting for Sandy Koufax.

As Kevin and Buck started for the outfield, an MG with two guys in the front bucket seats and two others perched along the back deck pulled in. Kevin recognized the driver as Corey Dickerson; just graduated from some private school, he'd heard. His parents had a large summer place on the south shore. The four jumped out of the car and joined the crowd on the visitors' side. What was it about them? Confident, that's what. It wasn't just that they were sure they were going to win the ball game. They were going to win at everything they did. And if you're winners, you need losers. They're Oreos, and we're Hydrox.

"Wake up, Kev," Buck shouted.

Cripes. They'd started, Kevin realized as a hot grounder came at him. He scooped it up and threw to second. Within minutes, Kevin was sorrier than ever he'd come. Gerry's pitches were drilled through the outstretched gloves of the infielders or smacked over the heads of the outfielders. Kevin imagined the headline on the sports page, *Tourists Trounce Townies: Humane Society Calls Game in Third Inning.* By the time the visitors finally inserted a couple of young kids that Gerry could strike out, Kevin wondered how soon he could slink away.

"Come on, guys, we'll get them back," Ade said to the home team dribbling off the field. "Remember Silky Sullivan. We've got them where we want them."

Yeah, sure, Kevin thought. He saw Linda talking to Corey Dickerson. First we get thrashed, and then they steal our girls.

"It's Frankie, Kevin and Duane," Ade called out.

Frankie struck out, and Kevin followed with a bloop single to right that rolled into the chairs on the visitors' side. A little girl picked up the ball and made an awkward throw back to the playing field. A dorky double, Kevin thought as Edgar Pierce, the umpire, waved Kevin to second.

When Duane swung for strike two, moans and razzing from the home side started. They're working on their excuses already, Kevin thought. From second base, he saw most of the visitors were talking to each other rather than watching the game. Self-assured. They won't even break a sweat. The women had pulled their chairs around in semi-circles as kid brothers and sisters played tag. The visitors' players standing closer to home plate joked among themselves.

Hitching up his jeans, Kevin felt his wallet in his back pocket: a couple of dollars, his learner's permit and the rubber he'd gotten from Buck shoved under the picture of Veronica Lake. Kevin thought he'd better take a closer look at it before the party. Do you put it on before you get a hard-on? He hoped not because he'd had one all day. Let's get this game over.

As Duane stepped back into the batter's box, a '56 red and cream Fairlane made a squealing U-turn on 28 and pulled onto the grass beyond third. Everyone on the field turned to look. The driver's door swung open, and Duke Duncan stepped out. He wore a tee-shirt, jeans and engineer boots. His black hair was swept back in a D-A. From the way Duke looked around with a sneer, Kevin thought he acted as if he'd missed the turn-off for Mel's diner in Raquette Lake. Then Chink Perrotti oozed out of the other side of the car and come around to Duke. They looked like a couple of extras in *Blackboard Jungle*. Conversations stopped, and, all the way from second base, Kevin could see *that crowd* written across his father's face.

Deputy Fisher marched over to Duke and Chink and pointed to the tire tracks on 28. Duke gave him a, "Yeah, I hear you," as he pulled a cigarette out from behind his ear and lit up. With Chink a step behind him, Duke strutted to the home side.

As Duke and Chink neared the players around Ade, Chink waved at Kevin. "Hey, Boyle. Act *sue -ave* out there. I'll knock you up – I mean in." Chink bent over giggling.

Shit. Kevin felt like two hundred eyes were on him. Chink was dumber than a moron joke. Kevin quickly knelt to carefully re-tie the laces on both his sneakers. Two weeks ago, he couldn't believe his luck with Chink and the other guys letting him into the Rock. Now he wondered if Chink was going to kick him out the next time he showed up. Did his father hear Chink? Everybody heard Chink. He stood and pretended to check out the shortstop: anything to not look at his father. All he needed now was for Maxine to come and yell to him about tonight's party. He was going to give himself a brain tumor or something.

Duane swung for strike three to end the inning, and Kevin trotted off second base to stand at the edge of the crowd gathered around Duke and Ade Harmon.

Buck jumped up and down, trying to get Ade's attention. "Duke can go in to pitch, can't he?"

Kevin saw Gerry Prindle catch a nasty look from Duke and shrug at Ade. "Duke Duncan is going to pitch," Ade said to Edgar Pierce.

"Hey Duke," Chink said, "I'll play short."

"Hank's at short," Ade said. "If you want to play, I can get you in right field."

Chink snorted. "Right field's for kids and crips."

"Hey, don't sweat the small stuff," Duke said. "Ain't going to need fielders when I pitch."

"Yeah. Don't sweat the small stuff," Buck said.

Kevin hadn't seen Duke and Buck together for a long time, and now he realized how much Buck looked like Duke and how he followed the trail left by his older brother and father. What would happen senior year? Would he and Buck still be best friends? Could he hang out at the Rock for the rest of the summer drinking beer, smoking, learning the wise guy phrases Chink and the other guys used and still be a part of the college crowd? He looked across the field at Linda. There was no way he would get from her what he was going to get from Maxine.

"Your team going to play ball?" Mr. Pierce called.

"Let's go," Ade said. "Duke, remember, it's not the sectionals."

"Yeah, sure," Duke said and strutted to the mound.

Kevin retook his position in center field. Buck grinning and pounding his fist into his mitt waved at Duke and Chink. Cripes. He acts like the Seventh Cavalry just rode in. Kevin cringed as Duke made a big show of smoothing the dirt around the pitching rubber while smirking at the visitors.

The visitors' first batter was a kid about twelve. Duke fired a fast ball down the middle of the plate, and the kid ducked away. A couple of men on the visitors' side turned from their conversations. Duke smiled, reared back and fired another fast ball, and the kid made a feeble poke at it as he backed away again.

"Hey, you!" a man yelled. "Take it easy."

"Don't have a cow," Duke said, then went into a full windup before delivering a slow looping pitch. The kid had seen the windup and had fallen out the box with a flailing swing before the ball reached home plate.

"Strike three," Mr. Pierce said and walked to the mound.

As Edgar Pierce, the sixty-something son of Pierce and Son Funeral Home, gestured at the visitor and home sides as though he was telling pall bearers where to stand, it was clear to Kevin that Duke wasn't paying any attention.

Someone on the home side called out. "Way to go, Duke. You knock 'em dead, and let Pierce lay them tourist stiffs out."

Kevin felt as though the temperature dropped ten degrees as conversations on the visitors' side stopped. That was smart, he thought, as a conference around the visitors' manager began. The next batter took a called strike one without taking his eyes off Duke. When Duke delivered the next pitch, the man brought the bat around in a snap and drove the ball deep into left field. He trotted around the bases as Buck chased the ball.

"Way to go, Garrison," one of the visitors said. "Still got the pop that put Dartmouth on top," another laughed as he hoisted his tumbler.

The next batter was Corey Dickerson. Duke kicked the dirt around the mound with his black engineer boots. "Dukie's going to kick some shit," Chink hollered.

Why doesn't he shut up, Kevin thought?

Duke reared back and fired a high inside fast ball at Corey Dickerson. Corey calmly pulled his head back and smiled.

"That's the ticket, Duke. Give him a Sal-the-barber Maglie," Chink yelled.

Duke nodded at Chink, then fired another high inside fast ball. Corey backed out of the box.

"Hey, pitcher," a visitor barked. "Let's keep this a friendly game."

Kevin winced as a man from the home side shouted, "Youse want it friendly as soon as our best pitcher comes in."

Duke made a show of hitching up his low-slung jeans and squinting in at the catcher. He wound up and fired another fast ball, and Corey's bat came around in a flash. The ball was so far gone the home team simply turned and watched it sail until it bounced down the slope and into the pines.

One of the guys who arrived with Corey Dickerson stepped into the batter's box. "Let's go, Skip," someone from the visitors' called.

"Give em your good stuff, Duke," Buck shouted.

"Yeah, *Duke*," a loud laugh came from the visitor's side. "Give us your good stuff."

"Talk it up out there," Ade said.

He couldn't just walk off the field, Kevin thought as he heard Buck yelling, "Let's go, *Skippie*, Let's go, *Skippie*" in a mocking sing-song. "Take it easy, Buck. It's only a game."

"Whose side you on?" Buck said.

Kevin turned from Buck to see Duke snarling at the batter. He couldn't make out what Chink was screaming at the visitors, but it had his mother and Mrs. Talmadge moving their chairs. Ade and a clot of home side spectators were crowding the third base line, yelling encouragement to Duke. On the visitors' side, the mothers gathered up picnic baskets. Their players had formed a line in front of them. They reminded Kevin of a picture in a history book; Roman Legionnaires with shiny shields getting ready to wipe out a gang of barbarians. "I don't know," he said in a soft voice. He glanced at Buck, edging in from his position, but Buck hadn't heard him. Kevin was surprised he'd said it aloud. "I don't know," he said again.

"Hey, peanut butter, don't wet your pants," Buck yelled.

"So, Piercey," Duke said, "like am I supposed to deliver meatballs?"

"Just pitch."

"Bring it," Skip called.

"Okay. If that's what you want." Duke delivered a pitch, and Skip smashed a screaming line drive back at the mound, which Duke missed with a stab of his glove and tumbled to his knees as the ball flew into left field. Buck froze, and the ball skittered off his glove and up his arm, glancing off the side of his head. Before Kevin could get to the ball, Buck had picked it up and thrown it to second base after Skip had rounded the bag and trotted into third.

"Asshole!" Duke screamed at Buck.

"That is enough of that!" Edgar Pierce said as he marched toward the mound.

"He's my stupid brother, Pierce. I'll call him anything I want."

"I don't care who he is. Any more of that language, and you're out." Mr. Pierce snapped his mask back on and turned back to home plate.

"You all right?" Kevin asked Buck, pointing to the blood oozing from the scrape the ball made along the side of his face.

Buck wiped his hand across his face. "I hope Duke beans the next batter."

Can't they call the game, Kevin wondered?

"Let's go, Jack," a man from the Visitors yelled as the next batter stepped into the box.

"Get Jack off," Chink yelled.

For crying out loud. Kevin hoped that Deputy Fisher would shut Chink up, but he was standing next to Ade. He wasn't cheering Duke, but was sandwiched between two guys holding beers and making threatening gestures at the Visitors. It didn't look to Kevin like he was going to cool things down.

"Come on, Duke," Buck shouted. "Drill em."

"Yeah, come on *Deuce*," someone yelled from the visitor's side.

"Deuce. Deuce. Deuce," kids chanted before a father shut them up.

Oh, Jeez. Duke threw a finger at the visitors. Buck was laughing and jumping up and down.

The batter looked at a woman who appeared to be in the direction of Duke's flip. "You better watch yourself, buddy, or I'll come out there and clean your clock."

"You better watch *yourself*, old man," Duke said.

Duke quick-pitched the guy and hit him on the left buttock. The man dropped his bat and stalked to the mound. Edgar Pierce was right behind him.

"I've had enough of your kind," the man said, closing in on Duke. Edgar Pierce rushed in behind him to put his hand on the man's shoulder, but the man got off a wild swing at Duke before Duke shoved him to the ground.

"Fight. Fight," Buck shouted as though he'd been waiting for this all along.

Buck ran toward the scrum around the mound, and Kevin followed. Maybe he should just leave. Would people see him? Would the guys on the home side call him a traitor? He joined the growing crowd around Duke, the man trying to get up, and Edgar Pierce.

Edgar Pierce grabbed Duke's arms. "What do you think you are doing?"

"Hey, fat ass here, threw a punch," Duke said.

The man started to get up. He'd gotten only to his hands and knees before taking huge gulps of air. A woman rushed out of the crowd and knelt beside him. "Jack. Jack. Just take it easy."

Several men from the visitors gathered around; a couple helped the man to his feet. "He's already had one heart attack," the woman yelled at Duke.

"Hey, lady, don't blame me if your old man takes a swing at me. He's lucky I don't punch out geezers."

Edgar Pierce was directing people away from the mound when someone from the visitors yelled, "Take on somebody your own age, *Deuce*."

"Fuck you."

"Shut your filthy mouth," a man said, "or someone will shut it for you."

Spectators from the home side began edging toward the mound from the third base side of the field, pushing Kevin in front of them. He couldn't get out.

"Which one of you pussies is going to try it?" Duke said.

Skip had come in from third base. He pointed his finger at Duke. "I'd be delighted to shut your mouth."

"He's not worth the effort, Skip," someone said.

Edgar Pierce stepped between Duke and Skip. "Game's over. Everybody go home."

Duke and Skip growled at each other. Kevin thought they would break it off, then Chink yelled, "Lucky for Skippy, or he would have had to back up his big mouth."

Skip turned red and took a step at Duke. "You would have been the one eating your words."

Kevin couldn't see who pushed first, but in a flash, Duke and Skip were delivering sharp shoves to each other's shoulders.

"Break it up," Edgar Pierce said, but Duke had pushed him away with his right hand as he hit Skip in the shoulder with his left.

"Let them settle it," one of the visitors said.

With that, the spectators and players from both sides stepped back to form two flanks. Kevin hesitated and for a second was left by himself. He couldn't walk over to the visitors. He didn't want to back into the home side. But he couldn't see a way out.

Duke wheeled around to face off with Skip. "Okay, Skippy-boy, lets...."

Before Duke finished, Skip lashed out with a quick right that caught Duke on the chin and staggered him. Duke stepped back, but Skip rushed him, landing blows on his head. Duke fell on his butt.

"He sucker-punched him," Buck said.

As Duke started to rise, Skip hit him squarely on the side of the face, and Duke fell back.

"Let him fight, you cocksucker," Buck cried.

Duke staggered up and tackled Skip. They fell into a tangle in front of Kevin.

"Break it up," Deputy Fisher barked as he pushed through the crowd. "Break it up." Duke and Skip, punching and kicking, rolled into Kevin and knocked him down.

"You stay out of it!" someone hollered as Kevin tried to untangle himself.

"It wasn't my fault," Kevin said as he scrambled to his feet, but everyone had turned to Duke and Skip.

Duke got up and landed a left on the side of Skip's face. Skip staggered, then ran at Duke, catching him under his chin with the top of his head. Duke's knees buckled, but before he hit the ground, Skip delivered two solid shots to Duke's head. Duke's eyes rolled back as he fell to the ground in a heap.

"You motherfucker," Buck yelled at Skip. Kevin watched Buck try to pull Duke to his feet. "You didn't fight fair."

Deputy Fisher pushed Skip to the visitors' side and stood in front of Duke and Buck. "That's it! It's over." He hitched up his gun belt and motioned for the crowd to leave.

Buck had his arms under Duke's shoulders, but Duke shoved them away. "Get off me, you athhole." He struggled to his feet. "Leth go, frat boy," he said through swollen lips. Duke ran his right forearm across his face and looked at the blood from his nose and cut under his eye smeared across it. A rivulet of blood trailed out of his left ear and down his neck. He brought his fists up.

Deputy Fisher stepped in front of Duke. "I said, it's over." He pushed Duke back. "Everybody go home. Out of here, or I'm writing tickets."

"This deuce is cooked," a laughing voice called from the visitors' side.

"He sucker-punched you," Buck said as he tugged on Duke's arm.

"Leggome." Duke shook Buck's hand away and hitched up his jeans. "Ain't seen the lath of me," he called over his shoulder.

"Duke will show you," Buck yelled at the crowd. Tears streamed down Buck's cheeks.

"Duke will show them," Buck sniffled.

Saturday Evening July 12

U. S. ASKS MOSCOW TO PUNISH AIRMEN FOR PLANE ATTACK
Learn Dancing at Home in 5 days or Pay Nothing.

"AND YOU HAD TO GET INTO IT," Kevin's father said as he paced across the living room floor.

"I told you. I wasn't in the fight. They knocked me down."

"That's not the way some people saw it."

"I can't help what they saw."

"But you stood there with *them*. You and that punk's brother."

"For cripes sake. Dad, I didn't start the fight. You've been on me all afternoon."

"I've had enough of your lip. After the game, Mike Yates asked me why you were on the other side."

"I wasn't on anybody's side."

"Jim Slade was hopping mad. Somebody yelled at his wife to go back where she came from. And that's the cleaned up version. Slade said he might just do that."

"Good," Kevin said. "If they can't figure out what happened, let them leave."

"Oh, that's smart. People start thinking we're in with local trash, and will have vacancies from here to eternity."

"It's not my fault. I'm getting out of here."

"You better not be hanging around with that Duncan kid or those other JDs."

Kevin grabbed his jacket and headed for the door.

———

KEVIN PICKED UP A STICK and whacked it against the "Slow Children" sign. It was seven-thirty, and he wasn't supposed to meet Maxine at Ricketts until nine. Was he going to spend the next hour and a half dodging anybody his father called local good-for-nothings? If he stopped by the Wentworth party, he'd have something to answer to his father's 'wheres?', 'whos?', and 'whats?'

At the end of Aspen Lane, Kevin turned in at the "Private" sign. He knew this place. After Labor Day last year, he and Buck snooped around these huge summer homes along the south end of the cove. Buck wanted to check out where the "richy-richs" lived, so they'd stood on wood piles to peek into windows and sat around on wicker chairs they'd unstacked on porches. With the water out, they ducked around into the front of the Wentworths' boat house where a mahogany Cris Craft was hoisted in a slip. They'd climbed up into it, and Buck, pulling on a white cap with a shiny black visor he'd found in the dashboard, yanked the throttle back and forth until the housing cracked and the handle bent. Then Buck swiped a seat cushion off a peg even though there were a several littered around his front porch. Buck had said he just wanted it. And he wouldn't put the yacht cap back, wearing it into town, waving and yelling at passing cars that Admiral Duncan was in charge.

Now as Kevin threaded through the cars parked behind the house, he felt creepy. Here he was tagging along as one of Linda's friends to a place he'd snuck into and robbed. Maybe he ought to find someplace else to hang out until Maxine picked him up. He patted his back pocket again, reassuring himself Veronica Lake was guarding the rubber.

"What do you want?"

Kevin jumped as a tall man appeared out of the shadows. The man took a long pull from the drink in his hand and gave Kevin a dirty look.

"I was looking for Linda Standish – and Todd Wentworth," Kevin said. He thought his voice sounded like he was lying. "I'm Kevin, Kevin Boyle." He held out his hand.

The man let Kevin's hand hang in the air. "Yeah? Well, I'm Sam Wentworth." He took another pull on his drink and looked Kevin up and down.

Cripes. Kevin felt like the guy was going to ask him if he was the one who trashed his boat and stole the seat cushion and cap. "She said Todd was having a party and I – her friends – were invited."

"They're around somewhere." He shrugged toward the lake.

He better say hello to Linda and get the heck out of here. Rounding the corner of the house, Kevin saw an ice-filled tub. He pulled out a Coke, picked up a church key from the table and flipped off the cap. From a record player on the porch, Pat Boone crooned 'writing love letters in the sand.'

Two guys grabbed sodas from the tub and reached around Kevin for the church key. One guy was so short, that Kevin could sight along the top of his flat-top. The other guy wore a madras shirt and cut-off jeans.

Flat-top stuck out his hand. "I'm Eric. This here's Corey."

Kevin recognized Corey. Linda had spent the whole game talking to him.

"Hey," Corey said. "I know you. You played center field for the townies."

"I live in Hawk Cove," Kevin said. "My parents own Iroquois Lodge."

"You know the guy – the one Skip punched out?"

"He's from here," Kevin said. "But he's not around town much."

Eric laughed. "Just shows up to bean old men and then get the crap knocked out of him."

He grabbed Kevin's arm and pulled him toward a group of people standing at the foot of the stairs to the porch. "Hey, Skip. I captured one of the home guys."

Kevin felt every eye on him. Linda stood between Skip and another guy. Did she take a step back when she saw him? Both guys were older than him. Probably more sophisticated, too.

"This here's Ken," Eric said. "The *Duke's* buddy. Came to offer a challenge. Switchblades at dawn."

Kevin pulled his arm out of Eric's grasp. "It's Kevin," he said. "I don't know anything about any challenge."

"Just kidding," Eric said as he slapped Kevin on the back.

Even in the dim light, Kevin could see a blue-black bruise on Skip's cheek.

Finally, Linda said, "Todd, this is my friend Kevin."

Todd, the one with the 'Groton Crew' tee-shirt, said, "You're the first of Linda's friends to show up. I suppose the fight's made it the Hatfields and the McCoys."

"Hey, Linda," flat-top laughed. "Did you invite the manager and that Chinkie?"

"That's not very funny, Eric. Don't judge Hawk Cove by the Duncans and their ilk."

Kevin was glad Linda looked annoyed. Serves her right for sucking up to these jerks. Was he supposed to show them he was a Hawk Cover who could chit-chat without burping or farting?

"So, Linda, do we do have to worry about getting jumped at the post office by Dukie and his buddies?"

"If he's still in town, he's probably sulking at the Rock." Linda looked at Kevin. "It's the hangout for the town's losers."

The word dropped like a plop of bird shit on Kevin's feet. He started to say something, but let it go.

"The *Rock*," Eric said. "Sounds like a *big* deal."

"It's an overgrown boulder sticking out of the lake," Linda said. "Where the guys with nothing better to do with themselves drink beer and pretend they're daring cliff divers at Acapulco."

"You know all about this rock," Eric said.

"Hardly. I've went there once or twice with some friends – in the daytime. Yuck. A scraggly clearing with a dirty beach, and a broken down lean-to."

"I don't know, Linda," Eric said. "You have an awful lot of inside dope for someone who's only been there once or twice – in the daytime. Ever been in the lean-to?"

Kevin tried imagining Miss Prissy-Pants in the lean-to. Fat chance of that. Too *yuckey*.

"I am *very* sorry I mentioned it. I'm going to find some other company until you boys learn to behave yourselves." With a flip of her auburn hair, Linda headed toward the house, then said over her shoulder, "Kevin can fill you in about the Rock."

As everyone watched Linda mount the stairs, Skip turned to Kevin. "Where is this Rock?"

"At the end of Cedar Road."

"Is diving off the Rock really dangerous?"

Kevin said, "Very. You have to go out far enough to miss the ledge at the bottom. And you only do it at night."

"You've done it?" Eric said.

"Lots of times," Kevin looked around at these guys staring at him like he was a strange animal Frank Buck had hauled back from the Amazon. What trick was he supposed to do next? "I've got to go."

"See you at the Rock," Eric called after Kevin.

As Kevin rounded the corner of the house, Linda was coming out the side door.

"You're leaving so soon?"

"I won't be missed."

"I'm sorry, Kevin. I shouldn't have said only losers go to the Rock. I was angry. I haven't seen you all summer."

Kevin nodded toward the front lawn. "You've got your friends."

"I know; they can be full of themselves. But they're nice once you get to know them."

"I doubt I'll get the chance."

"Don't be like that." Linda's auburn hair fell forward as she traced a circle in the sand with the toe of her white tennis sneaker. "I'd like to see you."

"Do I have to join up with those guys, or can I see you alone?"

"I would like to see *you*, Kevin. Give me a call when you get that chip off your shoulder."

———

NINE-FIFTEEN. Kevin watched another car pass Ricketts heading south. Ten cars, and he was leaving. A black Ford station wagon: one. A gray Dodge: two.

Linda wants to see him? Why did she wait until now to say so? He remembered the prom, his arm pinned to her side the moment his hand started to inch toward her breast. An image of Linda jumping in the air in her cheerleader skirt popped into Kevin's head. He'd never make starting guard. But there was Maxine at the Pearson Place, naked except for her panties, his fingers flicking over her nipples. Linda would never let him do that. Was he supposed to spend the rest of the summer trying to cop a feel off the Breck girl – or do it – really do it? Was it a sure thing; what they'd do tonight at Maxine's party? Hurry up.

Another Ford: three. *Cripes!* His father's car. No, wait, this Chevy's maroon. Where are they? Did that Chevy make it four or five?

"Hey, numb nuts!" Jimmie Nelson leaned out the window of his car, the red tip of his cigarette swinging back and forth along the door. "Where the hell you been?"

"I was here. I thought you'd be coming from Inlet."

"Get in, cripple dick," Jimmie said as Noel pulled the seat forward to let Kevin clamber into the back seat next to Maxine.

"You said nine."

"We were early, so we stopped by the playground."

"Jimmie, will you let up?" Maxine said and pulled Kevin closer. "We went down to your place. Your old man said you weren't there."

Oh, shit! Kevin remembered the look on his father's face when Maxine and Noel stopped by last time. He wasn't supposed to hang around with Buck, and now he was going to have to explain why Maxine was looking for him. "What did you say?"

"We said we'd find you, but I don't think he wanted us to."

As Jimmie made a hard right onto 28, Kevin's arm jammed tight against Maxine's breast. Her hair smelled like squeezed lemons. "There was this place I had to go, but I wasn't going to miss your party."

As they drove through Inlet, Kevin slouched down so he wouldn't be seen by anyone who'd tell his parents he was in Jimmie Nelson's car. A mile north of town, Jimmie swerved up a sandy road and pulled into the front yard of his house.

Kevin crawled out of the back seat and looked around. Patches of sky peeked through thick pines. A lamp threw a fuzzy halo of light over the steps to the screened front porch. No other houses were in sight. "We're all alone out here."

Maxine said, "Jimmie's parents and his sister are at his cousin's wedding in Utica until tomorrow." Maxine gave Jimmie a playful push. "And Jimmie was scared of staying all alone in the dark."

"Maxine," Jimmie said, "Get off it."

Kevin was glad they seemed so casual about being here, about what they knew they were here for. He was nervous as all get out.

"Let's go put out the horsey-dervies." Maxine and Noel scampered toward the house.

"You owe me two bucks for the beer."

"Yeah. Sure," Kevin said trying to sound as though he did this all the time. Did Jimmie see his hand shake as he pulled two dollars out of his wallet?

Jimmie punched Kevin's arm. "You up for this?"

"No sweat. I'm cool with it."

When Jimmie and Kevin stepped into the house Maxine and Noel were in the kitchen emptying a bag of pretzels and a bag of potato chips into bowls. Kevin's eyes darted around. He guessed the bedrooms were off the hall at the end of the living room, where a ten-point buck mounted over the stone fireplace stared at him. 'See instructions on carton,' rattled in his head. Was there something about the rubber he should have asked Jimmie?

Handing Kevin a beer, Maxine said, "Black Label okay with you?"

"My favorite." Kevin took a swig from the bottle and coughed on the bitter fizz that backed up his nose.

"We should have got them fancy beer glasses like they got at the Knotty Pine," Noel said.

Real cool, Kevin thought. He took another swig of beer. Jimmie had flopped into a stuffed chair near the fireplace. Jimmie popped a pretzel into his mouth and took a swig of beer. Maxine and Noel stood at the counter separating the kitchen from the living room. Kevin sat in the chair opposite Jimmie, crossed his legs. Was he supposed to do something?

"Hey. This is a party," Maxine said. "Let's have some music." She flipped up the top of a record player next to the couch and shuffled through a stack of 45's. "How about we start with lively stuff; Bobby Freeman, Paul Anka."

"Just put something on," Jimmie said.

Maxine leaned over Jimmie's head and held her fist to her mouth. "Ladies and gentlemen, it's the Chordettes. *Lollipop. Lollipop. Oh, Lolli, Lolli...*"

As Maxine's hips rocked back and forth, it struck Kevin she acted so much older than him. He was afraid she was going to turn around to see a kid choking on his beer, trying to ape Jimmie's every move and call it off.

"Do you want to dance under the moonlight?" Maxine sang as she put another record on. She pulled Kevin off the chair and swung him around. *"Do ya? Do ya? Do ya?"*

Kevin felt like a fool as he tried to follow Maxine's lead, catching Jimmie's smirk as she spun him around. He didn't want to dance. He wanted to do it – now – before Maxine realized what a mistake she'd made.

Jimmie walked to the record player. "I ain't got what it takes to do that jig-a-boo dancing." He fiddled with the record player. The needle hit the disk, and Connie Francis sang, *'Who's sor ry, now. Who's aching for...'* Jimmie jerked his head and Noel hopped off the couch and folded into his arms as they turned in a slow circle.

Maxine pressed into Kevin and laid her head on his shoulder, humming along with Connie Francis. "I'll bet you don't want to dance anymore," she whispered.

Kevin took in a deep breath of lemon and soap, felt her breasts against him, and pushed his face into her hair. "I want – I want to be with you."

Maxine lifted her head from Kevin's shoulder and nodded at Jimmie.

Jimmie tugged Noel's arm, and they disappeared through a doorway off the kitchen.

Taking Kevin's hand, Maxine led him down the hall and into a bedroom with two single beds. She pulled him toward the one closest to the door.

Kevin stared at the bed: not the backseat of a car, not on a rug in some camp, but her bed, right here, right now.

Maxine kissed him.

He felt his pulse in his temples as Maxine rubbed along the front of his jeans. Over her shoulder, the glass eyes of the teddy bear sitting on a bookcase stared at him.

As Maxine's tongue flicked along his lips, then into his mouth, Kevin cupped her breasts and squeezed.

"Easy. They're a little sore. My friend is on the way." Maxine pushed Kevin out to arm's length. "Slow. Remember?"

He wanted it to last all night. He wanted to feel every part of her, slowly. He saw a pink nightgown crumpled at the end of the bed, and he had to quickly look back at the teddy bear to keep from coming. Could he go slow? He grasped her sleeveless blouse and tugged it out of her shorts. Fumbling with the buttons, he finally managed to get if off her shoulders.

Maxine started to unclasp her bra.

"Let me." He wanted to remove each bit of her clothing and stand back to admire what he'd uncovered. As Maxine's bra slid down her arms, revealing the taut nipples and the blue veins under her skin, Kevin knew this is what he wanted.

Maxine smiled at Kevin as he managed to unbutton her shorts and let them fall around her ankles. As slowly as he could manage with trembling fingers, Kevin tugged her panties down. His finger traced the ghost outline the elastic left in her skin, first around her waist and then where its faint shadow arched across her hips and then between her legs.

"Now," she giggled, "I want you to think about puppy dogs and kittens and fairy tales while I take off your clothes."

Kevin stared at Maxine's fingers as she unbuttoned his shirt, undid his jeans, and pushed his briefs down his legs. Oh, God, he was going to come. No. He bit his lip so hard he could taste blood. As he kicked off his shoes and the jeans around his ankles, he fumbled in the pocket of his jeans until he found his wallet and the foil-wrapped condom.

Maxine took it from his hand and slid it over his erection.

As she pulled back the covers, a warm aroma of perfume and powder filled Kevin's face.

Maxine put her hands around Kevin's hips and drew him onto to her as she lay back, her hair spread on the pillow.

He wasn't a dumb kid. She wanted him. Slowly lowering himself, Kevin let Maxine take his erection in her hand and guide him into her. As he pushed in, he felt Maxine grasping his hips and pulling him further in. Then her hands pushed him away. "That's it," she whispered. "Gently push – then pull. Don't come yet."

As he pulled away, she whispered, *Push, now pull. Gently.* The sound of her making love to him, the sensation of her fingers pulling, then pushing, at his hips was like nothing he'd imagined. His eyes fastened on the grain of the wood in the headboard to keep himself from coming. But when he looked down and saw her smiling at him, the flecks of gray in her blue eyes, the shuddering behind his knees began.

Maxine's smile broadened, and Kevin felt her tighten around him. The feel of jangling nerve endings raced from his neck and his thighs, then crashed together between his legs. He pushed harder, felt her knees rise, and her fingernails dig into him. After a few more pushes he collapsed onto Maxine and lay there panting, a jumble of thoughts racing through his head. It was better – better than – better than anything. "Oh, wow. Oh, wow," he whispered over and over.

"I'm glad you liked it. Now I think you'd better get off me."

Kevin pulled his knees up and began to pull out of Maxine. As he did, he felt wetness spreading. He looked at the gloppy mess and stripped the rubber off into the palm of his hand. "Did this break?"

"It looks okay – I guess," Maxine said. "Don't worry. I'm due for my period any day. It's hard to get pregnant this close."

Kevin tried to push that word out of his mind. "What'll I do with it?"

Reaching behind her head, Maxine pulled a tissue from a box. "Here."

Kevin wiped his sticky fingers and folded the condom into the tissue and dropped it on the floor.

Maxine pulled Kevin to her side of the bed. "Let's snuggle."

Kevin let her pull him down next to her, then kiss him and put her arms around him. He twisted into a more comfortable position on the narrow bed.

Maxine stroked Kevin's cheek. "I'm glad I was your first time."

As Kevin pulled in closer to Maxine, he wanted as much of her body next to his as possible. He lay there listening to her soft breathing and tried to remember every moment of it. It was better than anything. And now he was lying naked in the same bed with a naked girl. Was he dreaming this? No, he was here. She was there. They had done it.

Maxine whispered. "Can you stay? Jimmie's parents won't be back until tomorrow."

"I can't."

"Jimmie's got to take Noel back. I guess you'll go with them."

Maxine ran her hand through Kevin's hair. Nobody had ever done that to him, and it gave him the shivers. *What the hell?* Lights flashed across the bedroom window set high on the wall. Kevin bolted upright. "I thought I saw lights." *Jesus. His father had tracked him down.*

"Lie down. It's probably heat lightning."

As Kevin started to lie back into her arms, he heard the sound of a door opening, feet, and voices. *"Somebody's here!"* Oh, Jesus.

A voice from the front of the house called, "What's going on?"

"Oh, shit! Hilda. It's Jimmie's parents!" Maxine croaked.

"Jimmie said they were staying in Utica."

Maxine grabbed a handful of clothes from the floor.

Banging his arm on the side table, Kevin jumped out of bed and looked around for his clothes.

From down the hall, a woman yelled, "This puts a cap on a great day!"

Maxine leaned against the bedroom door and turned the lock as she yanked her shorts on. "My bra. Where's my bra?"

Kevin couldn't find his briefs and had pulled on his jeans without them. "Here. Here it is." He tossed the bra to Maxine, found his briefs under the pillow on the floor but stuffed them in his pocket as he quickly pulled his shirt over his head and plunked on the edge of the bed to get on his socks.

"Let me in," a voice called from the hallway.

"I'll be out in a second," Maxine answered.

"It's my bedroom," a girl's voice said.

Kevin saw the crumpled tissue on the rug and remembered the used rubber. He grabbed it and stuffed it into his pocket.

"In a second," Maxine said.

"Who's in there?" a woman's voice called. "Open this door."

Maxine stuffed her foot into her sandal and tried to smooth down the blouse she'd buttoned in the wrong holes. "There. There," she hissed and pointed to Kevin's sneaker at the far end of the bed as Kevin wheeled around.

"I said, open this door."

Kevin had just managed to get the sneaker on as Maxine turned the key and stepped back as the door swung open. A red-faced Mrs. Nelson stood with her hands on her hips. He recognized Donna behind her, looking wide-eyed around the large woman's arm.

"I should have known!"

Maxine said, "We were just talking."

"Do you think I was born yesterday?"

Kevin and Maxine followed Mrs. Nelson's eyes to the tousled bed.

Mrs. Nelson said, "You're Tom Boyle's kid."

Kevin wondered if he could deny it, then shrugged and stuffed his underpants deeper into his pocket. His mind was melting down as it raced through possible things to say when everyone turned toward the shouting from the front of the house. At the sound of a loud wail, Mrs. Nelson glared at Maxine and Kevin and headed toward the ruckus. Donna gave Kevin a now- you're-in-trouble smirk and followed her mother.

"What do we do?" Kevin said.

Maxine quickly smoothed the covers on the bed.

More yelling came from the front of the house. "It's her," Mrs. Nelson shouted. Wailing that must have been coming from Noel filled the house. "It's that one in there. *Your* niece," Mrs. Nelson yelled.

Maxine said, "I'd better go out there."

Kevin looked at the push-out window high on the bedroom wall. "I might as well come with you. She knows who I am."

Cautiously following Maxine down the hall to the living room, Kevin saw Noel hunched forward in a chair, her face in her hands, sobbing. Jimmie, his father, mother, and sister turned toward Maxine and Kevin.

Mrs. Nelson pointed at Maxine. "I knew you'd bring your trouble here."

Jimmie said, "Mom, it's..."

"Shut up!"

"Mom, take it easy."

"We can't leave for a day without this going on. Turning our house into a, a..."

"Whorehouse?" Jimmie's father said.

"You shut your mouth too," Mrs. Nelson shouted. "I don't know whether I should be happy we had to leave early or not. Come home to find this."

"Why did you come home?" Jimmie said.

"Never you mind," Mrs. Nelson said.

"We had a fight," Jimmie's father said. "Me and Charlie."

"The two of you!" Mrs. Nelson said. "His daughter's wedding, and the two of you have to start the fight over your mother's furniture again."

"I didn't start it."

"I don't care who started it. You were both drunk. For crying out loud, your mother's been dead for fifteen years, and you and Charlie can't get through a funeral, a wedding – anything without one of you starting in on it. I told you a hundred times before we left, on the way there, just before the reception – don't start it. And if Charlie does, walk away."

"Jesus Christ, Hilda. Maybe after hearing it two hundred times, I got confused."

"Oh, big sense of humor – now that you've sobered up." Hilda turned to the others. "I had to drive home, and the doctor said I'm not supposed to drive at night."

"Hey. You're Tom Boyle's kid," Mr. Nelson said to Kevin.

"Hello, Mr. Nelson." Kevin quickly ran through the possible ways his parents might run into the Nelsons. They didn't go to St. Mary's. Still, this was such a small town. Mr. Nelson didn't look angry – but Mrs. Nelson looked like she was getting ready to kill someone – probably Maxine.

"My daughter's bedroom," Mrs. Nelson said to Maxine. "We bring you into our house. We share our daughter's bedroom, and you do this."

"I'm sorry," Maxine said.

"Mom," Jimmie said.

"What?"

"It's not Maxine's fault."

Mrs. Nelson shouted at Donna, "Go to your room. Now."

"How come you're yelling at me?" Donna whined. "It's not *my* fault."

"Shut up and do what I say."

"Oh, for crissakes, Hilda," Mr. Nelson said. "I'm dead tired, and I've got an awful headache. Can't we sort this out tomorrow?"

"What's to sort out? She's got to go," Mrs. Nelson said.

"I've got to go home," Noel wailed.

Everyone in the room turned toward Noel.

"If I'm not home by twelve, my dad will kill me."

Thank you lord, Kevin thought.

Jimmie said, "Let me take Noel home. And Kevin. I'll take Maxine along. Give everybody time to cool off."

"There's nothing to cool off about," Mrs. Nelson said.

Jimmie put his hand on Noel's arm. She rose from the chair sniffling and turning her face away from the others. Jimmie, Kevin and Maxine crept toward the door.

On the ride back to Hawk Cove, Maxine put her arm around Kevin. With his underpants stuffed in his pocket, and his jeans chafed against his crotch. He wanted to remember how it was, doing it with her. But as Noel kept wailing, "She'll tell my parents. They'll kill me. What am I going to do? Jimmie, please tell her not to tell my parents. My dad will kill me," Kevin couldn't push away the thought of what would happen if the Nelsons told his parents. It was special, his first time. It was great – and now this.

Sunday July 13

KEVIN PULLED HARD ON THE OARS and rounded the point south of the Lodge. He took two more pulls and let the oars trail in the water as he drifted a hundred yards off shore. Squinting into the afternoon sun, he could barely make out where the cottages lining the beach stopped at the edge of Injun Swamp and the sheer face of the Rock rose out of the clearing at the end of Cedar Road. A metal flag marked the line of underwater boulders that ended in the shallows he floated over. He could see the tops of the weeds just below the surface. Motorboats would steer wide, and fishermen wouldn't move into this area until dusk.

This time yesterday, he was at the game standing in front of Ade Harmon, waiting to be assigned his position, just like he'd done every year. This time yesterday he'd never done it. It wasn't like a mortal sin you could erase at Confession and start fresh again. I used to be a Red Sox fan, now I like the Yankees. You could start out as a Republican then change to a Democrat. My dad was a Catholic, and now he's not. He tried to think of all the things in life you could reverse. Today, he was different, and there was no going back to what he was.

In the corner of his eye, he caught a splash off the end of the boat. A sunny slurping a bug off the surface. How old was he when his father had first taken him fishing out here: six, maybe seven? A late spring afternoon, cooler than today. Pricking himself in the thumb with the

139

hook as he tried to not look at the worm squirming between his fingers; shivering as the goop oozed out when he'd finally managed to thread it on like his father had shown him. And then the tug on the line, his father telling him to set the hook, the jolting pulls as the line sliced through the water. His father laughing and shouting 'Good work, Kevin!' when the perch was hauled into the boat. Then watching the shuddering fish as his father tried to hold it still as he twisted out the hook; the lid-less eye staring at him, its mouth opening and closing as if it was trying to tell him something. No amount of tuneless humming blocked out the sound of the suffocating fish thwacking against the bottom of the boat.

They'd finally rowed home with four perch and two sunnies. After climbing out of the boat, his father had clapped him on the back and asked him if he'd had a wonderful time. A catch in his voice must have been what made his father put his hand on his shoulder, look him in the eye and ask, 'You really didn't like it did you?' He'd started to say he had, but a glimpse of the six fish hanging from the stringer in his father's hand stopped the words before he could speak. And then he'd cried. He remembered the scratchy feel of his father's sweater as he hugged him to his chest, telling him it was all right not to like fishing – but Kevin should always tell the truth.

Just like last night when he got in, Kevin thought. No, he hadn't run into the Nelson boy and those two girls. It wasn't as though he hadn't told a lie in the past ten years. Hardly. But somehow it was different. And, yes he'd had some beer. He wasn't about to add he'd also had real sex with a real girl for the first time, but there must have been something that took the starch out of his father. He didn't figure sex had made him bold as brass. In fact, as this conversation was going on, he'd been try-ing to not stare at the telephone – a bomb ready to go off with a call from Hilda Nelson.

His father blustered about how Kevin was too young to start drink-ing, but Kevin could see his father's heart wasn't in it. But it wasn't just that he'd lied and gotten away with it. No, there was something differ-ent about it that he hadn't figured out yet. Taking out a rowboat and sit-ting alone for a while would give him a chance to catch his breath. The phone hadn't rung last night, but every time it rang this morning, he'd braced, positive Mrs. Nelson would be on the line with the story of him caught in the bedroom with her husband's no-good niece. By noon, he'd figured if Mrs. Nelson hadn't called yet, it wasn't going to happen. Then he started replaying one of the biggest events of his life.

He wondered if he should risk calling Maxine. Had Mrs. Nelson kicked her out of the house; was she on her way back to Minerva, or up to Lake George? Kevin lifted the oar out of the oarlock, then let it slide back down. Remembering Maxine's whispered instructions made him stiff. One time he might have even taken it out and done it right here in the boat. Nothing he'd ever done to himself had felt like that.

Ouch! Kevin swatted at the horse-fly on his left arm. Another one cir-cled his head, and he thought he felt it land on the back of his neck. A slap there distracted him from one biting into his ankle. *Damn it!* They don't give up. He should have known that on a hot afternoon with no breeze they'd come out of the swamp and find him in the shallows. Black flies. Mosquitoes. Horse flies. This place was like the Amazon jungle. He grabbed the oars, swung the boat around and started pulling toward the Lodge. Maybe he'd find out more at the Rock tonight.

———

A LITTLE AFTER EIGHT, Kevin and Buck were at the end of Cedar Road and heading for the Rock.

"Come *on*, Kev. I'm not settling for that. Blow-by-blow. You agreed."

"I agreed when you gave me the rubber – the one I don't know came apart or not."

"It was probably okay. So, you get to Jimmie's. Then you're in her bedroom. And she's naked. I want to know how she got naked."

"She took her clothes off. I helped."

"Christ, that's as exciting as the physical we took for basketball tryouts."

"Wait until we get to the Rock." Kevin had been avoiding giving Buck the details. That would make it less special. It was his thing. "Is Duke still around?"

"He was at the house earlier. He won't leave town until he gets a piece of that asshole who sucker-punched him."

"He ought to let it go."

"You don't know Duke. Now start where you're first in her bedroom."

Kevin and Buck reached the end of the road. They stepped into the clearing. Puffy Russell and Hack Leroux were standing around the fire pit.

"Nobody around tonight?" Buck said.

"We're here asshole," Puffy said.

"Sure is quiet," Buck said.

Puffy laughed. "Didn't Duke say anything to you about finding those assholes and kicking their butts all the way to Tupper?" Puffy poured gasoline on a teepee of logs in the pit, lit a match and tossed it in. They stepped back as the logs burst into flame.

Headlights bounced off the trees as a car pulled into the clearing. "It's Chink," Puffy said.

Chink Perrotti climbed out of his car and joined the group around the fire. "Wow. Some night. Duke and me just left our calling cards at Richie Rich's Ranchero."

"What did you do?" Buck asked.

"While Duke was packing Limburger in the heater of one of them sporty cars, I took three paper sacks full of dog shit, added a little high test, and touched them off on the porch. This fat bitch comes out of the house. *Oh, my! Oh, my!* and stomps one. Then a guy comes out and puts his dancing slippers into the other. Just about wet my pants. Then we both laid heavy tracks across the lawn."

Another set of headlights came up Cedar Road, and Duke's Fairlane pulled in next to Chink's Hornet. Duke stepped out and walked to the water, bent and swished his hands around. "Whew!" He walked back to the fire pit. "Hail. Hail. The gang's all here." He shoved his hands in Puffy's face.

"Hey, those were big-time calling cards you left," Hack said.

"We'll see." Duke laughed. "Hey, you scare away all the broads? He grabbed Buck, put his head in a hammer lock and gave him an Indian burn. "Just kidding, buddy."

"You figure those guys will show up here?" Puffy asked.

"Who knows what those pussies will do." Duke sniffed his hands. "Man, I still smell like my brother's shorts." He looked around. "You chickens stop diving off the Rock when I left town? I'm going in and float this stink down to Boyle's place."

Duke kicked off his engineer boots, stripped off his jeans and pulled his tee shirt over his head. He wore a pair of tight black swim trunks. "Don't any of you fruitcakes get any ideas," he said as he tossed his clothes onto the grass and started toward the Rock. "Anybody going to join me?"

Chink goosed Hack. "Hack and me are going to have a couple of brews. Somebody's got to be around to drag the bottom for you."

"Come on," Buck said to Kevin.

Kevin and Buck followed Duke and Puffy around through the scrub pines to the back of the Rock. They clambered up the slope on a narrow path through the brush and low-hanging pine branches to the shelf of rock at the top. Duke grabbed Kevin by the shoulders and pushed him toward the edge. Kevin let out a yell as he looked down at the boulders twenty feet below at the foot of the Rock.

Duke laughed. "Don't wet your pants, Boyle." He gave Kevin another shove and pulled him back.

Kevin slipped around behind Puffy. Duke stood on one leg, waving his arms, pretending to lose his balance. He pivoted to face the lake, bent his knees and dove off. The guys stepped forward to catch his dive just beyond the boulders at the bottom. Duke surfaced, shook the water from his long hair and shouted, "Who – ee! That's colder than a witch's tit." He took two strokes and climbed onto a large boulder at the base of the Rock, then followed the hand and footholds along the crevice that ran up the far side. When he reached the top he shook his hair and sprayed the guys. "Who's next?"

Puffy said, "I'm in." He stripped down to his shorts, then leapt out into a cannon ball that created a large splash as he hit the water.

One of the guys at the pit fire let out a yell.

Puffy pulled himself back to the top of the Rock.

Duke reached out and grabbed Buck. "Come on. I don't want a sissy for a brother."

Buck slowly got out of his clothes and carefully stepped toward the edge.

"If you hit the rocks, we'll all come to the funeral," Puffy laughed.

Buck bent his legs, then Duke stepped next to him. "We'll hold hands. Dual-exhaust Duncans." The brothers leapt off the Rock and splashed into the lake. In the dim light, Kevin could see Duke trying to push Buck under.

"Hey!" someone yelled from the beach.

Kevin turned to see a car stopping at the end of the road.

"It's Skippy and the peanut gallery," the voice shouted.

"Hot damn," Puffy said as he headed down the path behind the Rock.

Kevin watched Duke and Buck treading water. One of them – Kevin couldn't tell from where he stood – started swimming toward the beach. The other turned and swam toward the crevice on the far side of the Rock. Kevin heard shouting from the beach. He looked down, but in the dark, he couldn't tell whether it was Duke or Buck climbing up the far side of the Rock. Not sure what he wanted to do, Kevin scrambled down the narrow path behind the Rock. As he ducked through the bushes, he could see three guys at the end of the beach. They were throwing something at those near the fire.

Puffy stumbled into Kevin. "Fucking horse balls. They've got bags of horse balls." Kevin ducked as something whizzed by his head. Over Puffy's shoulder, he could barely make out someone doing something to Duke's car. The guys around the fire had scattered along the beach. Two guys started toward where Puffy and Kevin were standing. As they neared, Kevin thought the first one was that Skip guy. He shoved Puffy into the brush. As Puffy fell, the second guy reached into a large paper sack and smashed a horse ball in Puffy's face. Kevin dashed into the scrub pines behind the lean-to. The sharp branches tore into his arms. A low branch knocked him down. He scrambled to his feet.

Stopping to gulp for breath, Kevin turned and saw the guy hadn't followed him. Should he stay hidden in the pines; keep going until he reached Spruce Road? He could hear more yelling, the sounds of scuffles coming from the beach. He realized he'd come around to the far side of the Rock and decided to get up on top. He found a foothold, then handholds along the back that brought him almost to the top of the Rock. He grabbed a branch and pulled himself chest high to the top where he saw legs: two guys standing close together.

"Fuck off, asshole," one said.

"You and your friends can eat shit – horse shit," the other guy said.

Kevin's started to slip, and he tried to gain another foothold. As he turned back, he saw the legs tangling, heard grunts.

"Bastard."

"Fuckhead."

Then a long *"Aaaaak!"*

"Holy Shit!"

Kevin only saw one pair of legs. Then a body from the waist down – in tight black swim trunks.

"Holy fucking shit!"

"What happened?" Kevin screamed.

"Oh, shit to high fucking heaven!" the bare-legged person croaked before heading to the side of the Rock toward the beach and out of Kevin's sight.

Kevin grabbed another branch and managed to pull himself onto the Rock. He crawled to the edge and looked down. *Ohmygod!* Someone was in the water; half in the water, half on the boulders. *Ohmygod!*. Kevin scrambled to the end of the Rock nearest the beach. "Quick!" he shouted. "Over here! Somebody fell off the Rock!"

Sunday Night and Monday July 13 &14

BRITAIN ALERTS TROOPS: MACMILLAN PUTS FORCES ON ALERT

Discover Your Self: Use mental tools to solve an amazing number of your problems.

WHO'D BEEN RUNNING behind him through the brush? Was that before the guy fell in, or after – when he was running away? Would anyone blame him? He must have been dead already. He looked dead: his left arm bent behind; head twisted way to the right; his other arm straight out over his head. He didn't look like anyone he had seen alive. The others came running as soon as he'd yelled. They were in the water as fast as he could have been from the top without jumping in himself. He'd scrambled down the back of the Rock, heard the shouting. What else could he have done?

Running through back yards, first toward home, then away. Out of breath, on his knees gulping for air, his thighs burning, the Prindles' back yard. People already out front on the road, looking toward the wail of sirens. He'd fallen in behind them heading to the lake, joined the growing crowd at the end of Cedar Road, just another bystander wondering what had happened. The rescue squad had pulled up. The volunteers grabbed the equipment off the fire truck, ran to the Rock. He'd watched the ambulance back in, craned his neck as the stretcher was loaded, guessed the answer to the question on everyone's mind when the ambulance drove away too slowly.

He'd tried to look as shocked as the others around him when he saw his father on the other side of the sandy road. What was he going to tell him? In the halo of the lights from the trucks, three boys in the middle of the clearing, hunched over with their heads in their hands, the ones with the kid who'd fallen off the Rock. Duke, Buck, Chink, and Puffy weren't there. He wasn't the only one who had run away.

Now, sitting on the end of his bed, still dressed, shivering, he stared at the rusty splotch of dried blood that had seeped through his sleeve. Had his parents seen the stain and scratches on his wrists before he'd dashed upstairs? What would he say to them? Could he explain that he wasn't really there, that he couldn't remember what happened? Would they blame him? He didn't do it. Still, he ran away – and lied.

———

WHEN THE PHONE RANG at seven-thirty, Kevin's eyes shot open. Hilda Nelson? Then the sting of the scratches, the ache in his shoulder reminded him. It hadn't been a nightmare. Dealing with Hilda would have been better than this, sitting with his father in the school cafeteria along with the others who'd been summoned for questioning by the State Police.

Deputy Fisher paced along the tray runner, empty steam tables, racks of dishes, and the cash register waiting for the first day of school. The click of the taps on his heels punctuated the anxious murmurs hanging in the room. Kevin thought maybe it wasn't bad that the firemen, most of the guys that had been at the Rock, along with their parents, and people who lived on Spruce Road all sat clumped in chairs taken off the long tables. Maybe he'd get lost in this crowd. As he stared at his shoe laces, he hoped he could come up with something to say to the troopers in Mr. Putnam's office: something that didn't make it his fault the kid died, something that explained why he'd run away. It was all a muddle. But as soon as a story began to form, his father pulled his chair closer to Kevin's. He scuffed his feet and jangled the big key ring, demanding to know why Kevin had even been anywhere near the Rock, why Kevin thought he was so stupid as to buy the lame excuses Kevin had been trying to sell since the phone call this morning.

"I told you if you went anywhere near that place, there'd be trouble. Now I want...." Did he want to get called next just to get away from one more angry demand?

"Hey, Fisher," Chink Perrotti yelled. "How long we supposed to wait here?"

Conversations stopped as Deputy Fisher wheeled around. "Until I say so."

"You ain't got nothing to say about nothing," Puffy shouted. He brushed his father's arm away as he stood and pointed in the direction of the principal's office. "Go ask them troopers whether we're supposed to spend all day cooped up while they figure what end's up."

Deputy Fisher hitched up his gun belt "Everybody who got called stays until they've been questioned."

"They paying my wages today?" Chink said. "Already lost a half a day. And where's those other guys?"

Stewie Rapp, one of the volunteers at the Rock last night, levered up his six-foot, four inch frame. "Why don't you two shut up? Nobody's getting paid for this – but you ain't dead either."

Thomas hissed at Kevin, "If you weren't there, then why did they call you?"

Across the room Buck sat next to his mother. Duke wasn't there. "It looks like they called half the town."

"Perrotti, Russell, Duncan. If it's half the town, it's not the better half. Were you there?"

"Kevin Boyle," Deputy Fisher called.

"No. I mean, not exactly. I was..."

"Boyle. Kevin Boyle," Deputy Fisher said loudly.

"We'd better go," Kevin said.

As Kevin and his father walked toward the double doors at the end of the cafeteria where Deputy Fisher waited, Thomas said, "If you're lying..."

Deputy Fisher held up his hand. "They said only Kevin."

Kevin ducked around Deputy Fisher, hearing his father's, *'You'd better...'*

Inside the principal's office, two State Troopers were bent over one end of Mr. Putnam's desk, their starched Stetsons aligned side by side on the other end. Without looking at Kevin, one pointed to the chair in front of the desk. As he sat with his hands clenched in his lap, the troopers ignored him while they scanned a map spread across the desk. He wished he'd gone to the bathroom. He had never been sent to the principal's office. He should have changed his shirt. He'd balled up the bloody one he'd worn last night and stuffed it in the back of his closet. He would ditch it in the trash later. Minutes crept by. He would explain he wasn't really there. Or there, but not so close he could see what happened. And he had left – in a hurry. Not exactly running away. Just going for help. That's all.

As if hearing a silent alarm, both troopers looked up at Kevin with hard expressions on their faces. Kevin tried to hold their gazes, but dropped his head. Silence. Finally, Kevin raised his head again. There was only more silence until one of the men spoke.

"You were there."

Kevin couldn't tell which one had said it. He opened his mouth, but no sound came out. He didn't know what to say. Tears filled his eyes, then dribbled down his cheeks. He wiped his nose with the back of his hand. The scratches on his wrist looked like ragged scars.

"Why don't you tell us what happened?" said the younger of the two troopers.

"Can I go to the bathroom?"

The men looked at each other. The younger one said, "Where is it?"

"Right down the hall. I'll be right back. I've really got to go."

"Make it fast," the older one said. "Don't talk to anyone."

A few minutes later, Kevin was back in the chair in front of Mr. Putnam's desk. Had anyone seen him as he ran down the hall to the bathroom? Did he look like he'd been crying? What was he going to say to them?

The older trooper identified himself as Sergeant Fleming and stood in front of Mr. Putnam's desk while Trooper Wilson remained seated at the table.

Sergeant Fleming said, "Kevin, I want you to tell me what happened. Where you were. Who was there. What you saw."

"I didn't see the kid get killed."

"Why did you say 'get killed?'"

"I don't know. I mean. He's dead. I didn't mean somebody killed him."

"Did someone kill him?"

"No. I mean. I don't know."

Sergeant Fleming put his hands on his hips and stared at Kevin. "Where were you when Skip Satterfield fell – or was pushed – off the cliff?"

Kevin tried to remember the stories he'd concocted. As he started to tell one, then another, they caught in the back of his throat. Finally, he said. "Yes. But only sort of." He told Sergeant Fleming he had been in the woods behind the Rock; he saw people, maybe only two people, on top of the Rock. They were talking – okay, shouting at each other.

"Was Duke Duncan one of the two?" Sergeant Fleming asked.

"I don't know," Kevin answered.

"Kevin." Sergeant Fleming snapped. "I asked you whether Duke Duncan one of the people on the Rock?"

"Maybe. But I'm not sure."

"Did Duke Duncan push Kent Satterfield off the Rock?"

Legs. Shouts. How could a person see with his hands slipping from the branches, gouging his wrists, his knee skinned on the jagged rock face? "I don't know. I couldn't see very well. I was slipping. Branches were in my face."

"You don't know?" Sergeant Fleming asked. "Or you won't say?" There was a knock on the door. "Who is it?" Trooper Wilson barked.

The door opened slowly, and Deputy Fisher peeked through the crack. "Sergeant, we've got a problem out here."

"What is it?" the sergeant growled.

"It's Perrotti and Russell. They say they're leaving, and the others look like they might go too."

"Can't you keep the situation under control?"

"It's – well. They might listen to you."

"Trooper, go with the deputy and settle them down."

Sergeant Fleming let out a long breath as the younger trooper left with Deputy Fisher. He looked at this watch and said, "What *did* you see?"

"Just legs. I didn't know if it was Skip. I was slipping off the back of the Rock."

Sergeant Fleming's eyes darted toward the sounds of voices on the other side of the door. He leaned close to Kevin and said very slowly. "Listen to me, young man. We're not through with this. You had better think long and hard about what you saw or didn't see. Understand?"

"Yes sir."

"You can go – for now."

Kevin started toward the door. As he grasped the knob, Sergeant Fleming's voice cut through the air like an arrow. "Kevin Boyle." Kevin turned slowly, afraid of what he might hear next. Sergeant Fleming was standing, his finger pointing at Kevin's chest. "Kevin Boyle. If I find out you are lying to me...." He let the words hang in the air as he held Kevin in a piercing stare until, after several seconds, he jerked his head toward the door. Kevin tried not to run. He glanced in the direction of the cafeteria, then headed for the side entrance. He'd tell his father that's the way the troopers told him to leave.

"Kevin!"

Thomas was quick-marching toward him. "What were you going to do, leave me there? What did you tell the troopers?"

"I told them I didn't see anything."

"Why would you not see anything if you weren't there?"

"I was around. Somebody. Maybe Chink Perrotti told them I was where I could see something."

"Perrotti?" Thomas spat. "I don't understand. I want the truth."

"Tom. What the hell is going on?"

Milton Standish, the Town Supervisor, stood a few feet away.

"I figured you'd know, Milton."

"I *ought* to know. But I don't mind telling you I am very, very upset. Sheriff Dawson messed this up royally, not getting the troopers down here last night. Sergeant Fleming told me Dawson didn't make it clear it might be a homicide. Said Dawson made it sound more like a drowning. By the time they figured out it was serious business, Dawson and Fisher had mucked up the scene, did some half-assed questioning, and let the other kids who were there leave town."

"What are they going to do? They just talked to Kevin. Looks like they got about everybody else who was there, except for the kid that got.... Did he drown?"

"We don't *know*. Edgar Pierce drove the body to Connecticut first thing this morning. You want to go down there and tell the parents we'd like to haul the body back up here for an autopsy; try to do one down there now."

"Does it matter whether he drowned or died from hitting his head?" Thomas said.

Blue polo shirt; khaki shorts; one of those moccasin shoes, top-siders, still on his left foot, the other on the rocks behind him. Wrist watch on the left arm twisted behind him. Kevin shuddered, tried to shake away the image of the dead kid, half in, half out of the water. He didn't want to re-imagine what had happened before; who he couldn't see on top of the Rock.

"All I do know is the State Police are thoroughly annoyed." Milton Standish stepped closer to Thomas and lowered his voice. "We were down to Wentworth's a week ago. Me and Alice and Linda. We met the kid's parents. The father's name is Talbot Satterfield. A top exec at Westinghouse. Very well-connected politically, according to Sam Wentworth. He seemed like a nice enough guy, but then his son hadn't been killed yet."

Killed. Murdered. Died. The kid that died. That's how he'd think about it. But he didn't want to think about it. He wanted to go home; do his chores; call Maxine. Get out of town.

"That family's got to be in a lot of pain right now, Tom. In a few days. Next week. That pain's going to be spread around if we don't figure out what happened right quick."

Tuesday July 15

KEVIN FLINCHED as a black spider the size of half dollar skittered under the box next to the one he'd lifted. He hated spiders. No matter how hot it was he wore his cap, work gloves and a long-sleeved shirt with the collar turned up when he cleaned the storeroom where hundreds of huge spiders lurked in the dark corners. Kevin stamped his feet and kicked at the next cardboard box. At least he was alone. For the past two days, every time he turned around, there was his father shooting suspicious looks or his mother doing her *this-is-the-end-of-the-world* sigh. As he carefully lifted the box, he thought he should have decided to cut back the brush in the parking lot. He'd be alone out there too, but in here he could take another peek at the sex book. He needed something to get his mind off the kid getting killed at the Rock. Last night in bed, he'd started to do it, thinking about him and Maxine in her bedroom. Then the sound the kid made as he fell and remembering how he looked crumpled at the base of the Rock jumped right into his head, and his thing went limp. *Jeez.* Even though he'd managed to do it ten minutes later, he worried this business would turn him into one of those eunuchs or something. Maybe he'd find something he could do with Maxine next time; show her he wasn't just a rookie.

After pushing a stack of cardboard boxes between him and the door, Kevin pulled *Ideal Marriage* from its hiding place. He thumbed through the book in the shaft of light from the window over the hot water tank. What about this one? 'Attitude of Equitation (Astride), the method of coitus which the Roman poet Martial considered so normal.' *Equitation, Roman poets.* Cripes. Forget about that. It was Maxine's soft cooing in his ear, 'In and out' that had his thing stiffening again. He flipped the pages. What's this? Sedentary Attitude (Vis-a-vis). *Vis-a-vis.* He liked the sound of that. Damn, just when he was starting to do it with Maxine, this mess at the Rock was going to screw up everything. He needed to see her soon; do it again.

The door to the storeroom opened, and Kevin slammed the book back behind the files.

"Hey, Kev. You in there?"

"Buck. What are you doing here?"

Buck stepped into the storeroom. "Whew. It's hot in here," he said. "What's with your father? He acted like I was a worm or something."

"He's mad about you and me being at the Rock."

"I need to talk to you about what happened."

"For chrissakes, Buck, I keep telling everybody I don't know what happened."

"Take it easy. Besides, that's the story Duke wants everybody sticking to."

"Duke?"

"He was at the house an hour ago. The troopers caught up with him in Star Lake. Duke said he told them he didn't know what happened to that Skip guy. He was on the Rock but dove off and swam to the beach. Said maybe Skip tried to follow him and couldn't make it over the boulders at the bottom. That's the story."

"That's ..." Kevin stopped. "Did they believe him?"

"Who knows? Duke says as long as everyone sticks to it, we're alright. It's our word against them others, and they were back on the beach throwing horse shit. Duke talked to Puffy and Chink. They're supposed to get to Hack. Duke told me to talk to you."

"Jeez, Buck. How do you know what they already said to the sheriff and those troopers?"

"What did you say?"

"Nothing." Kevin shrugged. "I mean I had to tell them I was there. But I didn't say anything about what happened. I told them I couldn't see what was going on at the top of the Rock."

Jabbing Kevin's arm, Buck said, "That's it! There was arguing and all that. But then Duke dove in. How could he know the jerk was going to try it without knowing about the boulders at the bottom?"

"I thought you… Never mind." Kevin paused. "What happens now?"

"Nothing – we hope. The troopers huffed and puffed some shit about sticking around for further questioning. Everybody keeps cool, and they can keep their fat asses up in Tupper."

"I don't think it's going to be that simple, Buck. That kid's father. The Wentworths. They're not going to let this go away."

"We'll see. I got to go to work."

"You're heading through Inlet?"

"Yeah."

"Maxine. She's waiting tables at the Acropolis. Could you duck in there, and see if she's still working?"

"You want me to tell her I'll pinch hit for you next time?"

"Fat chance. No, I just want to make sure she's still in town."

Buck laughed. "What did she do, take off when she saw your tiny dick?"

"Just tell her I said hello if she's there. I'll try to see her. See if she's okay."

"You owe me, Kev. If you don't come across with your promise to give me the skinny about what you're doing with her, I'm going to tell her you're queer."

"I promise. Just see if she's there."

"Okay. I got to get going before it rains. And remember – we all stick together."

———

AT THREE-THIRTY THAT AFTERNOON, Kevin dropped the book in the return box at the end of the circulation desk. Having books due was a good excuse to get away from his parents and everybody else who wanted to know about the *incident*. That's what the *Thendara Times* called it. Even the Utica *Observer-Dispatch* had a story on it: 'Youth Drowns in Hawk Cove. Investigation Continues.' Okay. So, he *was* there. He cringed at the recollection of crying when Sergeant Fleming said that. He was upset. Anybody would be. Besides, Sheriff Dawson and the troopers would love to tie Chink and Puffy and Hack – and especially Duke to this incident. They had him pegged as a sniveling kid on the edge of what happened.

As Kevin walked toward the periodical section, he was surprised to see Larry Needham and Mr. Marsh standing in the fiction room loading books on a cart. Kevin sat at the large oak table with the *New York Times*. Mr. Marsh walked toward Kevin.

"Hello, Kevin," Mr. Marsh said as he walked by Kevin.

Kevin muttered a "Hi" at Mr. Marsh's back. He acted like I was a nobody, Kevin thought. He wanted to be alone, but maybe it wouldn't have been bad to talk to someone who might understand the pressure he was under. Nothing. And what was Larry doing here?

Kevin got up and walked into the fiction room. "Hey, Lar. What are you doing?"

"Mr. Marsh gave me this re-shelving job."

"I thought you were working at Thibedeau's."

"Thibedeau wants me to work on Saturdays and Sundays for the rest of the season. I had to find something for Wednesdays and Thursdays, and Mr. Marsh had a part-time opening."

"Great. Well, I'll see you around." Kevin returned to the table in the periodical section and leafed through the *Times*. How come he didn't ask me? he thought. Mr. Marsh was busying himself behind the circulation desk, and Kevin waited for him to come over to talk to him as he usually did. Nothing. He's mad at me too, Kevin thought. Probably figures I'm just like Duke and Chink and Puffy and the other guys at the Rock who never set foot inside the library.

To hell with him too! Kevin stuffed the *Times* back in the rack and headed for the door. Just inside the exit, at pay phone hung on the wall. Four o'clock. Even if Buck had stopped in at the Acropolis, there was no way Kevin would hear anything until tomorrow. He leafed through the phone book, found the number, and called the Acropolis. Athena Dorakadis answered, and in what he hoped was a disguised voice, Kevin asked if Maxine was there.

"She working," Athena said.

"I just need to give her a quick message. It's important."

"I see if she around," Athena said in an annoyed tone.

A few moments later, Maxine said, "Hello."

"Maxine. It's me, Kevin."

"Hey." Maxine paused. "I hear you got a pile of trouble."

"I'm okay. When can I see you?"

"I need to see you, too. I got to go. Athena's waving at me like her pants are on fire. But we need to talk. Friday. Okay. Okay. *Jesus*, that woman is nasty. Your place?"

"No! Ricketts front steps. After he closes. Ten after nine. You okay?"

"I'll see you Friday."

———

AFTER DINNER Kevin pulled the wagon with the last load of trash cans to the back of the parking lot and spotted Slim's dog sniffing the barrels. "Can't you get a decent meal someplace else?"

The dog crept towards Kevin and whined.

"Alright, already." Kevin tipped the can over the lip the drum. "Let me see. No, you don't want corn cobs. Okay, here's a piece of hamburger bun. Wait, you're in luck, part of a hamburger. I hope you like ketchup." The dog snatched up the garbage scraps Kevin tossed. "I'm dying to get this done, and you've got me laying out a blue plate special."

Kevin continued picking out food scraps and tossing paper plates and napkins into the burn barrel. When he finished with the last can, he lit the paper and leaned against the drums.

"That's it. No dessert tonight." Kevin looked at the dog. "I am going looney tunes. I don't remember if Slim gave you a name, but if you're stupid enough to hang around here, I ought to give you one. You're a scruffy brown mutt, so you're Brownie."

The dog sat on his haunches looking at Kevin. Cripes, he looks more intelligent than half the guys at the Rock. "I'm in deep shit, Brownie. Right up your alley. Seven or eight certified assholes at the Rock, and I zoom to the top of those troopers' Ten Most Wanted list. Dad figures my excuse is right up there with the dog ate my homework. Yeah, I'll blame it on you." The dog moved closer to Kevin.

A shift in the breeze blew the smoke from the burn barrel at Kevin. "I'll never get this stink off me." He walked around to the far side of the fire, picked up a stick and poked a smoldering damp napkin back into the barrel. Brownie came around to the side and settled down a few feet from Kevin: the two of them watching the sparks fly up from the burning trash.

"They probably haven't buried Skip yet, and Buck's already on me with sticking to *our* story. I don't even know what the hell *my* story is."

Kevin poked the embers down to the bottom of the burn barrel. "You ought to find yourself a regular meal ticket." He grabbed the handles of the cart. "Nothing but garbage around here." Lifting the cart, Kevin started back to the Lodge. "At least Maxine wants to see me. I'm going to need three bars of *Life Buoy* to get rid of this smell before Friday."

Thursday July 17

DUCKING UNDER THE OVERHANG next to the workshop, Kevin shook the rain off his poncho and pulled it over his head. It hadn't let up since late yesterday morning, and it was going to be another ugly day. At breakfast, Kevin sensed his mother had convinced his father not to keep badgering him about the incident. But all morning, working close to his father on rainy day chores, he could feel the questions, and finally the anger, hanging like wet fog between them. Kevin drew his head into his shoulders as he listened to the undertone in his father's forced-jolly answers to the guests walking by the workshop: "Can't rain forever," "Should let up pretty soon," and "Radio says a high should be moving through."

And once each guest got out of ear-shot, Thomas said to Kevin, "One more goddamned question about the rain, and I'm going to tell them to pack up and leave! How do you think I feel being held personally responsible for the weather? They say, 'It's been raining for two days,' as though *I've* willed it to rain on their precious vacation. 'How's the weather look for tomorrow?' they ask as though I had a PhD. in meteorology or a direct pipeline to the gods of sunshine and rain. Damn." He looked at Kevin. "Why did you take off your poncho? We need to shovel gravel into those ruts in the parking area."

"I'm supposed to go to St. Mary's. The job for Father Donovan. I need to get cleaned up."

"Great! I'll shovel gravel, and you can lick stamps in the cushy rectory."

"I can quit. I can stay here and help you."

"No. You'd better go. Three bucks an hour. You could use the money, what with this..." Thomas paused. "Go. It'll make your mother happy."

———

Was he supposed to stand all the time, Kevin wondered as he reached for another newsletter? Father Donovan had greeted him brusquely at the door and told Kevin there was another stack of newsletters on the dining room table to fold and stuff into envelopes. No jokes about the Red Sox, nothing. Then Father Donovan said he had work to do in his office. Okay, Kevin thought. A couple of hours doing a job a moron could do and getting three bucks an hour – and being left alone would be great.

"Youth. The Prime Target of Communist Attack" was the headline of the story on the right side of the newsletter. Kevin read the first sentence. 'Communists, front organizations and fellow travelers craft their clever appeal to America's youth with promises to repeal the draft, support academic freedom and promote world-wide youth friendship for peace and democracy.' World-wide youth friendship. Sign me up for a trip to France, Kevin thought. I'll be a willing tool of Soviet indoctrination. France. He'd settle for Utica right now. According to his father, being involved with *the incident* put Kevin put on track for Canton Community College.

Kevin jumped when Father Donovan put his hand on his shoulder. *Cripes*. He didn't hear him come in.

"I'm afraid I startled you."

"That's okay," Kevin said. "I'm almost done."

"I see that. I'd like a word with you. Perhaps it would be best if you came to my office."

Kevin followed Father Donovan down the hallway. In the office, a large oak desk sat in front of a double window overlooking the small shrine behind the church. Two chairs flanked a round table. Father Donovan sat behind the desk and motioned for Kevin to sit in the chair next to the table.

Father Donovan stared at Kevin. His fingers formed a steeple under his chin. "Kevin, I understand you find yourself in a spot of trouble."

"There was this kid: Skip Satterfield. He drowned."

"Yes. I know. It appears you were in the vicinity – or so the story goes."

"I didn't see what happened."

"Still, it must be very upsetting," Father Donovan said. "With the investigation, the questioning, I don't imagine you've had much time to think about what I said last week."

"No, Father."

"I suspect a great deal of attention will be focused on you as this investigation unfolds."

"I told the troopers everything I know, Father."

"I'm sure you did." Father Donovan paused. "I had hoped our conversations about your spiritual and intellectual and physical development might evolve at a more studied pace."

"I guess."

"I don't mind telling you I hoped this job," Father Donovan said with a dismissive wave of his hand toward the door, "would also entail a discussion, a learned conversation – a symposium – in light of your intelligence and perspicacity."

"I don't know about that, Father."

The priest opened his hands in front of his chest. "Don't be modest, Kevin. You are special. I said it last week, and I'll say it again."

Kevin didn't know what he was supposed to say. He didn't think he was going to make the varsity, and certainly not as starting guard. Just because he knew the meaning of perspicacity didn't make him special. He hadn't been doing those exercises, and he wasn't listening for a vocation.

"You're talented in many ways. The physical and the intellectual," Father Donovan said. "And I have a talent, Kevin. God gave me this gift: the ability to identify those individuals who can join the elite of society."

"I don't think I'm in the elite, Father."

"I'm not talking about the country club set, Kevin. Millionaires. Movie stars. I'm talking about a small number of individuals who have special insights into the meaning of life: *gnosis*." He smiled. "I've got you on that one haven't I?"

Kevin nodded.

"It's Greek for knowledge. *Gnosis*. Socrates, Plato, Aristotle and the others laid the foundations of Western civilization. Kevin, I am not denying the truth of Christianity when I tell you they also illuminated another path; a virtually secret route; an alternative way of understanding; a supplement, a complementary approach to living in this tumultuous world." He paused. "Why am I telling you this?"

Kevin's nose itched. Greek philosophers and Roman poets? "I don't know, Father."

Leaning toward Kevin, the priest said, "I share this with you now because you will be tested in these coming days. I had hoped to bring you along more slowly. To let *you* see your specialness. You're confused, aren't you?"

"A little."

"I want to help you, Kevin. What I am trying to explain is those who follow this hermetic – another Greek word – path have special obligations and special dispensations. You understand dispensation?"

"Yes Father. It's like you get a free pass."

"Close. Permission or privilege might be synonyms. Let me use an example. Someone comes at another person with an axe. Is it permissible for the person to defend himself, even if it results in the death of the attacker?"

"I suppose so, Father."

"You're probably correct. None of these are easy questions or decisions. A family is starving. They have no money. Their children are in danger of becoming ill, perhaps dying. Is it wrong for the father to steal food: pick apples from someone's orchard; perhaps take a loaf of bread from a grocery store?"

"I guess not, but maybe the owner of the store would have given him the bread."

"Perhaps. The point, Kevin, is what seems to be a crime, even a sin, might not always be what it seems to be."

"Like if someone gave this starving family hamburgers, and it was Friday, and they were Catholics. It might not be a mortal sin if they ate meat."

"That's it. Indeed you do see the *nuances* involved." He sat back in his chair and stared at Kevin. "Until this unfortunate incident, I don't suppose you have had any experience with truly serious crimes."

"No, Father."

"I'm not surprised. I can say without violating the seal of the confessional, for most," he paused, "virtually all young men your age the struggle with temptations of the flesh result in the most serious sins."

Kevin looked down at his hands.

"Yet, someone with your inquiring mind, your intellectual capacity can understand the interplay among the philosophical, the moral and the physical elements in life. You see that don't you?"

"I guess so, Father."

"Don't be bashful about your confusion. Young men who are beginning their journey in life; who see a hint, a glimmer of the path and

165

aren't sure what it means; whether they should venture down it."

'Right now, there are a lot of things I don't see clearly, Father."

"Kevin. I want to be your friend. I want you to rely on me for advice. I want to be a shoulder you can lean on."

"Thank you, Father."

"You've been doing your exercises haven't you?"

"Gee, Father. It's been an awful week. What with the thing at the Rock."

"I understand." Father Donovan glanced at this wristwatch. "I see you still owe me thirty minutes. I propose we make this a win-win situation. You can do your exercises – on my time."

"I don't know, Father. It doesn't..."

"No. I'll take full responsibility for spending our benefactor's money. So, Mr. Boyle shall we begin with a few jumping jacks?"

"Here, Father?"

"Of course. I don't think you'll shake the crystal from the sideboard in the dining room from here. Stand up my boy!"

Kevin stood in the center of the carpet where the priest pointed.

"Okay. One, two. One, two."

Kevin managed a few awkward jumping jacks.

"No. No. You've got to set aside the intellectual and take on the physical. Get yourself focused on the physical. Pretend you're in the school gym. Take off your tee-shirt."

"My...?"

"Of course. You won't catch cold!"

Kevin slowly stripped off his tee-shirt. He felt a shiver, then a flush spreading across his stomach. Wondering what to do with it, he set it on the chair. He crossed his arms in front of his chest and wondered if he was supposed to wait for Father Donovan's count.

"Turn toward the door to the hall."

As Kevin faced the door, a flash went off. He glanced back over his shoulder to see Father putting something in the top drawer of the desk.

Was it Father Donovan's Polaroid? He remembered him taking his picture the day he started.

"Ready?"

Kevin nodded.

"Okay. One, two. One, two. One, two."

Kevin got into the rhythm of the jumping jacks by staring at the pine tree outside the window. After a few minutes, he was taking deep, labored breaths.

"Tired?"

"A little," Kevin said as Father Donovan's eyes zoomed in on his chest. Kevin stopped and concentrated on the flower in the pattern of the carpet.

"What's your best exercise?"

"Sit ups, Father. Last winter, I did two hundred in gym class."

"Okay. Then do sit ups."

Kevin lowered himself to the floor and lay back.

"Back farther. I want to make sure you're not cheating on me."

Kevin scooched further back on the carpet. He could see the priest's hands on top of the desk. Kevin laced his fingers behind his head and pulled himself up, then forward as his left elbow almost touched his right knee. Then down. Then up, right elbow almost touching his left knee. Then down. As he came up, Kevin saw Father Donovan was staring at him, but his eyes seemed glazed. He was rocking slightly in his chair. Back down. Then up. The priest's mouth hung open, and the tip of his tongue was thrusting against his lower lip. Back down. And up. Father Donovan's hands weren't on the desk, and his face had reddened. Back down. And up. The priest's eyes were squeezed shut. And down. And up. A long hiss of breath slid out of Father Donovan's lips. Kevin laid back, hesitated then slowly drew himself up. Father Donovan had a lop-sided smile on his face. His right hand was back on the desk top. "I don't think I can do any more," Kevin said. Father Donovan didn't seem to hear him. "Can I stop, Father?"

"Yes. Yes. Very good, Kevin."

Kevin stood and pulled his shirt back on. "It's my best exercise."

"You will be excellent at whatever you put your mind to." Father Donovan stood and came around from behind the desk to face Kevin. He held out his hand, and when Kevin grasped it, he drew Kevin into an embrace. "But for some problems, you need a special friend." He patted Kevin's back. "Lean on me, son. I'll help you."

Friday July 18

AT NINE O'CLOCK, Wendell Ricketts, locking the door of the Red & White, eyed Kevin suspiciously. "Waiting for someone?"

"Yes, Mr. Ricketts. A friend. Sh, ah, he ought to be here any minute."

"I would be vexed if you and your friends commenced to make the front steps of the post office a gathering place. Damaging or destroying federal property is a very serious offense."

"Don't worry, Mr. Ricketts. We won't be here long."

"I should hope not."

Fifteen minutes later, Kevin figured Maxine had stiffed him when a dented '49 Plymouth pulled into Simpson's. Someone got out, and the car pulled away with the driver beeping the horn and waving out his window. Maxine stood in the cone of light next to the pumps, then sauntered across Route 28.

"You're late," Kevin said.

Maxine let out a mirthless laugh. "I thought I'd never hook a ride."

"You hitched?"

"I wasn't going to walk." She glanced back toward the road. "I've never had to wait that long. I figured with this handkerchief of a dress Theo calls a uniform, I'd catch a ride right away."

"I thought you'd come with Jimmie and Noel."

"They went someplace. And I needed to talk to you right away."

"I was hoping to see you sooner, too. It's been crazy since Sunday with the kid getting killed. The whole town's in a stew."

"I'm late."

"That's okay. It's only nine-twenty."

"My *period's* late."

Her sharp tone surprised Kevin. Then he tried to think of something else Maxine could mean as he watched her eyes follow the taillights of a passing car. Finally, in a tone that fell between a question and a plea, he said, "Your period's late?"

"You gone deaf?"

"Like you might be – pregnant?"

"Like I might," she said. "Where can we go? I don't like standing here."

Kevin had been counting on Maxine coming with Jimmie, then going someplace for more of what they'd done last week. He'd even talked Buck into giving him the other rubber from his mother's room. "We can't go to the Rock. The town crew pushed boulders across the road to block cars from getting in, and the cops are cruising by every hour to hassle anybody who's walked in."

Maxine surveyed the closed buildings along Route 28. "Jesus, this place is duller than Inlet. Is *anything* open after nine around here?"

"Just the Trading Post and the Halfway House," Kevin said. But he didn't want to let her know he couldn't go to either. Then he remembered Buck's mom would be at the Knotty Pine until at least ten. Buck said he was going to Tommy Ender's until Tommy's parents got back from going out to dinner, and then over to Butch Sutter's when his parents went to the movies.

A few minutes later, Kevin and Maxine were slinking along the driveway leading to Buck's house at the back of the lot, when Sammy started barking. "I hope that dog's on a chain," Maxine said.

"Quick. In the bushes," Kevin said as the back door opened and someone stepped out into the yard.

"What's the matter, boy?" Mr. Becker called. "Who's there?"

"It's me, Mr. Becker," Kevin yelled.

"Nobody's home back there."

"It's okay. Buck Duncan asked me leave something for him on his porch."

"That you, Butch? Butch Sutter?"

"Yeah."

"Say hello to your dad for me. Sammy, you be quiet."

"Come on," Kevin whispered.

"There better not be any poison ivy in them bushes," Maxine said.

Kevin stepped onto the porch and pointed at the sofa. "We can talk here." But what to say? Even his view of Maxine's long legs as her short dress hiked up her thighs was crowded out by the memory of a very pregnant Jeannie Bailey waddling around town. "This thing. You being late. You sure?"

"This *thing* – like maybe you knocked me up, I can't be so sure about – yet."

"Then you might *not* be ..." Kevin was afraid that saying the word again would jinx the chance she wasn't.

"I kind of thought when we did it last week, it might get my period started, like it's done before."

"What do we do?"

"Pray."

Why would God fix this? *Please God, don't ... God, if you make this go away, I'll...*

His mother was right. There was something in his blood; something lurking in his genes all along waiting for a Maxine. Would his parents argue about whether it was the Boyles or Wards that made him do it? He just wanted some fun, and it was only once. Pregnant was what happened to adults – or girls like Jeannie Bailey. What would praying do? He perched on the other end of the sofa staring up Maxine's dress. Why not? Was God going to make this okay if he behaved himself *now*? "If your period doesn't come, do we have to – get married?"

"Christ, you *are* a funny guy. You're seventeen, and I'm nineteen, for crissakes. You planning on renting an apartment on your allowance, move in with your parents?"

"I don't know. I could get a job, I guess. I don't..." Kevin stopped. His voice cracked. "I never thought."

"Because you guys all think with your dicks." She reached out and put her hand on Kevin's arm. "Look. Don't get yourself too down. I don't know for absolute sure, but I figured we needed to talk in case."

As Maxine shifted her bottom and pulled up her legs, Kevin caught a flash of white between her legs. "Then what?"

"That's where you come in – *dad*."

"*Jeez*, will you stop with that?"

"Have a little sense of humor. One way or another, I figure I got to have some dough. Maybe five hundred." Maxine eyed Kevin. "Could be more – like a thousand."

"Dollars?"

"No, hickory nuts. What do you think I'm talking about? From what I hear, it costs a lot."

"Cost for what?"

"Whatever," she said. "A home for unwed mothers. There's this place in Plattsburgh. Girl I knew in high school – couple of girls actually – who had to go there. They take care of you for a few months. Then you give the kid up for adoption."

"That's a lot of money."

"You got a better idea? I figured it might take you a little time to get it together in case."

"I haven't got that kind of money."

"Come on. Your family's rich."

"I told you. They owe a lot of money. There's a mortgage on the Lodge, my mother's cousin...." Kevin stopped before going on to say what had popped into his head. *His college fund.* One-thousand, four hundred, and seventy-seven dollars and thirty-two cents in the savings account at Thendara Savings and Loan. But he couldn't use that. It was his sacred hoard. How could he? Could he?

"I ain't got the money either, and where I come from, you take the ride, you pay the toll."

"I'm not. It's just that. I've got to think. I need time to figure this out."

"If my friend doesn't show up pretty soon, you ain't got a hell of a long time to figure out where to get the money. The first morning I up-chuck, Hilda'll kick me out."

"Can you go back to Minerva?"

"That's a laugh. About the only person I knew really well in Minerva tried to kill me."

"I thought your mom lived there."

"Mom and her boyfriend moved to Rutland. And I doubt they'll stay there. Jerome passes too many bad checks to hang around anywhere for long."

"You're kind of alone."

"I got you."

Sammy started to bark. "Stupid dog barks at anything that moves," Kevin said. "When do you think you'll know for sure? I've got to figure out where I'm going to get the money."

"If nothing happens in a week, I'd be sure. Couple of years ago, I went almost three weeks late. But never more than that."

"In the meantime we wait?" Kevin didn't say *pray*, even though he thought it.

Maxine shifted around on the sofa to face Kevin. "In the meantime, we might as well – you know – do it. I either am – or amn't," she giggled. "A good fuck might shake things loose."

"*Jeez.* I don't know, Maxine." And if she isn't, he thought? A lot of good that old rubber did last time. God would really....

"This old sofa is pretty comfy. And we might as well enjoy ourselves until we find out how much of a pickle we're in."

Kevin froze as a pair of headlight came down the street, then let out his breath as they continued toward the lake. "What if Mr. Becker comes out or Buck's mom comes home early? And what if you're not?" As Maxine leaned back, bunching the skirt of the uniform at the top of her thighs, Kevin couldn't take his eyes off the shiny white triangle between her legs.

"You just going to look, or do you want to do something?"

Checking the street over his shoulder again, Kevin said, "Yeah. That would be great."

Maxine leaned back and drew up her legs. The short skirt of her uniform hitched over her hips. She started to hook her thumbs into the waistband of her panties, but Kevin put his hands on her wrists.

"Let me." Looking into Maxine's eyes, then at her panties, Kevin grasped the tiny frill of elastic around her legs and slowly pulled her panties down her legs and over her ankles, letting them drop on the sofa. As he kneeled over her, Maxine undid Kevin's belt and tugged his jeans and briefs down to his knees and leaned back. With one more glance towards the street, he lowered himself on her and let her guide him into her.

"Remember. Slowly," she whispered and locked her legs around Kevin's waist.

But Sammy began barking again, and as much as he tried to think only about pushing in, then pulling out as slowly as he could, Kevin couldn't shut out the racket the dog was making. Then, he heard the back door of Becker's open.

"What's got into you, Sammy?" Mr. Becker called.

Kevin heard the thunk of Mr. Becker coming down his back steps.

"Coons out already," Mr. Becker said. And after a moment, "Is that you still over there, Butch?"

"Oh, shit! He's coming." Kevin pulled out of Maxine, and as he did, his thing spurted on her legs. Pulling pull up his jeans, he kneed Maxine in the head as she yanked down her skirt and tried to scramble off the sofa. "Owww," Kevin yelped as the zipper on his jeans raked his penis. "Let's get out of here!"

With Sammy barking and Mr. Becker right behind him, Kevin and Maxine jumped off the porch and dashed around to the back of the house.

"This way!" Kevin grabbed Maxine's hand and pulled her through the bushes. After twenty yards of thrashing through stinging branches snapping at their arms and legs, they came out in the parking lot behind the Halfway House.

"Christ Almighty! What is with you? Every time we do it, we draw a crowd."

"I didn't know he'd come out."

"Jesus Christ, you came all over me," Maxine said as she hiked up her skirt and rubbed the insides of her thighs. "Shit." Maxine looked at her dress. "I'm a mess. Hey, where's my panties?"

"Huh? I don't have them." Kevin looked back at the tangle of bushes they'd scrambled through. "*Damn*. They must be on Duncan's porch."

"Great. Now what?"

"I don't know. We could find someplace to sit and talk. Maybe we could..." Kevin's voice trailed off as felt the stickiness between his legs and the sting of his raked penis. Maybe he could go jump off Hawk Mountain. Christ, what a colossal screw-up he was.

"Where the hell are we?"

"The parking lot of the Halfway House."

Maxine said. "Great. I could use a cold beer."

"I don't have a draft card."

"Who the hell needs a draft card? In Minerva, you can get a drink if you can reach the bar with your money."

"Not at the Halfway House. They almost got shut down last summer for serving underage kids. Nobody gets by the guy at the door without a genuine draft card."

Maxine made a face as she looked around the parking lot. "No place we can get a beer?"

As Kevin was thinking about where they might go, the sound of a band blared as two guys came out the back door. They stopped next to a two-door DeSoto a few feet from where Kevin and Maxine stood. To Kevin, they looked to be in their twenties. As one fished in his pocket for keys, the other eyed them. "Hi," he said to Maxine.

"Hey, you guys wouldn't be heading towards Inlet would you?" Maxine said.

The guy nearest the passenger side shook his head. "Old Forge."

"Damn. I need a ride to Inlet."

The fellow turned to his companion, and said something Kevin couldn't hear. Kevin said to Maxine, "You leaving already?"

"I got to get back to Jimmie's sometime." She paused. "And there ain't nothing we can do around here. Unless you got wheels, I need to hook a ride. I'd better get out to 28 and start hitching."

"But I thought we might..."

"Yeah," the fellow said. "We could do that."

"Look, I better take this ride," Maxine said to Kevin. "You better start thinking about what I said – what you got to do."

As one guy opened the front door for her, the driver looked over the top of the car at Kevin and smiled.

"Are you going to be alright?" Kevin said.

"I can take care of myself." She gave Kevin a quick peck on his cheek. "Don't forget to start gathering them hickory nuts – quick." Maxine ducked into the car and slid along to the middle of the front seat.

As the car swung around toward 28, one of the guys leaned toward Maxine and he thought he saw her laughing.

Saturday July 19

PRAY FOR US SINNERS now and at the hour of our death, amen. Kevin finished his tenth Hail Mary, kneeling in the pew at the back of St. Mary's. Ten Our Fathers and Ten Hail Marys: the usual penance from Father Petroska for impure thoughts and actions. When his mother had told him Father Donovan was out of town for a few days, he thought he would confess what he'd done to Father Petroska. But it was so awful, he was afraid even Father Petroska would blow his stack. He was in so far over his head, he couldn't think straight. How could he kneel here with his eyes squeezed shut, fingers tightly laced, and ask God to forgive him when he hadn't told the whole truth in the confessional? The whole truth and nothing but reminded him of those two troopers. He was going to jail – and hell – and God was going to make Maxine pregnant – and she was going want a *thousand* dollars, maybe more! Oh, God please let her period come.

———

THOMAS MET KEVIN AND HIS MOTHER in front of The Longhouse as they returned from Confession. "I knew they weren't going to leave it."

Joyce said, "What are you talking about?"

"The Satterfields. The parents of the boy who was killed. I was at the

177

post office and ran into Milton Standish. They've hired a lawyer, and he's already met with the State Police and the District Attorney."

LATER THAT EVENING, Kevin hopped up on the end of the picnic table at the town beach. "I can explain."

"Some kind of friend you turned out to be," Buck said. "I get home, and Mom's on the porch waving a pair of panties at me, wanting to know whose they were, what I was doing when she's off at work. Then Sammy starts barking, and old man Becker comes out and asks if I got what Butch Sutter dropped off for me." Buck shook his head and laughed. "And Mom wants to know what kind of sicko friends I'm hanging around with."

"I'm sorry."

"You ought to be," Buck said. "I didn't know whether to shit or go blind wondering the same thing. But I was at Butch's after we left Tommy's house, so I knew it wasn't Butch that left them panties. It took me about one second to guess who else might be messing up my life."

"I was going to tell you as soon as I could."

"You haven't told me anything. I've been waiting for the *detailed* description you promised, and all I've got is a used pair of panties and a really pissed-off mom. If she remembers those rubbers that aren't there, I'm really in the shit."

"You keep them?"

"You think I'm a perv? You want them back? *Oh, Maxine, honey,*" Buck said in a loopy voice. "I think you misplaced your undergarments. But my dear friend Buck has retrieved them."

"Enough."

"You don't look so good. I would have figured a guy getting it like you would be on top of the world."

"I'm in trouble. Maxine's period's late."

"Jesus. How long have you been doing it?"

"A week."

"One week, and she's already knocked up? You're a lucky guy, Kev."

Kevin climbed off the picnic table and walked to the beach. The lights along the shore began to blur. He choked back tears as Buck came over and stood next to him.

"Holy smokes, Kev. I don't know what to tell you." Buck picked up a handful of small stones and tossed them in the water. "Can't she do something about it? It's no big secret Duke got a couple of girls in trouble. One went to a place in Utica and had it. The other one took care of it."

Kevin looked at Buck. "You mean she kept the baby or...? Oh."

"There's doctors or nurses that do that. Duke gave this girl the money, and she went to Albany I think."

"That's not what Maxine is going to do – if she is pregnant. She's going to go someplace – Plattsburg and have the baby: give it up for adoption."

"Okay. So, it isn't the worst thing in the world."

"But I got to come up with a thousand dollars, maybe more."

"Holy smokes! Can you get it from your parents?"

"Are you crazy? I might have to get it out of my college fund."

"You're lucky you got a college fund." Buck put his hand on Kevin's shoulder. "Maybe her period will come."

"Right now, I feel like jumping in the lake and swimming to Alaska."

"Even I know you can't get there from here."

"Maybe I'll just jump in and..."

Sunday July 20

3 ENGINE ATLAS FALLS IN FLAMES IN CAPE CANAVERAL TEST
Packard Car Line to End This Year.

"Corpus Christi."

"Amen."

"Corpus Christi."

Kneeling at the altar railing, Kevin listened to Father Donovan coming closer as he distributed Communion. Years ago, in catechism class, he'd been told, "God answers all our prayers." Earlier, on the front steps of St. Mary's, he'd seen Mr. and Mrs. Downey and their five kids. If God answered all our prayers, why did He let little Richie Downey die of leukemia? Mrs. Downey must have made a hundred novenas; said ten thousand prayers. Maxine hadn't been gone five minutes from the Half-way House before he'd started whining, *Please, God let her period come.*

"Corpus Christi."

"Amen."

Please God – and what? He'd say a million Hail Marys, give up candy for a year, never jerk off again?

Out of the corner of his eye, Kevin could see his mother's head bowed. She *was* praying. She was a good person. Had his mother and father prayed in the winter of 1941? God answers all prayers. Why not his mother's, Mrs. Downey's, his? We pray hardest for the things that are most important, and the answer is, *No.* When he was a child frightened by a thunderstorm, his mother would come to his bed, hold him in her arms and whisper, *Everything will be alright.* Would he get a good grade on an exam, find the lost baseball mitt? *Say a prayer. Everything will be alright.* The storms passed, the mitt was never found, and sometimes he didn't get the grade he wanted.

It was Sunday morning all over the world, and he imagined millions of prayers floating upwards toward heaven like leaves caught in a whirl-wind; God snatching some out of the air. Give Kevin a good grade on his geometry exam; letting others fall away. Richie Downey dies. Another prayer – make Maxine's period come – dips and swirls in front of God's hand. Everything isn't always going to be alright.

"Corpus Christi."

"Amen."

His mother was twenty that winter in Canton. Maxine is nineteen. He squeezed his eyes more tightly closed trying to erase flashes of his mother's face and naked Maxine with her legs spread on her bed tumbling over one another. Maxine and his mother: two girls in trouble. Was Maxine praying?

Friday night Maxine called him 'Dad." His father was twenty-two in 1941. *Father, Dad.* Him and his father; Maxine and his mother.

"Amen."

The sound of his mother's voice startled Kevin. He watched as she closed her mouth and bowed her head.

WAVING SMOKE OUT OF HIS EYES, Kevin dropped the last trash barrel off the tailgate of the pickup. He hated spending every Sunday after supper at the dump, sucking thick, oily air through his clenched teeth. His father wrangled the fifty-gallon drum to the edge of the drop-off and tipped it on its side. Stinking wet garbage slid down the embankment into the smoldering heap at the bottom. Twenty yards away, Mr.

Robinson dumped trash from Idle-a-While Cottages. Beyond him, a man pushed a battered refrigerator off the back of a trailer, sending it clanging end over end until it snagged in a pile of tires. Trays tumbled out of the sprung door.

Kevin pushed the empty barrel his father had lifted onto the truck bed against the others and glanced toward the sandy access road. At dusk, the large clearing between the road and the embankment would fill with cars. Families would scamper for the best spot on the lip of the drop-off to scan the woods with their flashlights until a handful of black bears lumbered out of the woods to paw for food scraps in the mounds of rotting garbage. Kevin wondered when one of the bears would finally snap and clamber up the embankment to whack the nasty brat who'd tossed a can at him or take a chunk out of leg of the foolish father who'd lowered himself through the squishy orange peels to take a flash photo two feet from the bear's face. This must be the only town in the Adirondacks where the dump is a major tourist attraction.

Kevin opened the side door of the truck and tossed his gloves on the seat.

"Will you hurry up," Thomas said. "The truck will be full of flies."

"I never do anything right," Kevin said. He slammed the door, walked to the edge of the embankment and kicked a can over the edge. "Stinking, rotten place," he muttered.

"You coming?" Thomas called.

Kevin stared at the smashed ice boxes, bald tires, and ripped mattresses strewn along the tree line at the bottom. He sensed his father standing behind him.

"What's the matter?"

Kevin shrugged. "Nothing. Everything."

"I'm sorry I yelled at you." Thomas gave Kevin a friendly swat on the arm with his work gloves. "Come on."

Kevin picked up a rock and threw it into the woods. "You're always yelling at me."

"I'm not always...." Thomas paused. "All right, I yell too much. I'm worried about you getting mixed up in this mess with those Duncans. You don't need more trouble."

Kevin looked at a clump of wet tissues spilling from an empty Wheaties box. Even with his heavy work gloves, he hated it when a bloody Kotex fell out of the camp trash into the burn barrel. He'd do anything to know Maxine was wrapping one in toilet paper right now. "I can't stop being friends with Buck because his brother got into a fight."

Thomas gave Kevin a skeptical look. "This isn't bean-bag. It's going to get ugly, and people are choosing sides, Kevin. That's not the one I want you on."

"How many sides can you have in Hawk Cove?"

Facing Kevin, Thomas said, "Look, I've heard your, 'I'm blowing this two-bit town' act all year. Okay. That's what I expect a smart seventeen-year-old to do. But don't kid yourself. There's a lot of people like the Duncans who wouldn't mind seeing those of us who don't scrabble for our twenty weeks get a poke in the eye. If you want to stand here in this cloud of crap," he said looking around, "we can count how many warring tribes God created in Hawk Cove."

"Am I supposed to side with those people from Connecticut?"

Thomas looked at Kevin as though he was re-measuring his height. "They hate all of us, but they've got a lot of pull. They can cause us – and you a lot of trouble. Do something dumb, and you could be stuck in nowhereville, as you put it."

"Like you?"

"You watch your...." Thomas looked away. He and Kevin stared at the pines.

"I'm sorry," Kevin said. The wind shifted, blowing smoke back at them, making Kevin's eyes water. "Why not leave?"

"Being stuck is more than a place."

"Stuck with me – and Mom?"

Thomas started to say something, then shook his head. After a few moments, he said, "That's not what I meant. Your mother and I love each other and you." He coughed. "We're going to stink like garbage for a week. We ought to go."

Kevin stood still.

"I'm angry," Thomas said. "I suppose it comes out angry at you and your mom, but mostly I'm angry at me."

"Why?"

"Because I don't know," Thomas said.

"You don't know why you're angry?"

"Yes. No." Thomas let out a snorting laugh. "I know you want out, and I never thought I'd end up living in a place like Hawk Cove either. And to tell you the truth, I don't like teaching." Taking in the dump with a sweep of his arm, he added, "And it's no big surprise that I hate running the Lodge to make ends meet. And I know there has to be something out there better than this." He paused. "But I'm not smart enough to know what it is. That's why I'm angry."

"Why not take a chance; leave; try something else?"

"I ask myself that question a lot more than you'd imagine. I may not like it, but I've got a job that's better than most have around here; a decent place to live and a business – even if it's mortgaged to the gills. I can look around every day and see exactly where I am." Thomas took a deep breath and turned toward the drop-off. "I guess that's why parents put too much on their children some times." He put his hand on Kevin's shoulder. "Makes them angry when they see them not making the best of their opportunities. You got what it takes, Kevin. Don't blow it."

Kevin cast a sideways glance at his father's hand. "I won't," he whispered.

"Come on. If we stay here another minute, your mother won't let us back in the house."

Thomas started toward the driver's side. Turning to Kevin, he said, "You want to drive?"

"Sure." Kevin grabbed the keys Thomas had tossed and slid behind the wheel. He'd been driving the Chevy all year, but his father hardly let him drive the pick-up, explaining that the aging clutch needed to be babied.

Kevin eased the pickup over the bumps in the sandy road, pulling way to the right to let the first cars of tourists by. As he pulled out onto 28, he winced as the truck lurched, but his father was staring out the side window.

As traffic backed up in Inlet, they inched by the Acropolis, and Kevin concentrated on the tail-lights of the car in front of them.

"You still seeing that Nelson girl?" Thomas asked in an off-hand tone as he looked at the front of the Acropolis.

Kevin felt his face flush. "Nah." He shifted into second. "You going to wait until after Labor Day to put in a new clutch?"

Monday July 21

IN THE PARKING AREA beside Thibedeau's Hardware, Kevin set the last of the six gallons of paint in the trunk. His father had reached for the car door handle, and Kevin was about to close the lid when he heard, "Mr. Boyle? Thomas Boyle?"

A tall man, dressed in a blue and white seersucker suit and wearing a straw hat, stepped in front of his father.

"Yes," Thomas said cautiously.

The man took off his hat and extended his hand. "Gordon MacKenzie."

The lawyer. Kevin heard the lawyer had met with the State Police. And his gray Cadillac had been spotted outside Sheriff Dawson's office. Mysterious stranger in town: *Have Gun Will Travel.* Except with his thick mane of white wavy hair, the lawyer looked more like Chief Justice Earl Warren.

"I wanted to introduce myself," Mr. MacKenzie said.

"Why's that?"

"Actually, I was hoping to have the opportunity to talk to Kevin."

Kevin ducked under the trunk lid to rearrange the paint cans.

"Why do you want to talk to Kevin?"

Kevin closed the trunk and slid toward the far side of the car.

"As you might have learned, I've been retained by the Satterfield

186

family. They are understandably devastated by their son's death and want to ensure everything humanly possible is done to explain the cause."

"Fell off the Rock. Kids horsing around. That's what I understand," Thomas said.

"Yes, that's one version I've heard."

"Kevin told the sheriff and the state troopers what he knows."

Kevin wished his father would just open the car door and get in so they could leave.

"Of course," Mr. MacKenzie said as his eyes locked on Kevin. "But there are many reports, various accounts of the events of the fateful evening by those who were involved: differing accounts by the same person."

"Look. I don't know what you're driving at. Kevin had been there, but he left. That's it." Thomas pulled the car door open. "Now we got work to do."

"Mr. Boyle."

Thomas's head snapped around.

"Mr. Boyle," he said in a softer tone. "I don't want to be rude, but this is extremely serious. There will be a Coroner's Inquest, and that *might* lead to a Grand Jury if it is determined Skip Satterfield's death was unnatural – a *homicide*." He let the last word hang in the air for a few seconds.

Let's go, Kevin thought as he pulled the car door open.

"And anyone involved who does not tell the truth at the inquest will find themselves in very dire legal circumstances." The lawyer looked over the top of the car at Kevin with an intense gaze. "There are accounts – perhaps erroneous – which nonetheless place Kevin close to the immediate events that caused Skip Satterfield's death."

With a glance at Kevin, Thomas said, "Kevin told what he knows. I've taught my son to tell the truth. Now we're going."

"If you change your mind and decide to allow me to ask Kevin a few questions about his recollection of what happened that evening, please call me." He handed a card to Thomas. "I'm staying at the Wentworth's. Their telephone number is on the back. I will be in town looking into this matter for a few more days; collecting what I suspect will be other versions of the truth."

Wednesday July 23

EISENHOWER INVITES KHRUSHCHEV TO U. N. FOR SUMMIT

Girls on the Loose – The Shocking Story of Today's 'Beat' Generation

KEVIN PICKED UP TWO OF THE CHAIRS that had been pulled around in a circle for the book discussion group and shoved them under the table at the end of the room. When he showed up earlier that evening, they were all staring at him, even Mr. Marsh and Miss Weaver, like he was supposed to give them the inside dope on what happened at the Rock.

The library had been one place where he could get away; a place where books and magazines and newspapers held out the possibility of a life somewhere else – doing something besides nothing. Now, it was one more place for *Where did you go? What did you do? Who were you with?*

And the discussion was stupid. *The Affluent Society* by John Kenneth Galbraith. John Galbraith? Jack Galbraith? Why was Father Donovan so upset about this Harvard professor from Canada? The book didn't seem subversive. Maybe it was because there wasn't much affluence around Hawk Cove. Mr. Marsh wasn't making much sense about how big corporations get us to buy stuff we don't need. Their new television, even with all the snow, was a heck of a lot better than listening to the radio. He'd been thinking about whether he'd rather have a Thunderbird or a Corvette when Miss Weaver chimed in about the plight of the poor – and knocked him right back to remembering he had to come up with a thousand dollars or more for Maxine.

Then Mrs. Perkins started bouncing up and down in her chair like an overweight chimp, squawking at Mr. Marsh. What was wrong with people wanting nice things, she demanded? If her husband had to depend on only selling drugs in the pharmacy, they'd hardly make a living. And Mrs. Perkins was giving him funny looks. Was he supposed to back her up? Was she going to tell Father Donovan he wasn't reliable: a Communist sympathizer?

Kevin grabbed another chair and carried it to the table in the periodical section. He heard Mr. Marsh and Miss Weaver washing out coffee cups in the room behind the circulation desk and talking. Probably figuring out how to make him give them the inside scoop. He *didn't* know what happened. Maybe Duke pushed him. Maybe Skip slipped and fell. What difference did it make now? He's dead.

Swinging around, Kevin knocked Miss Weaver's book bag off the table. As he knelt to gather the contents scattered across the floor, Miss Weaver and Mr. Marsh poked their heads out of the back room.

"Sorry," Kevin said. "I hope there was nothing that could break."

"I don't think so," Miss Weaver said, coming alongside Kevin.

Next to a wallet, a package of *Tums* and a glasses case was a manila envelope, and spilling out of the envelope were two slim paperbacks.

Miss Weaver knelt next to Kevin and quickly began to shove everything into the bag, but not before Kevin read the title of the volume closest to him: *Howl and other Poems.* The other had slid further under the table, and Kevin reached for it at the same time Miss Weaver did. They both had their hands on the book.

"I'm sorry," Kevin said. *On the Road* by Jack Kerouac. "I read about the book in the *New York Times*. I didn't think it was in the library."

Miss Weaver stood and brushed off her skirt. "It's not. That's my own copy."

Kevin saw Mr. Marsh give Miss Weaver a strange look as she pushed the two books into the manila envelope. Something was going on. He looked at the envelope. *City Lights Books* was printed in the upper left-hand corner. "I'd like to read it sometime." Once again, Mr. Marsh and Miss Weaver looked at each other as though they were trying to make up their mind about something.

"I'm not sure that would be a good idea," Mr. Marsh said.

They'd asked him to join the book discussion group because they said he had *adult* tastes and appreciation of literature. Now they were treating him like a kid. "Okay," he muttered. To hell with them.

"Kevin." Miss Weaver put her hand on Kevin's forearm. "It's not like that."

"You might as well tell him," Mr. Marsh said. "Kevin may be involved."

"What does *On the Road* have to do with the kid that got killed? I told the state troopers I didn't see exactly what happened."

Miss Weaver's hand tightened on Kevin's arm. "No, not that, Kevin. It's the books."

"I don't understand."

"I ordered these from a bookstore in San Francisco, and we're pretty sure the envelope was opened before I got it."

Mr. Marsh said, "And I'm convinced that packages of books I've ordered have been opened as well. At first, I thought perhaps the envelope was roughed up in the mail. But when I mentioned it to Doris, she said she thought packages of books she'd ordered had also been opened." He pointed to the envelope on the table. "And we're positive this envelope was opened."

"How come? Who would do that?"

"Good questions," Miss Weaver said. "My friends tell me the post office spends a lot of time reading our mail; sending some of it to *their* friends at the FBI." She picked up the envelope. "Five weeks from San Francisco to Hawk Cove." She turned the envelope over. "And on this one, they made no effort to be subtle about it." With an angry edge in her voice, she said to Mr. Marsh. "They want us to know they're looking."

"I'm sure my last one was opened right here," Mr. Marsh said. "The note in my box about a damaged package; the smug look on Postmistress Ricketts face when she handed me the envelope."

"They open your mail? Here in Hawk Cove?" Kevin said incredulous.

Miss Weaver snorted. "You bet they open our mail."

"I didn't. I'm not involved."

"I didn't mean you were opening our mail. It's that priest and his subversive books," Miss Weaver said. "At first I thought he was just another windbag, but Gladys Perkins made a crack when she came in earlier. I was thinking of something else, but later I replayed it: a garbled thing about howling on the road. Was she letting me know she was in on it?"

"Doris," Mr. Marsh said. "Maybe you're reading too much into it."

"Maybe. But she's gotten very tight with that priest. You said she's been going through the card catalog with a list." She turned to Kevin. "Do you know anything about this?"

"No." How come he had to be involved in all these problems? He quickly turned and walked into the non-fiction section for the last two chairs – but not before catching the skeptical looks on their faces. He thought they were his friends. Nobody's my friend. He finished putting the chairs back and rushed out the door without saying goodbye. To hell with them and their stupid book discussion group. He pulled on his jacket and started across the parking lot towards Route 28.

"Kevin! Over here!"

What? Who was calling him? *Holy Smokes*. It was Maxine, standing next to a fifty-six Chevy Impala at the end of the lot near the pine trees. "What are you doing here?"

"I needed to talk to you. Right away,"

There was a guy behind the wheel, but Kevin couldn't make out who he was. "What's going on?"

"Look, Kevin," Maxine said, stepping between him and the car. "Now, I'm sure."

"Of what?"

"Do I have to spell it out? I tossed breakfast this morning."

Jesus. Jesus. Jesus. "You're positive?"

"As sure as I can be without killing a rabbit. Lucky for me Hilda had left early."

"Oh, shit. Don't you have to go to the doctor or something?"

"For someone who's at the library until nine o'clock, you can be dumber than a board. I don't need no doctor. And Hilda's one of those old bitches that think they can tell if somebody's pregnant five minutes after they roll out of bed. Since the night they caught us, she's been giving me the fish eye every day."

"When?"

"When what? When I'm due? When Hilda's going to give me the boot? When you have to come up with the money?"

"The money, I guess."

"That's why I tracked you down. Now."

"I don't have that kind of money around. I've got to figure out how to get it out of the bank."

"Christ almighty. You walk up to the teller and say, 'Give me my money.' Fill out one of them little slips." Maxine shook her head. "Get with it, Kevin. I need it real soon: end of next week at the latest."

"How much – exactly?"

"How much you got?"

"A little over fourteen hundred," Kevin blurted.

"Good. Fourteen hundred."

"Jesus. That's my whole college fund."

"You got any idea how much diapers cost; baby formula; them little booties?"

"Alright. Alright. How are we supposed to do this?"

"You give me a call at the Acropolis when you get the money. Don't leave a message with Theo or Athena. Make sure I come to the phone."

"Cash?"

"What do you think?"

"You don't have to act like I'm a kid, you know."

"Okay – dad."

"That's not funny."

Stepping closer and putting her hands on Kevin's shoulders, Maxine said, "I'm sorry. I'm upset." She kissed Kevin.

The man in the car rolled down the window. "You going to be all night?"

"I'll only be a second," Maxine said.

The guy tossed a cigarette butt out the window, "Make it quick."

"Who's that?"

"A ride. Nobody special. You don't have wheels, and I need to get around."

"Can we get together one night this week? I feel like we need to talk about what's going to happen."

"I don't know. Things are going to get complicated. I got to get my stuff together – you know if Hilda gives me the heave-ho." Maxine put her arms around Kevin's neck and nuzzled his face. "You get the money and give me a call. We'll see." She glanced at the car. "I got to go." She kissed Kevin and quickly ducked around to the other side of the car.

Kevin stared at the tail lights – heading in the direction of Old Forge.

Thursday July 24

As he listened to the sounds of his mom making breakfast, Kevin stared at the splotch on the ceiling over his bed where the leak had stained the beaver board. He wanted to stay in bed. And he wanted to get out of bed, out of Hawk Cove, out. By the time the rising sun began to lighten the room, he'd already imagined an alternate summer to the one he'd lived; one where he hadn't gone to the Rock; where he hadn't met Maxine; where he was just doing stuff. He couldn't remember why it had been so important to go to the Rock.

He was exhausted. He'd felt like a jerk standing in the library parking lot watching Maxine drive off. Who was that guy? And how was he going to get fourteen hundred dollars out of his savings account without his parents finding out? And what was going to happen if they did – when they did?

He couldn't stay in bed any longer. His mother had already called up the stairs twice. He dressed and looked in the mirror, positive everything was written clearly across his guilty face.

Ten minutes later, he was hunkered down behind a box of Cheerios.

"How was the book discussion?" Thomas asked. "You hardly said a word last night."

"Okay. Mrs. Perkins and Mr. Marsh got into an argument about whether people ought to buy stuff they don't need."

"I wouldn't want to tangle with Gladys. She reminds me of a bull-dog. I could picture her with her teeth locked onto Warren's shin, growling."

"Don't be silly," Joyce said as she sat next to Kevin.

He felt his mother's smile brush over him. What was going on? Just over the box top, he could see his father giving his mother an odd look.

"Your mother and I have been thinking, talking." His father paused to nod across the table at Joyce. "I guess we hadn't realized how difficult all this has been for you."

"It must be awful for you." His mother laid her hand over his. "I've prayed for the poor boy. I've even prayed for whoever was responsible for his tragic death. And then I realized how terribly upsetting it must have been for you to be there, to see something like that."

He looked at her hand covering and caressing his and couldn't remember her touching him like this since he was a young boy.

"Not that we've completely forgotten that by hanging around at the Rock, you put yourself...." Thomas took a deep breath. "We're your parents. We love you. And we want to stand by you in this. We just wanted to let you know."

"Everything's been happening so fast," Joyce said. "We hadn't taken the time to think about how you must feel."

"I'm okay." Why did they have to be nice to him now? It will only be worse when they find out.

"I don't want you to feel pressured," his father said. "I was thinking about the lawyer – MacKenzie. We can get our own lawyer, if you'd feel better about it."

"I don't know, Dad. I don't see why. Who'd we get?"

Thomas put his hand on Kevin's shoulder. "We can ask around."

"I hate to have you spend money on a lawyer if I don't need one."

Thomas gave Kevin's shoulder a squeeze. "You think about it."

With his mother's hand caressing his, and his father's hand on his shoulder, he felt as though he'd been diagnosed with cancer or something.

———

That afternoon, Kevin was at his job at St. Mary's rectory.

"I understand your book discussion group was lively," Father Donovan said.

He'd almost forgotten about the book discussion group, concentrating as hard as he could on the simple tasks of folding and stuffing, glad Father Donovan had seemed anxious to get right to putting together the newsletters. Did Mrs. Perkins tell Father Donovan he hadn't supported her, or whatever he was supposed to do? "I guess so, Father."

"The library may be one of the most lively, *interesting* places in Hawk Cove." The priest sat on the end of the dining room table and stared at him. "As a matter of fact, with the death of the boy, one might not notice just how interesting the library has become."

"I suppose. I mean I don't know, Father."

"You don't know, or you *suppose*? Which is it?"

"I mean..."

"Don't play games with me, Kevin Boyle."

"I'm not."

Sliding off his perch at the end of the table, Father Donovan pointed his finger at Kevin and said in a loud, sharp voice, "Do not take me for a fool. I am *not* another old priest stuck up here in this rectory without a clue about what is going on in this town."

"I, ah. No, Father."

"There's more going on at the library than John Kenneth Galbraith and his pinko tracts isn't there?"

"I don't know, Father. Really."

"*Really?* Allen Gins-*berg*? San Francisco commie presses? *Really?*"

"I didn't. Those weren't my books. They're not even the library's books."

"How do you know that?"

"I just… Miss Weaver said. They're hers."

"Then how did you know what books Miss Weaver has?"

"I saw them. They fell out of her book bag."

"How convenient. And did Miss Weaver offer to let you read them?"

"No. I mean I asked her if I could borrow *On the Road*. But I didn't. She didn't."

"Young man. You are involved in something that is way over your head."

He didn't want to be involved in anything. Couldn't he just be left alone? It's a book discussion group, that's all. He didn't care if he read that book. All he wanted to know was how he was going to get the money out of the bank. "I have to go to the bathroom, Father." Kevin stepped toward the hallway.

"Stop right there!"

"I really have to go."

"What's Larry Needham doing at the library?" Father Donovan demanded.

"Larry?"

"Don't play dumb with me."

"I don't know. I mean, he's re-shelving books."

"Is that all?"

"I don't know. Honest."

"I told you that you were special. Do you remember?"

"Yes, Father."

"What else did I say?"

"I'm not sure. A lot of things. My mind is all confused." He felt as though his bladder was about to burst.

"Special people – like us. We have unique privileges. Isn't that what I said?"

"Yes, Father."

"Privileges – *and* obligations. Obligations, Kevin. This entire town is looking at you. You are the center of everyone's attention. People are looking at you to get at the truth about what is happening in this town."

"I didn't see Duke push the guy off the Rock. And I *really* have to go."

Father Donovan loomed over him. "The subversion. The decadence. The sickness that has seeped into Hawk Cove: Kevin Boyle, you are right in the middle of it, and I want to know what you are going to do about it. "

Kevin pivoted toward the door, but the priest grabbed him by the shoulder and spun him back around. "Oh, Father, *please*."

"You need to pray for guidance." Father Donovan pushed Kevin to his knees.

"Father, I can't hold it any longer."

With his hands clamped onto Kevin's shoulders, the priest pulled him tight. "The chosen have to cut the rot out root and branch."

One hand was now on the back of his head – the priest's hardness pushing and rubbing against his face. "I can't. Help. My Mom and Dad. I don't know what to do."

"We need to help each other."

"I didn't. It might have been Duke. She said it would probably be all right. It's my whole college fund"

Father Donovan grasped Kevin's shirt and pulled him to his feet, then wrapped him in a tight embrace.

"I don't know anything about Larry. Honest, Father." Father Donovan's hand was on his head, smoothing his hair. "I'm sorry, Father," Kevin sobbed.

Putting his hand under Kevin's chin and lifting it, the priest said, "Everything will be all right. Trust me. You're special. We're special." He kissed Kevin and pulled him back into an embrace as his hands rubbed Kevin's back, the back of his head.

Kevin felt Father Donovan's lips on his head. "I don't know what to do. I can't." The priest's hand fumbled at Kevin's crotch. He wrestled out of the priest's arms and bolted toward the door. "*Oh, no!* I'm peeing my ... I couldn't hold it." He cried, feeling as though everything inside of him was emptying between his legs.

———

KEVIN STOPPED GULPING FOR AIR as he leaned on his elbows. As soon as he'd crashed out the door of the rectory, he knew Hawk Mountain would be one place he wouldn't see anyone on a drizzly afternoon. Running up the back trail to the overlook, he'd scraped his arms on the branches that grew over the path, then banged his knee as he'd slipped on the wet rocks near the summit. The inside of his thighs burned. The sound of something hitting the ground made his head snap around, but there wasn't anyone there. He didn't care that the rain on rocks seeped through the seat of his pants. Asshole. Sniveling cry baby. No wonder she went off with that guy.

Kevin flinched when a cold drop of water hit the back of his neck. He hunched forward. How could he let him do that? Kneeling in front of him. His thing rubbing on my face. Letting him run his fingers in my hair, kissing him.... Oh, Jesus. Special. Does he think....?

Another cold drop of water ran down Kevin's back. Hemlock Island was hidden by the clouds. There were no boats on the lake, and he could barely see the cars pulling in and out in front of the stores on 28. He was done crying. Get the money – and get out.

Friday July 25

BRITAIN TO TEST SOVIETS ON CAIRO

New Midget Miracle Fire Extinguisher: Make More than a $1,000 a month.

KEVIN HOPED THE DOG WOULD CHOKE ON HIS CHAIN as Sammy barked at him. "Hey, Buck," he yelled from the front step.

After a few seconds, Buck appeared at the screen door. "Go away. My mom says I'm not supposed to talk to strangers."

"Cut the crap, Buck."

"Oh. If it isn't Mister Kevin Boyle. It's been so long, I wasn't sure it was you." Buck stepped out and plunked down on the end of the sofa. "I stopped down at your place, the other day, and your old man told me to get lost."

"It's Duke he's really mad at."

"Sounded like he was mad at me," Buck said. "And I ain't seen you for over a week. Been hanging out with Linda and all her rich pals?"

"I haven't seen Linda, and all those people took off after the Skip – thing." Kevin paused. "I know I haven't been around, but I need a favor."

"That's the only time I see you lately."

"Jesus Christ, Buck. She's pregnant." Kevin's voice broke. He couldn't cry. Not in front of Buck. It seemed like he'd been crying five times a day all week. "Buck, I'm in shit up to my neck. I need help."

Buck let out a long whistle. "You said she might be. Now she's sure?"

Kevin stepped up on the porch, plopped down on the other end of the sofa, and rubbed the back of his neck. "She's sure."

201

"And you're sure you're the father?"

Kevin stared at Buck. "Yeah. That's what she said. And she needs the money – for Plattsburgh, I guess."

"What's this favor I'm supposed to do?"

"She's got to have fourteen hundred dollars. No later than the end of next week."

Buck coughed out a laugh. "You come to the wrong house for a loan."

"No. I've got to tap out my college fund. I need to get to Thendara Savings and Loan, and I was hoping you could ask Butch Sutter to drive me. He's the only one I know who's got a car, and he's more friends with you than me. I figured he'd do it if you asked him."

"We still friends?"

"Of course," Kevin said. "It's all this stuff. I can't keep anything straight. Can you ask Butch? Tuesday afternoon. Just a quick down and back. That's all."

"I don't know. I got to talk to him," Buck said. "Lucky for you, my mom didn't call up his folks to tell them Butch was in a panty stealing gang."

"Jeez, Buck. I'm sorry. I got to get back to the Lodge."

"Your old man don't know you're here, right?"

Kevin nodded. "You get Butch to take me to Old Forge on Tuesday, and I'll pay him. And I'll tell you everything."

"I need a favor too," Buck said.

"Anything. I'm in big trouble. I don't even know if this is going to get me out, but I'm stuck."

"Remember I told you we stick to our story: the one Duke told the troopers."

"Sure. I haven't said anything else."

"What about the big-shot lawyer? Son-of-a-bitch's been in town long enough to vote."

"I didn't tell him anything," Kevin said. "I told him I didn't see Duke push the guy off the Rock."

"How could Duke not push him if Duke was already in the water?"

"That's what I said. I mean I said I didn't see anything. Cripes, Buck. First it's those troopers, then this lawyer. I didn't say anything against Duke. I got enough on my mind with Maxine."

"You better get that taken care of, because the lawyer's asked just about everybody in town something," Buck said. "So, your hand washes my hand, right?"

"I guess."

"The favor I need is easy. You keep cool about what happened."

"I said I would."

"A lot of people *say* they will, but this lawyer's a smooth and nasty piece of work. Duke said he's threatening Chink's old man with a probation violation if Chink don't come up with a better story."

"You can count on me Buck."

———

"IT'LL ONLY BE A SECOND, Mr. Dorakadis," Kevin said into the phone. He peered out of the booth on the side of Simpson's Garage.

"Hi, Maxine. It's me, Kevin. I'm sorry. I told him it would only be a second. Can I see you tonight? I know you said to only call when I had it, but I need a couple of days. How about tomorrow night? Tuesday's the earliest I can get to Old Forge for the money. Can't we talk about it? Just talk. I got this ... Okay.... Well, I'm sorry, too. You just hanging around at Jimmie's? You're okay with Hilda? She's not kicking you out or anything? Okay. Okay. Tell Theo to hold his horses for cripes sake. All right, I'll call you then, but.....Maxine?"

Kevin stared at the receiver. Damn. Was he ever going to see her again – besides when he forked over his college fund?

As Kevin started to pull back the accordion door of the phone booth, a car pulled around the corner of Route 28 onto Beaver Pond Road. There was Larry Needham and, in the driver's seat, Warren Marsh. And Larry was laughing. Kevin couldn't ever remember seeing Larry laugh – even smile.

Saturday July 26

45 IN PLANE SAFE AFTER SEA MISHAP
Scratchex Stops Dog Itch

IN THE WOODS BEHIND THE PARKING LOT, Kevin hacked at the roots of a bush with the hatchet. A mosquito landed on his forearm and stung him before he could squash it with an awkward swing. A severed artery is all I need to make this a perfect summer, he thought. He'd been replaying over and over doing it with Maxine to take his mind off what happened with Donovan. But no matter how many times he heard her whispery voice guiding him into her, the feel of her wrapped around him – the sticky smell of Father Donovan grasping at him, pulling him, putting his hand there blotted it out.

Kevin swung the hatchet at the base of the bush. *"Cocksucker."* How many times had he heard that? Is that what they do? Did he think I'd do that?

Kevin wheeled around at the sound behind him, hatchet raised as if to fend off an attack. Brownie stood a few feet away looking at him. "You scared me."

Brownie moved closer and sat on his haunches.

"Don't get comfy. You don't want to be anywhere near me. Besides, I'm not doing the trash until after supper." Kevin swung the hatchet and cut through the roots of the bush. He tossed the branches on the pile of brush he'd cut and sat next to Brownie.

Kevin waved away the mosquitoes buzzing his face and sunk the hatchet in the dirt between his legs. "I don't know what to do, Brownie. Everywhere I turn I'm in big trouble. We only did it once – and a half. Lucky guy, Buck says. Big joke. Gives me a rubber that's been around since D-Day. She's *pregnant*."

Kevin pulled the hatchet out of the ground and began digging a small trench, pushing the dirt into neat piles along the edges. He patted down the ridges, then started another trench at right angles to the first. Brownie continued to stare at him.

"I never did *anything* that would give him that idea."

Leaning back on his elbows, Kevin took a long look at Brownie. "You find another place to eat? He spied the red plastic jug he'd carried from the Lodge. "Do dogs drink Kool-Aid? Let me figure this out." Kevin unscrewed the wide top and poured Kool-Aide into the up-turned lid. Brownie quickly rose and lapped up the juice. Kevin poured more, and Brownie drank until the jug was empty.

"I never said anything either. All that fancy talk about being special: physical fitness, moral fitness." A mosquito landed on his forearm. He started to swat it, then waited until it had plunged its needle-nose into his arm. Smack. The crushed bug lay in a splatter of blood.

Kevin sniffled. He ran the rough glove across his cheek. Another mosquito landed on his arm. He let it sting him. "I don't know why he picked me." Snot dribbled from his nose. "I didn't say anything – and I didn't do anything. It was him."

Sunday July 27

AIR FORCE HALTS HUNT FOR MOUSE
Queen Names Son Prince of Wales

IT ISN'T FAIR, Kevin thought as Father Donovan read the Gospel about the workers in the vineyard. Why should the guys who showed up just before quitting time get the same pay as the guys who worked all day? *It's not fair.* Those were Miss Weaver's books, not his. And even though his father hadn't exactly said it, Oneida standing empty in the last week of July was his fault too. His father's pinched face, talking to him like he wanted to say something else: everything that was supposed to not make him feel pressured was like a line someone had forgotten to untie from a boat pulling away from the dock.

His father had said, "We want to stand with you on this" If he only knew. Whether Duke pushed Skip or not was the least of the *thises*. His mother sat next to him in the pew. "I prayed for that poor boy," she'd said. Yeah. He's dead. I'm still alive, and – *Jesus*, he hadn't thought about that – you're going to be a grandmother. Maxine being pregnant was the first thing that came into his mind when he awoke – even though, in those drowsy moments he'd toyed with the idea that it was all a bad dream. And it kept him awake as he tried to go to sleep at night. And every day he'd see his father, other fathers around town, and he hadn't been able to connect these adult men with what he was going to be. His mother and father as *grandmother* and *grandfather* were too much to think about. One stupid mistake, and his entire life, his family's life was kicked topsy-turvy – ruined. *It wasn't fair.*

"Under the guise of *literary* pursuits, subversive tracts infiltrate our town's institutions," Father Donovan said from the pulpit.

Surprised Father Donovan had started his sermon, Kevin looked up at his self-righteous smirk. He made me piss my pants! Kissed me.

"The authorities have a moral obligation to take action *now*," Father Donovan said.

It's *his* fault, Kevin thought. If he'd let him go to the bathroom, it wouldn't have happened. It was only because he'd wet himself it happened. He didn't do anything to make him do that. He wasn't going back. He hadn't gone to Confession on Saturday morning like he'd told his mother. Instead he'd walked up to town and tried calling Maxine, but she wouldn't come to the phone. He was going to follow his mother right up to the altar railing and take communion. A mortal sin? What difference would it make?

————

As Kevin was about to get up from the table that evening, his father said, "Kevin, your mother said Father Donovan had this sermon about subversive books at the library. What do you know about this?"

"He's full of – it."

Joyce bowed her head as though she was sorry about bringing more pressure on Kevin.

"That may be," Thomas said. "But Milt Standish caught up to me in town this afternoon. He said Lester Perkins wanted him to call a Town Board meeting on the library situation. He said you were involved."

"I'm not involved!"

"What the....? Take it easy, son. I didn't. It was Milt, or I guess Lester said that."

Kevin started toward the door. "I'm going to go crazy."

"Hold on."

Wheeling around and on the verge of tears, Kevin said, "How come I'm supposed to be involved in everything that happens in this damn town?"

"Calm down. I'm not sure – even Milt wasn't sure – what this is about, but he said it had to do with the book discussion group."

"It doesn't. It has to do with books Mr. Marsh and Miss Weaver are getting from San Francisco." As soon as the words were out, Kevin felt like a tattle-tale. But why should he take the blame for whatever was bugging Gladys Perkins and Father Donovan? If they want to make a federal case out of some stupid poems and the other book, let them. They weren't his, and he wasn't involved. He had enough to worry about.

Tuesday July 29

PRESIDENT SIGNS NATIONAL AERONAUTICS AND SPACE ACT

Make extra money. Every business uses union label matchbooks.

ONE THOUSAND, FOUR HUNDRED DOLLARS. He'd never seen so much money in one place. He couldn't remember having a one hundred dollar bill in his hand – and here were fourteen fanned across the bedspread. Hearing a creak, he glanced at the bedroom door where he'd wedged a chair under the handle. Stupid. He was sure his parents were asleep. And as hyped-up as he'd been all day, he was afraid he'd fall asleep too from nervous exhaustion.

His hand shook so much when he made out the withdrawal slip, the prune-faced teller must have figured someone had forged his signature, even after he'd pushed his learner's permit under the brass enclosure. Then after looking him up and down for about ten minutes, like he had a Smith & Wesson 38 in the paper bag he'd brought along, the teller loudly announced such a large withdrawal would have to be approved by a supervisor.

After waiting for what seemed an hour, Mr. Craig M. Gibson, *Chief* Teller, stared at the withdrawal slip like he'd never seen one before shaking his head and initialing the back of the slip. Then Mr. Gibson asked him if large bills would be all right – like it was a trick question. *Cripes.* He hadn't thought about what one thousand, four hundred dollars and no cents would look like. By the time Mr. Gibson returned from another teller's cage, he was thinking more about finding a toilet real

210

quick than what big bills meant. When Mr. Gibson insisted on slowly recounting the bills – 'Can't be too careful with this much money' – he was sure someone who knew his family would come in the bank and see him making this huge withdrawal and immediately report it to his parents, if Mr. Gibson didn't get to it first. And who might overhear Mr. Gibson's too-loud voice – 'Five hundred, six hundred, seven hundred...' – and decide to knock Kevin on the head and grab it before he could get into Butch's waiting car? It was a lucky thing the trooper going south didn't wheel around and pull Butch over, the way he tore out of the parking lot like he was driving the get-away car in a heist. And how could his mother greeting him from the kitchen not notice a wad bigger than a dead raccoon stuffed into his pants as he dashed up the stairs? And what if....?

Kevin shuffled the bills into a stack and began peeling them off. "One hundred, two hundred...," he whispered. How many years had it taken to save fourteen hundred dollars? He'd been ten when his father started giving him five dollars a week for doing chores around the Lodge during the season. Fifty dollars for the whole summer. Even now his parents couldn't afford to pay him much more. There weren't any part-time jobs around town after Labor Day, so he couldn't make any of the fourteen hundred like that. He peered at a one-hundred dollar bill. All to save the absolute minimum to cover costs at a state college. What a joke – his father pushing him to hit up the guests for recommendations to Clarkson and St. Lawrence and the other privates. He'd need those and a hundred-mile-an-hour slap shot to cover first semester room and board at those places. Would he have to stay in Hawk Cove and work for another year – maybe two?

"That's what it costs," she'd said. She never said exactly what *it* was. A place in Plattsburgh her girlfriend knew about; somewhere to have it taken care of? He'd heard about that, but, maybe he should have asked. And he was sure she'd said five hundred or a thousand when she'd told him her period was late. Fourteen hundred didn't come up until he'd told her that was what he had in his college fund. What the hell was he going to do – call up Jeannie Bailey and ask her how much a home for unwed mothers cost; ask Buck to find out from Duke what 'having it taken care of' costs? *Jesus. Jesus.* How the hell could he think straight? Her calling him *dad* and going on about booties and stuff; his brain turning to mush trying to picture them – and a baby – living in a two-bit apartment in town. Maybe he could ask her about it tomorrow.

Thursday July 31

MOSCOW CHARGES PLANE INTRUSION

Imagine Making $5,000 a Year Writing in Your Spare Time.

THOMAS STABBED A STRIP OF BACON. "While you were at the cushy job at the rectory, I was getting an earful about the flap at the library."

Kevin looked up in time to see his mother's frown. Was she sending a reminder they'd agreed to go easy on him? Should he tell them now?

"Sorry," Thomas said. "I shouldn't take it out on you. But Wendell Ricketts caught me in town. Since he's on the Town Board, as though I needed a reminder of his lofty position, he felt he needed background on what he's calling 'the situation at the library.' He and Lester Perkins are pushing for an inquiry at the next meeting. Ricketts repeated the business about books that 'run down America. I suppose he's hearing that from Gladys, who's carrying Father Donovan's water."

Joyce said, "I doubt Father Donovan needs Gladys Perkins to carry anything."

"He told me," Kevin said and was sorry he'd opened his mouth. He should have let them argue about it and not remind them about the job at the rectory. "He just wanted me to go along with Mrs. Perkins in the book discussion group. That's all."

Thomas leaned back in his chair and regarded Kevin as though he was making up his mind about what to say next. "That's not all." Thomas glanced at Joyce before continuing. "Trying to figure out what Ricketts really means is a chore, but he's implying there's another bug up his fanny besides pinko books." His stare seemed to squelch the objection on Joyce's lips. "San Francisco. Warren Marsh." He gave Kevin a questioning stare.

"I saw a couple of books Miss Weaver got from a bookstore in San Francisco," Kevin said. "She said the package had been opened. Mr. Marsh said he thought his mail had been opened too. I don't remember if it was from the same place."

"Ethel Ricketts," Thomas muttered. "What kind of books?"

"Poems. *On the Road*. No Communist propaganda," Kevin said. "For crying out loud. That's why I quit."

"Quit what?"

"The job at the rectory."

"At three bucks an hour?" Thomas shook his head. "I'm glad you don't need the money."

"I do – but I thought Larry could use it more than me." He couldn't go back there, Kevin thought. Not for thirteen dollars an hour.

"What's Larry Needham got to do with this?" Thomas said.

Yesterday, before Butch drove him to the bank, Kevin had ducked into the phone booth outside Simpson's, took a couple of deep breaths, rehearsed what he was going to say one more time, and dialed the rectory. He'd hoped he could just leave a message with Mrs. Pulaski, but she'd insisted he talk to 'the Father.' Kevin repeated he wasn't going to be able to come today, and hearing the resignation in Father Donovan's, "I understand," Kevin had been emboldened to add, "And I think I won't be able to do the job anymore." When Father Donovan asked how he was supposed to finish the important work under way, Kevin didn't know what to answer, then said he knew someone who could do the job; that he'd ask him to take over. "Nothing. I mean. I couldn't do it. I don't know. I knew how much Larry needed the money, so I figured he might as well have it." Kevin watched his mother's face soften, glad to turn away from his father's skeptical eyes. He couldn't go back there. Did he let Father Donovan do that? Did he do something to start it? Was it his fault? "I'm not going to go nuts on you, Dad, but giving this job at the rectory to Larry takes one thing off my back."

Thomas stared at Kevin for several seconds. "Okay," he said. "We didn't want to put more pressure on you, but that doesn't mean you stick your head in the sand. Ricketts made a crack about the Coroner's Inquest; the lawyer for the dead kid's family stirring up trouble in town; how business of was off. Then he asked if you were going to testify – like the son of a bitch didn't know." Thomas stood and grabbed his gloves off the end of the table. "I think Ricketts and Perkins might be looking for someone to blame for a slow summer, so don't do something stupid." He stared at Kevin for several seconds. "The beach needs raking." As he headed for the door, he muttered. "The summer of fifty-eight is going to be one for the books."

Kevin turned from watching his father leave to see a look of deep concern on his mother's face.

"Is that all there is to this?" Joyce asked.

"Isn't it enough? With Father Donovan's subversive book thing, I didn't want to get in the middle – between him and Mr. Marsh."

"I realize there are many important things going on in your life right now, perhaps more than any seventeen year old can be expected to endure."

"I'll be alright – if I don't have to worry about Father Donovan – those subversive books and stuff." Seeing his mother's eyebrow raise a fraction, Kevin added, "And I can't sleep just thinking about seeing that Skip kid – dead." Was he laying it on too thick? What would he do next, crumple to the floor with uncontrollable sobs?

Joyce nodded solemnly. "All right. If that's going to help you, I understand." She paused, then put her hand on Kevin's forearm. "I hope you are making the right decisions on this – and all the other things going on in your life right now."

"I am, Mom," Kevin said pulling away. "I got to rake the beach."

"Kevin, I am not as unaware of these issues as you might think. You can talk to me – and your father – if you'd like our advice about these choices."

"I will, Mom," Kevin said as he dashed for the door.

———

LATER THAT AFTERNOON, Kevin stood on the shoulder of Route 28 with his thumb out.

A blue Chevy slowed, but Kevin waved it on, pretending he wasn't hitchhiking. Other times he would have taken the ride, but the fourteen one hundred dollar bills, counted and recounted, then carefully pressed into the envelope made him scan each possible ride as though the driver might be Willie Sutton. He knew local folks would pick up kids they knew hitching back and forth between Hawk Cove and Inlet, but standing just outside town for the past twenty minutes, he hadn't recognized any of the cars or pickups that had passed so far. His parents weren't crazy about him hitchhiking, but a lot of guys did it. Maxine was about the only girl he'd seen do it. Still, he couldn't wait all afternoon. Maxine had said to meet him at three at the head of the footpath along the Fifth Lake channel. And those dark low clouds looked like they could bring one more rainy afternoon.

A dark gray Cadillac approached. It slowed, and even though he didn't recognize the car, Kevin decided to take the ride. But the driver eyed Kevin and sped by. Kevin watched the car round the curve and wondered what there was about the driver that seemed familiar. He had to get there, and give Maxine the money. For the past two days, he must have moved the stack of bills ten times. Under the mattress, where it made a huge lump; in the bottom drawer under his winter sweaters, where he imagined a dozen unlikely reasons for his mother to get in there; in the back of his closet; inside his slippers. And every time he moved the stack and recounted it, the more he realized what it meant.

His entire college fund, printed on the bottom of the withdrawal slip hidden behind the bookcase, was now forty-three dollars and twenty-seven cents. So much was happening all at the same time, he hadn't had time to think. If he'd told Maxine he had a thousand dollars or five hundred dollars in the bank instead of what was really in his account, would she have said that was enough?

He'd sat on his bed staring at the money, trying to imagine what it meant. His college fund. What did that mean? He was more worried about what would happen if – no, when – his parents found out what he'd done then what not having money for college meant. College was in another life far off. Right now, his life was such a mess, he couldn't see to the end of the week. What if he crossed the road, stuck out his thumb, and hitched to Utica, Syracuse, San Francisco? He was sure Jack Kerouac didn't have fourteen hundred dollars in his pocket. If he wasn't going to college, he'd have to figure out another way to get out of here.

A beeping horn jolted Kevin out of his reverie. Claude Thibedeau's pickup had pulled onto the shoulder, and Kevin hopped in.

FIFTEEN MINUTES LATER, Kevin approached Maxine standing on the edge of the channel to Fifth Lake that ran behind the Inlet shops.

"You're late," Maxine said.

Kevin said, "My ride had to stop to make a delivery." Twenty yards away, two young kids were throwing stones into the water where the channel began. Unlike every other person he'd passed from the center of Inlet where Mr. Thibedeau had dropped him off, they didn't look like they were about to jump him and grab the envelope.

"You got the money?" Maxine glanced at her watch.

Kevin was about to pull the envelope out, but stopped. Maxine didn't seem happy to see him. He wasn't sure what to expect, but they were in this together, weren't they? "Can we talk?"

"Theo will shit a brick if I'm late for my shift."

Kevin couldn't help staring at her stomach for some sign. "Are you feeling okay?"

"Not too bad. Something frying does it, so I try to steer wide of the grill."

"You look good." All week, he'd been plagued by an image of Maxine waddling around like she was hiding a fifty pound sack of potatoes under her skirt.

"Thanks." Maxine looked at her watch again. "Something else we need to talk about?"

"Let's walk along the channel."

"Just a couple of minutes. I got to go."

Kevin and Maxine walked down the grass embankment to the gravel path that ran along the channel. The backs of the buildings lining Route 28 in the center of town were above them. "It's everything. Are you going to be all right? What are you going to do? I've got a million questions – and I don't know."

"I'll take care of it."

"It's my whole college fund."

"College ain't everything, you know. Lots of people do okay without going to college."

"I'm sorry. My brain's going to bust. I can't see a way out. This guy getting killed, and now this."

"Hey, I'm sorry about that guy, but that was then." Maxine patted her stomach. "This is now. Besides, you don't have to worry about college for another year."

Kevin couldn't imagine how he'd get fourteen hundred dollars in the next year. He couldn't imagine to the end of this week. "It's a lot of money: all I've got."

"You're not going to rat-fink on me? All I got is this." Maxine patted her stomach again. "Dad."

"*Jeez*, will you stop saying that."

"Okay. I'm nervous too, you know. I swear Hilda's going to give me the heave-ho any second. And even if Theo keeps me on, I only got another four weeks until Labor Day. Then what am I going to do? I ain't got rich parents to take care of me."

"Where are you going to go with the money?"

"I don't know." Maxine kicked a stone into the channel. "But I'll tell you one thing. I'm deciding what to do. It was "do this" and "do that. The bastard stabbed me because I wouldn't take care of it."

"Of what?"

"Jesus, you're dense. My baby. What the hell do you think I was talking about?"

"I didn't know you –you were pregnant before." Kevin paused. "What happened?"

"I damn near bled to death, and my baby died."

"Holy smokes. You've had..."

"I don't want to talk about it. With the fourteen hundred bucks, I get to decide what I'm going to do." Maxine looked at the sky. "I better get over to the Acropolis before it rains. You got the money, right?"

Kevin pulled the envelope out of his pocket and handed it to Maxine.

Maxine opened the envelope and flicked her fingers over the bills. "It's your whole college fund?"

Kevin let out a mirthless laugh. "I got forty-three dollars left."

Maxine stepped close to Kevin. "I'm sorry I've been hard on you. I got a lot of things on my mind. You've been a real stand-up guy on this."

"Considering it was only one time at Jimmie's. I guess I'm either a lucky or an unlucky shot."

"It was twice. On your friend's porch. The place with the dog."

"The neighbor came out before we finished."

"Oh, Christ, yes. And I did get poison ivy." Maxine turned her leg and pointed to her ankle. It's almost gone, but I remember it itched like hell." Maxine looked over her shoulder and sighed. "Tell you what. Seeing's how I've cleaned out your college fund, I'll give you something to remember me by." Her hand ran up Kevin's thigh.

"Right here? Cripes." Kevin looked up at the backs of the buildings, the path that curved toward the park. "What if someone comes?"

"It's up to you. I got to go pretty quick."

"Yeah," Kevin whispered as Maxine rubbed the crotch of his jeans. "Oh, Jeez," he muttered as she unzipped him and got his thing out of his briefs. He stared at her smiling eyes as she began pulling and squeezing his erection. Out of the corner of his eye, he saw movement through the trees, up the embankment, and froze. But Maxine kept pulling on him. As Kevin turned back, Maxine was slowly bending. Her tongue flicked over his thing. Then watching her duck lower, he felt her wet tongue sliding along one, then the other side of his erection. He was sure he was going to come and wondered if he should warn her. Then as he felt her lips close over the tip and slurp, his eyes rolled back and the image of one half of a black raspberry Popsicle being sucked raced through his brain. *Oh, Jeez.* Before he could warn her, his thing began throbbing in her mouth. But instead of pulling away, she sucked harder. *Oh, Jeez. Oh, Jeez. Oh, Jeez.* Finally, Maxine slowed, let his deflating thing slip from her mouth, and raised her head to grin at him. His stuff was dripping from her lips. "Sorry," Kevin said. "I didn't know I was coming."

Maxine wiped her mouth with the back of her hand. "I hear it's got a lot of vitamins. Probably good for the baby."

The sound of kids laughing came from around the curve of the path. "Shit." Kevin stuffed his dripping thing into his pants.

Maxine giggled as two young kids skipped by them. "I really got to go now."

"I'll walk you back to town."

As they waited for traffic to clear, Kevin said, "Can I see you this weekend, tomorrow, Sunday?"

"I got a lot of stuff to get together."

"Just for a little bit; anywhere. You name the time, the place. I'll get there."

"Call me," Maxine said over her shoulder as she ducked through a break in the line of cars.

Kevin watched Maxine disappear into the side door of the Acropolis. Did she want him to call her at the Acropolis or at Jimmie's? Kevin felt the mess between his legs start to stick and went around the back of Bob's Esso and into the bathroom to clean up. Five minutes later, with his damp briefs chafing under his jeans, he came around to the front of the station and looked up at the darkening clouds. He turned at the sound of a tire iron hitting the concrete floor and remembered it was almost the first of the month. There'd be a new pinup on the calendar at Simpson's Garage. Christ. A month ago, he was jerking off to pinups and bra ads. He was sure what she did wasn't in the *Modern Marriage* book. Something to remember me by. Damn. It was going to rain.

As Kevin stood on the edge of the wide shoulder on the hill leading out of Inlet, he wondered whether he should have stayed inside the gas station until the rain blew over. Where the heck had all the cars gone to? Over the top of the trees, he could see the storm marching up the lake. Wasn't that Ida Rayburn who drove by? He'd turned to dash down the road back into town, when a gray Cadillac pulled off on the shoulder. The driver was waving at him. Wasn't that the same car he saw earlier? He didn't know anybody with a gray Cadillac. Go back or take the ride? The driver blew the horn again just as fat rain drops began plopping on the road, kicking up the smell of dust. Raindrops pelted down, and Kevin dashed for the car.

As Kevin pulled the door shut on the drumming rain, he turned to see the lawyer behind the wheel. A startled "Oh!" shot out of Kevin's mouth.

"Kevin Boyle. I thought it was you," Mr. MacKenzie said. He turned on the windshield wipers. "It appears I've rescued you from the deluge." Sheets of rain were lashing across the road. The leaves on the trees were turned inside-out white.

Sunday August 3

ATLAS LAUNCHED SUCCESSFULLY

See the USA in your Chevrolet

"SHE NOT HERE. I got to go."

"Mr. Dorakadis. Wait a second, please," Kevin shouted into the phone. "When is she coming in?"

"I tell you. She quit. You see her, you tell her I want uniform back."

Kevin stared at the buzzing telephone in his hand. He felt tears welling. Oh, Jesus. He knew it. He just knew it. Friday: I can't talk right now. Saturday noon: give me a call later. Sunday at six: she left. Damn. And he had to piss. Kevin slammed the phone into the hook, and yanked open the door of the booth. Walking right by Mr. Simpson without buying a soda, Kevin went into the grimy toilet off the first bay and peed into the brown-stained bowl. A tear leaked from his right eye. I am not going to cry. Damn it. He sniffled and zipped up.

He'd been upset at the first call on Friday, but somehow he wasn't surprised. *Something to remember me by.* Kevin fingered the dimes in his pocket. Maybe, just maybe, she's at Jimmie's. He shoved open the accordion door of the booth, took a deep breath, and dialed Jimmie's number hoping to hear Maxine tell him she got another job, one where a Theo wasn't copping feels all day. Oh, and great news, Kevin. My period came. I won't need the fourteen hundred. Let's get together tonight. I'll give you back the money, and we can, you know.

"Hello."

222

Shit. Hilda. "May I speak to Maxine, please."

A dry snort. "Maxine's not here – thank goodness. Is this Kevin Boyle?"

"Ah, no. It's ..."

"I don't need more lies. Look Mister Boyle, I've got half a mind to..."

Oh, Jesus. Now he's poked a hornet's nest. Kevin started to hang up, when he heard, "Ma, give me that."

"Kevin?" Jimmie said. "Ma, just leave it. I'll take care of it. Relax will you? Kevin, that you?"

"Yeah, Jimmie. What's happening? Where's Maxine?"

"She left."

"Left, like left town?"

"Yeah. She took off this morning. She and that Dave guy."

"Dave? Who's Dave?"

"I thought you knew. She said you two broke up. This guy she's been seeing came by this morning. Maxine comes out of her room with two suitcases and the rest of her stuff under her arm and says goodbye. Just like that."

Kevin pressed his forehead against the cold glass of the booth. "Fifty-six cream and blue Impala?"

"Yeah. That's the one. Dave something or other."

"I don't suppose she said where's she's going?"

"Nope. She thanked my mom and dad. Said if her mother called, to have her leave a number or address, and she would try to get back to her."

Kevin didn't know why he wanted to dig at the wound, but he said, "This Dave. How long has she been going with him?"

"I don't remember exactly. Pretty soon after – you know – what happened that night here," Jimmie said. "You didn't know?"

"I knew. We sort of decided to cool it for a while. Thanks, Jimmie. See you around." Kevin replaced the receiver and stared out the glass booth. He tried to put features on the guy in the Chevy. Was he one of the guys from the Halfway House? Jesus, what a jerk. Cradle robber. Chump. Maybe it was better she was out of town. A very pregnant Maxine waddling up to the front door of the Longhouse had been one of his many nightmares.

"Hey, you taking a nap in there?"

"Sorry," Kevin muttered to the man standing outside the booth.

Monday August 4

CANADA MAY SEEK ATOMIC WEAPONS

Psychic Dominance. How to Rule Others with Your Thoughts.

KEVIN WALKED ALONG SPRUCE ROAD. A car approached from behind, and he stepped into the weeds to let it pass. The gray Cadillac pulled alongside him and stopped. Last Thursday in Inlet, he'd tried to back out of the car, but Mr. MacKenzie had already pulled onto the road. Three miles, and not a word. When they'd finally arrived at Iroquois Lodge, Kevin was out of the car before it came to a stop.

Now, the electric window hummed down and Mr. MacKenzie's eyes locked on his. "Get in."

Kevin slid into the leather seat. His hands shook as he pulled the door closed.

They drove down Spruce, but instead of turning onto Lake toward Iroquois Lodge, they went straight into the parking lot at the town beach and parked facing the lake. On this cool, overcast morning, there were only two other cars on the far side of the lot near the picnic tables. Mr. MacKenzie turned off the ignition. A fisherman cast from the floating dock and reeled the lure in; cast again; reel. What's to stop him from getting out of the car? He wasn't under arrest. But he remained glued to the leather seat.

"Maxine Nelson has left town."

Kevin looked quickly at Mr. MacKenzie, then back at the man at the end of the dock. The Jitterbug skittered along the surface. Stupid tourist.

Nobody ever caught anything off that dock. Was he supposed to say something? Finally, he nodded.

"Miss Nelson seems to be in a bit of trouble," the lawyer said coldly.

Kevin tried to not look at Mr. MacKenzie, but he was afraid the jerk of his head gave him away.

"Miss Nelson has important choices to make, but it seems she has found someone to help her through her troubles – a benefactor."

"I...."

"Shut up."

Kevin could feel the lawyer's eyes on him as he tried to squeeze into the door. Just open it and get out. But his hands were locked in tight fists his lap.

"Whatever Miss Nelson decides to do will have enormous consequences for you."

"It's not my..."

"Pay attention. I'm not interested in your pathetic whining."

Kevin looked at the electric window switch. There wasn't enough air in the car.

"If she decides to have the baby and put it up for adoption, you might be off the hook, so to speak." Mr. MacKenzie turned on the ignition, and the air-conditioning sent a cold, damp blast into the car. "But she may decide to keep the baby. Child support payments might be required."

A flash recall of Larry Needham standing in the dark cellar of Thibedeau's Hardware shot into Kevin's head, but it was Kevin stacking boxes. Then a picture of him carrying out the garbage from the back door of the Trading Post formed.

"If, on the other hand, she decides to have her problem taken care of, as the euphemism goes," the lawyer paused. "Well, that would be extremely unfortunate for someone who had paid for such a heinous and felonious deed: accessory to the fact and all. At the least, not what one would want included on one's college application."

"Wha....?"

Mr. MacKenzie held up his finger, and then pointed to the dock where the fisherman was reeling in a splashing fish. "Lucky fellow. *You* might get lucky. Or you might find you need assistance in extricating yourself from the predicament you've created."

Tuesday August 5

AS HE OPENED THE DOOR TO THE LIBRARY, Kevin felt as though the walk from the Lodge had been through wet cement. He'd lay awake half the night trying to figure out what the lawyer meant. All he'd been doing is waiting; standing on the sidelines while everyone else was deciding his life. He should get out – now.

He could hitch to Thendara and withdraw what was left in his bank account. Then he could hook a ride on one of the delivery trucks heading back to Utica.

He'd call his parents from Utica: tell them not to worry. If he bought a long-distance bus ticket, he could sleep on the bus and not have to stay in motels. He could buy sandwiches and cokes when it stopped for gas. Get a part-time job at a stop along the way when his money ran low. Where to? California. Why not? If you're going to get out, go all the way. San Francisco. Did you have to be eighteen to rent a room? Could he get a job? He could find City Lights Bookstore. Okay. Maybe not California. But he had to do something besides wait.

Kevin dropped the books on the circulation desk. At the end, Mr. Marsh looked up from the paper work in front of him.

"Hello, Kevin."

"My mom said you left a message. You wanted to see me when I came in."

Stepping closer to face Kevin across the desk, Mr. Marsh said, "I wanted to let you know the book discussion group has been cancelled until further notice."

"Just for a while? How come?"

"I thought someone as perceptive as you would have figured that out."

"Mr. Marsh, I didn't tell anyone about your books – the ones from San Francisco. I mean, Father Donovan already knew. He asked me. I couldn't lie to him. I even told him Miss Weaver wouldn't lend me one."

"Well," Mr. Marsh said with a sigh, "I don't think we need to get into who told whom. It's out, and I'm afraid it will involve more than the death of the book discussion group."

"I heard about the Town Board meeting. I'll tell them Gladys Perkins is a fat busy-body."

"I'm sure Mrs. Perkins' role in this won't be on the agenda."

"And I'll tell them Father Donovan ought to mind his own business, too!" Kevin saw the quizzical look on Mr. Marsh's face. "I don't know why he can't just leave people alone," he said more quietly.

"Yes, Father Donovan ought to leave people alone." He paused. "Larry's taken your job at the rectory."

"I'm sorry. I didn't think about you needing him here at the library."

"That's not important. What's important is what's best for Larry."

"Father Donovan pays three dollars an hour."

"I can't pay him that, and Larry could use the money. But some things – many things – are more important than money." Mr. Marsh took the books stacked in front of Kevin and set them up on their ends. He looked at the spines. "Is there any reason you think the job at the rectory might not be the best thing for Larry?"

"I don't know," Kevin said. "There's a lot of stupid stuff: newsletters about Communists hiding everywhere. I hope Father Donovan and Mrs. Perkins aren't going to start something like that about the library."

"That's it?"

"Yeah."

Wednesday August 6

KHRUSHCHEV, MAO MEET IN PEIPING
Burned Teamster Resists Questions: Uncle Disappears.

SHOVING HIS PLATE AWAY, Thomas looked toward the front door. A timid tapping at supper time meant one of the guests wanted to borrow a piece of kitchen ware. Kevin or Joyce might offer to see what was needed and assure the apologetic guest they didn't mind the interruption. The loud rapping they now heard signaled a backed-up sink or an over-flowing toilet – crises Thomas would have to solve.

"Damn it, I'm coming," Thomas muttered as he pushed his chair back and walked toward the insistent *rap-rap-rap.*

Kevin examined a piece of pork chop at the end of his fork, wondering if he'd be gagging it down in twenty minutes as he helped his father plunger-down someone else's shit. But then he heard a familiar voice. "I'm *terribly* sorry to interrupt your dinner hour." The instant he recognized the voice, snatches of the explanations he'd practiced sounded even more unbelievable. His mother cocked her head as if puzzled by the visitor's unfamiliar accent.

"Kevin," Thomas called. "Joyce."

As Joyce shrugged at Thomas' summons and stood, Kevin stuffed the piece of pork chop into his mouth and followed her to the living room.

Mr. MacKenzie had managed to slip inside the screen door still being held half-open by Thomas. The lawyer cast a broad smile towards Joyce as he swept off his straw hat. Kevin shriveled behind her.

"Mrs. Boyle," he said with a small bow.

"We were having…"Thomas said.

Stepping around Thomas, MacKenzie extended his hand to Joyce. "I'm delighted to finally have the pleasure."

MacKenzie gestured toward the sofa. Joyce sat and looked at Thomas as though expecting an explanation. Thomas let go of the screen door with a slam.

Smiling, MacKenzie said, "Mr. Boyle, if you'll grant me a minute or two of your time, I assure you'll find it to be exceptionally important to you and Mrs. Boyle and your son."

All eyes were now on Kevin.

Kevin surveyed the room, seeming to gauge each seat before joining his mother on the sofa. Thomas started to object, but finally settled into the chair MacKenzie was pointing to.

Although MacKenzie smiled, his cold eyes bored into Kevin.

Kevin stared at his two tightly knotted fists in his lap. *It was just that once. Maybe I can get a job over the winter to…I don't know what she's going to…She…*

"As I was starting to say, there has been an extremely significant development related to the tragic events of July thirteenth."

Kevin glanced up. MacKenzie was still looking at him. *Was that the date they'd done it? No, it was…*

"Since Kevin is so intimately involved," MacKenzie continued, "I wanted to bring you up to date on what I have learned."

July thirteenth? That was the night at the Rock.

"Unfortunately, the circumstances surrounding and following the death of Skip Satterfield have been more complicated than one could have imagined at the outset."

The kid that got killed. Not Maxine?

"As you may know, the Satterfields are a very old Connecticut family. And Satterfields have attended Yale since the college was founded.

Of course, they fully expected Skip would take his place at New Haven next fall."

"Why are you telling us this?" Thomas said.

MacKenzie held out a hand. "Please bear with me, Mr. Boyle. I'm afraid we attorneys can be loquacious." Turning to Joyce, he said, "A mother would surely understand, but I must confess I was ashamed of myself for my initial surprise when the Satterfields told me they were funding a scholarship at Yale in Skip's name. I wondered how a family could think to be so generous in their time of grief. But, of course, I know the family, and this is but one instance of their desire to do the right thing."

"This scholarship," Thomas said, "the person who gets it can only use it at Yale?"

Peering at Thomas over the top of his half-glasses, MacKenzie said through a frozen smile, "Forgive me, but few people who haven't had the privilege of attending an Ivy League school fully appreciate the opportunities Yale affords. Postdam State is a fine college. And Mrs. Boyle, you know St. Lawrence is highly regarded, so it must have been a grave disappointment to have to leave before the end of your sophomore year."

Kevin felt a sharp twitch and heard a tiny surprised squeak from his mother. His father looked as though the air was seeping out of him.

"Yale provides the best teachers. A Yale education is an entrée to the top law schools, medical colleges, and brokerage houses. There one associates with the finest young men from the best families, making friends and connections for life."

"This scholarship," Thomas asked, "would a person have to take a test for it?"

"Actually, no," Mr. MacKenzie said. "Its disbursement is entirely at the discretion of the Satterfield family." He paused. "But since you inquired, let me add one or two additional pieces of information the

Satterfields have chosen to share with me. Since it is possible the recipient might not have the resources a typical Yale matriculant might possess, the family has indicated the scholarship could cover room, board, books, and all other expenses one might incur."

"A free ride," Thomas said.

"One might say that," MacKenzie said. "However, we must keep in mind the Satterfields expect the recipient to be worthy of their generosity. Worthiness, in my humble experience, is never free. It's earned." Mr. MacKenzie's eyes bored into Kevin. "Well, I must be on my way. Thank you again for taking the time to assist me and the Satterfield family in this terribly difficult time."

Mr. MacKenzie stood and bowed again to Joyce. "It has been a pleasure, Mrs. Boyle. I am confident you can comprehend a mother's grief – and the redemptive power of generosity."

As Thomas stood, MacKenzie thrust out his hand. Thomas eyed it suspiciously for a moment before taking it. MacKenzie swept out the door. Joyce and Kevin sat silently. Finally, Thomas lowered himself into the chair. He rubbed his face and looked at Kevin. "Do I need to spell it out for you?"

"No," Kevin said in a hoarse whisper. "If I tell the Coroner's Inquest Duke pushed Skip off the Rock, I get a scholarship to Yale."

Thomas snorted. "I'm glad we raised such a smart kid. We won't have to waste our breath *parsing* MacKenzie's euphemisms." He paused. "What are you going to do?"

"Do we have to discuss this now?" Joyce said. "I can't cope with all this ..."

"It's been almost three weeks, Joyce. That ought to have been enough time for Kevin to get one story straight."

"Thomas..."

"That's okay, Mom."

Thomas said, "You've told several stories about what happened that night: you weren't there, you were there, but not really there, you saw two guys on the Rock, you saw Duke, maybe you saw a scuffle. You've got a bunch of stories. So why not pick one that does you some good? All summer I've been hearing you go on about getting out of Hawk Cove. Okay. MacKenzie just offered you a ride on the Reading, hotels on Park Place. It's time to stop whining and do something that will get you out of here."

"Thomas," Joyce said. "All Kevin needs to do is tell the truth."

"The truth?" Thomas said with a mirthless laugh. "What a joke. I spend every day from the last week in June to Labor Day lying. 'Good morning! Hope you have a wonderful day!' I have to shout every god-damned one of those seventy days. I have to grin and bear it when our guests want to spend all afternoon yakking about how much snow we got last winter, guests who expect you not to mind when they come knocking at your door at any time of the day or night. Do you think this is the life I imagined living?"

His mother's fingers clenched and unclenched in her lap.

"Don't worry, I understand," Kevin said.

Thursday August 7

FULBRIGHT LASHES AT FOREIGN POLICY

How to Make Money with Simple Cartoons.

"DO YOU THINK there are many requests for reservations in those?"

Kevin wheeled around and dropped the stack of envelopes he'd pulled from the Iroquois Lodge box at the post office. Mr. MacKenzie, wearing a blue poplin suit, red polka dot tie and straw hat, stood behind him. Kevin knelt to pick up the mail scattered at the lawyer's feet. As he stood, Mr. MacKenzie nodded toward the door.

"A word, if I may."

Kevin followed him to the front of the post office. The driver of a log truck blew the air horn at a Studebaker slowly pulling onto Route 28 from Simpson's Garage. "He probably thought he was backing up," Mr. MacKenzie said. "But unlike Studebakers not knowing whether they are coming or going, I imagine your life has become much less complicated."

"Why don't you leave me alone?"

"I should think you would be pleased to see me. After all, I can't imagine scholarships to Yale are thick on the ground in this lovely hamlet."

"Okay. I get it. What do you want, an oath signed in blood?"

"Don't be so melodramatic, young man. I'm confident you've had time to contemplate the enormity of the Satterfields' generosity – and influence. I suspect your parents also understand the importance of what is on offer."

"What are you going to do, tell them about Maxine if I don't come up with the right story?"

Mr. MacKenzie slowly shook his head. "I do hope the Satterfields are making the right decision. You suffer the consequences of living in a town, if not at the edge of the known world, within its sight. And yet, Miss Nelson's dilemma does continue to hang like the proverbial sword. Fortunately for you, I do carrots as well as sticks."

"You know, I might just tell you and the Satterfields and everybody else who's telling me what to do, to shove it."

"You see, that's the problem: the narrow limits of your circumstances. This small town righteousness gleaned from Gary Cooper movies, the dread of eternal damnation for eating meat on Fridays, a smattering of moral bromides from the *Saturday Evening Post*. Brittle. Likely to shatter under the slightest pressure."

"Screw you."

Chuckling, Mr. Mackenzie said, "And I thought we were only going to have to remind you to not pick your nose at your Yale admissions interview. Are there any other expletives you'd like to spew before we get down to business?"

"You think you're better than everybody else."

"Of course. What do you think this is all about? Many go to Yale because they already *are* better than anybody else. And some fortunate young men go to *become* better than anybody else: better professions, better incomes, better travel, opportunities to do whatever one wants. Or perhaps you dream of a simpler life."

"I'm not stupid."

"Then don't act as though you've fallen off a potato wagon."

"There are thousands of good colleges that aren't Ivy League," Kevin said.

"And given the chance, the overwhelming majority of their best students would stampede to New Haven and Cambridge in a thrice."

"If I don't take your offer, you think I'm going to spend my whole life feeling sorry for myself?"

Mr. MacKenzie sighed. "You see, my young friend, with a degree from Yale you go through life with the world assuming you are a well-educated leader among men – regardless of whether one is a legacy or the fortunate recipient of an unrestricted scholarship. After graduating from Yale, one has to strenuously demonstrate one's stupidity. On the other hand, a degree from, say, Potsdam State, and your lot is to constantly prove you are capable of buttoning your flies."

"What do you want?"

"Those envelopes," Mr. MacKenzie said pointing to the stack in Kevin's hand. "I doubt they hold any last minute requests for the many vacant cottages at the Lodge. In fact, at this late date in the season, it is extremely unlikely any will be rented."

"What are you going to do, get your friends from Connecticut to rent them?"

"Unless you have something intelligent to say, I'd appreciate it if you would keep your mouth shut and listen."

Kevin shuffled the envelopes.

"On the Monday following Labor Day, your parents have a loan payment due – one they are highly unlikely to make in light of the number of cottages they've rented."

Kevin opened his mouth to ask how Mr. MacKenzie knew, but closed it as he realized MacKenzie knew everything.

"But, my clients, understanding the strain on the local economy and your parents' business caused by the unfortunate events of July thirteenth, are prepared to extend a no-interest loan to your parents more than sufficient to meet their obligations to Mr. Ward."

Kevin couldn't remember his mother's cousin called anything except Cousin Bob. "Why didn't you tell my father yesterday?"

Mr. MacKenzie stared at Kevin. Then closed his eyes and sighed. "Because, *you* are the operative agent in this matter."

"So, if I...."

"Do shut up!" Mr. MacKenzie said. He paused then added in an even tone, "I trust we do not have to belabor the obvious."

"No, I understand." As Kevin watched Mr. MacKenzie walk toward his gray Cadillac he heard him mutter that he hoped Eli would forgive him.

Saturday August 9

WITH HIS HEAD STILL REELING with MacKenzie's offers of scholarships and loans, Kevin hesitated at the end of the library's sidewalk. He needed a quiet place to think, but he also hoped Mr. Marsh would assure him the rumors swirling about the town board and the books from San Francisco were bunk. As he started toward the door, Doris Weaver came out.

"*Saluton*, Kevin."

"*Saluton*, Miss Weaver."

"You don't look like you're in a one-world mood."

Kevin tried to sidestep Miss Weaver, but she planted herself in the middle of the sidewalk. "I'm okay."

Miss Weaver put her hand on Kevin's shoulder. "You're not okay." With her hand still on his shoulder, she guided him to the picnic table under the maple. After sitting quietly side by side for a minute, she said, "You look like your boat is taking on more water than you can bail. You want to talk about it?"

Which *it*, Kevin wondered: Maxine, what Donovan did, MacKenzie's offers? "I don't know what there is to talk about. I've got to tell this Coroner's Inquest what I saw that night at the Rock."

"But it's not that simple, is it?"

"No. I try to remember exactly what happened, but it's not clear."

"Maybe it wasn't clear," Miss Weaver said. "Not every problem in this world has a black or white answer."

"That isn't good enough for some people."

"I heard. The lawyer – the one the Satterfields hired – glides around in his Cadillac telling people he just wants to help those folks put their minds at rest. Baloney! It's revenge they're after. He's what Napoleon called Talleyrand, 'Shit in silk stockings.'"

"Whatever they're after, what happens is on my head."

"A lot of it, I suppose. But you don't have go around thinking everything depends on you."

"But what I say affects other people – Duke Duncan, even my parents."

Miss Weaver put her hand on Kevin's arm. "Indulge an old lady. My mother died in the influenza epidemic of 1918. Dad was *supposed* to die in no less than a year from the mustard gas he'd inhaled at Passchendaele. My brother, Jeremiah the second, grabbed his trust fund and took off to New York. Jerry went from being man-about-town to DOA after staggering in front of a milk wagon one early November morning." She paused. "And I got to stay home to spoon-feed my father applesauce and clean his soiled linen until he finally managed to die – in 1948."

Maybe he'd head for New York instead of San Francisco, Kevin thought. "I'm sorry", he said.

"Me, too. You ever hear people say they have no regrets?" Miss Weaver said. "Well, I've regretted staying here to care for my father every single day of the last forty years. It's no secret he left me enough money to live well, and," nodding toward the library, "do a couple of things for the town. But I should have given every red cent of the money away; hired somebody to take care of him. It wasn't as though I was leaving him in a shack up on the Uncas Trail."

Kevin pictured Doris Weaver's huge house overlooking Frenchman's Cove. Everyone said she had a ton of money. What did she know about being broke? "I guess you thought you were doing the right thing."

"For a long time I told myself I was I trapped. It wasn't fair. But when I finally got the guts to look at myself, I realized I was afraid. I didn't know what I wanted to do. I couldn't see a picture of me in ten years, even five years. It was easier being the good daughter. For a lot of people, it's easier not to choose, pretend they're doing the right thing – for someone else."

If it was only *one* thing, Kevin thought. He couldn't tell her because he didn't know where to start; there were so many things hounding him. "Thanks, Miss Weaver. I really appreciate you trying to help."

"It's your life." She nodded toward the library door. "I wish I could convince our friend of that."

KEVIN WASN'T SURPRISED the library was empty on the first sunny day in a week. Seeing Mr. Marsh behind the circulation desk, Kevin decided to chance asking him about what was going on. "Mr. Marsh, he said, "This thing with the town board – what will happen?"

Mr. Marsh pushed a stack of books toward the re-shelving cart. He looked at Kevin for a few moments as though deciding on which of several answers to choose. "I can't give you the details, but I can predict the outcome."

"I don't understand. They can't close down the library," Kevin said as though it was a ridiculous idea.

Mr. Marsh let out a snort. "You won't hear anybody say that, but you'd be surprised how many people would like to close down libraries. The English gave us the Magna Carta *and* made it illegal for the Irish to learn to read."

"Well, I don't care what Father Donovan and Mrs. Perkins say, Miss Weaver isn't going to let anyone close this library."

"You're right about that. No, there will be another outcome."

Kevin stared at Mr. Marsh. "They're not going to fire you, are they?"

Warren Marsh took a deep breath. "I may quit before they get the chance."

"You're serious? Why? I mean, they can't fire you for reading your own books. Those books – the ones you and Miss Weaver had – you didn't put them in the library. You wouldn't even lend them to me."

"I don't want to get you involved in this."

"Why not? I'm already *involved* in a dozen other things around here." Kevin nodded toward the door. "Miss Weaver's telling me I've got to choose, or someone's going to choose for me."

"Good advice." Mr. Marsh pulled a stack of books from the return box.

"Miss Weaver, my dad, the lawyer, everybody's telling me 'do this', 'don't do that', but it's my life, and I don't know what am *I* supposed to do."

"What are you waiting for, somebody to come along with the perfect plan for Kevin Boyle? Maybe you make it up for yourself."

Mr. Marsh's sharp tone surprised Kevin. If he couldn't get good advice from Mr. Marsh, where else could he go? He thought about dropping it, but decided to ask. "Did you?"

Opening a book, Mr. Marsh took out the card from the back pocket. "Overdue," he muttered.

"You chose to be a librarian, get a job in Hawk Cove. How can you quit – even before you see what the board does? They're a bunch of old blow-hards."

"You sound like Doris. He pulled another card from the back of a book. "It's not that simple." He grabbed the re-shelving cart. "I've got work to do."

Kevin remembered Larry had left his job here to take the one at the rectory. Donovan was part of this too, he thought. A picture of Father Donovan, Mrs. Perkins, and every other small-minded person in Hawk Cove sitting in a jury box shot into his head "You can't let those know-nothings change your life."

Mr. Marsh looked at Kevin for a few moments. "With me, it's different," he said in a hoarse whisper as he trundled the cart into the fiction room.

Monday August 11

POLISH PRIMATE ORDERS PROTEST

Play Guitar in 7 Days or Get Money Back.

As Kevin started back to the Lodge with the mail, he heard a siren. Turning, he spotted Deputy Fisher's cruiser heading south on Route 28 with its flasher on, followed closely by one of the town DPW pickups. He guessed someone had hit a deer. As he continued walking along Tamarack, Mrs. Pennhurst stopped her car to ask if Kevin wanted a ride to the Lodge. As he was about to get in, Mrs. Pennhurst said, "If it isn't one thing going on in the library, it's another. It's enough to give a body palpitations."

"What do you mean?"

"Well, I don't know why the sheriffs had to be called out, but I'm going to have a lie-down and a cold compress as soon as I get home."

"Thanks, Mrs. Pennhurst, but I forgot something at the Red & White." Kevin backed out of the car and headed for the library.

Kevin crossed the library parking lot. The cruiser was parked at the back door. He went in the front. Inside, one of the men from the town crew dumped something from a large dustpan into a trash barrel. Mr. Marsh and Deputy Fisher were next to the circulation desk, and Kevin started toward them.

"Careful," the man from the town crew called to Kevin.

Kevin looked to where the man pointed and saw a pile of glass and wood splinters. The wreckage of Mr. Marsh's rock collection was strewn across the room: display boxes lay smashed as though someone had knocked them from the shelves and stomped them.

The man asked Mr. Marsh and Deputy Fisher, "You want me to shut the front door?"

Deputy Fisher said, "Maybe you ought to close up today."

"No," Mr. Marsh said. "I'm sorry. I didn't mean to shout. I don't know why someone would want to do this, but I'm not going to close the library."

Kevin noticed the bandage on Mr. Marsh's hand as he gestured toward the smashed display cases.

Deputy Fisher said, "You sure you don't want to have that looked at?"

"I'll be alright," Mr. Marsh said. "I'll help clean up this mess. I don't expect much business today."

The deputy cast a glance at Kevin, then said to Mr. Marsh, "I guess I've got everything I need for my report for now. If you come up with any ideas of who might have done this, give me a call. I got a break-in at the South Shore Inn I got to check out." He shot a suspicious look at Kevin. "Kids. Busted the lock on the storeroom and hauled off five cases of beer." He hitched up his belt and went out the back door.

The town crewman said, "You want I should toss everything out?"

"No, I want the rocks," Mr. Mash said. "The cases are ruined. No sense keeping them. And watch the glass," he said, holding up his bandaged hand. He looked at Kevin as though he didn't know him. "What can I do for you?"

"I came to see what happened."

Mr. Marsh gave Kevin an annoyed look. "What does it look like? Someone, or ones, took an extreme disliking to my rock collection."

"But, why would…?"

"Must have something against rocks," Mr. Marsh interrupted. He turned and walked into the room behind the circulation desk.

Tuesday August 12

MISSILE FUNDS LAG, HOUSE UNIT FINDS
Whole Country Hoops It Up in New Craze.

STRADDLING A SHINY RED SCHWINN, Buck said, "It's a surprise, but you'll cream your jeans when you see the new hang-out."

Kevin looked at the three-speed Columbia leaning against Buck's porch. "Where did the bikes come from?" He pulled the bike upright and checked out the gears.

"We'll drop them off later," Buck said as he started pedaling out his driveway.

Kevin hopped on the bike and followed Buck. He hoped they weren't going through the middle of town with these "borrowed" bikes. As soon as Buck turned off Tamarack and started down the long dip toward Eagle Pond Road, Kevin guessed the location of the big surprise. He pulled alongside Buck. "What about the neighbors?"

"Only one other house on the road, and they took off for Ohio to help take care of their daughter's new baby."

At the bottom of the hill, they turned up the long driveway toward the Polka Dot Cottage.

Every time Brownie showed up, Kevin wondered what would happen to the cottage. Relatives somewhere out of state were planning to sell it. But it had been a couple of months, and he hadn't heard a thing. At the end of the long driveway, Chink's Hornet hunkered in behind Jimmie's Merc. On the other side of the sandy patch in front, a '56 red and cream

Fairlane sat by itself.

Duke's car, Kevin realized. Was there a rule about hanging around with him before the Inquest? Buck dumped his bike in the bushes. Kevin laid the Columbia alongside it, and followed him. Everyone from the Rock was there – except Maxine. On the porch, Chink and Puffy sat side-by-side on an old sofa fiddling with something. Jimmie, with Noel in his shadow, pushed through the screen door. A ripped "Keep Out. Sheriff" sign hung from the wall.

"Hey, Boyle. Long time no see," Jimmie said. He took a swig of beer. "Sorry about you and my cousin. There's beer in a cooler," he said with a shrug toward the door. "Grab yourself one."

Kevin wondered when Jimmie decided to act like a normal human.

"Neat, huh?" Buck said, jumping up onto the porch. "Let's get a beer."

Inside the cottage, papers and magazines were strewn around the floor of the small room. Cigarette smoke hung in layers. A rancid stink of butts in the dregs of beer bottles lingered. Two Coleman lanterns barely lit the room. At the far end, Duke lay sprawled on a cot, his back against the wall. His arm draped over the shoulder of a girl Kevin didn't recognize; his hand dangled over her breast. Kevin and Duke's eyes met for a second before Kevin followed Buck into the tiny kitchen where beer cans and bottles filled an ice chest.

"Duke's treat," Buck said, grabbing a couple of cream ales.

Kevin wondered how he knew that. They'd just gotten here.

Buck punched holes in the tops with a church key and handed one to Kevin. He pointed to a bottle of *Southern Comfort* perched on the back of the counter.

"That's Duke's drink."

Flies buzzed over dirty plates in the sink. A can of condensed milk and container of instant coffee sat on the counter under the one small cupboard. Slim had lived in these two small rooms: running water, but no bathroom, a privy twenty yards out back.

"Hi, I'm Nina," a girl said in a voice that was mostly whisper.

Buck had vanished, and Kevin struggled to look at the girl's face instead of the enormous breasts straining against her scoop-necked tee-shirt. "Kevin," he finally answered.

Nina put her hand on Kevin's wrist and pressed in close to him. "Duke told me about you."

Backed against the counter in the tiny kitchen, Kevin couldn't help but stare into her cleavage where a black lacey bra barely kept Nina's breasts from springing free.

Nina followed the trail of Kevin's stare, took a deep drag on her cigarette and blew the smoke out of the corner of her mouth. "No harm in looking," she said smiling.

Holy Smokes. She looks like she's been ripped off the cover of *True Detective*. Nothing subtle about Duke.

"Said you were a real cool guy. Maybe we could have some fun."

Wow, Kevin thought. Duke figures I'm horny, but he must think I'm dumb as a post. "I've got to give my buddy a message. Catch up with you later." Kevin slipped around Nina and out of the kitchen, sure Duke was watching him. "Thanks for the beer," he said, tipping his beer toward Duke.

On the porch, Chink and Puffy had pulled the sofa to the end so it faced a row of whirligigs set along the edge of the woods. Puffy pumped a BB gun. Chink held a pellet pistol in his hand.

"I oughta get at least ten feet closer," Chink said. "You got a rifle."

Puffy lifted a cheek and ripped off a fart. "Fuck you. The pellet gun's got more punch." He put the rifle to his shoulder and pulled the trigger. Sand kicked up in front of the cardinal on the end.

"You couldn't hit a fly off the end of your dick," Chink said. He steadied his shooting hand and knocked over the cardinal with a shot.

"Dumb ass luck," Puffy said.

Everyone on the porch turned toward the dog that had begun barking at them from edge of the woods.

Kevin hadn't seen Brownie in a week. Damn, he thought. He looks like he hadn't been fed.

"That's Slim's dog," Puffy said as he pumped the BB gun.

Brownie took a menacing step toward the porch. Lips pulled back, it snarled at them.

"Somebody oughta put it out of its misery," Chink said.

Puffy raised the rifle and shot. Brownie yelped and wheeled, licking the spot on its haunch where the BB hit. With a low growl, the dog charged.

Puffy jumped up and stumbled backwards as Brownie leapt onto the porch and sunk his teeth in his calf. "Get him off me!" he screamed as he tried to shake the dog loose.

Chink swung his boot back.

"Don't," Kevin shouted as Chink's boot connected hard into the dog's side, knocking it off the porch. Squealing, Brownie limped into the woods.

"Why'd you do that?" Kevin yelled.

Chink pushed Kevin aside and began prancing around the porch. "Get him off. Get him off," he yodeled in a girlish sing-song. "The bad doggie bit me."

"Asshole," Puffy said. "What if it's got rabies?"

"He's foaming at the mouth already," Chink called to the other guys.

"You think it's funny?" Puffy shouted, stumbling in the dim light. "What if I got to get shots in my belly? I'll kill that fucking dog." He lurched to the line of whirligigs and began stomping them into splinters.

"Hey!" Kevin yelled, but Puffy didn't stop until every one of the whirligigs was smashed. "What did he have to do that for?" he said to no one, then coughed to hide the pressing lump in the back of his throat. He scanned the woods, but there was no sign of Brownie. Turning to face the others who were watching Puffy kick the pieces into the weeds,

Kevin started to say something, but they all seemed to be enjoying Puffy's rampage.

"Steer clear of wild man," Chink said. "He's been on a tear all week."

Kevin asked, "What does that mean?"

"It means not a goddamned thing, buddy-boy."

"Did Puffy smash the rocks at the library?"

"Ask him," Chink said. "Hey, Puff," he yelled. "Cool your jets and get over here. Boyle wants to play 'I Got a Secret.'"

Puffy gave one of the crumpled whirligigs a kick and lumbered over to the porch. *"What?"* he snarled.

"G-man here wants to know if you had a hand in wrecking fairy-boy's fancy rocks."

Puffy stepped onto the porch and leaned his face, pitted with black heads and acne scars, inches from Kevin's face. "Where'd you hear that lie?"

"I didn't hear anything," Kevin said.

"Busybody Boyle's hearing things," Chink hissed in Kevin's ear. His breath smelled of cigarettes, beer and old cheese.

Puffy's eyes bulged with malice as he leaned in closer to Kevin's face. "Maybe his pansy pal cried on his shoulder."

Chink grabbed Kevin's arm and squeezed hard. "Puffy's a peace-loving guy. But he could go ape-shit if someone was spreading lies around."

"Yeah," Puffy added, stabbing a finger in Kevin's chest. "I don't know nothing about who broke up them rocks." He jabbed Kevin in the chest again. "But if Marshy-Warshy's feelings are so hurt, maybe he could go someplace friendlier to his kind."

Chink released Kevin's arm with a shove. "And if anybody….."

"Leave him be," Duke interrupted.

"We was just explaining the facts of life to Boyle," Puffy said.

Duke eyed the two guys until they were staring at their shoes. He made an almost imperceptible nod toward the door. "Why don't you two grab a couple of brews? Let me have a word with my man." Duke put his arm over Kevin's shoulder and steered him to the end of the porch. "Don't pay them no attention. I ain't going to let them beat up on the only friend I got in this town."

Looking over his shoulder, Buck was nowhere to be found. Everyone had moved into the cottage. "You got friends," he said.

Duke surveyed the wreckage of whirligigs. "You're right. But some got a screw loose."

"He didn't need to do that," Kevin said.

"Don't worry about them." Duke faced Kevin. He put his hand on Kevin's shoulder. "You don't have to worry about nothing – if you stay on their good side."

"I don't know about that, Duke. Maybe it's not such a good idea me hanging around with you what with the inquest coming up."

"I wish I had your brains. People could get the wrong idea, not understand it's all on the up-and-up. No sweat. All you got to do is tell the whole truth and nothing but. You know like on Perry Mason. It's them preppy boys that's got me worried. They're going to lie about me being on top of the Rock, pushing Skipper off."

"You're right, Duke. People could get the wrong idea. I'm going to head back to town. Thanks for the beer." Kevin slid out from under Duke's arm. "Tell Buck I had to go." He jumped off the porch and grabbed his bike from the tangle of bushes.

"Thanks for saying I'm right," Duke called out after Kevin pedaling down the driveway.

"Come here, Brownie!" Kevin shouted into the woods. "Brownie? Come on, boy."

Wednesday August 13

"IF THERE IS NO FURTHER OLD BUSINESS, shall we move to new business?" Milton Standish asked.

Behind him, Kevin heard feet shuffling; a couple of nervous coughs. Sitting in the fourth row of the town hall meeting room next to his father, he hoped the rumors had been false. Even though Kevin promised his father he'd keep his mouth shut, he might give these old farts something to chew on if they thought they could mess with the library. But Miss Weaver sat in the second row, right behind Mr. Marsh – the only person in the room wearing a jacket and tie. She'll give them both barrels.

"Mr. Chairman," Lester Perkins started in a phlegmy voice that had most of the people in the room clearing their throats. "It is perhaps a small item, but as chairman of the library and parks committee, I felt our policies needed clarification."

The chemical aroma from the mimeographed agendas and the sweat from an hour in the hot room left purple stains on everyone's fingers. The room was packed, instead of the ten or twelve regulars who usually attended the August meeting. All week, Kevin overheard guarded conversations around town about something "fishy" at the library. Dummies. Those books weren't the library's – and Mr. Marsh and Miss Weaver wouldn't lend him their copies. The only item listed under New Business was Vacation Policy. Maybe the storm had blown by. But Mr.

Marsh and Miss Weaver looked like they were at a wake, and whispered conversations were going on around the stuffy room.

"I perused the aforementioned policies, but could not find any reference to staff vacations," Mr. Perkins said.

Staff? There was only Mr. Marsh, Kevin thought. One of the guys from parks came by at the end of the day to sweep and throw the trash in the back of his pickup. And when Mr. Marsh went on vacation, Verna Nichols came over from the Town Clerk's office to fill in. Probably the only time she saw the inside of the library. Did all these jokers turn out for nothing? But why was that scum-bag Father Donovan sitting in the back row? Was he and Glad - ass Perkins trying to finagle their crusade about subversive books into vacation policy? He says anything, and I'll tell them... I can't.

Mr. Perkins said, "Perhaps you could enlighten us, Mr. Marsh. How many weeks do you take for vacations?"

Were they going to punish Mr. Marsh for reading *On the Road* and *Howl* by cutting his vacation? This town is so damned *small*.

"Two weeks," Mr. Marsh answered. "That's what I was told when I took the job eight years ago: by Mr. Standish."

"Mr. Marsh is correct in his recollection," Mr. Standish said. "I do recall I believed that seemed fair."

"But not actually, or exactly, written down in policy?" Mr. Perkins said.

"Correct," replied Mr. Standish.

Returning his gaze to Mr. Marsh, and shaking his head slightly as he pursed his lips, Mr. Perkins said, "Amply sufficient for your annual jaunt to Provincetown?"

"I don't see why that's....." Miss Weaver said.

"Please, Miss Weaver," Mr. Standish interrupted. "There will be an opportunity for questions and comments from the floor when Mr. Perkins is finished."

Mr. Marsh turned and slowly shook his head at Miss Weaver.

"I'm sorry, Miss Weaver. We're all friends here. And in a town as small as Hawk Cove, we don't have too many folks who have reason to get all the way to Provincetown." He chuckled. "I'm such a true-blue Adirondacker, I can't figure why anyone would want to vacation in Provincetown, Massachusetts. But to each his own." He paused and looked around the room.

As though a hornet's nest was in the rafters, a low mummer filled the room.

"I suppose you meet a lot of," Mr. Perkins paused as though trying to come up with the right word, *"Artists?"*

Miss Weaver angrily whispered, *"Really!"* and drew a cautioning raised finger from Mr. Standish.

"Sorry, I digress," Mr. Perkins said. "I want to ensure that any policy the board adopts would be fair to family men as well as – bachelors."

Kevin felt his father twitching in the seat next to him. Someone behind him muttered, "Get this over with, Lester."

"Then you find two weeks sufficient and would not object if I proposed the board make your vacation days official?"

"To this point," Mr. Marsh said, "I have been fairly treated by the board and the others associated with the library. I believe two weeks vacation would be sufficient for your librarian."

For crissakes, Kevin thought. Just because Lester Perkins has spent his entire life inside the blue line, he's going to beat up on Mr. Marsh because he hangs around with artists. Still, Kevin didn't like the sound of 'your librarian.' He didn't know squat about vacations, but if this dragged on, he was going to tell Lester Perkins Mr. Marsh was a great librarian, and what books he ordered on his own and where he went on vacation were nobody's damn business.

Forcing his mouth into an imitation of a smile, Mr. Perkins said, "Thank you, Mr. Marsh." He neatly stacked the papers in front of him, turned to Mr. Standish, then returning to look at Mr. Marsh said, "Oh, and one more thing. It's not directly related to the vacation policy, but would you clarify the employment of Larry Needham?"

Mr. Marsh's shoulders lifted, then settled before replying, "I hired Larry to help with the re-shelving of the non-fiction room."

"But, he's no longer?" Mr. Perkins asked.

"No. He took another job. At St. Mary's."

Mr. Perkins looked at Mr. Marsh, then around the room, until everyone had followed his gaze to Father Donovan who had been sitting in the rear. Nervous coughs punctuated the silence. Finally, Mr. Perkins asked, "And do you intend to employ any other – young boys?"

"No, Mr. Perkins," Mr. Marsh answered softly.

Staring at Mr. Marsh for several seconds, Mr. Perkins finally said, "Mr. Chairman. I have no other questions to ask of Mr. Marsh. I'm sure the board can deal with this situation to everyone's satisfaction."

"Well, then," Milton Standish said. "Does anyone have any questions or comments?"

Kevin looked at his father, who shook his head. He turned to see whether anyone in the room was going to say something, but most were looking into their laps. Miss Weaver: She'll give them a twelve-gauge blast, he thought. But she was staring at the back of Mr. Marsh's head.

"If there is no further business, do I hear a motion to adjourn?"

Harry Simpson snorted. "I so move."

"Second," said Wendell Ricketts. His frog eyes looked left to the end of the conference table, where Claude Thibedeau and Floyd Tucker nodded as they stared at the table top.

"Meeting adjourned," intoned Mr. Standish.

"Is that it?" Kevin said to his father. "Nobody said anything."

"Let's go." Thomas stood.

Warren Marsh remained seated in the front row, eyes straight ahead, a nerve along his clenched jaw pulsing. Doris Weaver, sitting directly behind Mr. Marsh, reached her hand toward his shoulder, and then drew it back. Her shoulders slumped. Kevin took a step toward them, but Miss Weaver saw him and shook her head. There were tear tracks on her cheeks.

"Is it going to be okay?" Kevin asked

Regarding Kevin as though she couldn't believe his question, Miss Weaver said, "No, it's *not* going to be okay." She turned away from Kevin and put her hand on Mr. Marsh's shoulder.

"I said, let's go," Thomas called to Kevin.

As Kevin followed his father out the door after the meeting, folks grimly nodded at each and made for their cars. "They didn't say a thing about those books: the ones from San Francisco. Nothing about the book discussion group. And Gladys Perkins put her husband up to it because she and Father Donovan are mad about John Kenneth Galbraith." Kevin stopped and said to his father, "I don't understand."

Thomas zipped his jacket and dug around in his pocket for his car keys. "Warren Marsh. He never said or did anything – inappropriate – did he?"

"He and Miss Weaver wouldn't even lend me those books they got. And this stuff about where Mr. Marsh vacations. What's that supposed to mean?"

"Never mind. Let's get home."

"Nobody said anything! Why are you acting like something's been decided?"

"Get in the car, Kevin. It's over."

"Vacations? This is crazy."

"Jesus, Kevin," Thomas barked. "Do I have to spell it out for you?"

That can't be, Kevin thought. He'd been so focused on the book thing, it never occurred to him. But recollections of articles he'd read in the *Times* and other magazines about Provincetown and Key West and San Francisco came back: how he'd finally decoded the veiled references. Not Mr. Marsh. It's Donovan, not Marsh. "He's not…"

"You sure he never did anything?"

"It was… No. Mr. Marsh never did anything like that. He's not like…" Kevin got into the car and slammed the door.

Thursday August 14

99 ON DUTCH AIRLINER LOST OFF IRELAND
Dacron – They Dry Neat, Stay Neat

SITTING ON THE JUNGLE GYM at the town beach, Kevin said, "No way!" His mind had been in a swirl the past two days. Fruitcake. Pansy. Queer. He wasn't completely stupid. But not in Hawk Cove. When Mrs. Eversall's son Otis left town a few years ago, he overheard Harry Simpson tell Danny Henderson that Otis had gone off to be a hairdresser; then flapped his hand from his wrist at Danny. Mr. Marsh wasn't like that.

Buck tossed a pebble toward the water. "That's what I hear – and it's not just Puffy Russell."

"I remember Puffy running around every Thursday seeing who was wearing green," Kevin said. "Maybe it's Puffy that's......" He slid off the end of the jungle gym and walked to the edge of the water. If it wasn't true, then why did Mr. Marsh leave town the next day? After struggling with what to do, Kevin had finally gone to the library. 'Closed. See Verna Nichols in Town Hall in case of Emergancy.' Cleared out of his apartment too. And Kevin spent most of Wednesday avoiding his father. What did he mean by '*inappropriate*?' Kevin had been so upset at the end of the Town Board meeting, he hadn't heard his father straight. Then, when he'd finally cooled down, it snuck back up on him; those articles, the jibes the guys made.

Buck stood next to Kevin. "Don't keep sweating it. He's cut out."

Was it over, Kevin wondered?

257

"Whether or not Marsh is or isn't, ain't the question I'm thinking about. Your big day is coming up."

"Why is it *my* big day. You were there. Eight, maybe ten others too."

"Yeah, but you were the one with the ringside seat."

"I wish it was tomorrow, it's giving me fits," Kevin said.

"Everybody wants it over with, especially Duke. What do you think he feels like, knowing those rich bastards are trying to pin that jerk's dying on him?"

"Has Duke been around?"

"He was here Tuesday night." Buck laughed. "Had to put some backbone in Puffy. Word got around Puffy was checking out expensive new wheels. Said he might be in the market after next week. Seems like this lawyer's been talking to everybody who might stick it to my brother."

"He's like a fly on a turd."

"Word's got around he's spent a lot of time with you."

Kevin wheeled around and pushed Buck "I'm goddamned sick of this town and the words that go around."

"Yeah. So what's he offered you?"

Kevin started toward the path to the parking lot. Buck ran up behind him and grabbed his shoulder.

"You selling out my brother, too?"

Kevin pushed Buck's hand off his shoulder. "I'm not selling anybody out. I'm going to tell them what I saw – or didn't see, and that's it."

"Sure. The lawyer'll get a hold of you, and you'll be crying for your mama; telling them my brother stuck him with a switchblade, kicked him over the edge."

"My brother: all of a sudden it's Wally and the Beaver."

"You ever hear about blood being wetter than water? Who are you sticking with, those swanky pricks from Connecticut?"

"I'm not sticking with anybody," Kevin said. "I'm telling it like I saw it, and that doesn't mean I'm saying Duke didn't push that guy off the

Rock."

"Good. Duke'll be glad to hear that."

"Don't go off and tell Duke anything. I didn't say I wasn't – or I was – or – shit my brain's gone to mush."

"When are you going to figure out whose side you're on: when you put your hand on the Bible – or when you see what you can get off the lawyer and that guy's family?"

"I'm not getting anything from them."

"Then why not help Duke out? What do they get out of this? It ain't going to bring their kid back. He's dead. Duke's alive. He might not be everybody's favorite guy, but he's not a bad guy. You tag him with pushing Skip off the Rock, and they'll indict him for manslaughter or something. Then he's looking at three, maybe five years in state prison." Buck poked his finger in Kevin's chest. "It's us versus them, and you have to pick a side."

Shoving Buck's hand away, Kevin said, "Don't tell me what I have to do! I don't need one more goddamned person telling me what to do."

Buck stepped back. "You've been bought, you asshole."

"You're full of shit."

"You get all high and mighty – nothing but the whole truth crap – when it comes to my brother. What do you care? You're out of here next year. You don't give a shit about people like us. You knock up Maxine, and you're crying because you had to give her your college fund. You got it made in the shade, you asshole. Daddy and your rich friends will bail you out."

Kevin swung and caught Buck on the side of the head. Buck dropped to his hands and knees. "Oh, shit. I'm sorry." He tried to put his arms under Buck's, but Buck shook him off.

"Get away from me, you cocksucker."

A trickle of blood ran from Buck's nose. "I didn't mean to. I...."

Buck struggled to his feet. His fists rose. Kevin braced, hoping Buck would hit him.

Buck glared at Kevin, then spit at his feet. "You're no friend of mine." He turned and walked back to the beach.

Friday August 15

AT THE TOP OF THE LADDER, Thomas gripped a section of rain gutter and looked down at Mr. White.

"The missus is afraid to turn on the stove, and I can't blame her," Mr. White said.

"I'll finish nailing in this section and be right over."

"She's got the kids on the front porch. I'd like you to do it *now*."

Mr. White jumped back as the clanging gutter dropped at his feet.

With a frozen grin nailed to his face, Thomas slowly climbed down, and without waiting for Mr. White, started toward Cayuga. "It's supposed to have a faint smell. They put it in on purpose – for safety," he said over his shoulder.

Kevin had gone with his father to check the fittings the last time Mrs. White smelled gas. When no leak was found, she'd let them know the water tasted rusty. And one of their brats piped in that it smelled like poo-poo in the back of the cottage. Yeah, Kevin thought, and the beaverboard smells like wet cardboard after a couple of days of rain, and you can sweep and shake all day, but you weren't going to keep the sand out of the sheets. The White's box on the schedule was already outlined in red pen – do not rent again.

Fifteen minutes later, Thomas pushed through the workshop door and slammed the crescent wrench on the bench. "So help me, I'm going to kill him before Saturday. Do it *now*. I don't think I can hold on until Labor Day when they all leave."

Kevin tried to get out of the workshop, but Thomas squared on him and shoved a finger into his face. "I am sick to death of every damn one of them!"

There wasn't anything Kevin could do except stand there and take the hit for the Whites – and every guest who'd been a pain since the season began.

"It's my fault if the mosquitoes are biting and the fish aren't. The lake is too cold. It's raining again. It's too hot. The dinner we had at the Knotty Pine wasn't good. I'm renting them cottages – not a god-dammed perfect life for two weeks." Thomas tossed his work gloves on the bench. "You know what my favorite time of the summer is? Those Saturdays when every cottage turns over, and I have four or five hours when I don't have to be nice to anyone." Thomas poked Kevin in the chest. "You've got the brass ring right in front of you. Get as far from Hawk Cove as you can."

"You don't have to yell at me," Kevin said. "You've been harping on it all summer." He remembered the first time they'd gone fishing. "Always tell the truth," his father had said. "I've taught my son to tell the truth," he'd said to MacKenzie outside Thibedeau's. He was juggling so many lies, he couldn't keep them straight. "I suppose it could have been like MacKenzie said."

"Suppose? Are you just jerking around; playing a game? I would have thought you were smart enough to know what's at stake."

"It sounds too easy. What's the catch?"

"Let me spell it out for you, Mister *New York Times*. First, you have to get out. Maybe you'll get a scholarship on your own; maybe you won't. Don't hold your breath waiting for another offer like MacKenzie's." Thomas grabbed Kevin's shoulder. *"Got it?"*

"I got it."

"Second, you're getting the chance to move to a world where you make the rules; where people need you; where you don't spend your life toadying to jerks like that..," he said pointing toward Cayuga.

His father was gripping his shoulder so tightly it hurt, hammering each phrase home with a push. " If you hate it here so much, why don't you get out?" Kevin was surprised he'd said it.

"Don't be smart."

"At the dump, remember. You said you didn't know what was out there. Is not knowing better than being angry all the time? Why not take a chance?"

Scowling, Thomas released Kevin's shoulder. He picked up the crescent wrench and put it in its place on the peg board. He straightened the containers of washers along the back of the bench. He re-arranged the screw drivers in their holders, then turned the hammers so all the heads faced in the same direction. Finally, staring at a pair of pliers he said, "I'm afraid."

Kevin could hear kids on the playground shouting, *Scarty cat. Scarty cat.* He didn't want his father to be afraid. "Could something different be worse?"

"I don't know." Thomas put his hand on Kevin's shoulder and gave it a soothing rub. "That's why I want you to be someone who's not always afraid of falling off a narrow perch."

Kevin felt his eyes sting. He could tell his father about the mess he was in. So what if he yelled at him. It was a terrible mistake. Maxine was pregnant. His father could understand: after all, back then, 1941. It would feel good finally confessing. And his college fund was gone too – but there was the scholarship and the loan. Why not? He was going crazy.

"Dad," Kevin said. He drew in a breath, the words formed, *This girl. Maxine. You see…* dangled, then fell awkwardly from his lips, "Dad, I'm afraid of a lot of things, too."

Saturday August 16

19 ON AIRLINER KILLED IN CRASH AT NANTUCKET

Learn Accounting at Home.

ACROSS THE ROUND MARBLE-TOPPED TABLE, Linda sipped her strawberry ice cream soda. Kevin had left the last quarter of an inch in his instead of slurping it up. A date with Linda. Into town and the Sweet Shoppe for ice cream sodas. Saying "hi" to the other kids; catching up with who's doing what, going where. A walk on the town beach on the way back to her house. A goodnight kiss?

Kevin wished he could turn the clock back to the end of June. It could have been like this all summer. No Rock. No dead person. No Coroner's Inquest. He smiled at Linda. Okay, no Maxine either. But was it worth it? He'd stopped jumping every time the phone rang: no longer sure each call was from Maxine – in Plattsburgh, in Lake George, telling Kevin she'd decided to move back to Hawk Cove to live with him and their baby. And lying in bed with his thing in his hand, trying, but not able, to recapture the feeling of her wrapped around him, her soft whispers of *Now push, now pull.* He wasn't going to be able to play the record backwards: forget about Maxine, somehow get the money back into his college fund, say something at the Coroner's Inquest that would please everyone, stay away from Father Donovan, be friends again with Buck.

Linda was the prettiest girl in the place, and it made Kevin feel better. When she'd said she'd love to go out for an ice cream with him, he wondered whether it was because the Wentworths and the other sons of the summer people had cleared out.

"Gosh," Linda said, "don't you feel the summer's almost over?"

"I wish it was the day after Labor Day, New Year's Eve, Groundhog Day."

"Oh. I almost forgot. There's that terrible inquest. Whenever my dad mentions it, I get the shivers thinking about the Spanish Inquisition and somebody being burned at the stake."

"Thanks for cheering me up."

Linda scooped the last of the vanilla ice cream with her long spoon. "I'm sure it won't be easy, but you'll tell them what happened, and that's that. Next year at this time, you'll be packing for college and you'll hardly remember it."

"I guess."

"You don't sound very happy about it. What are you going to do, stay in Hawk Cove?"

"I'm not planning on staying, but is college the only answer?"

"Join the Air Force, get some low-paying job?"

"That's the thing." Kevin picked up the stiff, shiny menu from behind the napkin holder. "Ice cream sodas, sundaes, banana splits." He flipped it over. "Hamburgers, hot dogs," he said as he shoved the menu back. "We don't have to choose from the menu."

"Oh, sure," Linda said nodding toward the waitress across the room. "Nancy, I'll have the strawberry shake – and pour hot fudge in it please."

"Why not? Have what you want – even if it's not what everybody does."

"Who thought that up, Chink Perrotti?"

"Mr. Marsh, actually."

Linda's face reddened. "If I were you, I wouldn't refer to *him* as an authority on anything."

It's like Mr. Marsh didn't live in this town for eight years, Kevin thought. Gone in a day, and if you mentioned his name, you got nasty looks. He thought about defending him, but decided to let it go. "I'm just saying we all think we have to pick one kind of life or another when we're seventeen," Kevin said. "Heck, you've been talking about going to Vassar and becoming a child psychologist since fifth grade." He laughed. "We're all telling Mrs. Tallon fireman, nurse, airline pilot and you with your *child psychologist*."

"I don't know why you find that funny. It just so happens my Aunt Jane *is* a child psychologist in Boston, and she did go to Vassar, and there is where I expect to go."

"Okay. If that's what you really want, do it. I'm just saying maybe there are other possibilities."

"All right," Linda said. "But the menu gets bigger and better if you go to college."

Kevin noisily slurped the last of his soda. "I was thinking about applying to Yale."

"Wow, Kevin. That's the tops. Yale, and the sky's the limit. I mean, you'd do well wherever you went, but – Linda's face darkened. "Gee. I just remembered talking to Skip Satterfield. He was going to Yale this fall."

"I heard."

"Really? Who from?"

Kevin shrugged. "Can't remember. Anyway, it's not like everyone who doesn't go to Yale and Harvard is doomed to teach driver ed at Hamilton High."

"Well, if you get the chance to go to Yale, you'd be a fool not to." Linda pulled the menu from behind the napkin holder and waved it at Kevin. "It's not sundaes or hamburgers, it's *crepes Suzette* and *filet mignon*. It's Paris and London. New York City. You're always yakking about getting out of Hawk Cove. How far are you expecting to go – Rochester?"

"Cheektowaga." Kevin thought about all the times he'd sat in the periodical section of the library, reading the *New York Times*, fantasizing living in New York, going to Europe, maybe having a job that took him around the world.

"Very funny."

"Maybe I don't want to do what I'd have to do to go to Yale."

"I don't know what *that* means. But I'd beg, borrow, or steal if they let girls in."

"Lie? Kill?" Was he just jerking off about going to Europe, or did he have what it takes to do it?

Linda stared at Kevin. *"What?"*

"Haven't you heard people say they'd kill to get something? I was thinking what a person would do – how far they'd go – to get something they desperately wanted." Kevin signaled Nancy for the check. He didn't know what it cost to go to Yale, but he knew it was a lot. Maybe he could strike a deal with the lawyer. Give me fourteen hundred dollars, and take your chances on what I'll say at the inquest. No way, he thought. That's peanuts to them. Last night he was awake thinking about being at Yale, sitting in a class room listening to a lecture. The door opens and two guys in suits, like FBI maybe, come in and grab him out of his seat. New evidence has turned up in the Satterfield case. You're under arrest for perjury. That's what he'd always been told. Murder will out. Do wrong, and you'll pay – eventually. But maybe people lied every day and got away with it. Got into Yale. Made a million dollars. Went to Paris and London. How did Skip end up at the bottom if he wasn't pushed?

Monday August 18

MOON SHOT FAILS; ROCKET EXPLODES
Poems Wanted to be Set to Music.

AVOIDING HIS MOTHER'S STARE, Kevin pretended the fried baloney sandwich required his total concentration. But he felt her eyes locked on him. He'd heard dogs could smell fear. Did guilt have an odor? He was positive he *looked* guilty. He took wolfing bites of the sandwich and gulps of the chocolate milk as though he had to bolt off to one of his father's absolutely-has-to-be-done-now chores. But his father had left for town ten minutes ago, and another day of brutal heat had flattened the guests into mute clumps along the breeze-less beach.

Besides the noise of the munching he was making with the last of his lunch, the buzz and plonk of a bottle fly banging against the kitchen window was the only other sound in the room.

He stole a glance over the top of his glass of chocolate milk. His mother was still staring at him as though he'd disappear if she glanced away. He wished he could. Everyone was staring at him. He was running out of excuses to avoid being alone with his parents for more than a minute or two. And he felt like he was on probation with Linda and his other friends as they looked at him as though he'd picked up a virus from what had happened at the Rock. In town, he sensed folks wanting to ask him the same question his father had asked about him and Mr. Marsh, even though they too would doubt his denial.

Kevin cocked his ear at the sound of a motor boat. "Sounds like one of those new Evinrude fifties."

Nothing.

He stuffed the last bite of sandwich in his mouth and started to push his chair back.

Joyce reached out and put her hand over Kevin's. "Kevin, what did you do with the fourteen hundred dollars?"

It was the question he'd been dreading, the one he knew was going to be asked in the dozen scenes in which he imagined being found out. Would it be his father storming in the door, clutching Kevin's bank book and demanding to know what he'd done? Or would he walk into the living room to find his parents sitting on the sofa with stunned, disbelieving looks on their faces? In each of these scenes, he heard accusations, tears, despair and predictions of ruin from his parents. He'd never imagined his mother calmly sitting across the kitchen table from him, a mild, quizzical look on her face, asking him that question in a tone as if wondering whether he'd remembered to throw his sheets into the laundry basket.

They'd tricked him, he thought, expecting to see his father, standing at the back door. "Ah, I..." He had no idea what he was going to say. "I didn't. I don't." Like a deflating inner tube, Kevin sank back into his chair.

"I imagine it has to do with that young girl, the Nelsons' niece."

"How did you find out?"

"I stopped by the bank, and Mr. Gibson came running over with a false look of concern on his face to ask whether you had made it home all right with the fourteen hundred dollars you had withdrawn." She let out her pursed lips, disapproving nose sigh. "I said everything was well in hand." She paused. "But it isn't, is it?"

In all those imagined scenes, he hadn't been able to concoct an excuse anyone would believe. And nothing came now.

"This girl?"

"Maxine."

"She's in trouble?"

"Does dad know?"

"Your father has other things on his mind right now. Do you still have the money?"

"No. I gave it to Maxine."

"To...?"

"She said that's how much she needed to take care of it. Go to Plattsburgh. She said her friend knew of a place she could go. Have the baby adopted," he added.

His mother's face was calm. She didn't seem angry, but her gaze shifted to something over his head and back to him again. "Mom, are you all right?"

"In 1941, it was three hundred."

All those nights at the listening end of the bed. The elopement story so lame they'd stopped telling it on their *anniversary*. "I don't need to know."

"It's a bit late for embarrassment isn't it – for either of us?"

It wasn't the same. Maxine even admitted she was a slut. And he wasn't the first one –that boyfriend who tried to kill her, and Dave in the Chevy, and those guys at the Halfway House. He wasn't special. He was a chump. But he couldn't push away the image of his mother lying on the bed at Jimmie's, *her* face smiling at him, his mother's voice coaxing him to go slowly in and out. All those nights he heard them, he quickly imagined doing something with Linda or Sue. "It's *not* the same."

Joyce didn't seem to hear him. "Fourteen hundred dollars," she said with a humorless laugh. "We didn't have the three hundred."

"I don't have to hear about it."

"Is she pretty?"

"No. I mean yes, sort of, but it doesn't matter. She's taken off with my college fund."

"Don't be cruel, Kevin. She's not the only one involved."

"Mom, do we have to talk about it. I'm so sorry, but…"

"But, Maxine has gone off to take care of it. When I think of what would have been if we had the three hundred dollars." She folded her arms in front of her chest and looked toward the window. "It cost the same, you know. Whichever choice you made, going to Father Baker's in Watertown – and you had to put your baby up for adoption – that was the rule, or the other thing, if you knew someone who could arrange it. Three hundred dollars and make your choice."

"But you didn't."

"I wanted to. I'm ashamed to say it, seventeen years later, but I wanted to. I didn't care. Whichever was going to make it – you – go away." She gazed at Kevin. "Here you are, my lovely son – and I wanted to make you go away."

What if he had been adopted by someone else? He wouldn't be stuck here with these problems and nowhere to run. "That was a long time ago."

"Yes, and I believe God has wiped away the sin of a foolish and frightened girl. But in all those years, I've often wondered what my life would have been like if I'd taken either path. Well, this is the life I'm living. What life will you live?"

"I don't have a choice," Kevin said. "She, Maxine, left town. I don't know what she's going to do. But there's the scholarship offer Mr. MacKenzie made. It's not like I have to lie. It might have been like he said – really."

"I would have lied. For three hundred dollars, I would have sworn the sun rose in the west."

"What should I do?"

"It seems your – and this young girl's – problem is out of your hands."

"About the money."

"You're up to your neck in a whole barrel of problems, and now you want your mother to tell you what to do," Joyce said with a trace of sarcasm.

"I want to do what's right."

Joyce gave him a skeptical look. "Perhaps your father will tell you what to do. You know what Mr. MacKenzie would like. I imagine your friend Buck wants you to protect his brother. I'm afraid Hawk Cove has railroaded your friend Mr. Marsh out of town, so he's not available for advice. Perhaps …"

"Mom, please."

"I don't think you understand what is at stake here, Kevin."

"I do know how serious this is. That kid is dead. I could send Duke to jail."

"Kevin," Joyce said forcefully. "It's *your* life I'm talking about."

"I know."

"Do you? It's not the scholarship, Kevin. Mr. MacKenzie and the boy's parents, Duke Duncan, your father, me, half the people in Hawk Cove have strong opinions about what you should do."

"It really could have been the way he said."

"Perhaps, but *you* have to decide, Kevin. And what you decide is going to go a long way toward defining what kind of person you're going to be."

"I see."

"I hope you do. It may change the course of your life. I wasn't much older than you, but I never got the chance to decide. I wanted to, but I couldn't. Five, ten, even twenty years from now, you may look back and say you made the right choice – or the wrong choice. But I don't want you to look back and say it wasn't your choice."

"I understand, Mom, but it doesn't have to be a forever thing."

"No, it doesn't. But once you start down a path, it becomes harder and harder to turn back and take another direction."

"Do you want to change – do something else? You're not old."

Joyce smiled and squeezed Kevin's hand. "Thanks." She paused. "It's hard, Kevin. I don't think I have the courage."

"Didn't you want to become an artist?"

Joyce chuckled. "But I am."

"Don't you still have dreams of other things, other places?"

Joyce got up from her chair, opened the kitchen window, and shooed the fly out. She stood behind Kevin, put her hands on his shoulders and kissed him on top of his head. "Dreams are done with me, Kevin."

Kevin felt his mother give his shoulders a squeeze before she stepped away. "Are you going to tell Dad about me taking the money out of the bank?"

"I'm not going to lie. He may find out for himself. But perhaps he doesn't need to hear it from me just yet."

"Were you very fond of her?"

Kevin stared at his mother. "Yes."

Wednesday August 20

ARAB LANDS OFFER NEW PLAN TO EASE CRISIS IN MIDEAST
A Smith-Corona Portable can help your child's education in seven important ways.

ON THIS CRISP, CLEAR EVENING, Kevin knocked on the porch screen door at Linda's house. He hoped being seen with Linda sharing ice cream sodas at the Sweet Shoppe and hand-holding through *The Bridge on the River Kwai* was making them a couple in the eyes of their old friends. As much as he wanted out, he still had to live in Hawk Cove until next summer. Could he make it through the next ten months as zombie-boy? Over the past couple of weeks, he felt people staring at him, then shying away. It was like the magnets he'd fooled with as a kid: feeling the unseen force pushing the two negative poles apart. The other day in the Red & White, he'd come up on Ade Harmon and Wendell Ricketts arguing. He heard Ade tell Ricketts, "they were looking for trouble" before they saw him and changed the subject – like the other Hawk Covers who clamed-up or looked at him like they might have something to tell him before quickly going about their business. At least Linda hadn't shut him out, but she didn't seem delighted when he said he'd pick her up at her house.

Mr. Standish came to the door and eyed Kevin as though he hadn't known him for the past seventeen years. "Oh, it's you."

Cripes, Kevin thought. Do I look like I joined the Jehovah's? "Hello, Mr. Standish."

"Linda," Mr. Standish called over his shoulder. "Someone's here for you."

274

Was it his fault it rained last week? How much of the drop-off in business in the gift shops could they pin on him?

Linda came out of the house and brushed by her father with a quick kiss on his cheek.

"We won't be back from our bridge game at the Chapman's until around eleven," Mr. Standish said as Linda joined Kevin on the front step. "Remember...." Mr. Standish said ominously as Linda grabbed Kevin's arm and pulled him down the sidewalk.

"Remember what?" Kevin asked

"No guests in the house when they're not home. I told him we were going to the town beach to watch for the satellite."

"At least there will be hundreds of witnesses he can interrogate after I take you off to join my motorcycle gang."

"Come on, Kevin. It's not that bad. Dad's worried."

"Whenever I run into him, it's like he's deciding whether he ought to run me out of town. I'm surprised he let you go out with me." Kevin kicked a pine cone along ahead of them.

Linda kicked the cone into a ditch. "I'm seventeen, and I'll make my own decisions."

At the bottom of the hill, Kevin and Linda stopped at the parking lot of the town beach. He remembered sitting here with Mr. MacKenzie. Now, the parking lot was full.

Kevin and Linda walked onto the beach. A bunch of their old friends started toward them.

"Hey, guys," Linda said. She leaned in closer to Kevin and gave them a wave that said she wanted to be alone with him.

Kevin said, "There are so many stars out tonight, I hope we can pick out the satellite."

"Oh, Gerry will be our guide."

Ten feet off, Gerry Prindle fiddled with a pair of binoculars. He'd been in Linda's thrall since second grade; carrying her books, doing her frog dissection in bio lab, and lurking close enough to be ready if she changed her mind and regarded him as something more than a "best buddy."

Looking around at the dozens of families on the beach, Kevin said, "Everybody looks so happy. Don't they understand they're here to see how far the Soviets are ahead of us?"

"That's the negative thinking this town needs to get over," Linda said.

Even at dusk, Kevin could make out the ghost of the scalloped top of her bra under her thin white blouse. He recalled playing Chutes and Ladders years ago. He'd managed to get to the top with Maxine. Now, he was back at the bottom, peeking through blouses. "Okay. Tonight I'm starting on the power of positive thinking."

Linda put her hand on his arm. "I'm sorry I snapped at you. I can't imagine how you handle the pressure so well."

"I'll be okay after next week – I guess."

"You'll come out of it okay. It's Hawk Cove, I'm worried about."

"Thanks a bunch."

"Oh, Kevin." Linda took his wrist in her hand and pulled him around to face her. Leaning close, she said, "I do worry about you. But I know you're smart and strong and will do the right thing. I wish I could say the same about the rest of the town."

"Everybody in town will be glad to get it behind them; make it to Labor Day, see if they can get in their twenty weeks."

"If only it were that simple," Linda said. "Dad's worried the inquest is pulling the town apart. Dad says he's heard from a lot of folks who think those other kids got free passes."

"Life's not fair."

"The Adirondacks are changing. Look at how many of the old hotels have closed. Fewer people are renting for two weeks. And Dad's worried that if Duke gets off, the people that still come for the whole season are going to sell out."

"They're already leaving. Hardly any of them come for the summer anymore. And how many groceries or dinners do they buy anyway?"

"But they add," Linda hesitated, "class. Okay, maybe I'm a snob, but if we don't have the summer people, what's the alternative: motorcycle gangs and weekenders from Utica."

"Cripes, Linda. We should have skipped *The Wild Ones*."

"I'm not joking. Are we going to be nothing but a bunch of bark-eaters living off scraps? Dad was up at Lake Placid with the chamber to see what's starting to take hold there: gourmet restaurants, upscale inns, nice shops – they're called boutiques in Montreal – selling something besides 'I cry for you and balsam' pillows. We can do that here too."

"Dad says this, and Dad says that. I thought you were making your own decisions." Kevin scanned the people on the beach. He nodded toward the road. "Let's take a walk."

Linda started to say something, paused, and then said, "Maybe later."

"Later?"

Linda looked away, then into Kevin's eyes. "I want you back with our friends – with me." She gave him a peck on the cheek. "Later."

Gerry Prindle walked up to Kevin and Linda.

"Did you bring your binoculars, Linda?" Gerry asked.

"I didn't."

"I brought an extra pair for you," Gerry said, handing Linda the binoculars and giving Kevin a smug smile. "The *Observer-Dispatch* says we should be able to see it moving from the southeast to northwest at around nine-oh-five: at the lowest point of its orbit. Let's get a place on the dock. We can see it better from there." Gary stared toward the dock. "Come on," he called over his shoulder. "We'll miss it."

Holding hands, Kevin and Linda followed Gerry across the beach to the long, narrow walkway attached to the floating dock. They stepped around mothers and fathers with kids in tow and made their way to the end.

Gerry had a Boy Scout compass and was pointing out where they should first see Sputnik.

"This isn't that the one with the little dog?" someone asked.

"That was Sputnik II," Gerry said.

"Those terrible commies: letting that poor dog die up there."

"Laika," Gerry said. "That was the dog's name. This one is Sputnik III, and it's huge, over thirteen hundred kilograms."

"Okay, Mister Wizard, what's that in American?" a man asked.

"Daddy, can we see it yet?" a young boy shouted. His father hoisted him on his shoulders and pointed across the lake toward the low hills on the south shore. "Over there. Soon."

"Remember when the first Sputnik was launched last year?" Kevin said to Linda. "October fourth. My birthday."

"You're a special guy," Linda said as she pressed in closer to Kevin.

"It's nine-oh-two. Which way should we look?"

"See the dock light to the left of Hemlock Island," Gerry said. "I calculate it will appear right over it."

"Hey, the science fair kid says to look this way."

"Is it here yet?" asked a man who came onto the dock holding the hands of two boys.

"Whoa," Kevin said as he pointed to the deck now six inches above the water. "I don't know how many more people this dock is going to hold."

"I think I see it."

"That's a star. It's not moving," the man next to her said.

"I think I've got it," Gerry said. "Yup, there it is." He held his binoculars in one hand and pointed across the lake with the other. "Just to the left of Hemlock Island. About two inches above that tall pine."

"Daddy, I can't see it."

"Over there, Emma."

"Do you see it Kevin?" Linda asked.

Kevin squeezed around behind Linda, put his arms over her shoulders and aimed her binoculars toward the tall pine. "Do you see it?"

"I don't... Yes. There it is. A tiny dot. It's moving!"

Someone pressed in behind Kevin and pushed him closer to Linda.

"I see it. I see it," a little boy shouted.

"Which way?" voices called from behind Kevin as he felt more people pressing onto the dock.

"Over there, near that..... Yikes!" Cold water lapped across Kevin's ankles. "The dock's sinking!"

The people on the dock, trying to move away from the water slopping across the deck, shuffled from one side to the other until too many had made it to the left side and the dock tilted up and they all slid, flailing into the cold water. Parents scooped up their children in the three feet deep water. Shouts of "Holy Mackerel!" "What the dickens?" and "The dock sunk!" filled the air. Then someone laughed. Then someone else. In seconds, two dozen men and women and children standing and sloshing around in the water and the people lining the walkway were laughing, even splashing one another. Gerry was standing waist deep, binoculars still pressed to his eyes.

"Kevin. There you are. Over here," Linda called. "I thought I'd lost you."

Linda was four feet away. Her auburn hair was plastered across her face. In the light cast by the lamps on the beach and along the walkway, her white bra was clearly visible under the now-transparent white blouse. Kevin stepped towards her, and they put their arms around each other and kissed. Hand in hand they sloshed toward the beach among the people still laughing and calling to each other. They stopped, ankle deep in the water. Linda looked down at her wet front. She shrugged and smiled, and Kevin slid his hands across her breasts as they embraced again.

Linda said, "We ought to get out of these wet clothes." She looked at her wet blouse again, following the arc of Kevin's gaze. "We could dry off at my house."

"Aren't your parents....?"

Friday August 22

SOVIETS REPORTED PLANNING TO SEND CHINA ATOM ARMS

L & M's - Less Tar, More Taste

KEVIN SHIVERED in the gray, pre-dawn light. He'd thrown on his jacket and stuffed his bare feet into sneakers, but his pajama bottoms didn't keep the cold from seeping through. The rotating red flashers from the fire trucks, ambulance, and police cruisers pulsed a lurid glow on the faces of the people gawking at the scene. He'd heard the first siren around three, glanced at the clock and rolled over. When he heard the wails of the second and third sirens and then his parents' voices downstairs, he met them on the doorstep where they realized the sirens had stopped in town. They jumped into the car and found a crowd milling at the end of the dirt road leading to the Needhams' trailer.

"Gas! Put out your cigarettes," Deputy Fisher shouted at the people headed for the scene. Behind him, a cruiser was pulled across the end of the road. A fire truck blocked Beaver Pond Road from the west. Firemen and police stood in a cluster twenty yards from the trailer.

Kevin had expected to see the firemen rushing with hoses toward the trailer; the pumper nozzle pouring a stream onto a fire. But the idling engine of the nearest truck was the only sound. Around him, people talked in anxious whispers. They seemed to know what had happened. He glanced at his father who shook his head and pulled his mother, who was sniffling into a handkerchief, closer.

From where he stood, Kevin saw the ambulance backed up to side door of the trailer, its flasher sending streaks of red along the long gray side. Then, he heard doors slam and saw the ambulance start slowly toward them. The crowd pressed in, but the driver shook his head as he made his way toward Route 28. Kevin hoped the driver would turn on the siren and race south toward Utica General, but the ambulance stopped to let a truck pass, then carefully pulled onto the road and drove off.

A few men from the crowd started edging down the dirt road toward the trailer. Deputy Fisher caught up with them. Waving his arms he warned them. "Stay back! There's still gas around."

"What happened?" Orin Matthews called.

"Can't say right now."

"We're not a bunch of tourists," Mr. Matthews said. "Was it Bunny?"

The deputy walked up to the front of the crowd. He glanced back over his shoulder, and then said in a lowered voice. "Both of them. Bunny and her son, Larry."

Kevin's mother buried her face in his father's chest. Larry *and* his mother? Dead? Kevin tried to imagine two stretchers with their bodies side-by-side inside the ambulance. He'd just seen Larry a few days ago at the library. How could he be dead? "Leak?" someone called after Deputy Fisher who was walking back to his cruiser.

He shook his head and kept walking.

"Probably a loose fitting," Mr. Matthews said. "You'd think Tallon would check when he delivered."

Kevin felt his father brush by him as he reached out and grabbed Mr. Matthews' shoulder. He pulled him around and shoved his finger in his face. "Jim Tallon's been delivering propane to Bunny for next to nothing for years. And Jim checks everything twice."

Mr. Matthews stepped back and put his hands up. "Don't have to get so riled up, Tom. I was just conjecturing about a loose fitting."

Kevin was shocked to see his father go after Mr. Matthews.

"Loose screw," someone muttered.

Thomas wheeled around as though trying to identify who'd said that. "It's got to be somebody's fault. Two people dead, and five minutes can't go by without choosing sides."

"Thomas, let's go home," Joyce said, pulling his sleeve.

As he watched his father turn and start walking toward their car, Kevin tripped at the edge of the grassy shoulder and stepped in a patch of ferns. The moment he breathed in the woodsy tang of the crushed ferns he knew he would never in his life smell that aroma without thinking, Larry and his mother are dead.

———

At nine that morning, Kevin's father returned to the kitchen. "That was Sheriff Dawson on the phone. He wants to come over to talk about last night."

Joyce said, "Why us?"

"It's Kevin he wants to talk to."

Kevin stared at the Cheerios stuck to the edge of the bowl. He hadn't gone back to sleep. Shivering under an extra blanket, he tried to imagine what it looked like inside the trailer: Larry and his mother in their beds as though sleeping – but dead. Not like Skip lying at the base of the Rock, his left arm bent at a crazy angle, his right reaching straight out, legs splayed.

Pacing across the kitchen, Thomas stood over Kevin and in an incredulous tone, said, "Are you involved in this? How? I mean why in the world would the sheriff want to talk to *you* about this?" He turned to Joyce, his palms up in gesture of surrender.

Kevin hunkered closer to the cereal box. Skip. Larry. Mrs. Needham. Dead people. He was too exhausted to try to make sense of it, but he wasn't surprised the sheriff wanted to talk to him. He glanced at his mother and father eyeing him as though he was the missing link in some unfathomable mystery. He shrugged. "Don't know."

———

FROM WHERE HE SAT ON THE SOFA, Kevin watched Sheriff Dawson bob up and down: first standing, then sitting, then standing again when his mother came into the living room. Kevin thought the sheriff looked more nervous than he did. He supposed he should be nervous. Maybe he was too tired: tired from being up all night; tired from … Too many things to think about. And with his last shred of alertness, he did wonder how he was involved in this.

Finally perching on the edge of the chair, Sheriff Dawson started to open the notebook he carried, then closed it. He looked at Kevin, then Joyce, and finally at Thomas. "I don't suppose you've heard?" Apparently seeing their puzzled looks, he said. "Bunny and Larry. The Needhams. It looks like suicide."

"Are you sure?" Thomas said.

"Rags," Sheriff Dawson said. "Stuffed under the door, around the window sills."

No one spoke as the sheriff nervously riffed through his notebook. Kevin wondered if the sheriff had lost the place where Kevin came in. How do you do that, he wondered? He pictured Larry and his mother busily ripping Larry's tattered tee-shirts and sticking the strips of cloth in the cracks in the sides of the trailer as though decorating the place for a holiday. Then what? One of them turns on the oven, and they jump into bed? Wouldn't be easier to hang yourself, or shoot yourself? He was getting nutty. He felt like telling the sheriff and his parents he was too tired to make sense and was going upstairs for a nap.

"Sheriff Dawson," Joyce said. "Do you know whether it was Bunny or Larry?"

"We can't be sure. Haven't had a lot of time to think about it, but, you know, it could have been either one."

Thomas said, "Why do you have to talk to Kevin?"

"Pictures." The sheriff quickly looked at his notebook again. He seemed embarrassed he'd blurted out that word.

Kevin felt as though he'd been jabbed in the side with a sharp stick but struggled to remain calmly seated, hoping he looked as puzzled as his parents. He was still too tired to think clearly, but it was though he could feel his brain working to make the connections that hadn't quite made it to where it made sense to him.

The sheriff looked at Joyce. "They're kind of sensitive."

"What do you mean by sensitive?" Joyce asked.

"There were these pictures in a manila envelope we found in the trailer. Polaroids mostly: the ones that slide right out of the camera and develop on the spot. Some were kind of incriminating," the sheriff said without looking up from the notebook.

Kevin remembered the picture Father Donovan took on the porch, the first day of his job at the rectory. Pictures? Those flashes when he was doing those exercises? Why would that make Larry or his mother kill themselves? Wait! Incriminating? He wasn't so exhausted he didn't catch the jump from "sensitive" to "incriminating." This was crazy.

Clearing his throat, Sheriff Dawson said, "There were a number of these pictures, and there were ones with Larry Needham in them. Other boys we can't identify." He turned a couple of pages in the notebook. "And there were three pictures of Kevin."

His mother and father were staring at him. Sheriff Dawson was still looking down at his notebook in his lap. "Three?" Kevin said loudly. He was surprised by the sound of his voice.

Sheriff Dawson nodded without looking up.

"Father Donovan, said something about wanting a record of the people working for him," Kevin explained. "The newsletter. He said somebody from Boston was paying for it. It was the only time I knew about."

Sheriff Dawson said, "Tom, you sure you want the missus here for this?"

Joyce said, "I will not be treated like some *idiot*!"

"I'm sorry, Joyce. This gets awkward." Sheriff Dawson reached inside his uniform jacket and pulled out a small manila envelope. "Here's the three pictures. State Police wanted me to make the positive ID. I was pretty sure it was Kevin, but you better see for yourself." He took out three Polaroid pictures encased in plastic and held them out between Kevin and his father.

Kevin and Thomas stood and approached Sheriff Dawson. Fanned out were three pictures: on the right, Kevin sitting on the rectory porch looking wide-eyed at the camera. The middle picture was one of Kevin's bare back. On the left, a blurry shirt-less Kevin, with his hands behind his head, eyes half-closed, pulling himself upright in a sit-up as he lay on the carpet in Father Donovan's office. Kevin felt his ears burning as he looked at himself. "That's the one I said." He pointed at the one on the porch. "I didn't know Father Donovan took the other ones."

Joyce rose from the sofa, joined the others looking at the pictures, and then returned to the sofa.

"You didn't know he was photographing you?" Sheriff Dawson said.

"No. I remember a flash when I was doing the jumping jacks and sit-ups, but I wasn't sure he was taking a picture."

"Where were you doing these jumping jacks and sit-ups?" Sheriff Dawson asked.

"In Father Donovan's office: at the rectory." The sheriff and Kevin's father exchanged a quick look.

Sheriff Dawson put the pictures back in the envelope. "Why were you doing exercises in Father Donovan's office?"

"Father Donovan, kept going on about being physically as well as morally fit."

Sheriff Dawson shifted in his chair and glanced across the room at Joyce. "Was that all: just exercises?"

Kevin was positive his flaming face gave him away as the recollection flooded back of him kneeling in front of Father Donovan, face pressed into his hard thing, pissing his pants, Father Donovan embracing him, running his fingers through Kevin's hair. "No," Kevin croaked. "Just the jumping-jacks and sit-ups." From the way both his father and the sheriff stared at the envelope, he knew they thought he was lying.

After several seconds, Thomas said, "What does Kevin and Father Donovan and these pictures have to do with what happened to the Needhams?"

"Tom, I can't get into it. The State Police asked us locals to see if we could identify any of the boys in the photographs. Like I said, aside from Larry Needham, Kevin was the only other person I recognized."

"Well, I demand to know what this is all about," Joyce said. "It's our son. Poor Bunny Needham and *her* son. I'm not going to sit like a stuffed animal while you and the State Police keep us in the dark. For goodness sakes, Sheriff, with everything that's been happening in this town, we'll all go crazy."

"Tony, we deserve to know."

Kevin was surprised to hear his father call Sheriff Dawson by his first name.

Sheriff Dawson seemed to slump in the chair. "It's...." His voice cracked and he seemed to be struggling to regain his composure. "Joyce, do you think I could have a glass of water?"

"I've got a pot of coffee on."

"That would be wonderful."

The sheriff seemed like a completely different person to Kevin as he sat back in the chair when his mother handed him a cup of coffee.

"I've got to tell you, it's been a summer I never want to see again," Sheriff Dawson said. "And those troopers swoop in from Tupper and act like we're dopes: treat us like nothing but go-fers. I just about had to get a court order to get into the trailer last night." He took a sip of coffee. "Thanks, Joyce. I think this is the first time I've had a chance to sit since about three this morning."

Thomas glanced at Kevin, then said to the sheriff, "What can you tell us? I know there's stuff you can't, but whatever you can, we'd appreciate it."

"I'm not exactly sure what's going on myself. And God forbid you should say anything to anybody. But seeing as Kevin is involved, I guess it's fair to tell you at least some of what we know."

"We'd appreciate it, Tony. And it won't go out of this room."

"Okay. Joyce, I'm old-fashioned, so you'll have to forgive me if this gets into sensitive territory. We get the call about three-fifteen." He paused. "After we got the gas cleared, we got into the trailer. I don't need to tell you how we found them, but on the kitchen table is this envelope, the one with the pictures. Pictures of boys." He took a sip of coffee and looked at his lap. "Some without clothes."

"Not me," Kevin said. Surprised everyone was looking at him, he added, "Just my shirt off."

"I understand," the sheriff said. "Those three were the only ones with you. But in others, I was able to ID Larry Needham."

Oh, Jesus! It is my fault. I got him the job. I didn't know Donovan would make him do that.

"In a couple," the sheriff continued, "was this man. Looked kind of familiar. It was my deputy who said it looked like Father Donovan, only younger. So, around eight this morning, Doug and I went over to St. Mary's. Father Petroska is *not* happy to see us. When we tell him we want to talk to Father Donovan, he says Father Donovan has left. Not just out for the day, but gone, gone. *Urgent diocesan business*, he says. Can't say exactly where, but he'll let us know as soon as he talks to his superiors in Ogdensburg. When he finally lets us in the door, he and the

287

housekeeper, Mrs. Pulaski, are shooting daggers at each other. I've been in this business long enough to see she's got something to tell us. And the father wants us to go to – Old Forge."

The sheriff paused to take a sip of coffee.

"So, we do interrogation 101: Doug takes the father into his office, and I get Mrs. Pulaski into the kitchen. In a second she's telling me she never liked *that one* from the start – by which she means this Father Donovan. It seems Larry has been doing work for Father Donovan, *whatever that involves*, she says. Yesterday, Larry comes, and Mrs. Pulaski hears a ruckus. She knocks on Father Donovan's door, tries to open it, but it's locked. She hears Larry yelling; Father Donovan's voice, loud. He, Father Donovan, tells her everything's under control; go back to work. More ruckus. She stays in the hallway. Larry comes flying out the door and out of the rectory. She looks into the office. Papers all over the place. *That one* looking like he'd been in a fight. Tells her he'd fallen. Everything's all right. Slams the door in her face."

Sheriff Dawson stopped to finish his coffee and glanced at his watch. "I'm supposed to meet the Major from BCI in ten minutes. Let him stew for a while."

"Would you care for another cup, Sheriff?"

"That would be grand, Joyce."

Holy Mackerel, Kevin thought. Larry and Father Donovan. What did he make him do? Boys – with no clothes. He remembered those magazines in Father Donovan's briefcase. Should he tell the Sheriff about them? But maybe they'll think....

"Thank you, Joyce," Sheriff Dawson said as he took the cup.

"That was all we got from Mrs. Pulaski, and Father Petroska keeps telling us he'll let us know about Father Donovan – soon. We left. Figured if Father Donovan was blowing town, he'd need gas. Sure enough, Bob at the Esso station tells us around five yesterday afternoon, Father Donovan's fills up; hat pulled down over his face; and Bob says it looked like he had a shiner on one eye and scratches on his cheek."

"Sheriff – Tony,' Joyce said. "Do you think Father Donovan was sexually molesting Larry and these other boys?"

Sheriff Dawson, Thomas, and Kevin stared at Joyce.

"It's nineteen fifty-eight," Joyce said. "It's not as though people are ignorant of these things."

"He didn't molest me," Kevin said. "Just the physical fitness stuff."

"I am happy to hear that," Joyce said.

Sheriff Dawson took a deep breath. "Well, now that we've put a fine point on it, was there anything that suggested he, Father Donovan, might be – molesting?"

"I don't know. I did feel kind of funny about it. The physical fitness stuff; him going on about special people. I quit. That's how come Larry got the job."

"Well, I guess I can explain to the *Major* I was working on the investigation instead of taking a well-deserved break." Sheriff Dawson opened his notebook. "Since you raised it, Kevin, were you aware of Warren Marsh having anything to do with this?"

"He had nothing to do with it!" Kevin said. It sounded to Kevin a though he was protesting too loudly. "He gave Larry the job at the library. He needed the money. When I quit Father Donovan's job, that's when Larry got it."

"Okay. It's just – well, you remember the flap. Father Donovan was involved. Got Warren Marsh kicked out of his job." Sheriff Dawson shut his notebook and lifted himself from the chair. "Two years, five months, and three weeks. Another summer like this, and I'll never make it to retirement in Fort Meyers."

Ten months more before he got out of Hawk Cove, Kevin thought. There can't possibly be anything else that would keep him here.

Monday August 25

As KEVIN LEFT THE POST OFFICE, still haunted by the images of the naked boys in those Polaroids, he heard the squeal of tires. Two cars had pulled off Route 28; their turn signals still blinking. Cars driving south flashed their headlights and edged onto the shoulder in front of Thibedeau's Hardware to allow the oncoming traffic to avoid a large object in the middle of the road. Seeing Claude Thibedeau calmly waving cars by, Kevin realized it couldn't have been a person. He walked quickly toward the incident with a knot of dread growing in his gut. A deer, he hoped as heads leaned out and quickly ducked back in the cars. In front of the Sunnyside Up, a man walking back said, "Lucky it was only a dog."

Kevin ran toward where the cars were pulled over and saw a mangled heap in the middle of the road. For a second, he tried to pretend the mottled brown fur streaked with gray belonged to another dog – but it was Brownie. Kevin dodged a car slowly pulling around the scene and dashed to where Claude Thibedeau and a man wearing Bermuda shorts were standing over him.

"Just darted out," the man said.

Kevin knelt beside Brownie who was panting as he tried to rise up, but then fell back squealing. A back leg was twisted under his haunches. Blood dribbled out his ear. "You hit my dog," he croaked.

"I tried to miss him. I'm real sorry."

Kevin tried to cradle Brownie's head in his arms. The dog's confused eyes fixed on Kevin, looking as though he thought Kevin could stem the pain. "He's hurt bad," Kevin said choking back tears.

Mr. Thibedeau leaned down and put his hand on Kevin's back. "It was an accident, Kevin."

"Wasn't going more than fifteen miles an hour with traffic this heavy," the man said.

Kevin appealed to Mr. Thibedeau, "What are we going to do?"

"Let's get him out of the road," Mr. Thibedeau said.

The two men knelt, but as one put his hand on Brownie, he snapped at the hand and collapsed with a tortured whine. "Can't pick him up."

Kevin stripped off his shirt and spread it carefully next to Brownie. "Slide him on gently, please." Kevin and the two men slowly levered the dog onto Kevin's shirt, keeping away from its snapping jaws. Then Kevin, cringing at every whimper, pulled the shirt heavy with Brownie across the northbound lane.

As Kevin and the two men stood looking down at Brownie, whose chest heaved with every labored breath, Kevin said, "We've got to do something."

Mr. Thibedeau said, "I don't think there's much we can do for him."

"We can't let him just lie here and suffer."

The man in the Bermuda shorts looked at his blood-spattered sandals and said, "I'm sorry, son. I hate to leave like this, but I got a car full of kids." He pointed to a packed station wagon in front of the hardware store. "Nothing I can do here, and I got to get on the road. One kid's got the croup; the missus and the others are sweltering in the car." He reached into his pocket, pulled out his wallet and held out a ten dollar bill.

Kevin stared at the bill and shook his head.

"Sorry, kid," he said and then walked quickly to the car and drove off.

Kevin looked up at Mr. Thibedeau. "We could take him to the vet in Old Forge."

"I'm no expert, but I don't think he'd make it."

Kevin stood and scanned the handful of whispering people huddled a few yards off. "Can somebody help me take him to the vet in Old Forge?" Heads shook before the crowd scattered. Kevin spotted Chink Perrotti standing next to his Hornet in the driveway of the Sunnyside Up. He ran toward the car. "Chink. I need your help."

Chink opened the car door and started to get in. "I ain't got time for a dead dog."

"I'll pay you. We can be in Old Forge in fifteen minutes."

"I can be there in twelve," Chink said. "But I ain't carting no road kill in my wheels." He slammed the door and sped off, gravel spewing at Kevin from the spinning wheels.

Kevin ran back to Brownie. "Mr. Thibedeau, I need your pickup to take the dog to the vet."

Mr. Thibedeau shook his head. "Hate to sound hard, Kevin, but it would be a waste of time and gas." He looked across the road. "Got to get back to the store. "

"We can't let him lie here and die like this," Kevin cried.

"Calm down, Kevin."

Kevin wheeled around. Deputy Fisher had put his hand on his shoulder. "Deputy." He looked at Brownie. He was barely breathing. Blood had started to puddle under his jaw. His eyes were glassy. Kevin sunk to his knees.

Deputy Fisher grabbed Kevin under the arms and lifted him to his feet. "Kevin, "he said softly, "why don't you walk up the road a bit. I'll take care of your dog."

Kevin stared at the deputy, then sighed. As he turned toward the post office, out of the corner of his eye he caught the deputy pulling his billy club out of his waist band. Kevin started walking slowly away. After he'd walked about ten yards, he heard a dull *Thwack*. He stopped. A few seconds later, he heard another *Thwack*. He stood staring at people getting back in their cars, those on the road slowing to see what was going on. Finally, Kevin turned around and walked back to where the deputy was standing over Brownie.

"It was the best thing, Kevin. No need for him to suffer."

Kevin nodded as he stared at Brownie, no longer breathing.

"You want me to call the town guys for him?"

"What will they do?"

"Probably take him to the dump."

"No," Kevin said. "I'll take care of him."

"You sure you'll be alright," the deputy asked. "I could take you where you need to go."

"No, I'll take care of him." He bent down and started wrapping his scuffed shirt around Brownie. He pulled the shirt over Brownie, lifted him and started walking toward Tamarack Road. As he got to the corner, people coming out of the Red & White quickly ducked back into the store. Brownie was starting to slip, and Kevin hefted him higher against his chest.

Walking down Tamarack, Kevin stumbled but caught himself before he fell. A sound like one of his mother's saddest sighs came out of Brownie, and Kevin felt wetness spreading over his arms. The stench of shit and piss gagged him.

By the time Kevin made it to the end of Spruce Road, he was staggering under the weight of Brownie. A car passed, and the driver slowed, then sped on as he saw Kevin and the dead dog. When Kevin reached the parking lot of Iroquois Lodge, his father and mother ran toward him.

"Kevin," his father said. "Deputy Fisher just called. "What ...? Oh my God."

His mother held her hands to her face. "Oh dear. How awful."

Kevin stopped and looked around. "Can I bury him over beyond the burn barrel?"

Thomas said, "I guess that would be alright." He looked at Joyce, then back at Kevin. "Can I help you?"

Kevin started to shake his head, but seeing the stricken faces of his father and mother, he said, "Yes." He looked around and said, "How about over there under the maple?"

Thomas said, "I'll be right back."

His mother whispered something to his father, then walked with him through the parking lot to where the trash drums and burn barrels sat. At the edge of the clearing, he knelt and let Brownie's body slowly slide down his arms to the ground. "Car hit him."

"We heard," Joyce said.

Thomas arrived with a shovel and a cloth rolled under his arm.

Kevin said, "Here looks good."

Thomas nodded, and Kevin began digging. After a few minutes, he stopped, too fatigued from carrying Brownie from town to continue. As he started to dig again, Thomas took the shovel and finished digging the hole. When he'd scraped the sides straight, he unrolled the cloth he'd brought from the Lodge; one of Joyce's good tablecloths.

Joyce knelt next to Brownie. Kevin tried to hold her back from the bloody mess, but she put her hand on Kevin and they both slid Brownie from the tattered shirt and onto the white table cloth, gently rolling it over him and tucking it neatly around his head. Kevin, Joyce, and Thomas lifted Brownie and laid him in the hole. Kevin and his father pushed the pile of dirt next to the hole over the draped dog.

"I think we should say a prayer," Joyce said.

Kevin, Joyce, and Thomas stood looking down at the mound of dirt as Joyce thanked God for the creatures of the earth who give us joy. She added that she wasn't sure about the theology but hoped that Slim and his dog would be reunited.

Kevin and his parents smoothed the dirt on Brownie's grave. When they finished, they silently looked at each other's bloody, smeared clothes.

Tuesday August 26

ARKANSAS CASE GOING TO HIGH COURT

Western Union is a written record: No mistake about it.

TAKING HIS SEAT in the town hall meeting room for the Coroner's Inquest, Kevin tried to recall everything about that night at the Rock. He supposed he should have been thinking about it all the time. Any other year, being mixed up with a homicide would have been the biggest thing in his life. But this summer he'd been mixed up in too many things messing up his life. And he worried they weren't solved yet. So far, he hadn't heard that the folks in Hawk Cove had connected the dots between him and Father Donovan and Larry and Warren Marsh. He trusted Sheriff Dawson, but it wasn't going to be long before folks began concocting a juicy story and giving him a leading role. Could he be out of here before then? At least Maxine was long gone. He hoped. Pervert or chump. He'd better concentrate because the Satterfield's offer was his only hope of getting out of Hawk Cove before he got named the village idiot.

But Kevin still couldn't make sense of exactly what happened that night. He tried picturing Chink or Puffy wearing the tight black swim suit, grappling with Skip in his madras shorts and loafers. But it never looked right. He remembered Buck in his white briefs before he jumped off the Rock the first time with Duke, so it couldn't have been Buck. Maybe somebody else came after he'd run away. But he could never make it sound like anyone but Duke yelling, "Fuck off, asshole," and then, "Holy shit!" before he scrambled to the top of the Rock and saw Skip at the bottom.

Now sweating in the tight, wool sport jacket smelling of mothballs, Kevin wondered if an inquest was like a trial. He pictured himself in a jury, listening to the witnesses' testimony. He would be impartial, fair. He'd listen to the evidence. Or maybe Duke would confess on the stand, just like on Perry Mason, and he wouldn't have to say whether he saw Duke shove Skip.

Maybe.

The door from the office opened, and two men and a woman walked into the meeting room. The woman sat at a small table and began fiddling with a machine that looked like a long, narrow typewriter. One of the men stepped to the front.

"Ladies and gentlemen, my name is Henry Meyers, County Coroner. This afternoon, I am going to conduct an inquest. I understand some of you have consulted with an attorney, so you may know what this is about. Regardless, I will explain."

Kevin's shirt stuck to his back, and he was sorry Deputy Fisher made him and his parents sit in reserved seats in front. On this first hot, sunny day in a week, these people ought to be at the beach instead of jamming this sweltering room. And how come they'd been put on the side where the Connecticut people were sitting? When he glanced behind him, there was Mr. Satterfield in a gray suit and Mrs. Satterfield in a black dress whispering with Mr. MacKenzie. Eric, Todd, and Corey sat behind them, wearing blue blazers, striped ties, and khaki slacks. He pulled the short sleeves of his jacket over his dangling wrists.

Out of the corner of his eye, Kevin saw Duke on the other side of the aisle, dressed in jeans and a plaid shirt, slouched in a folding chair. His thumbs were hooked into his wide black belt, engineer boots crossed over his ankles. He stared at the ceiling as a man in the rumpled suit whispered in his ear. The other guys who were there that night were scattered around the other side.

Kevin was sure the buzz in the room was Hawk Covers talking about him. He could feel their stares, and he was sure they'd figured he'd already made up his mind to tell the Coroner Duke pushed Skip off the Rock. How come Duke got to be the town hero, and he was the turncoat?

Maybe they should have gotten their own lawyer. The Satterfields had Mr. MacKenzie. The man next to Duke must be his lawyer. Everybody had someone in their corner but him.

"There are several reasons a Coroner's Inquest may be held," Mr. Meyers said. "I won't go into all the conditions in the law. The relevant sections of the statute in this case, *in re* Kent Satterfield of Cos Cobb, Connecticut are clear."

Kevin heard a laughing snort and saw Chink mouthing *corn cob* to Puffy, who made a face at the Connecticut people.

"I remind those present," Mr. Meyers said, "a Coroner's Inquest is a formal, legal proceeding authorized and conducted under the statutes of the State of New York. Any behavior that impugns this proceeding will be dealt with accordingly."

Kevin scrunched down as far as he could. He'd wanted to get into the Rock so he could be one of the guys. Like Chink and Puffy? Now he was stuck between his parents like a little kid in this stupid sport jacket.

Mr. Meyers cleared his throat and glanced at the black book he held.

"In this present case, an inquest must be held when there is reasonable cause to suspect the deceased died a violent or unnatural death, or a sudden death of which the cause is unknown." Mr. Meyers lowered the book. "It is apparent Mr. Kent Satterfield died a violent and sudden death."

Hearing a sniffle, Kevin saw his mother take a tissue out of her purse. Should he bow his head or something?

Mr. Meyers continued. "This Coroner's Inquest may find Mr. Satterfield's death was violent or sudden – and natural." He paused. "Or violent, sudden – and unnatural."

Mrs. Satterfield sobbed. One night at the Rock, and her son's life was over, Kevin thought. One night at the Rock, and the mess he'd made of his was just beginning. He should have stayed home that night. He wouldn't have met Maxine. She wouldn't be...

"This inquest is not convened to determine guilt," the Coroner said. "However, the findings will be turned over to the District Attorney, who may wish to bring them before a Grand Jury."

It isn't going to end here. The longer this drags on, the more everything else is going to come out.

Mr. Arnold Stern," the Coroner said, indicating the man standing slightly behind him, "is a magistrate and will be assisting in the questioning of the individuals called. I want to remind those who will be called to testify you will be under oath and subject to the laws of perjury."

Sheriff Dawson was the first person to testify. He described the scene at the Rock when he'd arrived. As he recounted finding the *deceased's* body, Mrs. Satterfield's wracking sobs were the only other sounds in the room. The sheriff's voice fell into a monotone as he read the details from the same black notebook he'd carried on the day after Larry Needham and his mother died. Kevin remembered the looks on his father's and the sheriff's faces when the sheriff pulled out the *other* pictures. Nobody would believe him. He'd be one of the boys with their clothes off.

When Mr. Stern asked Skip's friends to describe what occurred that night, each told a story about just happening to be around the Rock. Sure, they were angry about having dog excrement dumped on their porch and Limburger cheese packed into the heater of the car. Yeah, they'd brought along horse balls and tossed a few, but it was all in fun.

Lies cooked up by Mr. MacKenzie, Kevin thought. And so polite and respectful in their blue blazers, acting like they were taking a short break before going to lunch at their country club. Yes, sir. No, sir. He remembered the guy smashing the horse ball into Puffy's face, knocking Chink back into the fire. Watching them put on an innocent act made him want to puke.

The Coroner called 'Mr. Carl Perrotti,' and that set off a round of giggles. Chink said he didn't see Duke. All he could *recollate* was them guys throwing horse shit – "if you pardon my French."

When Mr. Meyers called for Wilbur Russell to come forward, the guys in the Connecticut crowd snickered. Then Puffy stood, bent over and ripped off a fart in their direction. That got a big laugh from Puffy's buddies and a number of the other Hawk Covers.

Mr. Meyers slapped the table with his hand. "This is a legal proceeding! Anymore of this behavior and I will ask Sheriff Dawson to remove the person or persons in question – *and* consider whether charges of disorderly conduct are warranted."

"Dogpatch," someone hissed.

A free ride to Yale: he'd take a free ride to Utica right now. He didn't have to end up like these stuck-up bastards if he went to Yale. His father will go bat-shit when he finds out about the college fund going to Maxine. Maybe he could get a part-time job at one of the state colleges and a loan. But he'd still have to come back to Hawk Cove in the summer. People looking at him all the time. 'You know: him and Larry Needham and the priest that left.' The free ride to Yale was a one-way ticket – out. The rusty iron taste from the glass of water he'd gulped before leaving the house was making his stomach turn.

Puffy didn't pretend he wasn't at the Rock that night. But, if you believed Puffy, he and his Boy Scout troop were roasting marshmallows over the campfire when set upon by a band of ruffians. Puffy might have seen Duke around. He couldn't tell for sure who else was there – what with being blinded by one of those hooligans what shoved horse *manure* in his eye. The magistrate didn't spend much time with Puffy.

When Buck was called to testify, Mr. Stern zeroed in on what Buck saw at the top of the Rock.

"That Skip kid," Buck said. "He tried to push me off the Rock."

"*You*, Mr. Duncan? Didn't the others who were there say you were already in the water?"

"I don't care what they said. Besides, Puffy couldn't see. I was on the Rock. It was Duke that was in the water."

"Was anyone else at the top of the Rock?" Mr. Stern asked.

Buck's eyes darted toward Kevin.

They've decided to pin it on me! Kevin tried to read Buck's cold stare.

"Mr. Duncan. Was there anyone else with you?"

Buck shook his head. "Just me. Me and that Skip. He tried to push me in."

Wow. What a stand-up guy. Or was Buck saying that so he wouldn't tell the magistrate he saw Duke there, wrestling, maybe pushing the kid off the Rock?

"What did you do when he tried to push you in?"

"I jumped in – after my brother. That's why some must have been mistaken. That Skip was coming after me and probably didn't know you had to dive way out to miss the boulders at the bottom."

Even though the magistrate asked Buck several variations of what happened at the top of the Rock, Buck repeated his version until Mr. Stern, shaking his head, dismissed him. When Buck sat, Puffy leaned forward and gave him a friendly shove in the shoulder.

With all the smiles, and not just from Puffy and Chink and Duke, Kevin felt like everybody in the town thought Buck's testimony was great. Were they sticking up for Duke, too? He remembered the baseball game: us against them. Would they stick up for him no matter if the truth and nothing but the truth didn't come out so clear as Buck's testimony? With his college fund on its way to who knew where, he could be stuck in Hawk Cove for long time.

Doris Weaver sat over near the windows. He remembered their conversation outside the library just before Warren Marsh got railroaded out of town. Labels and opinions formed fast and stuck in small towns like Hawk Cove, she'd said. The queer librarian. What nickname would they come up for him: altar boy?

Duke was called next. He strolled to the front of the room as though he couldn't be bothered. As he slumped into the chair, he checked his watch. Kevin heard grumbles from behind him. "It was like my brother *Daryl* said. I was in the water."

"How do you account for the witnesses who said it was *you* at the top of the Rock with Kent Satterfield?"

"It was dark. They were attacking us. And me and my brother, we look a lot alike. Maybe they were mistaken – or maybe they wanted to get back at me for punching out the guy at the ball game. Who knows?"

'Lying punk!'

Heads turned toward Mr. Satterfield. His wife had his arm in a tight grasp.

"This is my *final* warning! Deputy, please remove the next person who disrupts these proceedings."

SEATED AT THE FRONT OF THE ROOM, Kevin tried to stare only at Mr. Stern. He didn't remember his name being called or walking to the chair.

As Mr. Stern peppered him with questions, Kevin tried to answer as best he could, but he was confused. Who was there? Where did they stand? Where were you? Was the magistrate trying to trip him up? It wasn't his fault.

"You ran away," Mr. Stern repeated when Kevin told him what he'd done. He made it sound like Kevin was guilty.

"But I came back," Kevin said, but his tone sounded whiney – and guilty– to him.

"I want you to tell the Coroner *exactly* what you saw when you came back."

"I was behind the Rock, and…."

"How far behind?"

"I, ah, think it was…."

"You aren't sure? Concentrate. How far from the end of the Rock were you?"

Was he holding on with his left hand or right hand? Was the Rock slippery or easy to climb? How far up had he managed to pull himself? *Cripes*, was he going to ask him how many leaves were on the bushes?

As Mr. Stern walked over to the Coroner to whisper something to him, he dared to look at the audience. Everyone was staring at him. He tried not to look at Duke, but there he was, his legs stretched out in the aisle, a smirk on his face. Buck looked down. There was Mr. Standish, but he was glad he didn't see Linda or any of the other kids they hung out with. Would the guys at school think he was a chicken for running away? Maybe he should let it out about him knocking up Maxine so they wouldn't get any funny ideas when stories about those Polaroids got around town.

He finally glanced toward his parents. His father looked like he was sitting on a nail. Maybe he should have told him about the loan MacKenzie offered. He'd been thinking he'd tell his father at the same time he told him about Maxine and the college fund. 'I've taught my son to tell the truth,' he'd said when Mr. MacKenzie came around the first time. Connections. Recommendations. Mr. MacKenzie's offer was a hundred times better than a half-baked letter from one of the guests who went to Colgate twenty years ago.

His mother was smiling at him. *Smiling*. Here he was up in front of the whole town trying to explain why he was hanging around with a bunch of jerks, running away from a homicide, and not knowing whether to shit or go blind about what he saw, and Mom looks like she was watching him read the Declaration of Independence at a school assembly. He was the reason their lives were so messed up. It would have been better if he'd never been born. *It's your choice.* He didn't want a choice. He wanted to shout at her: what do I say?

Mr. Stern walked back to stand in front of Kevin. Gazing intently at him for several long seconds, he finally said, "Kevin Boyle. What *exactly* did you see occur at the top of the Rock?"

"I saw two people. Standing close together."

"Just standing?"

"They were sort of wrestling."

"Wrestling?"

"Well, no. I can't exactly say that."

"Were they or weren't they?"

"They were grunting. Swearing at each other."

"And can you say they were grappling, wrestling, whatever you might call it?"

He stared at the buttons on Mr. Stern's vest. Sweat trickled down his back. He wished to be out of here in the worst way; up to his neck in the cool lake, alone, treading water way out beyond the dock.

"Mr. Boyle? Kevin? Were these two people wrestling?"

"I can't say exactly what they were doing."

"And who were these two people?"

There was Mr. MacKenzie staring at him over the tops of his half-glasses, smiling and nodding.

"One was Skip, Skip Satterfield. I didn't know it was him until I finally got to the top of the Rock and looked down, and he was at the bottom."

"And the other person: the one who was *grunting* and *swearing*?"

The polka dots on Mr. Stern's bow tie seemed to dance. "I can't say exactly."

Gasps ricocheted through the room. Mr. Stern looked at the Coroner, then back at Kevin. "Mr. Kevin Boyle, I want you to be absolutely sure of what you are saying."

"Yes sir." He smelled the rank odor from his sweat. A free ride out. A ninety degree turn to a different life. Could he say *exactly*? "I'm absolutely sure I can't say exactly who the other person was."

"And did you see this person you are *unable* to identify," Mr. Stern said, shaking his head, "push Kent Satterfield off the Rock?"

"No sir. I didn't see anyone push anyone."

LATER HE WOULD RECALL the surprise on their faces and the peculiar sense of satisfaction it gave him. The magistrate repeated the question, and he repeated his answer. But he'd already slipped into a twilight zone as he stared back at them. First, Duke and Buck with their mouths hanging open, sure he was going to sell them out, wondering what the catch was; the Satterfields angrily turning to Mr. MacKenzie; Mr. MacKenzie shaking his head as though he'd stupidly slammed the door on the best offer he'd ever get in his life. His mother's proud smile remained. His father's face had screwed into a question mark, knowing he'd forfeited the scholarship, but wondering if he'd had done something unaccountably honorable.

But he hadn't. As the seconds seemed to stretch into minutes, he imagined telling the magistrate he'd made a mistake, misspoken; saying it *was* Duke on top of the Rock; he *did* see Duke push Skip off. He imagined what those faces would look like then. Like a child with a mechanical toy, he could push a lever and make Duke's face go from anger to relief and back again. Or he could play a version of Mr. Potato Head and paste his mother's smile on Mr. Satterfield's angry face; slap his father's drop-jawed gape on Mr. MacKenzie.

Mr. Meyers dismissed Kevin. He tried to not look at either side as he retook his seat. Still, he heard a whispered 'Atta boy' from someone sitting near Duke; sensed the glares on the faces of the Connecticut families; and caught the dumbfounded look on his father's face as he stepped over him to sit down. His mother patted his knee. He sat in his chair and stared straight ahead – wondering.

Mr. Meyers said he anticipated a finding shortly, and he, Mr. Stern and the stenographer adjourned to the office.

Kevin stared at his knees trying to block out the laughing chatter from the Hawk Cove side, the grumbles and hissing from behind him, and the voice in his head that kept asking why he'd said he didn't see anyone push anyone.

Finally, the door to the conference room opened. Mr. Meyers stepped to the front of the room. "I have determined that Kent Satterfield's death was accidental and natural. My findings will…"

Before Mr. Meyers finished, Duke and his buddies stood and cheered. Mr. Meyers shouted *'Order,'* but he was drowned out by crashing chairs as Mr. Satterfield lunged across the aisle and took a swing at Duke. Chink grabbed Eric in a hammer-lock and was pounding the top of his head. Corey shoved Puffy backwards into a folding chair that collapsed, sending Puffy sprawling.

Sheriff Dawson and Deputy Fisher waded into the scrum and hustled the Hawk Cove side toward the front entrance and ordered the Connecticut crowd to the back. Shaking fists, middle fingers thrown, and shouts of 'Go back to where you came from,' and 'You punks haven't heard the last of this,' shot around the room.

Kevin was blocked behind his father. When the two groups had been pushed apart, he turned to see Mr. MacKenzie sitting in his chair with his knees crossed, still shaking his head at him.

Tuesday September 2

SOVIETS SAY THEY RECOVERED TWO DOGS SHOT 281 MILES UP
Sha-nah-nah. Doobie-whah- whah.

STANDING NEXT TO THE FIRE PIT at the Rock, Kevin poked the burnt stick with the toe of his sneaker. A crumpled wad of wet tissue lay inside the circle of rocks. Scraps of paper littered the ragged grass and hung in the bushes. At the water's edge, an empty can of Utica Club rolled in and out of the oily waves. He wondered if any of those who'd been here that night had come back. Right after it happened, the town crew unloaded four huge boulders to block the end of the road so no one could drive in. It didn't look as though the fire pit had been used much. He heard an abandoned deer camp on Sixth Lake had become the new hangout.

He walked to the far side of the clearing for a better look at the face of the Rock. He guessed the distance from the top to the first boulder at fifteen feet, twenty tops. If a person didn't jump out far enough to miss the boulders, he could easily break an arm or a leg – but that's if he knew he wasn't going to make it into the water. Skip probably figured he was headed for a cold dunking in the lake when Duke shoved him – then *whack*. "Accidental and natural," the Coroner ruled. Either way dead, and there wasn't anything natural about the way Skip looked sprawled across the boulders. He wondered if Duke had come back for a look around. Duke hung around the Trading Post until the guys got sick of buying him beers and listening to his story about fighting off two, then three or maybe it was four, guys at the top of the Rock.

His testimony hadn't stopped roiling through his head as he struggled to make it sound more believable. It was accurate – wasn't it: exactly what he didn't see? He could have said while he hadn't seen the underwear and swim trunks of every one of the guys, he'd deduced the person in the black trunks was Duke. And, in light of the wrestling and swearing, it was highly probable that Skip had been shoved off the Rock. But, he didn't. "Duke shoved him," he finally said aloud.

"No sir. I didn't see anyone push anyone." Was uttering that one sentence going to be the most important event in his entire life? Would everything good or bad find its way back to the summer of 1958? His father seemed to be still dumbstruck by the double whammy of the scholarship on its way back to Connecticut and his college savings off to who knows where with Maxine. But how angry could his father stay, when he'd been in the same pickle? "You're on your own," he'd said. "Some of the state colleges aren't bad. And they've got work-study programs that'll help." And when his mother told him how proud she was of him for standing up under all that pressure, it made him wonder if she had looped back to 1941. He glanced at his watch. Buck had called and insisted that they meet at the Rock this afternoon, didn't want to talk on the phone.

"Hey, Kev," Buck said as he popped out of the bushes at the edge of the clearing. "It's great to finally lay my peepers on you. I've been trying to run into you ever since that trial. You jump into a barrel of disappearing ink?"

"I didn't think you'd be looking for me."

"How come? After what you did for Duke?"

"Remember, at the town beach? I punched you, and you said I wasn't your friend anymore."

"Oh, shit, that. You had a lot on your platter."

Kevin picked up a stick and flipped it into the weeds. "Why meet here?

"I figured it was kind of important. If we could make up and be friends again, I figured we'd do it where we had our big scene. Put everything back to where it was before."

"Christ, Buck. That kid's dead. And I'm not in great shape either."

"That's what I figured. You need friends. Someone to *buck* you up," he laughed. "You should have come for the party. Man, it was great. We picked up beer, and old man Paquette even threw in an extra quart of Genny."

Kevin heard about Duke and the guys tying ribbons and cans on their cars and racing around with their horns blaring; hanging out of the windows yelling like they'd won the state championship. "I didn't think it would be a great idea."

"Okay, so things are cooling over. We got a new great spot – with a cabin. And Noel's cousin Jeanette's been asking about you."

He shook his head. "Just what I need." He could hear Maxine's whispering, 'Now, in, now out. Easy, slow." Was getting mixed up with the crazy Dupleiss clan worth it?

"Come on. The guys have been asking about you. We're in like flint. My mom even said I might snag her car sometime. Or Jimmie or Chink will give us a ride."

"I don't know if it's a great idea to be hanging around with Chink and Jimmie."

"You thought it was a good idea back in June. So we skidded through a rough spot. Yesterday, this town emptied out faster than goosed lightning. Who you going to hang with now? Linda and the stuck-ups?"

Buck was right. It hadn't taken long for what happened with Maxine to get around town. He was going to be radioactive with that crowd: parents forgetting to pass on his phone messages; no invitations to their parties; and a hundred excuses for not going out with him. "Do I have to only hang with one crowd?"

"Yeah. Who's going to go to bat for you when you need help?"

"Who says I need help?"

"Everybody needs help some time. Somebody to pull a string; give you a boost." Buck gave Kevin a playful punch on the arm. "You going to be a guy with no best friends? Come on. I can get mom's car Friday night and pick you up around eight. We'll be at the place on Sixth Lake in a flash."

"I'll give you a call."

Buck stared at Kevin. "We aren't going to be best friends anymore, are we?"

"Sure, we are. Why not?"

"Yeah. Why not?" Looking away, Buck said, "I got to get to work."

"I'll walk you to the corner."

Kevin and Buck pushed through the underbrush and ambled wordlessly along Cedar Road.